TEMPTING DARKNESS

JESSICA HALL

TEMPTING
DARKNESS

$\mathcal{S}$OMETHING FELT OFF THIS morning. I didn't know what, but something felt different as I glanced around the crowded room. Leering eyes watched me from where I sat alone in the mess hall. My usual spot was taken, preferring to be closest to the exit where I remained mostly unnoticed. Closer to the door was safest because it gave me an escape route.

Their sleazy gazes had me on edge as they watched me hungrily. I hated this place. There were no other women here. Most of all, I hated being the subject they loved to torment. All made worse by the fact that I was powerless to stop them.

In a room full of men, I stuck out like a sore thumb, and I did my best to keep to myself. The surrounding chatter quieted down and made me quickly glance around before I ducked my head when I noticed them. Darius had entered the room with my other three mates. They walked to the back of the room and took seats at the back, which I thought was a little odd; I rarely saw them here. It appeared they had something to talk about with their recruits because Darius spoke about some crap that I showed no interest in knowing. Keeping my head down, I ate quickly, wanting nothing more than to get the hell out of there.

However, the moment I stood up and went to throw my trash in the bin, my muscles spasmed, my feet faltered as I tried to take a step away from the table, and my entire body locked up with

"Aleera, freeze," came a voice. I recognized the voice instantly and dreaded what he would do this time.

My entire body stopped at the command. I couldn't move an inch, and everyone erupted with laughter. Oh, how I tried, but I couldn't so much as wiggle a toe. What were these savage men going to subject me to this time? They never usually went this far. Usually, they tormented me, chased me, hurt me. However, this was the first time they used compulsion on me, and it felt wrong as every muscle in my body tensed.

My eyes went to my mates at the back. Darius, Tobias, and Lycus watched from the far table. They were always happy to witness my suffering. Kalen, however, glanced around the room before he looked at me and dropped his head.

My stomach dropped when Zac, one of the recruits under Darius's thumb, got up from his seat. My lungs constricted at the cruel smirk plastered on his face. Zac sauntered over before he stopped in front of me. His eyes hungrily looked me over from head to toe. Zac was the worst out of all the recruits I had come across here. The vile bastard had no boundaries. He was usually behind my worst degradation. Zac walked around me slowly and plucked the sandwich wrapper from my fingers while I remained unmoving.

"Stand up straight," he ordered, and I gritted my teeth. My forced body was doing as commanded as Zac's cold magic caressed me. A violent shudder ran through me in repulsion as I tried to fight against the command, but it was pointless. I was a puppet on strings, and he was the puppet master.

"Nothing to say, Aleera?" he chuckled, and the entire room erupted with laughter. Except for my mates, who watched from the back with expressionless faces.

"Nothing I say will stop you. Did you want me to beg? Beg for you not to do whatever vile thing it is you intend to do?" I spat at him.

Being trapped in this place, I learned quickly not to beg. It just made the torment worse when I did. They didn't care that I was a female; they didn't care I was powerless. All they cared about was the control they had over me.

"You're right. It wouldn't stop me. The guys and I want you to put on a little show for us," Zac said in an amused tone. I glanced around the room to find the men were all leaning forward eagerly; one even winked at me while another licked his lips.

My eyes darted to the table where my mates sat. Not a scrap of emotion was shown on their faces for what I was about to endure. They would not help me, not that I expected them to. They never did. If only they had just told them who I was to them, if only their soldiers knew. I wouldn't have to deal with this shit daily. However, I knew they would deny it if I spoke up. Darius had threatened to kill me if I told anyone here who I was to them. So I had kept my mouth shut. They hated me, and the feeling was mutual. Yet, I couldn't bear to see them hurt, so how could they watch my humiliation with no expression at all?

My eyes went back to Zac, who looked me up and down. *Was he going to make me dance? What did he mean by a show?* I was already on display. How much worse could it get?

"You could always say no?" Zac teased before he scoffed. "Oh, that's right, you can't. Poor helpless Aleera, always so easily influenced, so easily overpowered. Must truly suck being the weakest form of fae," he mocked. His demonic eyes ran the length of me in a sleazy, obscene way. His gaze stopped at my breasts, and I felt my stomach drop somewhere deep and cold within me. I knew

My fingers twitched toward the mark with their fours names branded into my skin. I was going to call on them, which felt like a low-frequency buzz over every inch of my body, making me want to go to my mates. I had ignored that buzzing feeling for six years, and now it felt more like an itch. One I just couldn't reach to scratch.

A growl behind me made me jump, and I watched my entire life flash before my eyes in that split second as they closed in.

Lifting my hand, I placed it over the markings and sent a spark of my magic into it. Each of us had the same markings. Yet they only appeared when our powers manifested. My wrist burned painfully, making me scream and clench my teeth. The sheer agony in my voice made the wolves back off, wondering what had gotten into me.

The mate symbol glowed red and throbbed. I knew it only hurt like this because I waited so long to answer their call for me.

The world around me spun violently, and I fell to the ground. Both my hands and knees were driven into the road painfully. My power had become too low. A few more minutes, and it would fade out.

Teeth bared and snarling, a big black one rushed at me, and I closed my eyes and waited for my death. The surrounding air rippled, and the turbulent noise made me cover my ears. I recognized the whooshing sound of a portal opening up. Keeping my head down, I opened my eyes.

Four sets of feet hit the ground before the colored light of their magic was all I could see. It swallowed my vision. Their closeness made my reserves shudder, and I had to stamp down the urge to pull on it before they realized. Flames missed me by millimeters, the heat so hot, I cried out when it burned the flesh on my arms when it rushed past me.

When the howls and whimpers stopped, everything fell silent. My heart was pounding in my ears. Their domineering auras surrounded me threateningly as they took up each side of me and made me want to flinch away.

Can I take it back? I choose death. I choose fucking death fates. Nothing good would come out of me calling on them. The angry ripple of energy surrounding me told me they were livid, and these men were not ones you wanted to anger.

Paralyzed by fear, I remained frozen until boots stopped next to me. I clenched my hands into fists to stop them from trembling. They stepped closer, caging me in with their legs, making me feel tiny where I sat at their feet.

CHAPTER 2

THEY COULD KILL ME, and I felt like they genuinely wanted to crush me like a bug beneath their shoes. I have never felt so small in all my life.

"Six years, Aleera. Six fucking years, and you have the guts to ask for our help? We should have let them fucking kill you. Have you got any magic left? Because I can't feel it," one of them screamed at me.

I have never feared anyone more than my mates. I knew who they were and what they had done. Now, I was second-guessing my decision to call them.

One of them grasped my hair, my head ripped back, forcing me to stare at the eyes of the one I feared most. Darius Wraith. His name was constantly in the media; nobody in the world feared anyone more than they did Darius Wraith.

And to think he was one of my mates—not that the three others have stellar reputations. No, they were just as dark and twisted as he was. I never understood how I could be fated to be theirs. They were pure dark magic while mine was not like theirs; mine was... well... I wasn't exactly sure, but it was both, yet I felt a far stronger urge to my pure white magic. It made no sense why the fates chose to punish me this way.

They could not get their hands on my magic. It would be dangerous in the wrong hands, and their hands would be the worst. They didn't need more power, especially Darius. He was a demonic fae, and they were the strongest of our kind. He, too, like myself, was the last of his species.

Demon and fae, and here I were, the last of my kind, and mates with the last of his. What were the odds, two dying species fated to each other as if we should create a more incredible monster?

"Fucking answer me, Aleera! Say something!" he bellowed as I clutched at his hand, trying to free his tight grip. He yanked my head back harder by my hair, and I cried out, my hair ripping painfully from my scalp.

"Please, just let me go," I begged him, now wishing I'd chosen death. I was an idiot for even calling on them. A fate with them would be worse. Darius laughed at my pleading, but he let go, shoving me back to the ground. His presence was suffocating me already.

"Never, you belong to us, Aleera. We gave you time, and we could have come for you when you were thirteen, but we didn't. You ran from us. We are your fucking mates!" he yelled. His hands glowed with anger, and I watched as he clenched them into fists. I was readying myself for the blow.

"Bloody monsters," I whispered before I could stop myself. *Stupid no brain-to-mouth filter*. I instantly regretted the words I never intended to speak out loud.

"What did you say?" Darius snarled. I shook my head, not wanting to repeat myself, knowing that it would be a mistake, when someone suddenly nudged me from behind. His foot connected with my thigh hard, and I could feel my thigh bruising.

Kalen's obsession with her almost killed him last time when she never answered our call, and by the time we got to her school, she was gone. We thought she needed time to get her head around the idea of us, but after a few hours, we realized we had misjudged her.

"She is in the cells," Tobias answered him with a sigh before rubbing a hand down his face like he was tired, and he was. The anniversary was coming up, and he never slept much this time of the year. I would have to exhaust him or put him under when he went too long without sleep. Tobias would become unstable and driven by his instincts. We had lost a few men to his grief. Having her here was going to make him worse.

I watched Kalen as his head snapped up before he realized I was watching him. His face shut down, instantly recognizing his mistake. He was our weakness, and we couldn't drop our guard around her. I nodded to Lycus, and he patted Kalen on the shoulder and nodded toward the door. Kalen reluctantly got up and followed him. I would have to pull him in line later. We wouldn't lose him to her again. She had taken enough from us, and I wouldn't allow her to do it again. She either fell in line, or she would rot in that cell for the rest of her life.

"We should have let them kill her," Tobias muttered. He reached for the bottle that sat on the coffee table between the armchairs that circled the fireplace. Moving toward him, I watched as he twisted the cap off the bottle before bringing it to his lips, swallowing down the amber liquid. My hands fell on his shoulders, and Tobias flinched, only relaxing when I squeezed gently. He knew I would never hurt him. We'd been friends long before we became mates. I trusted this man with my life, and he trusted me with his.

"She will pay for what she has done," I told him, and he dropped his head back to look up at me standing behind him.

"I want her to hurt, and I want her to bleed like we have all done for her."

"Then make her," I told him.

Tobias turned his stare back at the fire burning for a second, his green eyes reflecting oddly from the flickering light of the flames. His expression darkened as his mask slipped back in place. The same icy demeanor that had made people run just at the sight of him. He could be cruel; he was nearly as sadistic as me, and he knew it. Aleera should fear him just as much. Tobias could be cold, and family meant the world to him before she destroyed his. Now, he would return the favor and destroy her.

"Aleera will wish for death long before we grant it to her." He chuckled softly, shaking his head before tipping the bottle to his lips. I took it from him, making him growl at me. His drinking had become worse, making me worry he was developing a drinking problem. My jaw clenched at the angry look on his face as he glared up at me.

"You want revenge, fine. But do it sober," I told him.

"And after?" he asked, and I stood upright. My lips pressed in a line as I stared at the flames, my mood plummeting further. Sometimes I hated the mate bond, hated it with a passion. It was the worst feeling, craving someone but hating them simultaneously.

She nearly ruined all of us; Aleera nearly killed Kalen. We almost lost him because of her selfishness. We just need to remember everything she took from us.

"Then we kill her. We don't need her."

"Are you sure that is a wise decision? We need her. I fucking hate her and wish nothing but death on her, but she is our power keeper. She would strengthen us, complete us."

"We have survived this long without her, and I don't want her touching my magic. She doesn't deserve to after what she has

"How about you tell them I am eating and drinking like a good evil minion, and they will be none the wiser?" I told him, rolling my eyes.

"I can't do that when they ask every day about you, so if you die and they find you, they will blame me for not telling them."

"Instead of asking you, they could check for themselves, so run back to your master," I told him, shooing him away with my hand, the movement taking way too much energy than it should.

"You have no idea. I warned you," he said, rushing out. I sighed, reaching for the drink bottle and tossing it through the bars so I wouldn't be tempted to drink it.

CHAPTER 5

HOURS PASSED AND I spent most of the day sleeping on the cold concrete floor. I was too lethargic to move. My ass went numb hours ago, my legs were asleep, and they had pins and needles. Yet, moving them felt like too much effort. My teeth chattered as my temperature plummeted, and the day turned into night. The coldness of night seeped into my bones, making them ache worse. I was asleep when I heard the steel door open.

"And you are back. Is it morning already?" I murmured. Hearing the cell door open, I instantly knew something was wrong as he never once came into the cell. My eyes flew open to see Darius standing in front of me.

"Oh, shit!" I cursed under my breath.

"'Oh, shit' is right. Why aren't you eating?"

"Not hungry," I told him, and my traitorous stomach growled at the mention of food. His eyes flickered, and he glared down at me. He walked over to me, and I had to fight the urge to shrivel into a ball.

Darius growled before reaching down and grabbing my hair. He jerked my head back painfully, but I couldn't even fight to loosen his grip. My entire body felt like a dead weight. He sneered at me, looking me over.

"Fucking disgusting," he said, letting me go and shoving me against the brick wall. My back hit the wall so hard it knocked the air from my lungs in one short wheeze.

"Just let me go. You don't even want me, so why keep me?" I asked, trying to catch my breath.

"You're weak. Eat, or I will force-feed you," he said, kicking the plate toward me. It resembled toast, only white with no color, but it was as stiff as toast. I turned my face away, looking back at the brick wall.

"I am going to give you three seconds, or I will make you eat," he said coldly. "One… two… three…"

I glared at him—a big mistake when his foot came down my shin. I screamed. The sound echoed off the walls and made my ears ring as the bone broke under the impact.

Pain radiated up my leg, and I blinked back tears while staring at his foot on my leg, his foot crushing it still as I panted. He counted slowly again, and I could only gasp and stare at him in horror at what he had done.

His face was expressionless, like hurting me meant nothing to him. I supposed it did mean nothing, or he wouldn't be doing it.

"One… two… three…" He twisted his foot, earning another scream from me, yet I was too weak to stop him, and my magic was all but gone; I highly doubted he would give me any to renew mine.

"Stop! Stop! Stop, Darius!" My scream was filled with agony, and I tried to clutch my aching leg, only for him to stomp on my hand. I heard the sickening crack of my three middle fingers. Bile rose in my throat before I threw up the emptiness of my stomach.

Acid burned my throat while I gasped for air as bile spilled from my lips onto the ground beside me.

He removed his foot off my hand, and I clutched it to my chest when the door opened behind him. My entire body trembled, and Darius stepped away from me, looking toward whoever entered. The pressure on my leg faded, but it was bent inward in the middle. Just moving caused me pain, and my blood coated the floor beneath it. The bone jutted out of my skin, and I fought the urge to throw up again at the gruesome sight.

I could only stare at my leg in horror at what he had done. The pain receded, and I knew I was in shock. I welcomed the shock, anything to replace the pain, but I knew it would wear off any minute, and it did.

"What's going on?" asked Tobias, making me look toward him, but I couldn't see him, with Darius blocking my view.

"She wouldn't eat. I was making her," Darius said simply as if he did this sort of thing every day, and it was merely some annoying chore to him.

"Just leave her be. Hopefully, she dies. We don't need her," Tobias said coldly, and it was like a dagger in my chest. Tobias stepped to the side and glanced at me with an expressionless face. His eyes darted to my leg and the blood pooled below it. I watched his Adam's apple bob as he swallowed, and his eyes went to mine fleetingly before he turned his attention back to Darius.

Darius grunted but added nothing else before closing my cell door and leaving me as he followed Tobias. The moment the steel door shut, I fell apart; uncontrollable sobs wracked my body, causing more pain as the floodgates opened. I could no longer contain it.

My hand shook as I tried to use the one that wasn't broken to pull my pant leg up, the fabric catching on the jutted-out bone.

"Kalen and I don't like leaving the castle," he finally stated, but my brain was still stuck on the word "castle." Did he mean like an actual castle from fairy tales? Did they still exist? Was I in a dungeon of sorts? That explained the weird-ass shackles on the walls. I thought maybe they were some twisted Halloween decoration, or perhaps they were into BDSM, but now I was looking at them differently. I wondered briefly how many people hung up by them.

"Aleera, hurry before I heal," he said before groaning, and I turned my gaze to his wrist that was closing up before my eyes. His eyes turned silver again, his canines sinking into his wrist. He tore the flesh away, which made me pull a face when he didn't even flinch. *Oh, how I wish I had his pain threshold.*

Right, back to escaping. Blood to heal, then siphon, and run like my ass is on fire. I could do this. I hoped it wouldn't hurt him, though. I knew I shouldn't care, but I didn't want to hurt him. The pull to his power and him now I recognized him was growing stronger—*stupid mate bond.* Couldn't the fates have made them as ugly as their shitty personalities? Seriously, they get to be sick depraved assholes and get godlike looks. How is that fair?

Grabbing his wrist with my good hand, he flinched, and I had a strange feeling he was fighting the urge to pull away from me. Like my touch repulsed him. I realized he wasn't healing me because he wanted to, but because he felt guilty. Anger coursed through me, and he looked away as I pressed my lips to his wrist, letting his blood flow into my mouth. I could feel his magic in his blood as it coated my throat and tongue, making them tingle as I healed.

Healing quickly, I wiggled my fingers before grabbing him with both hands and pulling. No, that was the wrong word for it. It was like turning on a vacuum, and I felt his magic slip into me. The more I took, the higher chance he would notice.

I wiggled my toes, and I let his wrist go. He wiped his wrist, cleaning my saliva off with his shirt, but I didn't waste any time. While he cleaned his wrist, I lifted my foot and kicked him straight in his pretty face. I hoped I hadn't damaged it. The shock would have been my only element of surprise, and I jumped up as he fell backward. Not expecting it, he clutched his nose, which now sprayed out blood.

But I didn't have time to feel bad when I blasted him with the magic I'd just stolen from him, which wasn't much but enough to shove him backward until he smacked into the metal bars, which knocked him out.

His face fell slack, and his shoulders slouched. I hesitated, feeling guilty I'd hurt him, but that wore off quickly as I looked to the open door and my escape route.

Running, I took the steps two at a time. Once I made it through the door and reached the top, I found another door and pushed it open slightly, peeking out. Blinking, I was taken aback by the fact the place was indeed something out of fairy tales. It was a castle with high ceilings, enormous chandeliers, massive staircases, and… was that a ballroom?

Oh, no, that was the mess hall. But it must have been a ballroom, judging by its sheer size. It had a very modern look for a castle; one of them had good tastes.

Pushing the door open, I could see a vast corridor across from me, but that meant running across to hide at the base of the stairs, which meant running past the wide-open double doors to the mess hall. Men seated at the long tables made me wonder if I would go unnoticed—*only one way to find out.* So I ran like crazy.

The screeching of chairs alerted me that I did not go unnoticed, and a fierce growl echoed off the walls. Still, I tried racing toward the double arched doors at the end of the long corridor.

This place was a maze, corridors leading everywhere, but I had no time to explore while I raced toward the doors, praying they would lead outside to freedom.

My blood ran cold when Darius suddenly materialized out of thin air, and my feet screeched on the floor. He appeared in front of the doors I intended to run out of. I was forced to stop and back up a step. Turning, I ran in the direction I'd just come from when I saw Tobias behind me. He had a menacing look on his face before I saw his hand whip toward my face a second too late.

It took another second to register as darkness swallowed my vision. Tobias punched me. He knocked me out, I thought. Though I shouldn't be surprised, he was exactly like Darius. Darkness engulfed me, and I begged the fates not to let me wake back up this time.

CHAPTER 7

Darius

TOBIAS'S FIST CONNECTED WITH her jaw. It happened so quickly that I barely caught the movement until she started to fall. Tobias hesitated to catch her, like he would let her hit the marble floors, but he moved at the last second, catching her limp body.

Lycus stormed out of the dungeons, looking extremely pissed off, and his shirt was coated in blood. Kalen was at his side in an instant, fussing over him. Lycus's shirt was saturated with blood, his nose bleeding, and Tobias turned, noticing my gaze was directed over his shoulder. Lycus smacked Kalen's fussing hands away as he stormed over to us.

"Fucking bitch stole some of my power and hit me with it," he growled, rubbing the back of his head with his hand.

Kalen's eyes looked to Aleera in Tobias's arms, his expression conflicted, before reaching his arms out for her.

"No, we have talked about this. You are to stay away from her," Tobias told him. Kalen looked at me, and I could see the pleading in his eyes. He wanted to hold her, feel her close.

"She is unconscious. She can't hurt him," I told Tobias, giving in to Kalen.

Tobias growled but shoved her toward him and let Kalen take her limp body in his arms. Lycus growled, not wanting Aleera near him. None of us did, and I worried this might start up the obsession again. I was pretty sure letting him take her would be just the beginning and a mistake on my part.

Kalen was already attached to her, and he hadn't even spoken to her yet. She looked small in his arms, hugged close to his chest. How could he still want her after it nearly cost him his life? He almost threw it away for her, and yet he was so tender with her. I hated it, and Tobias's deadly glare said he did, too.

"Put her back in the cells," I told him when he turned around with her in his arms. He froze, turning back to face me.

"Darius, please." His voice was a soft murmur before he looked down at her in his arms. Lycus walked over to him, stopping in front of him.

"Put her back in the cells, Kalen." Lycus's voice was a menacing growl. He was pissed off, but I wanted to know why he went into her cell.

"No! She isn't going back down there!" Kalen snapped, and Lycus's eyes went to his, his lips turning to a frown.

"She attacked me. She just tried to run. Put her back in the cells, or I will!" Lycus threatened him. Lycus was never like this with Kalen. He had never challenged our mate, but Kalen was the weakest of us, and the fact he would go against us showed his obsession was already returning.

We all knew he loved Aleera. He spent years talking to her. Without her knowing who he was to her, her running affected him the most. Now she was here. I was worried about his mental state. Stepping closer, I was about to back Lycus up when Tobias spoke beside me.

"Put her in her own room in our quarters. Kalen, if she runs again, I will kill her," Tobias warned him, and Lycus pressed his lips together, and his jaw clenched.

"She won't," Kalen answered, rushing off with her before Tobias changed his mind. We all struggled with saying no to Kalen. We were terrified of losing him again.

"What are you doing? We all agreed he was to be away from her. I don't want her near him," Lycus growled, his eyes flickering to silver, burning brightly as the beast that resided in him tried to take over. The savage side liked to terrorize its prey. Right now, I knew Aleera was his prey. *Good. She deserves no mercy.*

Lycus was usually calm. Aleera attacking him seemed to set him straight. He hated violence unless it was to protect one of us. He spent most of his childhood and teenage years fighting for Kalen in the orphanage they grew up in together. Aleera was a threat to Kalen, one he wanted to eliminate.

"You said she used your magic against you?" I asked him, and he looked away guiltily before making sure Kalen was out of earshot.

"Did you have to break her fucking leg and hand? I couldn't leave her like that."

"Well, you should have. So, don't blame us because Kalen is with her," Tobias scolded, but his eyes darted to me. We weren't usually violent toward women, but I had a particular spot reserved for Aleera. I had no qualms hurting her like she did all of us.

"You healed her," I scoffed before shaking my head.

"She was in pain. You said we make her suffer. You never said about literally breaking her bones."

"She was suffering. I see no difference," I answered.

"Don't let Kalen see you hurt her like that," he said, turning and folding his arms across his broad chest to glare at Tobias about to rant at him.

"He would have sat down there with her, don't look at me like that. You know I hate him with her just as much as you do, but I won't have our mate withering away in a cell with her or sneaking down to see her. It is better this way. We can monitor both of them," Tobias said before Lycus could shout at him about letting Kalen take her to our quarters. Lycus snarled, clearly not happy, but said nothing else on the matter.

"This may be a better idea, anyway."

"Why is that?" Tobias asked.

"Because tomorrow she can start classes. Let's see how she fares when she goes up against an entire castle of pure demons." Tobias chuckled at my words, knowing exactly what I was thinking.

"But she has no magic," Lycus said, and Tobias chuckled, dropping his hand on his shoulder.

"Exactly, we don't have to make her suffer. They will do it for us," Tobias said before stalking off toward the stairs.

"Where are you going?" Lycus asked him.

"To get Kalen away from her before he does something stupid, like confessing his undying love for her," Tobias tossed over his shoulder.

"So, what will you tell the men about her?"

"No, we will tell them nothing, only that she is our prisoner. Let them think what they want about her. I will just tell them she is an enemy we want to be kept close," I told Lycus.

"Good. I don't want them following her orders just because of what she is to us," Lycus replied while watching Tobias walk up the stairs to our mates.

"No, I have a better idea. Whoever breaks Aleera first wins the ballad for a ranking officer," I told him, and he smirked.

"Well, that will be enough motivation for them, but she is not to be in any of Kalen's classes," Lycus said, and I nodded my head in agreement.

"I know you're worried about him—" He raised his hand, silencing me.

"Don't. You didn't find him. You didn't have to cut his body down from the rafters. Worried is not the word I would use to describe how I feel about Aleera being near him," Lycus growled before turning on his heel and walking away from me.

My jaw clenched at his words. I wasn't there, but luckily we got back in time. Luckily, Tobias could revive him and heal his broken neck. A few seconds later, he would no longer be with us. We would have never let him die, but resurrection could be tricky. It tainted the soul, and not in a good way. She wouldn't destroy us this time. No, she would break and when she did, she would understand the torment she had caused us.

CHAPTER 8

Aleera

MY HEAD THROBBED, AND the back of my eyes ached but not nearly as much as my jaw did. I groaned, forcing my eyes open when I realized I wasn't on the hard concrete floor of the dungeon. No, I felt warmer and more comfortable. I blinked, trying to clear the blurriness of my vision to find a man sitting next to me. I was in a bedroom… on a bed.

The man stared, like he was looking through me as I jerked upright and pulled away from him. He had blond hair that looked like he had just run his fingers through it only moments before. His blue eyes were the lightest shade I had ever seen, so pale they were almost white. If it weren't for my enhanced eyesight, I would have assumed they were until he blinked. The color returned to them. I wondered where his mind had gone as the color returned, and his eyes were now a startling cerulean blue.

"Drink, please," he said, reaching beside me for the tall glass of water. He handed it to me, and I clutched it with shaky hands. "Please," he repeated, and for some unknown reason, I didn't like the idea of upsetting him, so I quickly obeyed, bringing the glass to my lips. The icy liquid poured into my mouth, which was so dry that I gulped it down before nearly choking on it.

"Slow. Not so fast," he murmured, gripping the glass. My fingers tingled where his bumped mine. He slowly tipped the cup up, allowing me to drink what was left in it.

He went to open his mouth to say something else when the door opened suddenly. He turned his head to look at who had entered, and so did I. Tobias was leaning on the doorframe. I quickly looked away from him, back to the man sitting beside me, and I knew who he was.

"You are Kalen?" I whispered, and his face turned back to me. He studied me for a second before shifting closer to me, his hand outstretched, and I wondered if he would hit me, but he didn't seem like he was going to. I didn't have time to find out when Tobias spoke from the doorway.

"Kalen, Darius wants to speak with you," Tobias said while pushing off the doorframe. Kalen dropped his hand and sighed.

"Why?" he asked, turning to look back at Tobias. His voice was deep yet not cruel, and it didn't make me want to cringe upon hearing it, like Darius and Tobias's voices did.

"You know why. Now, don't make him wait. You know he hates waiting," Tobias told him, his voice different, softer as he spoke to Kalen. Kalen's shoulders dropped as he got up off the bed. I didn't want him to leave. He was the only one that didn't appear to want to kill me. Yet as he moved around the edge of the bed and toward the door, I noticed Tobias would not follow him.

"Close the door," Tobias said, and my heart rate picked up at his words. I glanced toward Kalen, who nodded before giving me a sad smile and shutting the door behind him as he left. Tobias stepped slowly around the edge of the bed, and I moved to the other side, getting ready to run if needed.

He chuckled as if he found my fear of him amusing. He stopped next to the dresser that sat along the wall.

"I would remain where you are, Aleera. Don't tempt me because it will only end in pain for you," Tobias said, the softer, kind voice he'd used with Kalen now replaced with a harsh cold one that held a warning. I hesitated to place my foot on the gray carpet. He turned his head to the side, and I brought my leg back onto the bed before tucking both to my chest.

"Good. You can listen," he said as the door opened again. My other three mates walked in. Darius was the most imposing among them. The second was Tobias, but they were all intimidating. Darius and Tobias commanded your attention effortlessly just by their presence alone, and if looks could kill, Lycus would have turned me to ash.

He had changed his shirt to a white one. Darius had black slacks and a white button-up shirt, the sleeves rolled to his elbows. Not only was he menacing, but he also looked the part, with the way the shirt hugged his body like it was tailored to him. The fabric did nothing to hide the bulk of muscle beneath it.

Kalen had on jeans and a black shirt. He was leaner than the others yet still muscular from what I could tell by his arms and the ridges of his abs pressing against his shirt. Lycus, however, was all muscle, having werewolf genes mixed with his fae ones—typical shifter genes.

Lycus's eyes had changed again, making me wonder if they changed with his temperament. He looked pissed off, yet his eyes' color was now amber. Maybe it was the light down in the dungeon. I knew werewolf shifters had deep silver eyes in a semi-shifted or shifted state, so it must have been a trick of the light, which meant this had to be the natural color of his eyes.

Darius folded his arms across his chest, glaring down at me, and I dropped my gaze, unable to handle its intensity; it burned into me with a hatred that made my stomach twist.

"Nothing to say, Aleera?" Darius asked. What could I say? What excuse would he accept that was good enough because clearly murdering my parents and burning my family home down wasn't a good enough reason to run from them? If I told them the other reason, they would probably pin me down and use me to destroy the world as their personal power source.

Movement caught my eye, and Darius suddenly appeared next to me before gripping my face. His fingers dug into my cheeks as he forced me to meet his demonic eyes. Darkness was all I saw in them. He was evil incarnate.

"I asked you a question," he said, his voice deadly calm when he shoved my face away. I rubbed my cheek where his nails dug in a little too hard, breaking the skin.

"You will remain in this room between classes. If you leave this castle without permission, you will find yourself back in the cells, understood?" Darius asked.

"Don't try to run, Aleera. Our room is right next door, and I will have guards stationed on the stairs. They have permission to use force if necessary," Tobias said, and Lycus walked over to a door I hadn't noticed before.

He opened it, and I saw it was a bathroom. There was another door on the other end, which I guessed led into the room next door.

His words suddenly registered. *Did they all share the same room?* I stared at them but said nothing when Darius leaned down, making me tilt backward as his hands dropped on the bed on either side of my hips.

My eyes went to the faint outline on his neck, three marks overlapping each other. I blinked in shock, wondering if I'd imagined it. *No, it couldn't be.* I was their keeper, and mates didn't mark each other; usually, they only marked their keeper. I was the link between them, yet why did he have all three of their marks on his neck? I wanted to know if they all shared each other's marks.

"Is that understood, Aleera?" Darius asked, and I tore my eyes away from his neck to look at his face. I quickly nodded.

CHAPTER 9

DARIUS WATCHED MY FACE for a second, and I swallowed as his eyes ran down my body and to my lap, making me shift uncomfortably. He growled; the noise gave me goosebumps as he towered over me.

"Lycus, go get her some clothes. Kalen, go grab her a shirt until Lycus comes back so she can shower," Darius said before pushing off the bed away from me. Lycus nodded to him before walking out, and so did Kalen, leaving me with Darius and Tobias.

"You attend every class. Someone will pick you up from your room in the morning to take you down to the mess hall, where all meals are served for those who live here."

"Where am I?" I asked before I could stop myself. Darius didn't like being talked over as he took a deep breath, and I watched his hands clench into fists at his sides before looking down.

"Meals are in the mess hall. I will have some books sent in here. Under no circumstances are you to tell anyone here you are our mate. If you do, you will wish you were in the cells. Am I clear?"

"Crystal," I told him.

"Also," Tobias said, stepping closer to the bed and moving to stand beside Darius, "you will steer clear of Kalen. Stay out of our way, and if you can behave and do as you're told, you will have a bit more freedom."

"Why can't I go near Kalen?" I asked, confused. He appeared to be the only one who didn't outright condemn me.

"Don't question us. Just do as we ask. It isn't up for discussion," Tobias said just as Kalen walked back into the room. He had a folded shirt in his hands, and he placed it on the end of the bed with a towel.

"Now go shower; you're filthy. Tobias will bring you something to eat when you are out of the shower," Darius said before turning on his heel and walking out. He stopped at the door, looking expectantly at Kalen, who turned around when Tobias touched his shoulder, nodding toward the door. Kalen left. He looked like he wanted to say something but kept it to himself. They both left, and Tobias stayed behind, looking down at me.

"Count yourself lucky we haven't killed you yet, Aleera. Be careful not to give us a reason to. Kalen may not want you dead, but the rest of us do. Just remember that," he said before walking out and closing the door behind him. I heard the lock click in place, so I didn't even bother checking it as I got up and walked into the bathroom.

A shower sounded excellent. I hadn't had a hot shower in god knows how long, usually washing in lakes or streams. It wasn't the same. You never really felt clean with only cold water, and I was lucky to find soap when I could. *I suppose that's what happens when you leave the fae community and are forced to live in the wilderness among monsters, never catching a whole night's sleep and jerking awake at every noise.*

Walking into the bathroom, I stopped in front of the mirror above the basin, furrowing my brows when I noticed it had five sinks. A shower took up an entire wall behind me, and there was a colossal bath that could easily fit five people in the middle of the room. A toilet was in the far corner, and I wondered if they'd specifically made this room for the five of us before I ran.

Guilt gnawed at me as I placed the shirt and towel on the basin before looking at myself in the mirror. I looked different from what I remembered. My face had changed; it was slimmer. I didn't look like the same eighteen-year-old girl when I left the boarding school. I looked older, drained of life. I was skinnier, my hair dull and lifeless. It was so much longer now. It used to sit on my shoulders; now, it was halfway down my back, having grown out.

The door leading to the other room opened, and Kalen wandered in.

"There is shampoo and soap in the niches and a spare tooth-brush." He walked over before bending down and opening the cupboards under the sink basin and reaching into it.

He pulled out a hairbrush and toothbrush before handing them to me.

"Thank you," I told him, observing the man. He nodded, and I heard talking in the room he had just walked in here from.

"You all share a room?" Kalen looked at the door before nodding and looking back over at me.

"Strange, huh?" I shrugged, unsure what others did when they had multiple mates. I stared at his neck, finding the same markings I saw on Darius's. Kalen placed his hand over it, pulling my attention back to him.

"I should go. They won't be pleased if they catch me talking to you."

I chewed my lip as I watched him slip out of the bathroom. Turning back to the mirror, I peeled off my hoodie and shirt before dumping them in the basket.

The clothes were stained and holey, but I wasn't sure where my bag was, and I believed I had left it behind in the city—vaguely remembering it slipping off my shoulder when I called on them. I unbuttoned my jeans and stepped out of them before unclipping my bra. I placed it on the sink basin, knowing I only had one.

Turning around, I hurried to the shower and turned it on, my hand placed under the water as I waited for the temperature to heat before stepping in. It was like heaven, and I sighed, bracing my hands on the tiled wall—the dirt, grime, and blood washing down the drain as I pressed my face under the spray.

Opening my eyes, I reached for the soap in the niche before slathering it on my skin. I didn't want to get out but knew I had no choice; the effort it took to remain standing was becoming intolerable. Hunger made me feel weak and shaky; I needed to eat soon. The steam made me dizzy, and my hands hadn't stopped shaking since I awoke. Shutting off the shower, I jumped when I heard a knock on the door before the handle twisted.

CHAPTER 10

PANIC HAD ME RUSHING over to my towel and snatching it off the sink basin. The door opened while I was trying to wrap it around myself, barely managing to cover myself when Tobias walked in. He sneered at me before his eyes ran the length of me while I stood clutching the towel awkwardly. My fingers were clutching the towel tightly, and I watched as his face twisted in disgust like he couldn't bear to look at me. Shame washed over me. How could I be so stupid as not to check if the door was locked? I would have saved myself this sort of humiliation. I didn't think I was horrid to look at, nothing that warranted the look of disgust he gave me.

If I repulsed him with just a towel on, I would hate to see the look on his face if he got a good look at the burns on my back. That was something I consciously made sure was covered, my back permanently mutilated because of Darius. Gym class was the worst at school. I hated it. The girls would stare in pity; they never said anything but a look could sometimes express more than words could and to think my mate had done that to me when he killed my parents—he branded me permanently.

"Hurry up. I haven't got all night," he snarled before slamming the door as he walked out and back into the room they'd placed me in.

The bang of the door made me jump before I scrambled to dry myself and put on the T-shirt Kalen had given me to wear. It fell to my thighs, but I had another issue. I had no panties, and I couldn't put back on the ones I was wearing—a little nasty to wear them again after having them on for days while in the dungeon.

Tugging the shirt down as far as it would go, I sucked in a breath, trying to calm myself as I opened the door to see Tobias sitting by the fire.

He pointed at a bowl of something that smelled delicious. "Eat." His voice was cold as he turned his attention back to the fireplace. Frankly, anything would smell delicious at this point. Seven days without eating would make the grossest food smell and look appealing.

"Now, Aleera or would you prefer I bring Darius in here to force you to eat?" he asked, turning around from where he sat in the chair by the small fireplace. Shaking my head, I forced my feet to move, slowly walking past him toward the tray on the bedside table. Nausea swirled in my stomach at the smell. *Maybe I should have eaten the bread*, I thought as I watched my hands tremble as they clutched the bowl before placing it on my lap.

The spoon rattled against the porcelain as I grabbed it, trying to scoop the soup on the spoon. Most of it spilled back into the bowl as I brought the spoon to my lips. Seven days without eating, and the smell of hot food showed how weak I had let myself become. I couldn't even remember the last time I ate hot food, mostly living off fruit and veggies I could scrounge up in the forests. It was the first time that I had stepped into a city in months.

I wouldn't have even left, but the cold and snow had frozen my water source, and most of the vegetation was frozen or dead. At that point, I had no idea how much further the human communities were, and I was too weak to continue walking, so I dared to go to the city in search of water and food. Only that was a mistake because look at where I ended up… in the clutches of men who didn't want me.

Movement made me flinch as Tobias moved toward me, his aura rushing out like a protective barrier. Except it wasn't for protection. No, he wanted me to know he could hurt me, inflict pain on me if he wanted, as he stopped in front of me. I swallowed nervously before I strained my neck to look up at his angry face.

"I warned you, and you fucking still refuse," he spat at me before walking toward the bedroom door and disappearing into the hall. The door clicked shut behind him, and I wondered what he meant; I was doing what he asked. Turning back to my chicken soup, I placed the spoon down before glancing over my shoulder, slightly embarrassed before I drank the soup straight from the bowl, having managed to get none in my mouth with the spoon from the trembling of my hands.

They still shook as I brought the bowl to my lips and the warm liquid spilled into my mouth. A moan escaped me at the first mouthful, and some ran down my chin. I nearly choked as I hungrily gulped it down when I heard the door handle rattle. I pulled the bowl away from my lips and hastily grabbed the spoon from the bedside table so they wouldn't think I was some pig with no table manners, but it would have gone cold long before any made it to my mouth.

My belly felt warm from the chicken soup, and I tried to scoop some onto the spoon when a shriek left me as Darius appeared next to me, his hand reaching toward me. I scrambled back, nearly spilling the bowl onto my lap. Tobias grabbed it before it ruined the bed and splashed over my legs just as Darius gripped my hair.

Kalen nodded, holding the bowl up and pressing it to my lips. My hands grabbed it as he tipped it up, and my hands shook violently as I gripped his hand on the bowl, so I wouldn't choke as he poured the soup into my mouth.

"That's it," he said as I drank straight from the bowl. Soup ran down my chin and spilled onto his shirt.

"Slow, you will choke," Kalen told me, pulling the bowl away for a second and letting me catch my breath.

"When did you eat last?" he asked as I reached for the bowl. He brought it back to my lips, and I drank the remainder of it, my stomach feeling heavy and full for once when he pulled it away once I had drained it.

Kalen held his hand out, and I noticed Lycus had my towel in his hands. He passed it to Kalen, who handed it to me. I used it to wipe my face and his shirt, where I spilled some of the soup on it.

"You didn't answer," Kalen said, and I looked at him, my brows pinching as I tried to remember if he'd asked me something.

"Better?" he asked, and I nodded, giving the towel back to him.

"When did you eat last?" Kalen asked.

"Seven days ago," I told him.

"Bullshit, you have only been here three days," Darius snapped, taking a step toward me, and I cringed.

"That's why you were in the shifter city," Kalen stated, and I nodded.

"Yeah, everything froze over, all the vegetation and the stream. Most of the water sources were polluted. I didn't realize it was a shifter city. I was hoping it was a human one. I was desperate, mainly for water. I could have lasted longer... I have lasted longer but not without water," I admitted.

"You expect us to believe you were living in the forests and homeless all this time? Bullshit! Aleera, who did you run off with?

We saw the surveillance footage, and you left with someone? Who is he?" Darius snarled and Kalen glared at him. Did he seriously think I ran off with some man? That I would run away for someone else? Clayton had only helped me get out. That was it; we were not friends, merely acquaintances.

"I don't care what you believe, Darius. I know the truth, and that is all that matters. Whether or not you believe me is up to you or you could ask Tobias. He should be able to tell if I am lying or not. I have no magic left to mask myself," I told him. Darius looked over at Tobias, who was observing me like a complicated math equation.

Tobias moved around the bed stopping behind Kalen before reaching his hand toward my face. I pulled away when he suddenly pinched my chin between his fingers.

"Repeat it," he said, his eyes boring into mine.

"I hadn't eaten before now in seven days, drank anything in nearly as long. I ran because Darius killed my parents," I answered him, and he let my face go. He sighed, pinching the bridge of his nose and exhaling.

"Well?" asked Darius.

"I was wrong. She is telling the truth."

"So you called me in here for no reason?" Darius snarled at him.

"How was I supposed to know? I thought she was refusing to do what she was told."

"By fucking asking. Did you bother to ask her?"

"You deal with her then. I didn't even want to be near her," Tobias said before storming out of the room.

I looked down at my hands, my throat restricting at his words. The mate bond made his words sting, even though the feeling of hatred was mutual. Their outright blatant rejection was like a slap in the face, making me remember they didn't want me. I

"I can go?" he said, and he rolled about to get out of the bed. When I gripped his arm, he stopped. He didn't want to go, and honestly, I didn't want him to leave. It had been years since I met someone I wanted to be around.

Kalen was the first normal interaction I had had since leaving school. Being the strange girl who stuck to herself in school didn't win me any friends, and for years the only friend I had was a stranger I spoke to online. It was the only way to vent my frustrations, and I regretted leaving my tablet behind. I wondered if I could get access to a computer here. I knew it wouldn't be anytime soon if they did agree, and I doubted they would let me use it to speak to my friend over the internet, whoever they might be.

Kalen lay back down, and I observed him the best I could in the darkness, yet curiosity was eating at me.

"You're not like them. You don't seem to hate me."

"Because I don't. I figured you ran for some reason."

"And if I just ran?" I asked him. He shrugged. "I can't say I blame you. Darius scared the crap out of us when he found us." He paused like he was locked in his memories, his aura turned depressive, and I held my tongue, thinking it might be best not to ask what upset him.

"So, I still couldn't hate you for running even if you had no reason," he said simply before wriggling closer to me.

His hand reached toward my face slowly, and he hesitated once again before I grabbed his hand, his magic coming to life beneath mine, yet I didn't take it. I couldn't bring myself to break his trust. If I was going to be stuck here, I needed a friend to survive my mates, so why not keep the only decent one close?

Kalen let out a breath when I placed his hand on my cheek. His thumb brushed beneath my eye softly, and I closed my eyes. Sleep finally took me.

When I woke up, I found the spot where Kalen had been empty, looking around the room. A prickle up my spine alerted me to someone in the room before his voice did.

"Looking for someone?" Darius asked, and I shook my head, scooting up the bed.

I yawned. Darius watched me or rather glared at me. "Get up. You have five minutes to get dressed. Put these on," he said, throwing some clothes at me.

He then stormed out, and I looked to the window to see the sun was barely up. I groaned, wondering where he wanted to take me. I slipped the jeans on, which fit perfectly, and a white blouse. How did Lycus know my size? I shook the thought away before realizing I had no shoes. I looked around the room for some when the door opened.

"Time is up," Darius called, pushing the door wider. I glanced down at my feet. I only had socks on, and I quickly glanced around again but found no shoes. Darius, however, didn't care as he suddenly walked off. Was I meant to follow him even if I had no shoes on?

"Now, Aleera," Darius snapped, and I rushed out after him. His long strides had me jogging to keep up. My feet were cold even with the thick bed socks on. Darius walked down a flight of stairs, and I became lost with all the twists and turns. I could hear the murmuring of men behind doors, and I raced to keep up with Darius before we went down yet another set of stairs to a floor I recognized from when I'd tried to escape.

Darius walked to the mess hall, where I saw all the men gathered the other day. It had a few tables full when we walked in. All of them looked up, and I froze. More men filed in behind me, bumping into me, and Darius gripped my arm, his nails digging into my tender flesh. He dragged me over to a table and dumped me on a chair.

Glancing around, I noticed something quickly. They were all demons. These men weren't fae. The other thing I noticed was that there was no woman in this room. Looking up at Darius, he was smirking cruelly at me.

"Welcome to hell, Aleera. Don't think my men are your friends or will be your friends. No one likes a traitor." Darius leaned down. His stubble brushed my cheek, and I held my breath at his closeness.

"And all of them think you are and don't go looking for any woman. You will find none. You are the only one," Darius said before standing upright. Darius turned to leave.

"Wait!" I reached out, grabbing his hand, and he growled at me. I jerked my hand away and took a step back at the frightening look he gave me.

"You can't… Are you leaving me here?" I asked, petrified. Demons fed on fear or any emotion, really, and I knew I would be a nice treat to these men. *An emotional buffet.*

"Why? Are you scared, Aleera?" I looked around, their demonic eyes watching me, and I gulped before looking up at Darius. He chuckled, the sound mocking.

"I wanted to kill you, but now seeing the look on your face, I know this was the better option," Darius said, and he looked around at all the men. He smiled. I didn't like the look he wore on his face. It was off, severely off.

"Zac, come here," Darius called out and waved a man over.

"Keep Aleera company and take her to your first lesson."

"Be my pleasure, my King," the man taunted, his smile growing bigger as he stared down at me.

"Just don't kill her. I want to watch her suffer. I don't want you to incinerate her before she has," Darius told him before walking out of the mess hall. He left, and I remained frozen before turning to face this Zac person who grabbed my arm, hauling me over to a table with three other men.

CHAPTER 13

"DARIUS CAN BE A dick. He will settle down," Zac said. I stared at him, confused. He almost seemed normal, nice even, as he slid a food tray over to me. Zac sat across from me, grabbing another before digging into his food.

The man beside him was a huge burly-looking man with a short beard and dark hair, and he tapped my tray. "Eat. If you're training with us, you will need it," he said. I looked down at the tray to find it had scrambled eggs on it.

"I'm Satish, that's Zac, as you know, and that one is Deacon." The other man waved; he had blond hair, a boyish face, and was clearly the youngest at the table. It was impossible to tell the actual age of full-blooded demons; they could be hundreds of years old or precisely the age they appeared.

"And that one at the end is Lyle." The man nodded, but his lips pulled back in a snarl. *Note to self, stay away from the unfriendly one.* I went back to my food, scooping up some egg on my fork.

"So, Darius and the others don't eat down here with you?" I asked. Zac snorted and shook his head.

"No, this place belongs to Darius. He owns and runs it."

"So, he bought it then?"

Zac shook his head before leaning back in his seat. "You don't know much about them."

"About Darius and the others? No, only what I managed to hear on the radio or see on the news of their killing sprees."

"Darius grew up here, and this was his home. Darius turned it into a dark-arts training facility. They are all teachers in a way. Who better to teach dark magic than the Demon King himself?" Zac answered.

"So, you all like it here?" I asked, glancing around at the table, wondering if I could get an idea of where here was.

"Well, we all volunteered, so yeah. We may be demons, but we want to catch the ones responsible for releasing that plague and taking over the world also sounds promising," Zac answered, and I nearly choked on my food.

"Wait, Darius is building an army?"

"Why else would we be here?" Satish said with a shrug. Suddenly an alarm blared loudly, and everyone jumped to their feet.

The silent instruction had me scrambling to my feet after them, and I followed Zac, dumping my half-eaten breakfast on the bench like everyone else as they filed out.

Zac grabbed my hand, pulling me after him, and a few people trod on my feet by accident. I hissed when I felt my toenail bend back. Zac stopped, looking back at me, and I looked down at my sock, blood staining the toes. I ripped the sock off quickly, knowing the tugging would make it annoying. I pressed my lips together for a second to stop from swearing. My toenail was half ripped off. *I could live with that.* I quickly removed my other sock since everyone appeared to be going toward the main entry doors.

"Man, you must have really pissed him off for him not to give you shoes," Zac said, tugging me toward the door leading out.

Excitement bubbled in me; this could be my chance to escape. That thought instantly died down when I stepped outside and saw vast fields with different obstacle courses and then nothing but dense forest, making me stop.

"Hurry up. Tobias doesn't like tardiness. The first lesson is with him," Zac explained, and I nodded, trying to keep up.

"What does he teach?" I asked, trying to hide my disappointment at not seeing a road leading in here.

"Hand-to-hand combat and the tracks," Zac said, and I stopped completely.

"As in fighting, like in combat?"

Zac looked at me like I had grown two heads before he laughed. "Well, that is why it is called hand to hand." He held up his fists.

"Don't worry, I'll go easy on you," Zac said, and I let out a breath of relief before letting him pull me along after him.

"So, how many men and women are here?"

"Six hundred men."

I waited for him to tell me Darius was joking about there being no women, but when he added nothing else, my stomach dropped a little. "Wait, there is really no other woman here?"

"Nope, you are the only one. Lucky you, aye?" he said, tugging me to an empty place on the field. Men started getting into different stances, and I looked around nervously. A few were stretching, and some were just chatting among themselves.

"Well, I thought you would be a complete asshole since Darius asked you to show me around, but I am glad to see he was wrong about you," I told Zac as he led me over to his friends.

"He ain't wrong about Zac. He is the cruelest of us all," Satish said, clapping a hand on my shoulder. I looked over my shoulder at him, and he took a stance behind me when I saw Deacon move to my side and Lyle come up to the other.

The four men were boxing me in. Looking over at Zac, he had a smirk on his face.

"What?" I asked, my voice trembling, suddenly feeling uncomfortable with how they were all staring at me.

"Darius told her to her face that we would make her miserable, and yet she thought we could be friends." Zac laughed, and my stomach dropped.

What the heck just happened? But they were nice a few seconds ago. Satish sniffed the air deeply, and I spun to find him directly behind me, too close. I took a step back only to be shoved.

I landed in the mud, losing my footing and headbutting the ground hard enough that black dots danced in front of me before I hauled myself up onto my hands and knees, only to be kicked in the stomach. The air left my lungs in a long wheeze. I could hear them laughing and braced myself for another blow when a whistle sounded. They all stopped, and Zac kneeled next to me while I gasped for air.

"We told you our names, not because we want to be your friends, Aleera, but so you know who to whine to Darius about," he sneered before shoving my face away. The whistle blew again, and a pair of boots stopped in front of my face. I looked up with my blurry vision.

"Get up. Why are you on the ground?" Tobias spat at me. I looked over at Zac, who smirked.

"Tripped," I told him, and Tobias reached down, seizing my arm and yanking me to my feet. I tried to wipe some of the mud off using my hands but only managed to smear it worse.

"Fucking disgusting," Tobias growled before stalking off, and I gritted my teeth, fighting back the urge to cry. I couldn't let these monsters see me as weak; I had to learn to block them out. At least until I escaped.

"Twenty laps, then the obstacle course, no one-on-one today. You have your prep exams," Tobias called out to the men.

I gulped when I saw the men start running toward a field. I made my way over, trying not to slip on the mud, and the tiny sharp rocks dug into my feet. I made it halfway to the field before stopping. The mud was too slippery, making me wonder why this side was all mud and slippery.

What could you possibly do while sliding around? I clutched my knees, trying to catch my breath and also fighting the urge to throw up the little breakfast I got to eat. The backs of my legs were burning from having to unstick my feet and legs from mud. This was ridiculous; the mud was now up to my knees.

"What do you think you are doing?" I looked up and saw Tobias stalking toward me. I flinched when I saw his hand reach toward me. Losing my footing on the slick surface, I fell backward, slipping in the mud and landing on my bottom.

"Get your ass over there with the other men."

"I have no shoes."

"You need something, you fucking earn it. Clearly, Darius doesn't think you earned them yet. Now, get up!"

"Well, can I at least have mine back?" I asked. Tobias reached forward, gripping my arm, his nails sinking into my soft skin, and I could feel the entire outline of his hand. His grip was so tight, I knew it would have been bruised.

"You don't speak to me unless spoken to, understood? You weren't supposed to be in any of my classes, but here you are, so shut up and quit whining." I nodded before he shoved me forward, and I only just managed to stay upright as I clambered to the field. A sigh escaped me when I found my feet on solid ground.

However, my relief was short-lived when I noticed the track running a circle around the obstacle course was all gravel.

CHAPTER 14

"Move it, Aleera! Twenty laps, now!" Tobias roared behind me.

Despite not wanting to run, my feet started moving, the rocks digging into my feet painfully. It didn't take long before the men overlapped me. Around a hundred or so barging and shoving past me. What the heck was their problem? I didn't even know them and they took no care when they came too close.

"Aleera!" I heard Zac's voice behind me before looking over my shoulder in time to see him running straight at me. I tried to step out of his way when he dropped his shoulder and barreled straight into me, diverting slightly off track to hit me deliberately.

My body was tossed across the gravel, and I felt like I was being skinned alive. My face burned as I skidded across the loose gravel, my hands I used to try and brace myself grazed, and I felt battered and bruised all over.

"Up, Aleera! You have only done three laps!" Tobias called from the center where the obstacle courses were. I hauled my body up to my hands and knees, trying not to cry out at my pain and discomfort.

It was agonizing, I kept going, and by the time I finished the laps, the men had completed theirs plus the obstacle course. The rest of the class moved on to their next lesson while Zac had been told to make sure I finished the course.

His sneers and name-calling were starting to get to me. I was starving, and the sun was cooking me alive. I wondered how long I had been out here when the blare of the alarm sounded; it was time for lunch.

Someone brought Zac out some food while I tried to navigate the climbing wall. My arms could not take my weight much longer and shook as I tried to haul myself up when I felt something smack me in the center of the back. I was about five meters up when pain rippled up my spine, and I lost my grip, plummeting to the ground below.

A shriek left my lips as I grasped the air frantically, hitting the ground with a thud before darkness swallowed me.

The sound of angry voices pulled me back to my surroundings. A furious growl had me blinking, and I found the sun was no longer directly above me, the sky now painted in orange and pink hues as I tried to remember what had happened.

"If she runs again, I swear I will fucking kill her," Darius's angry voice boomed. I groaned, rolling on my side, my head pounding to its own beat and every muscle aching. My back was killing me, and my skin felt sunburned.

"You know she wouldn't be able to find her way through the forest. She wouldn't even know what direction to go in," I heard Lycus's voice answer.

"Wait, I can smell her scent," Lycus growled, and I pulled myself up to my hands and glanced around to see them coming up over the small hill from the castle.

"Found her!" Tobias called out, pointing at me. My vision was blurry, and I squinted about to get to my feet when suddenly Darius gripped my hair, yanking my head back. He moved with speed that made the air rush around me. One second he was over on the crest of the small hill; the next, he was beside me.

"You think you can skip classes, Aleera?" he snarled as I clutched his hands and cried out. My hair ripped painfully from my scalp, and I would need to find some scissors. The taunts and bullying I could deal with. The hair-pulling was a low act and very demeaning. I suddenly cursed being a girl.

"Let go. You're hurting me," I choked out, and he laughed before shoving me forward back in the dirt.

I rubbed the back of my neck and noticed Kalen was nowhere to be seen, which at least gave me comfort, knowing the only person who had been decent to me since being here wasn't hunting me down to inflict more injury when my brain backtracked. He was one of them. He could be looking for me elsewhere.

"Get up! You have power placement with me. If I ever have to come searching for you again because you have missed class—"

"Ah, finally you found her," Kalen said, cutting Darius off as he jogged over to us and a look of relief crossed his features as he let out a breath.

"Had me worried for a second. I thought you left us again," Kalen said, and his smile faltered when he looked at me. Kalen turned and looked at Darius before he shoved him. "Why is she bleeding? What the fuck did you do?" Kalen snapped out in an angry growl.

Darius ripped Kalen toward him by the front of his shirt. "I haven't done anything but take that tone with me again, and I will make you watch her punishment," Darius growled at him.

Lycus gripped Darius's arm, and Darius looked at him. "We have enough going on. We don't need to be fighting each other, especially over her," Lycus said before glaring down at me. I remained quiet, not wanting to draw any more attention to myself. Kalen, however, didn't.

"Punishment for what?" Kalen demanded.

"She skipped my class and Lycus's."

"Come on, give her a break. It's her first day," Kalen said, offering me his hand. I reached for it, and Darius slapped my hand away.

"She can get up by herself. She survived for six years, holed up god knows where or with whom. She can get herself up," Darius snapped at him.

CHAPTER 15

ALEN FROWNED AND APPEARED to be thinking. He went to speak before closing his mouth. A dark expression crossed his features before turning on his heel and walking off.

My stomach sank, wondering why the sudden change in his attitude. Surely, he didn't believe what Darius had said, but then again, I didn't really know any of them well enough to judge their behavior.

A kick to my leg pulled my gaze away from a retreating Kalen. I hissed at the sudden pain radiating up my leg.

"Get up, and get to your next class!" Darius spat at me. The look of pure hatred on his face made me cringe away. My eyeballs pulsating in my head, along with the pounding headache, and all I wanted to do was find somewhere to lie down and rest for a bit.

Climbing to my feet, I staggered. The ground felt like it was moving, and my vision blurred. Touching the back of my head, I winced, quickly pulling my fingers away to find blood had stained them.

"I said, get to the next class!"

I flinched at his closeness and forced myself to move. "Wha

time is it?" I asked as I tried not to limp. Each footfall caused pain as the rocks stabbed and sliced my tender feet.

"Lunch just finished," Lycus answered, and I nodded. My stomach growled hungrily at the mention of food. I couldn't believe I had been out here for hours. Zac had just left me there. That thought stung a little at the knowledge that not a single person here cared if I suddenly dropped dead.

"Where are your shoes?" I didn't bother answering Lycus, and Darius growled behind me when I stopped to glance back at him.

"I don't know where I am going," I admitted. *Let alone what class I had next.*

"The mess hall. Now, get moving," Darius snarled. Lycus moved toward me and gripped my arm. Tobias and Darius both growled at him.

"For fuck's sake, Darius, look at her feet. She can barely fucking walk."

"Well, if she didn't skip classes, I may have given her shoes," he retorted.

"I didn't skip. I fell off because of that jerk—" I argued but stopped, not seeing the point in debating my tardiness with him.

"Because of whom?" Tobias demanded, and I glanced at him to see Darius glare at him. Tobias quickly looked away and added nothing else when my feet suddenly went from under me. I shrieked, not expecting it, and Lycus grabbed me, scooping me up in his arms.

"Lycus!" Darius roared, and I felt the energy rush out of him, which made me suddenly want to run. Terror filled me, and I wanted Lycus to put me down before Darius did something. Lycus just held me tighter and started walking when I smacked into Darius's chest while in Lycus's arms. Lycus stopped, staring at him.

"She can walk," Darius told him, but Lycus held his gaze unafraid of him while I pushed closer to Lycus. The movement was not missed by Darius, who glared at me.

"She is done for the day," Lycus said, his voice even as he barged past him, walking around a furious Darius.

Everything ached. There wasn't a single part of me that didn't hurt, and I had never felt so relieved to be locked back in my room; I would take this prison cell over not having to face those men again. Lycus had placed me on my feet just inside the room before shutting the door. He'd locked it. I heard the door click and heard him storm off up the hall.

He didn't say a word to me, yet I could tell he was second-guessing getting me out of classes after we got back to the castle. Every time my skin touched his, he would tense like he couldn't even bear the thought that any part of me was near him. His jaw was tense as he climbed the stairs before placing me in the room and leaving. I kind of hoped I could see Kalen. I couldn't understand the strange vibes I got from him.

Like I needed to protect him, but from what? Like he was fragile somehow. I noticed they were super protective of him, but I wouldn't hurt him. I had no magic to even if I wanted to. It fizzled out, and until they either gave me some, which was unlikely, or I managed to sneakily obtain some, I was utterly defenseless, and that thought scared me.

As I moved toward the bathroom, pain rippled up my legs. It caused agony through the bottoms of my feet, but I needed to clean them. I winced when I placed my foot on the cold tiles, my foot sliding as my blood stained the tiles, making them slippery.

I made my way over to the bathtub and sat on the edge, planning to rinse them under the tap and assess the damage, when the door suddenly opened. I looked up to see Kalen step in with

burn my house with them in it to the damn ground," I snapped angrily, and Lycus stopped.

"If that is why you left, then you are a bigger idiot than I thought. Darius didn't kill your parents, Aleera," Lycus growled at me before taking a step forward. He stopped, and his eyes flickered with anger.

"You would know that if you bothered to fucking ask, instead of nearly killing us all," Lycus spat at me.

"I saw him. I know what I saw."

"Then what you saw was wrong. Darius and Tobias didn't murder your parents, Aleera."

"What are you talking about? Tobias wasn't even there," I argued.

"Who do you think dragged you out? So, if that is why you ran, then you deserve everything they do to you."

"Lycus!" Kalen murmured behind him, and Lycus growled before turning on his heel and shoving Kalen out of the bathroom. He then slammed the door so hard it made me jump.

CHAPTER 17

Darius

Lycus was in a terrible mood when I came up to the room. Pushing the door open, Lycus was yelling at Kalen, which was rare; he tried never to raise his voice around Kalen. We all knew how fragile he was. We had all had to pull him back from the brink at some point, yet walking in, I had no doubt that Aleera was the reason.

"What's going on?" I asked, opening the door and shrugging off my jacket. I tossed it over the back of the chair by the fire. They were both glaring at each other, yet neither answered.

"This has something to do with Aleera?"

"Who else? She needs to go," Lycus snapped at me, finally turning away from Kalen.

"What is this about? What did she do?"

"She did nothing. Lycus is the problem," Kalen said before storming toward the door.

"Where are you going?" I asked him.

"Out."

"Kalen!" I growled at him, and he stopped with his hand on the door handle.

"No, Darius. We are mates. You don't get to control all of us."

"If it is to do with your safety, I do. You leave this room before I know what is going on, I will have her placed back in the cells. Now sit your ass down," I growled at him. Kalen's knuckles turned white on the door handle, where he gripped it before he slammed the door. I raised an eyebrow at his anger.

I watched as he went and lay on our custom-made bed. Finding a bed that fit four men was impossible, so we made one. Lycus watched him and moved to the couch by the fireplace. Despite his anger, Kalen's behavior was as expected, and I could feel a hum of satisfaction come through the bond when Kalen lay down, snatching Lycus's pillow to use.

I wasn't even sure he noticed he'd done it, but it was always the same when Kalen was in a mood. He would just lie in bed and sulk or stare off blankly when he was depressed, clinging to our pillows like they were a safety net. I watched, amused, as he rearranged our pillows so he could steal our scents from them.

Tobias walked in and paused at the tension in the room. I turned to him, and he nodded, letting me know he'd dropped Aleera's dinner off to her. He glanced at Kalen. I shrugged, and he rolled his eyes before climbing on the bed and sitting next to him. Kalen rolled instantly, placing his head in Tobias's lap. Tobias leaned back against the headboard and brushed his fingers through Kalen's hair, and I could feel Tobias's magic oozing out and calming him.

The tension left the room, and guilt flashed through the bond. Both Tobias and I looked at Lycus, knowing it was coming from him. Kalen was our weak spot in more ways than one, and we hated upsetting him. His mind was fragile. One minute he was fine and overly excited and bouncing around. The next, he refused to get out of bed, would harm himself, or try to kill himself. Over the last six years, I'd lost track of the number of times he wanted to end it, the number of times he actually did, and we had to pull him back from death. Each time we brought him back, he was more mentally unstable.

It was not natural to die and come back so many times. The last time was the worst. We actually thought we had lost him for good. Twelve minutes he was dead for. For twelve minutes, he hung from the rafters unmoving. I had all the cameras pulled down that week. When I checked the footage, it sickened me. I couldn't unsee it. Kalen on that damn tablet wondering why she'd never opened his message, staring at the screen when he tossed it aside. He spent weeks begging her to come back or let him know she was okay.

I didn't see the rope around his neck until he jumped off the staircase.

It was the last class of the day. He had planned it perfectly. He knew no one was in the castle. He knew we wouldn't get back in time. Luckily, Lycus went back, feeling sick. Before he walked into the castle, Kalen was dead, and Lycus found him hanging from the second floor. He cut him down and performed CPR until Tobias got back. We all felt his bond sever, yet Tobias didn't stop. He kept feeding his blood to Kalen, and by some miracle, his heart started up, and Tobias's blood healed his broken neck. Since then, for the most part, Kalen was fine until he wasn't.

We finally got him to a good place recently, and then she called on us. Kalen had never been happier until we had to remind him she could leave again, not to get his hopes up.

Lycus crawled on the bed beside him before tucking his arm over him.

I shouldn't have taken his magic; it always made him worse. I couldn't believe I was stupid enough to take it from him, blinded

"You need my blood to heal, so kiss me." I shook my head, horrified at what he'd asked. *He couldn't be serious.*

"So, you would rather walk around with your feet like that?" My eyes darted to my throbbing feet, which now seemed to have their own pulse. My blood stained the cream-colored sheets from my thrashing.

"Maybe you could get one of the others?" I didn't want to get that close to him, just being in his presence was bad enough, let alone close enough to touch him. Darius growled at my words.

"Then forget it," he said, turning on his heel to leave the room. My feet ached, the swelling making my skin shiny, and I would have to walk around on them. But why did I have to kiss him for him to heal me?

"Wait!" I blurted out.

He was my mate, so it wouldn't be that bad. I didn't want to waste my first kiss on this monster, but my feet ached, and surely it wouldn't be that unpleasant, right? The bond zapped to life as my thudding heart pumped faster at what I'd agreed to do. Darius stopped and looked over at me. He smiled before walking back toward the bed. He stopped looking at me. I stared at him. Why was he making it more awkward?

"Haven't got all day, Aleera," Darius said tauntingly. My eyes darted to his full lips as his tongue darted out. He smiled, and I hated how my heart skipped a beat at his sight. I hated that he could hear it, too.

"Aleera," he said, annoyed.

My face flushed, and I hesitantly kneeled on the bed. Darius just stood there, waiting. Couldn't he bend down or something? He sighed and raised an eyebrow at me. Moving off the bed, I stood before him. I hissed as pain rippled across the bottoms of my feet that felt spongy to walk on. The bond zinging in my blood urged me to go to my mate, wanting me to touch him even though he hurt me.

Yet he was still too tall, so I looked up at him. I chewed my lip, feeling very uncomfortable despite the bond urging me closer. *Stupid bond.* Placing my hand on his shoulders, I stood on my tippy toes, and Darius gripped the back of my neck. I sighed, relieved that he wouldn't make me humiliate myself more as he tilted his face toward mine. I felt his breath fan my lips and his fingers tangle in my hair. His nose brushed mine softly. My heart hammered harder as his scent overwhelmed me, and I leaned closer when he started laughing.

My head was yanked back painfully by my hair. My hair tugged so hard I cried out, clutching his hands as I tried to lessen the pain.

"I wouldn't kiss you if you were the last person on this earth. You don't deserve love, only pain."

Hurt rippled through my chest as the bond went berserk at his rejection, and my stomach sank at his words. I didn't want to do it in the first place, yet his words stung more than they should, like he'd just reached into my chest and crushed my heart in his hand.

"But it was entertaining watching you struggle with the bond you ignored for six years," he snarled at me. He bit his wrist before jamming it over my mouth. His blood flooded my mouth, and I choked when I couldn't swallow fast enough. Sputtering, he shoved me away and laughed before turning away and heading to the door.

"All meals from now on are in the mess hall. The less we have to see you, the better," he spat at me. I wiped my mouth on the back of my hand, and he slammed the door, locking it and leaving me gasping for air, clutching my chest as pain rippled through me. The moment he was gone, hot tears flooded my eyes and spilled over, running down my cheeks. I hated him.

CHAPTER 19

SOMEONE HAD PLACED AN alarm in my room when I left. I thought a fire alarm was going off because it scared the crap out of me when it started blaring. It took me a few seconds to realize the noise was coming from beside my head on the bedside table. Looking at the screen, it read, "Breakfast, get up."

No doubt it was Darius's doing. I couldn't even shut the damn thing off and had to wait for it to shut itself off. My ears were ringing as I pushed open the bathroom door to pee. I also wanted to have a quick shower to wake up, as it was only 6:30 AM.

The moment the door opened, I realized that someone was already in the bathroom, judging by the steam. I froze when Tobias looked over at me before turning back to the mirror while he continued to shave.

"Sorry," I told him, backing out of the room.

"What?" he asked as I went to close the door. I shook my head.

"Aleera…"

I paused. My eyes ran the length of him. He only had a towel draped low on his waist, and I could tell he had just gotten out of the shower.

"I will be out in a minute but if you wanted to shower, I would stay if I were you. The moment I step out, someone else will come in," Tobias said, not bothering to look at me.

I nodded, stepping into the room and standing by the wall furthest from him.

"Did Darius give you some shoes?"

I shook my head, and he nodded, tilting his head to shave under his chin. I glanced at him before doing a double-take. His entire back was covered in thick burns, making me think of what Lycus had said. I opened my mouth to ask but quickly closed it. However, the movement of my lips was not missed by Tobias. He glared at me through the mirror when the door opened up, and Kalen walked in.

I couldn't help the smile that split onto my face when I saw him walk in. He didn't notice me at first and instead kissed Tobias's shoulder before plucking the razor from his fingers and sitting between the sinks next to Tobias.

"You're up," Kalen said excitedly, moving toward me. Tobias growled, and Kalen sighed before moving back toward Tobias. He sat between the two sinks before grabbing Tobias by the towel and moving him between his legs. Tobias placed his hands on Kalen's thighs. It was strange seeing Tobias pulled around by Kalen and letting Kalen pull him around. Kalen turned Tobias's chin up.

"Darius give you some shoes?" Kalen asked me as he started shaving Tobias's face. Tobias growled, so I didn't answer. Kalen gripped Tobias's chin and turned his face toward his. "Darius said he would get her some," Kalen told him.

Tobias's eyes softened, and I looked away like I was intruding on some intimate moment between them. I was beginning to realize that they all treated Kalen like he was made of glass; they were gentle with him. Even Darius was protective of him.

"I'll speak with him," Tobias told him, and Kalen smiled before turning his face back up and continuing to shave him.

"What classes have you got?" Tobias's eyes went to mine in the mirror, but I had no idea what classes I was meant to attend or where they were.

"She has Theory with me," Tobias answered. Kalen nodded like we just had an everyday conversation.

"Why not with Lycus?"

"Lycus refused the classes with her," Tobias answered, and I swallowed.

"I will shower later," I told them, about to leave the room. I felt somewhat awkward when Tobias hissed as Kalen jumped off the sink basin.

"Oh shit, sorry," Kalen said.

"Aleera, the tissues," Kalen said just as I was walking out. I stopped, looking to where he was pointing at the windowsill above the toilet in the niche. I grabbed the box and walked over to him. Kalen had sliced Tobias's chin. He repeatedly apologized to him, and I plucked a tissue out, handing it to him. I placed the box on the basin beside him and turned around.

"Don't leave. I don't know when Darius will let me see you again," Kalen whined, gripping my wrist. They had all warned me away from Kalen. My eyes went to Tobias's in the mirror, and he rolled his eyes.

"You can stay."

"See? Tobias isn't so bad. Just a big blood-sucking teddy bear," Kalen laughed. *Odd way to describe someone*, I thought to myself. I remained where I was, but I could tell by how tense Tobias was that he didn't want me anywhere near him and was only tolerating me because of Kalen. I swallowed, wanting to leave but also not wanting to upset Kalen.

I found my eyes trailing over Tobias again. My brows furrowed at the thick burns, which had me wondering if they were from the fire. But if they were, why didn't they heal? His power would have manifested by then. They were eighteen at the time of the fire, and he could have healed himself, or Darius could have healed him. Kalen happily talked away; he seemed extraordinarily bubbly and upbeat this morning.

"Did you take your medication?" Kalen's eyes darkened, and he cut off mid-sentence and glared at Tobias.

"Did you?" Tobias asked him. Kalen didn't answer, and Tobias sighed.

"I hate taking them."

"Go take them. Aleera needs to get ready, or she will miss breakfast," Tobias told him. Kalen went to argue when Tobias leaned forward and kissed him.

"You can see her later," Tobias said, tapping Kalen's legs.

"I can't once Darius gets back."

"I will take you to see her, but only if you take your medication," Tobias told him, and Kalen's brows furrowed, but he nodded before hopping off the sink basin. Kalen moved toward me, and I expected Tobias to stop him, but he didn't as Kalen suddenly grabbed me, crushing me against his warm chest. He buried his face in my neck, and I sighed, hugging him back before he let go and walked back to his room.

"You like Kalen," Tobias stated as I went to leave the bathroom. Was I supposed to answer that? I found it hard not to like Kalen. I think anyone would find it hard not to like Kalen.

"Kalen... he can be erratic," Tobias said.

"You mean, fragile? I have noticed how you all are with him. What sort of medication is he on?" Tobias nodded and chewed his lip.

Chapter 20

"Aleera!" he called, and my blood ran cold. I raced down the steps, quickly disappearing among the other demons. As I got to the bottom of the steps, someone shoved me, and I hit the ground. I looked to see who it was, but there were too many men to pinpoint which one. I cried out when another stomped on my fingers.

"There she is," I heard Zac's voice just before a fireball rushed toward me. I shrieked, barely managing to move, and it evaporated as it hit the ground where I was.

"Let's see how pretty she is without all that hair," Zac's voice said, making me look up the steps. Zac smiled, and his eyes burned with evil as he played with another fireball, bouncing it in his hand. I took off running down the corridor. I didn't stop running until I ended up in a hall on my own. I had no idea if he was still intending to burn my hair off when I stopped to try and catch my breath.

"I think she went this way," I heard Deacon's voice. I cursed and started trying doors, finding most of them to be rooms set up with bunks. Besides, I figured it wouldn't be a good idea to hide in one of their rooms. I could hear the screech of their shoes as they ran toward me before I burst through another door and quickly shut it.

Looking around, I found it was a classroom. I could hear them opening and closing doors in the corridor and looked around for somewhere to hide before spotting a jar of pens and noticing some scissors. I grabbed them before darting under the desk.

If I get out of this, the hair is going. I was going to chop it off. My heart stopped when I heard the door open. I clutched the scissors in my hand as I heard footsteps walk toward the desk. The chair got dragged out, and my eyes met with Tobias's. He went to no doubt curse me out when Zac's voice reached my ears, and I jumped, bumping my head on the top of the desk.

Tobias growled and sat down just as the door burst open. I froze, holding my breath.

"What?" Tobias snapped, pushing his chair in and caging me in with his legs.

"Shit… Sorry, sir," I heard the door creak, like Zac was about to leave before it stopped. "Have you seen the traitor bitch?"

My heart skipped a beat at Zac's words.

"No, now get out of my fucking classroom."

"Sorry, sir," Zac said before I heard the door shut. I let out a breath, but Tobias didn't move. Glancing at the scissors, I quickly pocketed them before tapping his leg. Still, he didn't move.

"Tobias?"

"You never answered me this morning," he said, pushing the chair out a little to look at me but not enough for me to get out.

"You would know if I lied, so I didn't think it was worth answering." He growled.

"Um, can I get out?"

"You missed my class."

"I couldn't find it."

"You know Darius won't be happy when he finds out." He pushed his chair back further, and I scrambled out before being trapped between him and his desk.

"Unless…" Tobias said. I swallowed, and my thoughts went to Darius last night and his cruelty playing with the bond. All night I was restless from the pain of being rejected and humiliated for falling for it.

"Unless what?"

"I won't tell him, but I want something in return."

"I am not doing anything sexual with you," I snapped at him, trying to push past his leg blocking my way. Tobias stood towering over me. His eyes flickered and turned blood red. He pinned me against the desk by placing his hands on either side of me, and I leaned away from him.

Tobias growled, and I watched as his fangs slipped out. "What if I want something else, like your blood?" he asked, and my heart rate quickened.

"You want to feed on me?"

He nodded, sniffing me before grabbing me and burying his face in my neck. "You smell fucking divine," he growled.

I felt his tongue run over the pulse in my neck, and I tried to shove him off and failed miserably when he let me go.

He grabbed my wrist, bringing it to his nose. "You smell sweet like Lycus," he whispered.

I felt his magic rush over me as he paralyzed me. My body froze as my thoughts ran rampant, and my heart thudded painfully.

"Lycus knows," I blurted out, petrified of him feeding on me. *Would it hurt? What if he killed me?* Vampires weren't the best with control.

"I will take care of Lycus. So, what will it be, Aleera? I tell Darius, or you let me feed on you? I promise to be gentle," he said, running his teeth against the inside of my wrist. My eyes widened before thinking of what Darius would do if he found out, but what was stopping Tobias from still telling him? Then again, what was preventing him from feeding on me if he really wanted to anyway?

"Tick-tock, Aleera. Darius will be back soon. Your next class is with him, so make your mind up, or you will be late."

"And you won't tell him?"

"I won't tell him. Besides, he would be pissed off if he knew I fed off you, so it will be our little secret."

My heart thudded so hard I could hear it, but I found myself nodding anyway, more frightened of what Darius would do if he found out. Apparently, my nodding must have been enough consent because I hissed as his fangs sank into my wrist in the next second, breaking my delicate skin. Initially, it hurt before my wrist and hand tingled. Warmth spread through me, making me realize he was using his magic so it wouldn't hurt. He didn't feed off me long.

Tobias then pulled his fangs from my wrist when the siren sounded, signaling the next class. I glanced at the clock behind him to find it wasn't a clock, but some strange moon wheel, with different phases of the moon.

Tobias wiped his mouth with his thumb before sucking my blood off it. His eyes glistened, and I watched as he pricked his thumb with one of his fangs before running it over the two punctures on my wrist. They closed instantly, and he brought my wrist to his mouth. I thought he would bite me again when he ran his tongue over it, licking up the blood that spilled down my wrist. His eyes flickered before going to mine, and he smirked.

"You taste sweeter than Lycus, though."

"Is that a bad thing?" I asked.

"Not for me it isn't, but for you, it may be…" He chuckled darkly. "Let's just say I have a sweet tooth."

I took a step back when his eyes glowed redder, and he laughed before flicking his wrist, and a portal opened up beside him.

"Get to class," he said, shoving me through it.

I gasped, feeling his magic swallow me along with the portal before I found myself spat outside on the fields. I landed on my hands and knees. I looked around the vast area to get to my feet and saw all the men and Darius walking in my direction. He stopped, cocking his head to the side.

"You decided to show up on time. Thought you would have run when you found out your next class was with me." He laughed as he stopped in front of me. The men moved out onto the field, and I was thankful it was all grass. However, that was short-lived when I realized they were using their elements, and this was a magic class.

Fuck! I cursed, knowing I had no magic. All fae had an element, and I knew I was about to come out of here battered because I wasn't dealing with fae but demons, who only had one and the most lethal element—*fucking fire*. Whereas I was an elemental harmony fae, which was not only rare but extinct, holding not only one but all elements, plus some other odd gifts I couldn't explain or have dabbled much in. Still, being an elemental harmony fae was no good to me now with no magic.

"Partner up!" Darius called out. I looked around at all the men, and one smiled at me. The man was a giant, tall with dreadlocks to his waist and mocha-colored skin. His demonic eyes ran the length of me, and I took a step back as he stalked toward me.

"I will take the traitor," the man said. *Traitor…* why does everyone keep calling me that? Darius nodded to him, and I looked at Darius. Surely, he didn't expect me to fight without magic? I would get destroyed in seconds.

"Let's see how pretty you are without your hair," the man sneered. What was it with everyone trying to ruin my hair?

"Her hair is off-limits. Burn her hair off, and I will take fucking your head," Darius told him, which shocked me.

"But she is a traitor…"

"I don't care; her hair is off-limits," Darius said. Maybe he liked long hair because I knew he didn't like me. *Well, he will be in for a rude shock when I cut it off later tonight with the scissors I stole.*

I spent most of the class dodging his fireballs, which I was glad was all he used. He could have turned me into a raging inferno but seemed more amused with just tossing them at me. Yet, I noticed Darius stayed close for some reason.

My clothes were singed, my arm was burned, and one hand took a nasty blow. I was exhausted, having spent all my time dodging while the men laughed and watched. Some even sat on the grass, watching my torment as I tried to avoid the flames. Dodging another, my lungs were burning as I ducked, falling to my knees when suddenly flames erupted around me, boxing me in with fiery walls. I jumped to my feet, looking for an escape, panic gnawing at me as they drew nearer. I hated fire, hated it, and nothing scared me more.

"That's enough!" Darius growled.

"Don't worry, I will only burn her a little," the man taunted as the flames grew closer. My heart rate skyrocketed as the flames grew closer and closer. I coughed on the smoke and could feel the heat blistering my skin.

"I said, enough!" Darius growled before the flames were blasted with water. I looked through the smoke to see Darius turn and attack the man I was partnered with, drenching him, too. Wait, how could he use a water element? I saw him use fire last night?

"My word is law. Defy me again, and you will find yourself in the dungeons," he snarled as I choked on the smoke from the extinguished flames.

Images flickered in my vision, the smoke ridiculously thick, and my eyes burned from the smoke. I remembered this feeling, the choking, as each breath burned my lungs. I tried to suck in a breath, my vision tunneling as I was brought back to the night my parents were killed. I stumbled, cursing under my breath, realizing I was having a panic attack.

Gusts of air suddenly blasted me as I became dizzy. The smoke was pushed away, and I blinked, my brain trying to register where the air magic had come from. Then all I saw was black, and I heard the snickering laughter of the men surrounding me as I fainted and collapsed to the ground.

CHAPTER 21

Darius

ALEERA WAS LITE ON her feet; I'd give her that. She could move when needed, making me wonder how much time she'd actually spent running. She moved quicker without magic than some of my men here who had been in training for years. It was like she anticipated where the next attack would come from, like she could sense it. I found myself absorbed as I watched her.

Even some of the men had stopped to watch. Most laughed, but most of them were floored with how she moved, and she remained almost in the same spot, never stepping out of the barrier. This class was a defense class. You had to block your opponent; yet she had no magic to block with, but she watched. I figured out pretty quickly she was studying the flick of his fingers, the way he stood. It was almost as if she knew what he would do before he did it just by examining his stance.

Mikhail was one of our best; he never missed a target, and at first, I thought he was holding back, but the longer it went on, I could see his frustration. He really was trying to hurt her; he just couldn't touch her.

I knew I should have stepped in. A pit formed in my stomach when he decided to partner up with her. I was initially going to be partnered with her, but he stepped forward, eyes locked on his target. Still, I was ready to step in if needed.

I wouldn't have hurt her, knowing it would upset Kalen and Lycus. Scared her, yes, but hurt her probably not with how this stupid bond grew stronger each day. Ignoring the pull was becoming harder until I remembered what she had inflicted. Which infuriated me even more, feeling the pull to her, feeling my mates' pull to her. But she deserved it. God, did she deserve pain for what she had caused us, but when I noticed her getting tired, I knew I needed to stop it.

The bond called me to protect her, going absolutely haywire when I saw her get boxed in. Just like the night we'd found her in her burning room. The entire place was a raging inferno; she had tried to escape but was passed out on the bedroom floor. The moment we stepped into her room, we knew something was amiss. We tried to get back out, but a barrier had been placed on her door and window. Tobias and I barely got her out in time before the roof caved in. Tobias had used his body to shield her and sustained severe burns while I broke the damn barrier spell placed on it.

It took nearly all our power that night to heal her and put the cloaking spell on her and her grandmother so she would be protected. Little did we know it also cloaked us from her once she came of age.

I always felt bad that I couldn't heal Tobias. His back was destroyed, and he refused to let Lycus and Kalen heal him, knowing our reserves were almost completely depleted. We were literally running off borrowed time.

Two and a half years, Tobias and I went without power before we figured out another way to power-share. All of us agreed that Aleera was not an option. She was too young, and her powers hadn't manifested. Besides, none of us were comfortable knowing what that meant for her—to power-share and transfer our power among all of us. It would have been plain disgusting. We were monsters but not that sort of monsters.

They tried to kill her. We should never have left that day. We simply wanted to tell her parents she was our mate and that we would wait for her to come of age. We never thought they would try to kill her. But as the flames got nearer, I could see her panicked state as she gasped, and I knew that was where her mind took her. I could almost feel her panicked state even without marking her. I heard her heart racing, so I extinguished the flames just as she collapsed to the ground.

Mikhail was warned, so I felt nothing toward him when I drove my hand through his chest and melted his heart. A few men gasped around me as his lifeless body fell to the ground at my feet.

"When I say enough, you fucking stop," I told them, letting fire engulf my hand and burn off the blood residue. Shaking the flames away, I looked down at my mate on the grass. I couldn't help the snarl that slipped through my lips as I scooped her up.

I didn't want to touch her, but I wouldn't leave her unconscious with these men. They could truly be monsters, but none got away with defying me. Yet as I picked up her limp body… Damn, she smelled good, felt good in my arms. I shook the thought away and opened a portal to her room before stepping through it. *Get a grip, idiot*, I reminded myself.

Placing her on her bed, she stirred, blinking up at me dazedly, stuck wherever her mind had taken her. I needed to get out of this room, away from her, when she rolled on the bed, and I saw

"Can either of you feel him?" Tobias asked. I glimpsed over the banister. I was on the third floor, and they were on the ground floor.

"What happened? What did you do to set him off this time, Darius?" Tobias said, gripping Darius's shirt.

"What do you think he did? He probably did something to Aleera. You know how he gets when it has anything to do with her," Lycus snapped.

"Fighting with me is not helping to find him. I did nothing. I only asked if he took his medication because I could tell he hadn't."

"Shit!" Tobias cursed.

"What is it?" Darius demanded, and I looked over to see Tobias clutch his head.

"I told him if he took them, I would let him see her tonight."

"You what?"

"She won't hurt him, Darius. I think she even likes him."

"If she liked him, she wouldn't have run the first chance she got," Lycus scoffed.

"I don't know, but she is different around him…"

"How so? I swear if she has done something, I will fucking end her," Darius snarled.

"No, not that. Like she can sense the shadows on him. I can't explain it, but she is different when it comes to him," Tobias argued back. "Maybe?"

"No!" Both Lycus and Darius bellowed at the same time. I turned away, having heard enough. I wasn't sure what was going on with Kalen, but I needed to find him, the bond pulling me toward him and urging me to get to him.

I had no idea where I was going, but I seemed to have wandered into an almost empty part of the castle. This side was cold, and the draft told me it had been closed for a long time. Dust clung to the walls and the sparse furnishings. Pushing the door open, I slipped inside.

The cold draft washed over me and sent a chill up my spine. This place looked untouched, and I wondered how long I had wandered before coming to this blocked-off part of the castle. It was eerily silent over here, and it gave me the creeps. Walking down the large hall, I looked at the high ceilings and the chandeliers covered in cobwebs. This place looked like it was out of some medieval movie. Like I stepped back in time to a different world. I ran my fingertips over the hallstand before brushing the dust off.

Even without magic, I could tell this place had been abandoned and forgotten for a reason. Something terrible must have happened within this part of the castle. Moving further down the hall, I stopped in front of a massive portrait of a man. He had a startling resemblance to Darius before my eyes fell on the teenage boy at his side. Reaching up, I swiped the dust off his face, and it was indeed Darius. The man had his hand on his shoulder, and Darius appeared to be about thirteen or fourteen. Both were dressed in a suit, and he shared his father's features, the same cold eyes and expressionless face.

Giving it one last look, I let the bond pull me to another corridor lined with doors, yet I never got the urge to enter any of them as I passed them. Instead, my feet took me to the end, to a large door with a silver knob.

CHAPTER 23

I TWISTED IT, HAVING TO push my weight against it as I shoved it open. I coughed and choked on the dust, and the draft here was so much colder. Ice cold, and it made me shiver. Stone steps ed up. Climbing them, I stopped halfway up the spiraling stone steps in front of a stained glass window.

I peered out and saw the back of the castle lands, but that wasn't all I noticed. It was a road. I was high enough to see over the forest, and I could just make out a road snaked between the forest as a car drove along the narrow-looking path.

That could be my escape, yet I wondered how it led into the castle grounds or if it did. Ascending further up the steps, I found myself in a round room. The pointed ceiling told me I had found my way to one of the castle towers. By the time I got to the top, was covered in cobwebs and dust.

The wooden floorboards creaked as I stepped inside. Boxes covered nearly all of the floor when I noticed a figure that looked out of place among the boxes. Kalen lay on the floor, his cheek pressed against the floorboards. He was murmuring to himself in language I hadn't heard before, or maybe it didn't exist because his words made no sense to me.

"Kalen?" I murmured, but he didn't move, and the feeling I got from him was cold and numb, shadowed with darkness.

I called out his name a couple of times before giving up and lying on the ground beside him; I lay on my side facing him. His eyes were closed, and his lips moved as he spoke to himself in a barely audible whisper. I reached out and brushed his cheek gently with my hand. His eyes flew open, going to mine. I didn't think he had heard me calling his name or felt my presence. He seemed to be in some trance-like state before I touched him, or maybe he still was; I was unsure.

He grabbed my hand on his cheek, kissing my palm, and he looked so vulnerable, desperate as he clutched my hand. My hand cracked in his tight grip, but I just gritted my teeth through it instead of jerking it away.

"You're here. Are you really here?" he whispered, kissing my wrist and hugging my arm and hand to his chest. "You feel real. I can even smell your scent."

"I'm real, Kalen," I told him, but he mumbled to himself incoherently. His behavior scared me. He almost seemed insane.

"Why are you up here? It is freezing," I told him.

"I don't think it's cold. Is it cold?" he asked.

I wasn't sure if he was talking to himself or me. His eyes stared at me, but it was like he was looking through me.

"I don't want to go with them," he mumbled.

"Go with whom?" I asked him, and he wiggled closer.

"They want me back. I shouldn't be here. They want me back with them."

"Who wants you back? Darius?"

"No, they won't let me near you. They took you from me."

His words made no sense because I was right in front of him.

"Now, I can't see you…"

Darius's rage at what I had done. I remained still, unmoving. Lycus looked at his hand when I felt Darius grab my arm in his grip, and I knew he was about to take it off me when Kalen made a strangled noise. My eyes darted to his as he blinked at me, like it was the first time seeing me.

His lips parted, and I knew he could sense Lycus's magic running through me, yet I remained still. Not moving, knowing if I did, Darius might just kill me for what I'd accidentally done. But the moment Lycus tried to force me to take it, my bond latched onto him like a starving person getting its first-ever meal and absorbed it completely.

I know that wasn't Lycus's intention. He would have only wanted me to take enough so that Kalen could feel me beside him.

"You're glowing," Kalen murmured, and I chuckled, yet his words made me stop.

"You have color in your aura."

I swallowed, wondering what gifts he had that he could see it. I focused on the power running through me, fighting the urge to let the bond change it, trying my best to ignore it as it tried to seep in deeper and mingle. I felt like I was back in school, fighting to keep my secret.

Fighting myself so no one would notice, I forgot how much strain it was to stop the light from mixing with the dark and morphing into something else entirely. I couldn't control my aura for those who could see it, but only one other person I had come across could see someone's essence within it.

Yet this other person died when we were attacked. I didn't even know his name, but he saved me and sacrificed himself to do it. I still remembered the look on his face. *"Well, don't you burn brighter than the sun? The first time I have seen a rainbow aura. I knew there was something special about you,"* he had said, then smiled before the bloodhounds came for us.

I tried to save him, but he shoved me through a portal when we couldn't run anymore.

"They will come for you!" he screamed when the portal sucked me in. When I tried to portal back, I couldn't; it was as if he'd blocked me from returning to help him.

"Why did you do that?" Kalen asked, pulling me from my memory.

"Do what?" I asked him without thinking.

"Change it to dark. Can you make the color come back?"

I ignored his question but could feel everyone's eyes watching us when Kalen reached his hand, brushing the air around me, his fingertips touching my aura. I could feel him through it. I couldn't see my own, but I could feel him touching it; it was an odd sensation.

"What are you?" he asked suddenly.

"I'm like you," I told him, and I noticed Tobias tilt his head to the side, observing me. I swallowed, wondering if he could tell I lied, but I hoped I had cloaked it enough. Kalen went to say something, but I cut him off. I needed him to be quiet. It would raise suspicion if he kept talking of my aura or whatever he sensed. He wasn't of sound mind right now, so I could play it off by letting them think it was his ramblings.

"We should get you back to your room, Kalen," I told him.

"They will take it away."

"Take what away? I am right here?"

"He means his power. We won't have a choice now. Not until he is stable enough to have it back," Lycus explained.

"I don't understand," I admitted.

"Of course, you don't. How could you when you weren't here?"

"Darius, not now," Lycus warned him. Darius's grip on my arm was tight still when a thought flicked through me, and I realized why Kalen's aura was so cold and dark.

He had died. It wasn't darkness but shadows of death. I suddenly remembered doing classes on it in school. The more someone was brought back, the more fragile they became mentally. It was also why the keeper of mates was so important. They could cleanse the shadows or share them with their mates until they dissolved.

"I... could..." I stopped, knowing they would disagree. I already had Lycus's power running through me, and I knew that made them nervous since they weren't sure exactly what my gifts were.

Darius growled as I moved and gripped Lycus's shirt while he tried speaking to Kalen. Everyone froze at my actions. Darius's hand was suddenly wrapped around my throat in warning. Not tight, but like he was seeing what I was going to do.

Lycus's eyes were on mine, and Tobias was on his feet faster than any other. My hands shook as I let his shirt go before touching his face. I gave it back; I couldn't believe I just willingly handed his magic back to him like I was giving him a piece of paper. He gasped as it rushed out of me, my hand glowing with the darkness of his magic before it fizzled out of me, leaving an emptiness inside me.

They all looked at me dumbfounded. Kalen tilted his face up, and I could feel his confusion at the sudden deadly tension in the room. I knew I only had a second before Darius ripped me away from all of them. I wouldn't have time to take it without him willingly giving it to me via touch. I knew that. So I acted quickly.

My lips crashed against Kalen's hard, so hard I hurt myself, but the moment they did, the bond flared to life, devouring the shadows tainting his magic completely. So cold, and I took it way too fast. Darius ripped me away and tossed me to the ground within seconds of touching him. I choked, gagging on its taste as I crawled to my hands and knees. My back ached, yet the pain running through me from his magic hurt way more. Smokey and twisted, I had never felt anything colder before in my life.

A scream left my lips, and I didn't know how Kalen coped with it as I gasped for air, feeling like I was dying. The air in my lungs turned ice cold. I tried to suck in a breath, but I couldn't get my lungs to work; I didn't know how to function anymore. My vision tunneled as the room darkened around me. Everything was numbing with the coldness of it.

"Wait, he still has his magic. She didn't take it, Darius!" Lycus screamed. I passed out just as he grabbed my hair. My body fell limply on the hardwood floor. I needed air. I couldn't breathe; I needed to breathe. These were my last thoughts as I succumbed to the darkness.

CHAPTER 25

Lycus

I TRULY BELIEVED DARIUS WOULD have to knock her out before she handed my magic back to me. Aleera gripped the front of my shirt as I leaned over Kalen, trying to make him come back to the room with us. Tobias could usually compel him to follow before we would douse him in our magic to cleanse the darkness away, and he would finally release it to us. The medication helped him, but something had set him off. I hadn't seen him like this since his last suicide attempt.

Darius caught her movement and gripped her throat. We all thought she would attack. Why wouldn't she? This was her chance to escape us again. The furious look on Darius's face as his hand wrapped around her throat told me he wouldn't hesitate to snap her neck if she did anything.

That would kill Kalen, but I knew Darius wouldn't allow harm to come to us, especially when we weren't sure exactly what she was capable of. Aleera froze, and my eyes were locked onto her sapphire ones. Her hand trembled as she reached for my face; her fingers barely touched me, but it was enough. She was our keeper

keeper of our souls and magic, so that small touch was enough to send my magic hurtling back into me with an alarming speed that stole the breath from my lungs and sent me backward.

Although, when she returned it to me, I felt it was different. Something about it felt different, but that was soon forgotten when she smacked her lips against Kalen's. A growl tore out of me when I saw her steal his magic. How could she take advantage of him while he was in this state?

Within seconds, Darius tossed her, and I moved forward, smacking into Kalen, who gasped. His eyes flew open, stunned before they flashed brighter, recognition returning, and the buzz of energy rippled across his skin and zapped me. She didn't take it. She didn't take his magic. Tobias, also realizing that, gripped my shoulder as he stood up. Darius stalked toward Aleera, who was choking on the darkness she had just taken from him.

Horror washed through the bond because she had no power to cleanse it from herself. It usually took all three of us to contain the shadows that had tainted Kalen, yet even we struggled because it always came back no matter what.

She crawled to her hands and knees, clutching her throat with one hand as she wheezed. An agonized scream tore out her, and her eyes burned brightly before the color faded, and they turned white.

"Wait, he still has his magic. She didn't take it, Darius!" I screamed as Darius grabbed her hair. Her eyes fluttered, and her face fell slack just as Darius looked over at us. I didn't see Tobias move when Darius was shoved by his magic, forcing him to let her go. Darius smashed against the window before the floor shook as he crashed back to the ground.

Tobias rushed toward her and dropped to his knees at her side, gripping her face. Kalen wailed as he scrambled across the floor to her. He snatched her away from Tobias.

"Don't touch her!" Kalen snarled. His entire body rippled as his aura tried to smother Tobias's, but he was no match for the Vampiric Fae King. Tobias ignored him. His fingers pried her eyelids open, and all I saw was white as I walked over and kneeled beside her. Darius groaned as he got to his feet and shook off the blast of Tobias's magic. No doubt, Tobias would later pay for attacking him.

"Help her! Fucking help her!" Kalen wailed as he tried to force her to take his magic to cleanse the shadows that writhed beneath her skin. The black veins wiggled under her pale skin as life drained from her when Tobias leaned down.

"Tobias, no!" Darius snarled as he rushed to get to his feet just as Tobias sank his teeth into her neck below her ear. Darius, realizing he wasn't marking her, let out a breath, and Aleera's body jerked as he clutched her, feeding off her and trying to pull the darkness out of her blood.

The dark veins below her skin's surface moved toward his bite mark when he jerked away, unable to absorb any more, and he began to choke, dropping her into Kalen's lap. Still, Aleera didn't wake.

"Darius, please!" Kalen begged, and I looked at Darius, who stared at her, unmoving.

"Darius!" I snapped when he didn't move to help her. I knew he struggled the most with her. Just as much as Tobias did, I truly believed he would never forgive her. But right now, she was dying; he couldn't let her die for helping our mate.

I understood his hatred toward her. I did. But she was our keeper, and even though I hadn't forgiven her for what she did, I didn't feel it was worthy of death. Darius killed his father for her and us. Doing that turned him cold. He hadn't always been so bloodthirsty and emotionless. Darius would never admit it, but

I knew he loved her just as much as he hated her; he just liked to blame the bond. Honestly, we all did. None of us could deny the pull we had toward her. He blamed her because he wouldn't have had to kill his father if she hadn't run. His father would still be here with him.

Tobias gripped Darius's pant leg, and Darius looked down before growling. Darius was a demon, the shadows affected him, but he could contain them. They just made him murderous when he took them, volatile, and his magic would become numb.

"Please," I gasped as Kalen wailed, rocking back and forth with her clutched in his arms. We only had seconds left before she would be lost to us. Darius's eyes softened as he watched Kalen. He kneeled beside her, gently taking her from Kalen. He brushed her hair back from her face. Being part incubus, Darius could give and take magic from all of us, but it required emotion.

Darius had been forced to become our keeper, and it was lucky he was an elemental, or we all would have perished when she left us. Though its consequences cost all of us everything, not that Kalen and I actually had anything before our mates. It cost Tobias and Darius the most since they were both straight before she left us. Tobias was also next in line to become Vampiric King. His entire family shunned him except his twin brother.

His lips covered hers, his thumb on her chin holding her mouth open, but I wasn't sure how it would work when she was pretty much dead in his arms—no emotion for him to feed off to take it. A tear slipped down his cheek. This man never cried, or if he did, it was never in front of us, and that was when I realized he wasn't taking the darkness. He was washing his magic through her and devouring his own power again, removing the taint, which would indeed have some consequences.

Color returned to her face, and her eyes turned blue again. Darius stumbled back on his hands, gasping before wiping his hand across his mouth and glaring at her. I saw the flicker of relief cross his features and zap through our bond before he masked it when her eyes fluttered and she sucked in a sharp breath.

"Aleera..." Kalen choked, crushing her against him. Her body was all floppy in his arms, and she would probably remain like that for a few hours. We were usually comatose whenever we cleansed Kalen. Although glancing at Darius and Tobias, they appeared alright, even after taking it from her. Yet Aleera showed no visible signs that she was still holding onto the shadows.

Tobias was breathless but still conscious. Darius, however, who had taken the most, was rippling with anger that usually came with absorbing the darkness. He rose to his feet before storming off, and I knew it was to stop himself from hurting us or hurting her in front of Kalen.

"I will check on him. Are you right to get them back?" Tobias asked me, sounding as breathless as he looked, and I nodded. Kalen was kissing her face while Aleera stared vacantly at the pointed ceiling.

"Kalen, we should get her back to her room," I told him, touching his shoulder gently.

"She could have died, but she still did it."

"But she is alright now."

"Darius, he was going to kill her," Kalen told me, and I pressed my lips in a line. I hated how much Kalen cared for her, but she did just help Kalen and gave my power back. My brows furrowed, wondering why she would still help after everything we had done or maybe it was just a ploy to get us to trust her so she could escape.

"You all hate her. Just get away from us," Kalen snapped, and jealousy flared through me that he would choose her over me after everything we had been through together.

"I don't hate her, Kalen," I told him, and as I spoke the words, I realized it was true. I didn't hate her, but I didn't lose as much as Tobias and Darius had, only Kalen. Although if she had taken him from me, I probably would have told Darius to let her die. Kalen was mine, always had been since my father abandoned me in the orphanage.

Kalen was the only pure dark fae in the place, the weakest, and he had been tormented relentlessly and even abused by the teachers. My parents were both pure dark fae. I should have been like Kalen, the weakest of the fae. That was until my mother died, and with my grief, I shifted. I was my mother's bastard. My father soon realized I wasn't his and dumped me on the orphanage doorstep. Literally tied a leash around my neck because I didn't know how to shift back yet. He tied me to a chair like a dog until the orphanage opened the following day and found me curled in a ball on the footstep covered in snow.

Looking at Kalen now, I saw the same thing in his eyes that I felt the first time I saw the other kids kicking the crap out of him. The same way my father kicked and punched me when I shifted. I wanted to protect him. He was so small compared to the other kids. So I did. No one dared touch him when I was near after that, and I made sure to stay by his side until we ran away. Kalen had that same look. He wanted to protect her, but he also knew he couldn't. Not against Darius or Tobias.

"Kalen?"

"No, Lycus. You need to choose a side. I won't lose her."

"And I won't lose you. You know what she has done. They won't just forgive her."

"She doesn't know. No wonder she hates us. We don't deserve her," Kalen told me. I looked at her limp body in his arms.

"She is cold," I told him, and he looked down at her. Her lips were blue, and her breathing was shallow.

"You don't want her to freeze to death, do you?" I asked him, and he shook his head.

"But, Darius…"

I gritted my teeth, already hating what I was about to say. "We will stay with her until she comes to."

Kalen turned his head to look at me. His eyes scanned mine for any deceit. "You will help me?"

I nodded, looking away from her. Darius would be furious about me letting Kalen near her, but she'd just risked her life for him, and maybe Tobias was right. Perhaps she wasn't a threat to him. Until we were positive, I would speak to Darius about letting him near her under supervision.

CHAPTER 26

Aleera

HUSHED VOICES WOKE ME. They sounded angry as I opened my eyes. The last thing I remembered was choking on the shadows and Darius grabbing me; I felt myself dying, and, in some ways, I even prayed for death. At least I wouldn't feel like this. I felt hollow. I had tasted their magic only briefly before they took it from me. My bond screamed angrily, writhing within me for it to come back.

"Darius, just leave him be. I am right here with them."

"Anything happens to him, and it is on you. It will be your fault," Darius growled before I heard the door slam. I jumped at the sound, and my eyes opened to find Kalen beside me, asleep. He looked so peaceful, and I gently brushed his cheek with my fingertips. His stubble was rough and scratchy when I felt the bed dip behind me, and I glanced over my shoulder to see Lycus sitting next to me.

"You are awake," he said, and I turned to face Kalen. I tried not to let his emotionless tone upset me. He didn't seem too pleased that I was awake.

"Thank you," Lycus murmured, and I chewed my lip and nodded at his words. It actually sounded like it physically hurt him to say it.

"Why did you give it back?" he asked. I briefly wondered the same thing. It was clear that nothing would change, even with me helping Kalen. I had just tossed my only opportunity to escape out the window. Yet the thought of Kalen being the way he was, I knew I would have done it again.

"Darius is angry," I stated, ignoring his question.

"He always is," Lycus replied before he leaned against the headboard of my tiny bed.

"Kalen struggles to cope. He hasn't had an episode like that for a while. It has made Darius more anxious."

"He blames me for it?"

"We all do. He has been fine for almost a year, then you show up, and he backtracks," Lycus growled before he sighed. "Sorry, I didn't mean to snap at you."

"How many times?" I asked Lycus, rolling onto my back to look at him.

"How many times he had tried to kill himself? Or how many times he'd done it successfully before we brought him back?"

I swallowed.

"Brought back eight times. Lost count of how many suicide attempts he's had," Lycus answered, and my heart sank. Kalen was far from alright.

"You did something to my magic," Lycus said, and my heart quickened at his words, making him glance down at me. He watched me, waiting for my answer.

"What do you mean? I did nothing to it."

"It feels different, stronger."

I let out a shaky breath. "I'm your keeper. Of course, it does."

"Yeah, but I didn't expect it to feel as strong as Darius and Tobias's power. You may be a keeper, but you are supposed to pass and share our energy among us, so we are all the same strength. Yet when you handed mine back, for a while, it wanted to challenge Darius's."

"Because I never shared it. It is the bond," I told him, and he nodded.

"Yeah, and I bet it is playing havoc with my magic out of your system and Darius's. Although it makes me wonder what you would be capable of if you shared all our power along with your own."

"I never touched Darius's magic," I told him.

"Why do you think you are alive? Tobias fed off you and tried to clean it from your blood. His saliva had magic in it, but he couldn't take it all. Darius flooded you with his power, so I bet you feel pretty uncomfortable now. Once a keeper shares power the first time, your bond will crave it for a bit until it is out of your system, which happens to Darius sometimes."

"Well, you all seem intent on keeping me defenseless. So, of course, I feel like crap."

"That wasn't the original intention. It didn't need to be this way," Lycus told me. Lycus went to say something else when Tobias walked into the room.

"Where is Darius?" Lycus asked him, but Tobias was too busy staring at me. "Tobias?" Lycus snapped, and Tobias shook himself before he looked over at Lycus.

"Huh?"

"Darius, where did he go?"

"Where do you think?" Tobias snapped at him. Lycus growled before running his hand through his hair.

"I know it's not you, but I just copped it off, Darius. I don't need you starting on me too."

"I was just checking on Kalen. I'm not here to argue," Tobias said.

"He is fine, as you can see. I won't leave him alone with her."

"Oh, for fuck's sake, I won't hurt him," I snapped as anger rippled through me. They both stared at me, stunned, and, honestly, I was surprised I voiced those words because I didn't mean to.

"Is that so? Fine, answer me this then."

I rolled my eyes, and Tobias was on top of me within seconds, his fingers squeezing my face.

"Tobias, what are you doing?" Lycus snapped at him and gripped his arm.

"She said she wouldn't hurt him. Let's see how true it is," Tobias said, glaring at Lycus, who shrugged. Tobias's fingers dug painfully into my cheeks as he stared at me.

"If given the opportunity would you run again?" Tobias asked me, and I felt my heart skip a beat which earned a growl from him.

"Answer me!" Tobias growled, and Lycus sat up more, looking down at me. What kind of question was that? What answer did they expect to get?

"If you were in my place, would you stay?" I asked instead.

"I wouldn't be stupid enough to run from my mates. I wouldn't risk killing them. Now, answer the question!" Tobias growled.

"You already know the answer, or you wouldn't be asking just to catch me lying, Tobias. Now, let me go." The noise that escaped his lips made goosebumps rise on my skin before he shoved himself off me.

"Still think she won't hurt him?" he asked Lycus. Lycus sighed.

"Now, get him to bed. Make sure you lock her door. I knew she only helped him to regain our trust."

"That is not true. I like Kalen. It's the rest of you I can't stand."

"You don't like him enough to stay for him, though, do you?" Tobias spat at me. He turned on his heel and stalked out of the room.

"You had to ruin it," Lycus snapped when he left. Lycus climbed off my bed before walking around to the other side and scooped Kalen off the bed with one swift movement. My heart hammered in my chest as the bond cried out for him.

My hand gripped Kalen's before I could hold myself back, and Lycus's eyes flickered angrily. "Wait, you don't need to take him. Just let him sleep here," I blurted, needing him back where I could feel him and know he was alright.

"Thank you for bringing him back to us, but Tobias proved you only intend to hurt him again. I won't allow that," Lycus said.

He walked out, taking Kalen, who remained unconscious, with him. His energy left the room, and I suddenly felt cold without any of them in there.

Time slipped by, and the cold set into my bones. I would take their wrath if one would come back and stay, anything to chase the cold of the empty bond away. One taste of their magic and my bond ached for them, only now they were gone.

I tucked the blanket up as I shivered, needing their magic or some of my own. Why was I so cold? Why did it hurt like this? Being the keeper, I required their magic, but I lived without it for so long, deprived of it for so long, so I didn't understand how after one encounter, one taste, it felt like they were tearing me apart piece by piece when they took it away.

No matter how close I sat to the fireplace or how many blankets I surrounded myself with, I couldn't warm up. My teeth chattered, and my entire body ached. I hoped it was just an after effect of the shadows, yet I had a nagging feeling it was them, and Lycus was right. I just hoped he was also right about it wearing off.

The door opened, and my bond leaped with joy as I turned around to see who had entered. I tried to slow my heart rate as he stepped into the room.

"The effects of you touching our magic will wear off. Give it a day or so, and you will be fine," Darius said.

"Maybe you could?"

"Not a chance," Darius said without looking at me. "We will never give you magic. That was a once-off, Aleera. As I said, it will wear off."

I turned my attention back to the fire and tried to warm up. He didn't even have to give me much, just enough to settle the bond until the effects faded.

This was torture in itself, and I promised myself that I would run as soon as I was able. I would rather battle it out there than live with this torment. Kalen would learn to survive without me, or maybe I could convince him to come?

Darius walked over to me and dropped a box beside me on the floor.

"Shoes. Don't be late to class tomorrow."

"Socks?" I asked, hopeful.

"In the box," he called out over his shoulder as he left. My hands snatched the box up, instantly rummaging through it for the socks to place on my cold feet. I would hardly call them shoes. They were flats—nothing special or even protective for my feet—and the soles were paper-thin but better than nothing. *Little victories*, I told myself, and if it were shoes, I would take any triumph right now.

CHAPTER 27

I HARDLY SLEPT A WINK throughout the night. Yet as the alarm went off, it cut out before I could even open my eyes. Fingertips gripped my wrist, and my eyes flew open at the sharp sting of fangs piercing my skin. My heart thumped in my chest, and Tobias growled before euphoria rushed through me as his magic caressed over me, stifling the scream that was about to tear out of me.

His blood-red cat-like eyes watched my face, his finger placed on my lips in warning, and I wondered how long he had been in here and why he was suddenly feeding on me again. My eyelids fluttered, and I was completely frozen with fear. I was prey against its predator, who was using me as his personal juice box. He licked my wrist before healing it, placing it on the bed, and walked out of the room when he was done. I stared after him, but he didn't say so much as a word to me. Instead, he just left.

I glanced over at the clock and groaned before rushing about the room and skipping the shower. I wanted to get to the mess hall before the others so I could grab something and slip out back to my room. It seemed like the safest option, and I knew I would

Retrieving my flats, I slipped them on while pulling my hood up over my head. I felt unsteady on my feet from the blood loss and very shaky after rushing around. I was forced to clutch the banister on the stairs, feeling slightly light-headed as I descended. Tobias's actions confused me. Why would he come and feed on me when he had three mates sharing a room with him that would provide him with blood?

My heart twinged at the thought of them, and my mind wandered to Kalen as I peeked into the mess hall. Relief washed over me when I saw I was the first one there. I rushed over to the display of food and scooped up some bacon and two pieces of toast before voices at the other end reached my ears. I would have to see if I could change the alarm to a little earlier. With my few pieces of bacon and two slices of toast, I escaped when more voices could be heard. Looking around, I glanced at the door of the cell I was kept in and groaned. Eat in peace, or try to make it back up to my room without being spotted? I chose the cells.

I pushed the door open, and the cold draft made me shiver before I sat down on the second step listening to the voices slowly filling the mess hall. My stomach growled hungrily, and the loss of blood didn't help. I was starving, and those two slices of toast and bacon didn't even touch the sides, but I was just grateful for anything in my stomach right now.

This morning, my first class was with Tobias and at the stupid obstacle course. I shook my head at the thought. No way would I ever complete that damn course. My mind wandered to Kalen again as I wondered if he was alright. I sighed, thinking about the men the fates had decided to bond me to.

Even on the run, I'd never felt this lonely, and this time I was surrounded by people. Not good people, but still people. I had spent so long on my own and thought I was lonely then, but despite being alone, it never felt this cold and unwelcoming. I reminded myself of the aftereffects of the bond and the shadows, trying not to let it get to me.

Yet the ache to go to them, beg them for just a taste of their magic, was still intense. Although, at least the agony of last night was over. It made me wonder how they power-shared with each other. Being the Keeper, I only had to touch them, but why did I have a feeling it wasn't that straightforward with them?

I didn't even think it was possible, but I also didn't believe any elemental fae other than myself existed. That was one thing I pondered while I had gotten dressed. The memory of power I had witnessed Darius use left only one conclusion. Darius was a dark elemental. Demonic elemental fae. I had never even heard of it before, but I knew I was right, which explained why everyone feared him. Still, Kalen's powers were odd, too. I had only met one other person that could read aura the way he did.

We all saw auras to some degree, but they were essentially manifested energy we could get a feel for. However, Kalen could clearly see them and even see the essence and soul that resided in them. That was a dangerous trait for him to have because this meant that if I obtained power in any way, Kalen would notice straight away. He would also realize what I was, and now he was stable. I knew he would ask questions and possibly tell the others.

I waited for the siren to go off and then waited some more before I heard the hallways clear of voices before I quickly raced out to join the class. I was determined not to piss them off today because I wanted to see Kalen. I needed to know if he was alright because not knowing was driving me insane.

That dreaded fucking climbing wall… I had never despised anything as much as I did that damn wall as I stood staring up at it. Once again, the men all passed me, but I was alive and still kicking. Sore and every muscle ached when the siren blared, signally the recess break.

The others had already finished the course, and I started climbing the stupid wall when a pair of arms wrapped around my waist, and I screamed and thrashed.

"Shh… It's me! Stop!" Tobias growled below my ear. His hand clamped down on my mouth to stifle the scream of fright that threatened to deafen me. I thought it was Zac, assumed he was the one that would be ensuring I completed the course.

Tobias removed his hand from my mouth, and I glanced at him behind me before he placed me on my feet. "Go eat and get to your next class," he said, straightening his shirt.

"I can go? But the others can't unless they finish it?"

"I fed off you. There is no way you will complete the course, and I know you are hungry. So, go before I change my mind." He didn't have to tell me twice. I hated that damn wall. Nodding my head once, I quickly walked off toward the castle when Tobias caught up with me.

CHAPTER 28

H E GRIPPED MY ARM, making me stop, and I almost groaned. *Was that some bullshit trick?*
"About this morning… It never happened, okay?" Tobias said, and my brows furrowed in confusion. *Pretty sure it did, but why did he seem so nervous?*

"Yeah, whatever," I told him. I was about to stomp off and try to find my next class, so I was not late. There was no way I was going in that mess hall, and I would just wait until dinner.

Tobias grabbed my arm with a growl and yanked me back. "Say it didn't happen," Tobias snapped at me. I thought his behavior was odd, his grip tight when realization dawned on me. He was forbidden to feed on me, and Darius would be the only person I could see him fearing.

"Why not compel me to forget?" I asked, and he tugged at the neckline of his shirt.

"Forget it," he said, stalking off.

"Fine, it never happened, but I want to see Kalen," I called out to him, and he stopped. A growl tore out of him, and he moved at blinding speed, gripping the front of my shirt. I gasped at how close his face was to mine, and his fangs protruded.

"Don't try to blackmail me," he snarled.

"The way I see it, the only reason you haven't compelled me is that you plan on using me as your blood bag. But by the way, you keep insisting it never happened. You don't want Darius to find out," I snapped at him. He let me go but glared at me.

"If I compel you too much, Darius will sense my magic on you, and so will Kalen."

"So, you do want to continue feeding on me," I told him, and he looked away but nodded.

"Why not use the others?"

"Does it matter? I will let you see Kalen. Once, and that's it," Tobias snapped.

"I see him once while you get to use me as your personal buffet?"

"You aren't in a position to negotiate," Tobias growled.

"And by how worried you are, you aren't in a position to say no to me."

Tobias gripped my throat, clearly not liking me arguing with him, and my hands clutched his.

"What's going on?" Lycus's voice reached my ears, and Tobias let me go. He stepped away from me, and I glanced at Lycus.

"Your next class is with Darius. I suggest you get going, Aleera," Lycus said, although his eyes remained on Tobias. I nodded before I rushed off to the next class.

❧

Thank goodness Darius's class was a theory lesson. Although I would have preferred being anywhere else and away from Darius's glares, surprisingly, I was left pretty much alone. Maybe because he insisted on putting a table next to his desk, like I was the naughty student that needed extra supervision. Everyone worked off tablets, and I looked down at the paper in front of me before scouring the pages on elemental magic while everyone did their pop quiz.

How was I supposed to fill it out when I didn't even have a pen? I glanced over at his desk when he suddenly passed me a pencil without even looking over at me. Thankfully, the class was uneventful; not even a murmur while Darius spoke and explained things. Everyone seemed to be nervous around him. Not that I blamed them; he made me nervous, too, with his explosive temperament.

When the class ended, I waited for everyone to leave before getting out of my seat. Darius watched me for a few seconds while I cleaned my desk and handed him the paper.

"Tobias messaged me earlier and asked for you to see Kalen this afternoon," Darius told me. He took the paper from me and glanced at it before placing it on his desk.

"After dinner, you can come to our room to see him. I don't want you alone with him."

I nodded and walked out, surprised Tobias even asked. Not that I was keen to go into their room. I was hoping Kalen could come to mine, but I would take what I could get.

I wandered around the campus grounds, bored. I wasn't supposed to wander off, but I knew their recruits were in the mess hall or recreational rooms, and I didn't feel like sitting in my room. Besides, I wanted to scope the grounds out and see if I could find the road I'd seen from the castle tower.

I was just about to turn the corner when I heard voices. A loud squawking noise reached my ears. The sound was terrible, and I peeked around the corner to see four demons laughing before noticing what was on the ground at their feet.

My heart sank. It was a phoenix, and I ran out to save it but stopped myself knowing it would probably only end up with me getting hurt or having to explain myself to Darius. Luckily, they seemed to get distracted before they inflicted more pain on the poor thing. One of them kicked it, and a sob left my lips, which made me cover my mouth with my hands. I watched them walk off, laughing and chatting among themselves. Once they disappeared, I rushed over to the fallen phoenix. It was only a juvenile. My hands were shaking terribly, and it snapped its beak at me, probably thinking I was here to hurt it some more.

"Shh, shh… I won't hurt you," I said. The bastards burned his feathers off, and one of his wings looked broken.

"You have to be quiet. I will help you," I said, trying to get close enough. Phoenixes hated dark fae, all dark creatures, in fact. Phoenixes, however, loved white fae and also contained magic themselves.

But being a juvenile, he had no such power or healing ability. Phoenixes also could power-share with their bonded. They bonded to their owners, primarily white fae or other phoenixes. I scooped him up, and he squawked loudly, so I grabbed his beak.

"Shh… They hear you and they will kill you," I said while holding its beak closed to stop the noise. Watching my surroundings, I raced back to the castle, making sure to remain unseen. But now what? Where could I hide him until he healed? Phoenixes hunted food, but he wouldn't even be able to fly for god knows how long.

I glanced at the stairs leading to the rooms and the cell door. I could try to hide him down there, but they may hear him if he squawked. However, my room joined my mates', and Darius might sense him. He had no power yet, but he definitely would be able to be felt once he did.

The cells it was. I rushed to the door, escaping inside before getting caught. I flicked the light switch on, lighting up the rancid place before descending the stairs. When I got to the bottom, I looked at the cells. I refused to look at the one I was in. The memory of Darius breaking my leg and hand down there made bile rise in my throat.

CHAPTER 29

WALKING TO THE ONE next to it, I placed him on the bed. At least this cell had one. The phoenix stared at me and nestled against it. His eyes looked sad, and I could tell he was in pain. I wished I had magic so I could heal him. Maybe I could try to siphon some from somewhere? Taking my jumper off, I cringed. I only had one and two changes of clothes. Hopefully, it wouldn't get too cold, but he needed it more than I did. So, I made him a makeshift nest out of it.

"I have to go," I told him, patting his head. He watched me and nestled into his bed. But when I tried to leave, he squawked, and my heart raced at the noise.

I rushed back, clamping my hand on its beak. "Shh, shh... They will hear you. You have to be quiet. I will try to catch you some mice or find some food, but you have to be quiet," I told him, and he made a cooing sound but dropped his head, tucking it under his good wing.

I patted him for a few seconds on the orange-red feathers that remained on his neck before giving him a kiss. He ripped his head out from under his wing, and I thought he would bite me, but he pressed his big beak to my cheek, and I brushed the few feathers on his head.

"I will be back," I told him. He stared with eyes far too intelligent. My mother used to have a phoenix before she died. After my father brought her back and turned her into a dark fae, I remembered it hated my father, constantly pecking him and snapping at him when he got too close to her, but it loved my mother. After she changed, it turned on her and attacked her, so dad killed it. I loved that bloody bird and cried for a week straight.

The phoenix appeared to realize I was trying to help him. He nestled down in my jumper, and I raced upstairs. I went back to my room, trying to find anything I could to help him and see if I could find something to feed it. I smiled when I laid eyes on the bandages still sitting on the dresser. They were filthy, but I might be able to use them to wrap his wing and part of his torso. Phoenixes grew quite large; fully grown, they stood at about five feet. My new little friend was a juvenile and was only around the size of a macaw right now, so I knew he would grow much bigger.

I grabbed the bandages and my pillowcase before deciding to smuggle the entire pillow out for him. I remembered how cold it got down there. Deciding to shower before dinner, I retrieved one of their shirts. I always thought it odd that I found a new one in the room to sleep in every night. I only had two pairs of pants and two shirts plus my jumper, so I was excited because now I had socks and some flats to add to my tiny wardrobe.

Just as I was about to walk into the bathroom, I noticed the glint of steel on the bedside table. I totally forgot about the scissors I'd smuggled, but why were they on the dresser? One of them must have found them, yet they left them, which surprised me.

Let's see them rip my damn hair out when I have none to pull on. I snickered at my thoughts, snatching the scissors off the top of the dresser and walking into the bathroom.

I tugged my jeans off and placed them on the counter since I still had to try and go and steal some dinner from the mess hall, and I certainly wasn't going down there in just one of my mates' shirts.

Looking in the mirror, I stared at my long, raven black hair. It was unruly and hung to my waist. My grandmother and father had the same color hair, and it saddened me that I was about to chop it off. But at the same time, I was sick of it being the first thing they grabbed. Grabbing the scissors, I hacked at one side. As I held up the handful of hair I'd just lobbed off, my stomach sank. Tears streamed down my face at how short it was, sitting just below my shoulders.

Placing the hair on the bench, I tugged my hair up in a pony-tail, chopping it off. *You can do it.* Besides, I had already cut one side that looked like I had tried to cut it with a fork; it was so uneven, and the scissors were blunt. So I couldn't back out now. I raised the scissors and gripped my hair at the top of my head, close to the scalp. I started chopping at it when the door opened. I didn't even have a chance to see who it was before the scissors were snatched from my hand, and my head was yanked back by the very hair I was trying to get rid of.

I cried out and clutched my hands before spotting Darius in the mirror.

"What the fuck do you think you are doing?" Darius snarled as Lycus wandered in behind him. Kalen's voice reached my ears, but Lycus quickly slammed the door and locked it.

"Darius…" Lycus hissed.

"She was—" Darius looked at me in the mirror before noticing my hair on the countertop. "Why would you chop off your hair? What the fuck is wrong with you?" he said, thrusting the scissors at Lycus's chest.

"Because I am sick of everyone fucking grabbing it," I snapped at him, and he quickly let go. He seemed shocked at me yelling at him. I rubbed the back of my neck and the top of my scalp. It felt tender as strands were yanked out on the crown of my head.

Chapter 30

"You are not cutting it. You will look like a boy," Darius growled.

"That's the point, asshole. I would rather have no fucking hair than have you ripping it out every chance you get!"

Kalen banged on the door, demanding to know what was going on, and Darius growled and looked over at Lycus.

"Deal with him while I deal with her," Darius snapped. He reached over, snatching the scissors from Lycus, who looked at him worriedly.

"Go deal with him," Darius said, his aura rushing out and making the room hot with his anger. Lycus sighed but opened the door. He had to grab Kalen as he tried to force his way in before the door shut and Darius locked it. He turned to face me, and I took a step back away from him when he went to step closer with the scissors clutched tightly in his hand.

"You ruined it," he snarled, and my heart rate skyrocketed at the evil look in his eyes. It was just hair. Why the hell did he care about whether or not I had hair on my damn head?

"Sit on the edge with your feet in the bath," he snapped, pointing at the bathtub. I glanced at the bathtub, and he growled at me, which made me move to do as he'd asked before he commanded me, giving me no choice.

"Don't cut your hair." He paused, and I felt his presence behind me but didn't dare look at him. I felt fingers run through its lengths as he growled at my hack job before dropping the scissors beside me.

"Wait here," he said before walking out of the room. I wondered what my chance was of escaping whatever punishment he was about to inflict when he walked back in. I looked over at him only to see Tobias with him. Tobias sighed and looked at Darius.

"Fix it!" Darius snapped at him.

"Do I look like a hairdresser?" Tobias asked him. *Not to me.* He looked more like someone that would scalp me, not fix hair. Darius dropped some pouch on the ledge of the bath beside me and rummaged through it.

"You do our hair all the time," Darius told him.

"That involves clippers, not scissors, and I am not sure I can fix that. You do it. You are used to cutting long hair. I have never done a woman's hair before," Tobias argued. That surprised me. I couldn't really picture any of them doing hair. Darius growled at him, but Tobias shook his head.

"Nope, you want it fixed, do it yourself. You used to do your mo—" Tobias stopped, his words cut off abruptly with the thunderous growl that left Darius. Tobias glared at him and walked out, and I looked at Darius, who was fuming before he scrubbed a hand down his face and looked over at me. I flinched when he stepped closer, but he only reached down and grabbed the comb.

"Just sit still," Darius said. He turned my head straight, so I had to look at the tiles. Frozen with shock when I felt him combing my hair, I stared off at the tiled wall. I was curious to know what Tobias would have said before being cut off by Darius.

"You like long hair?" I blurted the words before I could stop myself. *Fuck, Aleera. Curiosity killed the cat. You are the cat in this situation*, I tried to remind myself. However, I was shocked when he answered.

"Yes, Lycus used to have long hair. But it annoyed him, and he cut it off not long after we found him," Darius said. I felt him brush up against me as he continued to comb the knots out. He reached beside me, pulling a clip out and piling my hair on my head, leaving sections.

My hair started falling away as he cut it, and I glanced down to see it was cut just below my shoulders before he pulled another section from the clip and combed it.

"Were you a hairdresser in a past life?" I chuckled at the thought.

Darius huffed. "You believe in that past life crap?" he asked.

I shrugged, unsure what I believed or if I believed in anything after death. "Not sure," I answered honestly. I jumped when he placed the scissors beside me and walked off before rummaging under the sink. He returned and wet my hair with a spray bottle, which made me jump again at how cold the liquid was.

Darius, distracted while fixing my ruined hair, almost seemed like an average person, or maybe it was the bond. His aura remained threatening. But he wasn't being cruel, so I figured he must have had some shred of humanity in him. I tried to contain my laughter at that thought when I remembered him telling his recruits my hair was off-limits when they threatened to burn it off.

"I will try not to grab it, but don't cut it again. It is now short enough," Darius said behind me, and I almost turned to look at him, but his fingers forced my face forward before I could.

"Stay still," he snapped, and I swallowed.

"I can't picture Lycus with long hair," I admitted, and Darius chuckled.

"When we found them, it was really long, almost as long as yours."

"So, you liked doing his hair?" I pried.

"No, he cut it off. I was furious, but—" He stopped, like he remembered who he was talking to.

"Do you even care? Or are you just trying to make small talk?" he asked.

I thought about it for a second because it was kind of both; I cared because if he was talking, that meant he wasn't killing me, but I was also curious why he was so upset about hair.

"Just curious why you got angry when you seem so intent on ripping mine out," I told him honestly. He paused his cutting and cleared his throat.

"Don't try to cut it, and I won't grab it," he finally said, and his aura dropped, which allowed my shoulders to relax.

"My sister used to have long hair."

"I thought you were an only child?" I asked him.

"She died when she was seven."

"What was her name?"

"Molly. She was my mother's illegitimate child. She had an affair, and my father found out."

I chewed my lip at that bit of information. That definitely wouldn't have gone down well—especially if he was anything like Darius.

"He forgave her, but when the plague hit my sister, she died, along with the rest of the fae."

"Wait, your sister was a white fae?"

"No, a harmony one. Both my parents were dark-demonic. Molly's father was a white fae."

"Wait, but the fae plague hit before I was born," I told him, and he hummed in agreement.

"Yes, but the second wave hit seven years later. She would have been the same age as you."

My brows furrowed in confusion. I couldn't remember a second wave being talked about. Besides, how did I survive it if there was one?

"It wasn't like the first one. They poisoned the water system. We ran off town water. When the rumor started about the plague, my sister and mother went into confinement under the castle. She survived the first wave because it was airborne. My father had strict protocols on who was allowed in and out. They lived down there for three years before we realized they could come out. Mom wouldn't leave her down there by herself. Yet, when the second wave hit, no one saw it coming, and the water supplies were poisoned. She had a bath and fell ill."

"So, you used to do her hair?" I asked him.

"No... My mother's. After Molly died, she became depressed and couldn't look after herself. I looked after her until she died," Darius answered. I swallowed, not knowing what to say, and he didn't tell me anything else, just kept cutting my hair.

When he was finished, he tapped my shoulder for me to turn around before gripping the ends. His face was in deep concentration as he cut some of the hair around my face before making sure the ends were the same length.

He then nodded and stood up before he walked out. I stared after him before shaking my head and dusting off my shirt. Looking in the mirror, he cut just below my shoulders. Darius returned a few seconds later and placed some hair ties on the counter, not saying a word before he walked out again, leaving me alone. I quickly locked the door before cleaning up all my hair and dumping it in the bin. I then showered fast to get to the mess hall early and then back to my feathery friend.

CHAPTER 31

*I*RUBBED MY ARMS AGAINST the cold night air that drifted through the castle doors as I went downstairs. It was freezing tonight, and I worried for the phoenix since he was almost completely featherless and hoped he would be warm enough. Voices in the mess hall made me cringe as I approached it, but I needed to eat something; I was beginning to feel quite shaky. I couldn't survive off toast alone.

I kept my head low as I made my way into the line, wishing I still had my hoodie to obscure my face. The smell of the food made me ravenous, and my stomach growled hungrily. The man in front of me turned and looked down at me before snarling and looking away. Retrieving a tray and plate, I made my way down the line. Only whenever I stopped at one of the stations, the server stationed there would close the lids, not allowing me to retrieve anything.

I rolled my eyes and went to lift the lid off of the last one, not really caring what it was. Only the moment I did, the demon stationed there slammed the piping hot lid on top of my hand, and I felt his magic make the lid vibrate as he used his magic to turn the steel red as he forged heat into it. I cried out and tried to jerk my hand free, but he growled and pressed harder. The steel lid burned my flesh, and I could feel the bubbling of my skin.

"Traitor!" he sneered at me while I held back the tears that threatened to spill. I would not let him see me cry. Gritting my teeth, I jerked my hand out, bringing the ladle with me full of what looked like stew, and tossed it at his face. He shrieked loudly, but *fuck him*. If I had my magic, I would have scorched the bastard alive and watched him burn for the shit they kept doing to me.

I silently promised myself that I would get my revenge and when that time came, these men would know who they fucked with. I had no idea when that would be. Today or tomorrow? Years down the road? However, when I came for them, they would wanna beg because I would burn this place to the ground with them trapped in it.

He clutched his eyes as the boiling hot liquid splashed on his face, and I examined my skin. Blisters bubbled on the back of my hand, and the outline from the pot melted my skin and tore my flesh away when I jerked my hand out. I turned away to leave when someone grabbed me by the back of my neck. I screamed and tried to fight back, but he was behind me as he dragged me closer to the bubbling stew. I clutched the sides of the bench as he tried to force my face into the boiling bubble.

Those present laughed, and my hand slid into the pot. Pain seared up my arm to my elbow. I hissed and yanked it out, only for my face to press too close. I could feel the heat against my face when I threw my boiled hand back and connected with something that made him let go. A shocked collective gasp filled the room as I turned on my attacker and looked at him. Clutching his manhood, he had dropped to the ground. *Good to know I hit somewhere painful.* However, that was short-lived when I got a good look at his face.

"You're a dead bitch," he choked out, and I looked in horror at the person I'd tossed the soup at. It was Deacon, one of Zac's friends. I quickly ran from the room as I heard chairs screeching and didn't bother looking back as I ran for the stairs. *Fuck, I knew it wouldn't end well.* But what choice did I have? Once on the top floor, I knew I was safe or as safe as I could be in this dreadful place.

I had noticed no one other than my mates ever came up to the floor where my room was. Like it was off-limits to the rest of the recruits. I was thankful for that for once. My hand and arm seared with burning pain, and I rushed to the bathroom and turned the faucet on, placing my burned limb under the cool liquid. My hand looked like bubble wrap; the skin was that blistered. Tears welled in my eyes, and I knew that was the last of my dinner outings. It looked like my only meal would be breakfast if I could get there early enough.

I would have to manage until I found an escape out of here, but what would I do with my phoenix? I needed to find a way to get out of here and figured I would wait until he got better. If I carried him, it would slow me down, and if they caught me, they would surely kill him. So I needed to make sure he could fly on the off chance they did catch me. At least he could escape and be free.

When the pain subsided a little, I walked back into my room and flopped on my bed. I could try to sneak out tonight if they left my door unlocked. I could rummage through the bins for something for the phoenix to eat. He had to be hungry. I knew I was, but I wasn't at the point where I was going to start eating everyone's leftovers, not that I hadn't dumpster-dived before. How did it get to this, my life becoming this nightmare? I knew it was because I'd called on them, but now I saw that for what it was:

stupidity. But what about Kalen? Could I really abandon him after getting to know him?

I tried to light the stupid fire; the room was freezing, and whoever kept opening that damn window needed a swift kick up their ass. I glared at it before trying to yank it shut, and I actually managed it this time. The window slammed with a loud thud. I cringed, hoping they didn't come in and think I was breaking the place up.

Turning back to the fireplace, I tried to get the coals to light a piece of wood on fire. They could at least leave me a lighter. *Seriously, who uses a flint?* I thought, picking it up and examining the ridiculous thing. I shook my head when the door opened, and Tobias stepped in. I jumped to my feet when I saw the hungry look on his face; his fangs protruded and before I even had a chance to find something to defend myself with, he had me pinned against the dresser. A feral growl left his lips as he pressed his face in the crook of my neck.

Chapter 32

Tobias

WE HAD JUST FINISHED eating dinner, yet I was craving something else. Someone else. I should never have fed on Aleera. I was only allowed to feed on Lycus and Darius, and I knew the reason for it but her blood had been calling me from the moment I laid eyes on her. I told myself just a taste, but I knew I was done for when I fed on her and tried to take the shadows from her.

Lycus watched me; he had been looking at me strangely all day since he found me arguing with Aleera.

"I need to check the wards in the forest. Do you want to come?" Darius asked, getting up from his seat.

"No, I will wait here," I told him. He tilted his head to the side, examining me. I always went with him, and I knew he was suspicious of me, too. They all were. My hunger was insatiable, one of the reasons I was only to strictly feed on Lycus and Darius. They could fight me off. Kalen and Aleera, not so much if I lost control.

"When did you last feed? You seem to be in a mood," Darius asked before his eyes flicked to Lycus.

"Earlier off me, twice actually," Lycus answered, and Darius turned his gaze back to me. I noticed Kalen get up to head towards the bathroom, and I growled in warning at him.

"Sit, Kalen. I will take you to see her later," I told him. He sighed but sat back on the bed, yet Darius still didn't leave.

"Are you struggling since feeding on her the other night?" Darius asked me, and I shook my head.

"No, I am just drained," I lied. He didn't look like he believed me, but I also knew Darius had an obsession with the wards, and my mood wouldn't keep him here much longer; I just needed to wait him out.

"Lycus, do you want to come?" Darius asked him.

"Can I?" Kalen asked excitedly.

"I thought you wanted to see Aleera?"

"I can't until you come back anyway," Kalen huffed.

"Lycus can go. I will see if Aleera is back and take Kalen to see her," I told them, and Kalen's eyes lit up. My lips quirked in the corners, loving his excitement, and I wished he always looked so happy. Why couldn't we be enough for him? Why did she bring out this more optimistic side of him?

"No, Tobias. He needs to wait."

"I will be with him," I told Darius, and he sighed and rubbed his temples. Kalen pouted at him and gave him a pleading look, and I knew Darius was going to sway. He had trouble denying Kalen unless it was going to harm him. Darius knew I wouldn't allow her to hurt him. Understanding that, he sighed and turned to me.

"Don't leave him with her, and don't let her touch anything."

"What, you still want to bring her in here?" I asked him. I didn't think he was serious about that. Darius looked away, and I knew he was just as affected by her presence as we all were. He was just better at hiding it.

With me, her scent was all I could think about and the taste of her blood. I hated her more for wanting her, and I couldn't help but glare at the floor.

"Fine, we won't be gone long, but stay with them. Don't leave them alone together," Darius snapped before opening up a portal.

Lycus groaned, and I knew he hated leaving Kalen. Nighttime was pretty much the only time we were all together in one place, and I knew he missed Kalen most.

We all did; he was our glue. But Lycus and Kalen were together long before Darius and I joined the party. At first, the idea of marking them disgusted me, and I could have lived without the power-sharing. I could retrieve magic by drinking blood alone in little dribs and drabs, but I wasn't sure I could part from them after finding them.

After the fire, Darius and I cloaked her, which was stupid on our part. We cloaked her so well we couldn't even find her if we wanted to. If she left, the chances of finding her again were pretty slim. The cloaking spell had turned into a permanent shield on her. The only way to break it was by marking her, which Darius would never allow.

And damn how we had searched for her, following lead after lead. We weren't sure power-sharing was possible without our keeper, not until we witnessed it ourselves.

Kalen and Lycus were sleeping on the streets when we found them, and Lycus had become sick after accidentally ingesting wolfsbane, which made Kalen call on us. I still remembered how filthy and skinny they both were, and Darius and I were furious at how they were living. Finding out they had been living on the street for two years together startled us.

So when they called on our eighteenth birthday, we came to them and brought them back here. Just before learning Aleera's parents had tried to kill her, we sensed her distress. How we sensed her was beyond all of our reasoning. It was almost like she had called on us. She wasn't bonded to us yet, but we all had an inkling she was in trouble, and our marks burned our wrists.

I shook that memory away and watched Lycus grab Kalen's chin and kiss him. I smirked, watching them before Lycus let him go and followed Darius through the portal. That was also how we realized we could power-share. We walked in on Lycus and Kalen fucking and felt the magnitude of power in the air, so Darius did some research, and we learned that we could share our energy by marking each other.

It was taboo and only accepted if the keeper was dead. Ours wasn't, so it caused a lot of issues. Mostly with mine and Darius's family.

So, we marked each other, but it didn't work. We were back to square one, but Lycus and Kalen continued having power somehow when we realized how they were transferring it. Emotion. It repulsed Darius and me when we figured it out.

We realized that if we wanted to remain strong, we actually had to bond, which meant mate each other and commit to an actual relationship. Lycus and Kalen had no such issues, but Darius and I were straight. Completely straight. She gave us no choice when she ran, and we were forced to forge the bond. Kalen and Lycus were both patient, and they never pushed us past our comfort zones. When Darius got injured, protecting me from bloodhounds, we had refused for years to share power the way Lycus and Kalen did. But while hunting for her, we were set upon by the hounds, and neither of us had enough ability to take them down, forcing us to run.

He had sacrificed his life for mine, and, in turn, I kissed him. Didn't even think twice about it. He saved me, and I owed him, and I realized it worked better than feeding him my blood. After that, it became a non-issue. I was okay with it as long as nothing went near my ass. Well, for the first few years until the bond was forged, and I started craving them all. That craving extended to any way I could have them.

Darius was the most powerful. His power was potent, and I had never met anyone that yielded or controlled magic the way he did. Darius sort of became our keeper. He had particular gifts. We all found ourselves more inclined toward him. When we needed power, we usually went to him for it. His was the most potent and charged us quicker. Good thing he had good stamina. I chuckled, not realizing I did out loud.

"What are you laughing at?" Kalen asked, making me look up at him.

"Nothing, just when we all first got together," I told him, and Kalen smiled deviously before crawling to the edge of the bed. I could see he also remembered the orgy fest it had turned into.

His eyes sparkled. "I was wondering why your aura changed."

"Changed? How so?" I asked him while getting up from my seat. I walked over to him, and he leaned back to look up at me. He shrugged with a coy smile on his lips.

"More color in it?" he said before his brows pinched together.

"Well, that is new. Since when do I have color in my aura?" I asked him, knowing mine was usually a smokey gray color.

"Since you took the shadows from Aleera," he shrugged.

"Well, she is our keeper. I suppose her aura would be vastly different."

"I swear I saw something in hers, though. Hers was different, something about it—"

"You were manic, Kalen. You know you see weird things when you are like that."

He nodded when I tried to feel for his aura. His was surprisingly stable. I couldn't see it but felt it was the most transparent it had ever been. Like he was before he tried to kill himself the first time… before the shadows clung to him.

"You took your meds?" I asked him, and he looked down at his hands. I placed my knee on the bed beside him, forcing him back as I crawled on top of him.

"Is that a no?" I asked, nipping at his lips. His hands went to my sides and under my shirt. Sparks rushed across my skin when he tugged me closer, so I was pressed between his legs. His breathing became heavier, and I inhaled his scent deeply before kissing him. He tasted sweet, not as sweet as Aleera's blood, but I swear I could taste her on him.

Like she had tainted him in some way. Kalen responded to my kiss instantly. His tongue played with mine when I pulled away and kissed down his jaw and neck. I could feel his pulse under my tongue as I licked his mark, and I pressed my lips together when I felt my fangs slip out.

"Tobias?" Kalen murmured, and I heard his heart rate pick up, sensing the cologne of his fear seep from his pores. I shook my head and pulled away. He stared at me worriedly, and I pushed myself off him.

"I will go get Aleera for you," I told him before hopping off the bed and walking out. What was wrong with me? My fangs refused to retract as I moved toward her door. I could hear her cursing under her breath through the door, and I sucked in a breath, trying to will my hunger down, trying to control the bloodlust as it tried to consume me.

Thinking it was under control, I pushed her door open and closed it behind me, but the moment her scent hit me, a growl escaped me. Aleera looked at me startled and stood up, yet all I could hear was her blood pumping through her veins. She gasped as I pinned her against the dresser and buried my face in her neck. A hungered growl escaped me when she dropped her chin, trying to stop me from getting to her neck. Her words were not registering as she spoke in what I could tell was a panicked tone. My fangs grazed over her skin, and my mouth watered at the delicious scent permeating her.

"Tobias!"

CHAPTER 33

Aleera

"T OBIAS!" I SHRIEKED, DROPPING my neck when I felt his teeth slice over my flesh. He growled, and his grip on my arms was so strong I thought he would break my bones.

I lifted my knee between his legs when I felt his teeth prick into my skin. He groaned and clutched his manhood. The feral snarling growl that left him made my eyes widen, and I shoved him away from me, glancing around and looking for something to use to defend myself. I grabbed the poker for the fireplace and brandished it as a weapon.

"Kalen!" I screamed at the top of my lungs. Tobias lunged at me, and I jumped on top of my bed before jumping to the other side.

"Aleera?" Kalen yelled and banged on the door. It was locked when I felt the shudder of a portal opening up. Gosh, how I wish I could do that; it would be handy in a situation like this. Kalen appeared behind him, stepping into the room. His eyes were wide as he took in the scene. Tobias turned and growled at him before his eyes flicked back to me.

"Tobias, you need to focus on me," Kalen murmured with his hands out like he was trying to cage a wounded animal. Yet Tobias's eyes didn't waver from mine. Almost like he was locked on my scent and in a trance. I had heard of it at school but had never seen someone blood-crazed before. He was tracking my every movement.

Kalen tackled him, but Tobias moved too quickly, and Kalen hit the ground before I was tossed through the air. I didn't even see him grab me, only felt his nails slice into my soft flesh as he yanked on my arm. I smacked into the bathroom door when I felt his teeth slice into my upper arm like a savage as he pounced on me.

My scream echoed off the walls, and I noticed Kalen get up off the floor and shake himself. His head turned in my direction, and I reckoned the horror on his face mirrored mine. Kalen rushed over when another portal opened up in my tiny room, and Darius stepped in. He quickly assessed what was going on just as Lycus walked in behind him seconds later. I grunted when Tobias jerked me forward, his teeth sinking into my shoulder. Lycus growled and shoved Kalen through the portal while Darius gripped Tobias's shoulder and threw him backward. His teeth were torn painfully from my skin, ripping off a chunk of my flesh.

Tobias snarled and tried to attack him. Lycus intercepted just as Darius grabbed me, shoving me through the open portal. I gasped at the sudden movement. The air wheezed from my lungs as I fell through it into a new room. I landed on top of Kalen, knocking the wind out of him.

The room tilted a little, and I rolled off him and looked at the ceiling, trying to catch my breath as I sucked in deep breaths. He attacked me, and the only thing I could think of was, what if Darius and Lycus hadn't arrived? Or what if Kalen had no magic to portal in? Banging and growls could be heard from the room next door, and I sat up and looked around at my surroundings.

The room was dim; the only light provided came from the lamps that sat on either side of the enormous bed, which had to be the size of two kings.

"Are you alright?" Kalen asked me, and my head whipped in the direction of his voice. Kalen looked me over, and I glanced down to see blood gushing down my arm and spilling onto the black stained floorboards. I nodded, not knowing what to say. I felt cold, freezing, and Kalen moved toward me and gripped my arms. My head felt foggy, and my stomach woozy.

"You're shaking," Kalen murmured.

You would be, too, if someone tried to eat you and drain you of your blood. The banging in the other room slowly stopped when Lycus walked in through the bathroom door.

His hands gripped my arms, and the shock must have worn off because I threw up. Lycus looked down at his knees and shirt covered in bile since I had nothing in my stomach. Kalen gripped my hair as I retched when Lycus moved, picking me up. At first, I thought he was about to lose it because I threw up all over him, but instead, he scooped me up in one swift movement and walked me into the bathroom. My head was spinning, and I was still bleeding profusely. I could feel the blood draining out of me as I fought to remain conscious.

"Take her for a second," Lycus said; his tone was surprisingly gentle. Kalen took me from him, and I leaned my head heavily against his shoulder when I heard the sound of skin tearing before getting a whiff of Lycus's scent beneath my nose.

"Open your mouth," Lycus said, pressing down on my chin with his thumb. I obeyed, too weak to do anything else besides trying and hold myself back from retching again. Lycus had pressed his wrist to my lips; the taste of his blood breached the barrier of my lips, and my mouth opened, allowing his blood to flood in. I could feel the bite marks healing, although it did nothing for the blood already lost.

The sound of running water told me Lycus had turned the shower on. Seconds passed before I was pressed against his naked chest. Feeling water drench my face made me gasp as I breathed it in. My eyes flew open, and I jerked in his arms.

"Sorry," he said before sitting down. His back hit the tiles with a thud since he couldn't place his hands down because I was currently wrapped in his arms. I leaned heavily against him, and my eyes fluttered.

"Stay awake. Darius will be in soon."

All I wanted to do was sleep, and gosh, I felt cold. Icy cold but also numb; it was an odd sensation to feel. Kalen gripped my face before tapping my cheek, but I couldn't keep my eyes open.

CHAPTER 34

"ALEERA, STAY AWAKE FOR me," Kalen murmured. His voice became more and more distant, and I felt my clothes tugged off. My limbs were floppy, and Lycus moved me around like a puppet, yet the feeling induced by the blood loss had me not caring about anything as I focused on breathing. It seemed like a mammoth task—one I wasn't sure I wanted to keep forcing because it was too much effort.

A sharp prick in my arm told me someone had jammed a needle in me, yet I couldn't open my heavy eyelids.

"I don't get it. Why does she need blood? Lycus healed her," came a voice.

"She has no magic, Kalen. She might as well be human. She will be fine," Lycus murmured, and their voices grew louder.

"She looks so pale," Kalen said. Their voices became more explicit as my surroundings came back into view. I had no idea how long I'd been out for, but I was aware that I was no longer in the shower. Tingles spread up my arms from the fingertips that brushed up them lazily.

"Left some nasty scars, but she is getting some color back," Kalen murmured, and I groaned.

"She is waking up," Kalen said. The excitement in his words made my eyes flutter, and I opened them to look at the ceiling. The same ceiling I saw when I fell through the portal. Kalen hovered above me, looking down at me as he leaned over, pulling my eyelids up and making me blink rapidly.

He sighed before dropping his head onto my collarbone. My hand went to his hair, wanting to reassure him I was fine, when I felt the tug in the crook of my elbow. When he lifted his head, I looked at my arm and the line in it, giving me blood. I followed the line to find Darius staring at me. He moved, twisting something and cutting it off as he leaned forward. He placed a cotton bud over the canular stuck in my arm before pulling it out.

He said nothing when I looked for the blood bag, only to find the other end of the line attached to him.

"You gave me blood?" I asked groggily. He didn't answer but yanked the needle from his arm.

"We don't have an infirmary here. Not much need for blood here either besides Tobias, so we had to make do. Probably not the safest way if you were human." Kalen chuckled, cupping my face in his hands.

"Don't worry. His blood is clean and since we all share the same blood type, no harm done." Kalen shrugged.

"Huh?" I asked groggily before clutching my head.

"We're mates. Don't they teach this stuff in that boarding school you went to? I thought mates and fates were common topics in schools. They even taught us about them in the orphanage," Kalen continued to ramble. Darius had wandered off, so I turned my attention to Kalen, trying to listen to what he was telling me. However, I knew it took me a second to register what he was rambling about.

"I thought you would know about how the fates chose our

mates. Though a little iffy, if you ask me."

"I do know. Sorry, you just caught me while out of it," I mumbled.

"Then you tell me, can be a memory check of sorts," he chuckled.

I rolled my eyes before noticing he was staring at me expectantly. *Oh, he was serious.* He wanted to know if I indeed understood how the mate bonds worked.

"Um…" I shook my head. "Ah, they are determined by the time of birth, the position of the moon, and the date," I groaned. Why did my head still hurt?

"Yes, that is why all of us share the same birthday. You are the exception, though, since we are all twenty-nine, and you are only twenty-four. So, we were all born at 01:11 AM on the nineteenth of May. You, being our keeper, didn't appear until five years later. Although you share the same time of birth and have the same birthday, all mates share the same birthday. However, when I looked into it, no girls were born on the nineteenth of May, the year we were born, which is quite odd if you ask me."

"What, no girls were born on that day?" I asked, having not known that.

"Not one. Only boys and the three of us were born at the same time, setting our fates. The next turnaround for that time was five years later, and that was you."

I honestly never looked into our bloodlines or fate information, to be honest. I was too busy running from the fate that was bestowed upon me.

"But boys can be keepers," I told him.

"Yes, and most are male. But we got you since you were the only person born on that day when the moons aligned. None of us were born with keeper gifts," Kalen chuckled.

"I couldn't have been the only person born on the nineteenth of May that year. That seems impossible."

"You forget that is when the plague hit. It is also when many fae lost a mate and eventually their magic, seeing as the majority of fates were paired with harmony or white fae. We just got lucky a lot were forced into a human lifestyle," Kalen told me.

I nodded, knowing full well of the effects the plague had had. However, his words made me wonder about my mother. She survived the plague, but then Darius told me that there was a second wave, making me wonder if that was what had killed her.

"When did the second wave hit?" I asked. For some reason, my mind seemed to lock onto that thought.

"Seven years later. You would have just turned seven by then. It wasn't as bad, since some did survive, though only a few like Darius's sister."

I tried to figure out roughly how old I was. I knew it was a couple of days after my seventh birthday, yet I couldn't remember her falling ill before she died. Her death was sudden. I just remembered coming into the living room, and my father jammed a needle filled with his blood into her heart.

I remembered wondering why he had a random needle with his blood. I thought it strange, but she was sick for a few days afterward. Dad wouldn't allow me in the room with her, although I begged, not believing she was fine. A few days later, she just walked out while I was in the living room like nothing had happened. She was different after that. Dying had done something to her; it was an odd memory.

With a shake of my head, the memory faded.

"Your aura is so dark," Kalen murmured, whisking his fingers around my face.

CHAPTER 35

"REMINDS ME OF DARIUS. His is as black as coal." Kalen chuckled.

"Probably because she is full of my blood and my magic is tainting her. It should wear off in a few hours, but until then…" Darius said, coming over to me. He gripped my wrist and clamped something on it. It looked like a silver bangle, and I examined it.

"Until my magic fades out of your system, you wear that," Darius said, and I instantly felt its effects as he locked it in place. It sent a shock wave of exhaustion through me like a mood tranquilizer.

"Come on, Darius, was that even necessary? She hadn't even noticed she had magic," Kalen growled. *Fuck.* In my grogginess, I completely forgot. Though absorbing it from his blood in my system was a little harder than me absorbing directly from them by touch.

"Regardless, I won't take the risk."

"Exactly what do you expect me to do if I had magic? I have no idea where I even am."

"Open a portal and leave. That is what I expect."

I sighed. I would probably do that without question if given a chance again, but I had my phoenix here. *Shit! My phoenix!* I sat upright, and Darius growled at me. Lycus sat silently, watching us from the chair next to the fireplace.

I looked around for Tobias before my eyes landed on him sitting in the corner of the room. He must have felt my gaze on him because he lifted his head. My blood drenched his shirt, and once my gaze met his, I couldn't pull it away, locked in a trance as the memory of the savage look on his face came back to haunt me. Tobias looked away as if he was almost regretful of his actions. I was thankful when he did because I couldn't bring myself to look away from him until Darius stepped into my line of vision.

"Kalen, go get her something to eat," Darius told him, and Kalen nodded, getting up when I noticed I was actually in their bed. How it took so long for that to come to my mind confused me.

Kalen left, and my stomach dropped when I found myself alone with the three of them. I looked down at my clothes to see I was wearing only a shirt. Vague memories of being placed in the shower flooded my mind, and I looked over at Lycus as I tugged the front of the shirt. I leaned down and sniffed it. Kalen's scent was all over it.

"Darius dressed you," Lycus answered the question that came to my mind.

I nodded. No point crying over them seeing me naked; it was already done. I was just glad I was unconscious when it happened.

However, Darius's next words shocked me, and I swallowed my tongue. I wanted no part of this.

"Tobias will need to feed off you until he can control his blood-lust," Darius said before glaring over his shoulder at Tobias on the floor in the corner, his arms over his knees and his head rested on them.

"But—"

"It isn't up for debate. Lycus or I will be with him when he does until he can control the urge to kill you anyway."

"Why can't he feed off one of you?" I asked.

"He has been, but unfortunately, you are our keeper. Now that he has tasted your blood, he will withdraw from it. It's safer if he learns to control it than going cold turkey," Lycus said, also not looking happy about the situation. My eyes glanced over at Tobias, who was now clutching his hair, looking rather stressed out.

Darius followed my line of vision before speaking to him. "We asked you earlier if anything was up with you, and you lied," he scolded.

"I had it under control," Tobias said.

"Well, could have fooled me. This wouldn't have been an issue if you had told me you had been struggling since trying to take the shadows from her. I could have cleansed your blood," Darius snapped furiously.

"I thought I had control," Tobias growled. Darius growled at him, and I scooted to the edge of the bed before placing my feet on the ground.

"Where do you think you are going?" Darius said, his head whipping in my direction.

"I need to pee," I said, pointing to the bathroom door. He nodded, and I got up; vertigo washed over me. I clutched the bedside table as I stumbled before noticing a photo. At first, I thought it was Tobias until I saw an almost identical man beside him in the picture. Was Tobias a twin?

They looked the same age, and I could swear I had seen him before. I tried to rack my brain. My hand moved to pick it up when it was suddenly gone and placed in the drawer. Looking up, I noticed Tobias was beside me, and he was the one who'd snatched it before I could touch it.

He glared at me, and I looked away before he watched me stagger into the bathroom. An exasperated breath left me as I locked the door only to hear them lock it from their side, too. I shook my head before quickly using the toilet. When I was finished, I washed my hands and twisted the doorknob after unlocking it, only to find it still locked. I sighed with relief.

Obviously, they decided I could remain in my room. The sound of their arguing stopped when they heard the door, but I turned on my heel and walked over to the one leading into my room. Just as I stepped inside, I listened to the lock click on my bedroom door. I sucked in a deep breath waiting for it to burst open.

Chapter 36

I waited, thinking someone was coming in, but whoever it was had moved back to their room. Rubbing my arms at the coldness of the room, I made my way to the fireplace to see if I could light it. Kneeling in front of it, I got a sense of déjà vu, which sent a shiver down my spine and made me glance at the door.

No one came in, and I turned back to the fireplace. I looked for the flint and tried to get the fire going. Stacking the kindling in and some wood. Just as I was about to light it, I heard the door. My heart skipped a beat as it unlocked, and Kalen stepped in.

He looked upset as he carried a tray in his hands. The smell of hot food wafted to my nose, and a few seconds later, Darius walked in behind him. He tossed a fireball at the fireplace, and I jumped when it rushed past me before he sat down in the chair.

"Can't she stay in our room just for tonight?" Kalen pouted at him.

"I prefer to be in here," I told Kalen before Darius could answer. Kalen dropped his head and walked over to me while Darius moved to sit on the small armchair in front of the fire. Kalen placed the tray in my lap.

"You should eat," he said, and my stomach growled hungrily as I looked down at the plate, which contained vegetables and some steak. Real food, and it smelled delicious. Yet when I went to take the knife off Kalen to dig in, the plate was removed along with the knife. I sighed before looking at Darius, who then cut up the meat, and I rolled my eyes and looked over at the fire.

"Seriously, Darius?" Kalen whined at him. Darius ignored him before handing the plate back to me but keeping the knife. I took it from him, feeling like a child that I wasn't even allowed to use a knife like a normal person. He placed the knife on his lap.

"She could do just as much damage with a damn fork."

My fork was suddenly plucked from my fingers. "Thank you for pointing that out," Darius growled at him.

"Darius, I didn't mean for you to take it from her," Kalen snarled.

"Quiet, or you can go back to your room."

"How do you expect her to eat?"

"It's fine, Kalen. I spent most of my time in the woods anyway. No cutlery there," I told him before picking up a piece of broccoli off the plate.

Darius leaned back and closed his eyes while Kalen watched me eat and talked to me. He was very talkative, and I preferred this sunny side of Kalen as he animatedly told me about different things.

"So, you spent most of your time in the woods?" Kalen asked, and Darius scoffed, making me realize he had sat up to listen to our conversation. I plucked another piece of meat off the plate. The sauce was making my fingers sticky.

"No, mostly traveling. I was trying to find a human settlement or city to bunker down in."

"Why a human one?"

"Because I was running out of magic," I answered.

"The man on the footage from the school, who was he?" Kalen asked.

I glanced up at him from my plate. His expression darkened, and I could tell he was quite upset over it.

"I didn't know there was footage, but he wasn't boyfriend if that is what you were wondering. I never ran off with anyone, Kalen."

"Then who was he?" Darius growled, and I jumped at the tone of his voice. Kalen stared at me expectantly, wanting me to answer.

"An acquaintance. I hardly knew him. He was also running from his bonds. I overheard him speaking on the phone in the library to his girlfriend. He wanted to be with her, so he planned to find her."

"So, he just helped you escape?" Kalen asked.

"Yes. We needed two people to break the wards, so I offered to help him break them if he gave me a lift into the city. We parted ways at the bus depot," I told them.

"Then where did you go?"

I shrugged. "I had $43, and that was it. So, I told the bus driver to get me as far as he could, heading north."

"Why north?" Darius asked, and he genuinely sounded curious. I dropped my gaze, knowing my answer would probably anger him.

"Why north, Aleera?" Darius's tone of voice was more of a demand than a question. I looked at Kalen, who was studying me.

"I was trying to find a place called Astrid." That seemed to surprise them as they both looked at each other.

"Have you heard of it?"

"Yes, but we aren't telling you where it is. Why were you looking for it?" Darius asked, folding his arms across his chest and sitting back. He looked at Kalen, who sighed, also refusing to tell me where it was.

"Answer the question, or I make Kalen leave," Darius growled. I nibbled on my lip, not willing to say, and Kalen looked at Darius.

"Fine, come on, Kalen," Darius said, hopping up.

"Aleera, just answer. I want to stay."

Yet I didn't want my answer to upset him or for him to get the wrong idea.

"Kalen, now!" Darius snarled before bending down and gripping his arm.

"Just a little longer, please."

Darius glared at him and hauled Kalen to his feet, and the look Kalen gave me broke my heart.

"I was looking for someone," I blurted, and they stopped.

Darius turned to look down at me, and Kalen looked at Darius.

"She answered. Can I stay?"

Darius's lip pulled up over his upper lip before he sighed and nodded, and Kalen sat down again.

CHAPTER 37

DARIUS WATCHED ME FOR a second before taking his seat.

"Who were you looking for?" Darius asked, and I looked away from him.

"Someone I used to speak to through a chat link online," I answered, rubbing a hand down my face. When I looked up, Darius had leaned forward, bracing his arms on his elbows.

"So, you were seeing someone?"

I shook my head. "I never met them. I am not sure who they were, but we talked for years from the time my grandmother died."

"A man?" Darius asked, and I shrugged.

"I am not sure. We became friends. That's all I know. I never met them or saw them, not even a picture. I have no idea if they were male or female. Could have been anybody."

"Yet you went looking for them instead of calling on us," Darius said, leaning back in his seat. He turned his gaze to Kalen. "What was this person's name?"

"Does it matter?"

Darius shrugged and since they didn't have a name, I didn't see the harm in telling him.

"I only know his login name. It was part of the chat group.

We weren't allowed to use our real names, kind of like a pen pal. HTIARW," I answered.

"You still remember their login credentials?" Kalen asked.

"Well, I spoke to them every day for nearly four years, and they never changed it, so yes."

"Why would you go looking for someone on the internet?" Darius asked, his eyes darkening.

"Because the person mentioned if I was ever in Astrid to look for them. I was hoping when I got there I could get access to the internet and track them down, but I never found the place. I gave up after a few years. It wasn't on any map, and I figured they gave me a fake name for that, too." I shrugged.

"But you have heard of it, so it must be real?" I asked, wondering if I was indeed sent on a wild goose chase.

"It's not on any maps because it isn't a town or city. It's the name of a place," Kalen answered, and Darius growled at him.

"What sort of place?" I asked, but one glare from Darius prohibited him from answering. Kalen looked down at his hands and picked at his nails.

"What about friends at the boarding school or from your previous school? Did you keep in touch with them?" Darius asked me. I shook my head.

"Mom mainly homeschooled me. It wasn't until high school that dad convinced her to let me attend a real school. That only lasted a few months before they died, and I was shipped off to live with my grandmother," I said. That thought saddened me as I remembered my parents.

"You didn't like my grandmother?"

"Hmm, she was the best. She reminded me of my father. He looked a lot like her, stern like him, too. But she was good to me. I miss her," I said, glancing at the fire.

"She died only a few months later. She used to visit when I was a kid, never missed a birthday or Christmas. She was the only family I had besides my parents."

"We looked into your family background but only found your father's side. Your mother's records didn't exist, and we also thought it odd nobody knew her," Kalen said, scratching the back of his neck. I knew no records existed. My father went to great lengths to hide what I was, and that meant getting rid of everything on my mother's bloodline. My brows scrunched together, wondering how he'd managed it.

"Your father was an important person, worked for the fae government," Kalen said. *Now, that surprised me. That I didn't know.*

"Really?"

"You didn't know?" Darius asked me.

I shook my head. "I thought he was just a businessman. Mom told me he worked for the bank?"

"No, he worked for the dark political party," Darius answered. "He was one of the chairmen like my father."

"Your father worked with mine?"

"Yes, but on opposite sides, though. They hated each other."

"What did your father do?"

"He was an advocate for white fae." *Now, that shocked me further.*

"But you're dark fae."

Darius nodded. "Yes, my father was shocked when he found your father actually had a daughter. You were his best-kept secret. We didn't even know he had a wife, let alone a daughter," Darius answered.

"Hang on. I am still confused as to why your father was an advocate for white fae, being that he was dark?"

"Molly, his stepdaughter," Kalen answered.

"That didn't anger him that your mother had an affair?"

"Oh, it bothered him, but he loved Molly regardless. After she died, he started fighting to have those responsible for the plague brought to justice."

"Did they get brought to justice?"

"Some were caught and killed, but we never found how the plague originated, only that it was fae-made," Darius told me.

I nodded, not wanting to pry too much since he was being civil, and I didn't know how quickly that could change if I asked the wrong question. I picked up another piece of cold meat and plopped it in my mouth.

"I have another question?" Kalen said, and I looked at him.

"Why didn't you try to contact your internet friend before you left to tell them to expect you?"

"Honestly, I panicked. By the time that thought arose, I was already gone."

"So, you never tried to contact him after that?"

"Why do you keep assuming it was a man?" I said with a click of my tongue.

"Well, I was just assuming…"

"I am pretty sure they were female or gay, either one," I told him.

"Why would you assume that?"

"Because of how they spoke. They seemed pretty gender-neutral."

"Well, that is stereotyping," Kalen chuckled.

"Yeah, I suppose it is. It doesn't matter now, though. Not like I will speak to them again."

"Would you if you could?"

Darius growled, and I looked over at him. His hands clenched the arms of the chair, his knuckles turning white. I swallowed, not bothering to answer.

"Well, if they are gay or female, what does it matter if she spoke to them?" Kalen snapped, and Darius seemed to think.

"And you had no other friends?" Kalen asked, pulling my attention back to him. I shook my head.

"So, you spent six years alone?"

"Bullshit!" Darius scoffed.

"I was doing fine on my own, and yes, Kalen," I answered.

"So, you met nobody else?"

"Well, of course, I met people along the way, but I mostly stayed away from cities unless I thought they were human ones. I just never found one."

"Six years, and you never found one?" Kalen asked incredulously.

"Not one."

"If you weren't attacked the night we found you, would you have called on us? Eventually?" Kalen asked, and I looked away. I swallowed thickly.

"You wouldn't have, would you?" Darius said.

"Well, what did you expect after you killed my parents?"

"You say that like I am some monster and killed them in cold blood," Darius scoffed.

"You are!" I screamed, and he seemed taken aback by my outburst.

Darius glared at me before leaning forward, and I pulled away from him. "I was fucking protecting you from them!"

"My parents were good parents. I sure as hell didn't need protecting from them."

"So good they tried to kill their only child."

"They would never hurt me," I told him, looking away.

"That may have been true before they found out I was your mate!" he yelled at me. Darius stood up and gripped Kalen's arm, yanking him to his feet just as the door to the bathroom burst open.

"What's going on?" Lycus asked, rushing in.

"Nothing, we were just leaving," Darius said, shoving Kalen toward the door.

"Wait, what do you mean?" I asked Darius, but he continued walking without so much as a glance back at me before he slammed the door.

CHAPTER 38

HAT WAS IT? HE wasn't even going to attempt to explain what he meant? The loss of their presence was instantly felt. The coldness of the bond slowly evaporated into the air, and I sighed, wondering if I would ever get used to it every time one of them stormed out.

It was making it increasingly difficult to hate them when the bond played havoc constantly when they were around. Darius's words made no sense. Why would he have to protect me from my own parents? I knew what I saw, if only briefly. There was no doubt in my mind that he was the reason they were dead.

I tried to remember that night, but nothing stuck out or showed that my parents had anything to do with the fire. Stoking the fire, I got up before picking up the plate that I had purposely eaten slowly, wanting to save some of the meat for the phoenix.

My eyes moved to the door. With a glance over my shoulder, I walked over to the main door and twisted the handle, and my heart leaped with joy when I noticed it was unlocked. It was odd for them to forget to lock me in. Usually, I would wake up to the door being unlocked, but they always locked it when they went to sleep.

As quietly as possible, I rushed around the room, grabbing my supplies. I grabbed a tissue and wrapped what was left of my dinner in it before retrieving my old bandages. Grabbing one of my pillows off the bed, I snuck over to the door, listening for any noise out in the hall. When I thought the coast was clear, I turned the knob slowly so it didn't grind. My heart hammered in my chest at the thought of being caught sneaking out.

Once in the hall, I glanced down the dimly lit hallway toward the stairs. I rushed to them with hesitant steps and only stopped at the top to look back the way I came for any sign of them. They hadn't noticed, and I slipped down to the bottom level. It was clear everyone was tucked safely away in their dorm rooms because I saw nobody wandering about. The place was dark, and I noticed the glow of the door handles that led outside in the foyer area. They glowed a fluorescent orange, and I wandered over to them.

It took only seconds for me to recognize them for what they were: wards. Darius's magic emanated from them, and I wondered if he spelled the castle every night. My head turned back to the stairs, and I reached out before pausing as I went to grip the door handle. I wanted to see if I could siphon it, but I also didn't want to risk him noticing. I also wasn't sure if I would be blasted like an intruder by touching it. Definitely worth investigating later on, but I needed to check my phoenix for now.

The doors to the mess hall were closed as I approached the cellar door leading to the cells. With a pull, the door opened, and I descended the steps while feeling for a light switch. It wasn't until I reached the bottom that I found it, and I quickly flicked the light on. The bird cawed a yelp before calming when he noticed me.

"Shh, it's only me," I whispered to him as I stepped into the cell. He observed me carefully, and I knew he was unsure of me. Phoenixes were brilliant birds and could sense power. Even without magic, I could tell he knew something was different about me being a harmony fae. They could feel it. Phoenixes were almost drawn to the white fae, making me wonder if he had sensed me here, wherever here was. Just like Darius and I, phoenixes were a dying species. They were killed off by the dark fae and considered pests because they hated the dark fae and were known for attacking them. So, most were killed, which was sad because they were amazing creatures. They were just a little temperamental when it came to the dark fae, but they were still amazing despite their hatred for my brethren.

Sitting beside him, I opened the tissue and pulled out the cut-up meat. I tried to wipe some of the sauce off, but he didn't seem to care, pecking at my open palm, wanting to eat it. I held up a piece to his beak, and he pinched it before tossing his head back and gulping it down.

His beak nudged my hand, wanting more, so I continued to feed him. I was hoping to gain its trust because I wasn't looking forward to being bitten after watching its beak slice through the beef like a knife through butter. Its snake-like tongue slivered out, turning the beef strip this way and that as he hungrily ate.

"Do you have a name?" I asked it. The phoenix tilted its head to the side. I tapped my chin, trying to think of one.

"What about Flame?" The bird tilted its head the other way.

"Scorch?" It shook its head.

"Ember?" It appeared to huff, puffing out its chest and making the feathers stand upon his head.

"How about Ryze, with a 'z?'" I offered, and it blinked at me before nudging my face with its giant beak.

"Ryze it is then," I chuckled.

"Now, are you going to bite me when I try to wrap your wing? If you are, a warning would be nice, but I will try to be gentle,"

I told him while scratching the top of its head. The phoenix watched me unravel the bandages, and I carefully plucked him from where he sat on the bed, placing him on my lap. He whimpered, and his snake-like tongue slivered out to lick at my hand placed under his chest.

"I'm sorry. I am trying to be gentle," I told Ryze. I bandaged him up, placed him on the pillow, and tucked my jumper and pillowcase around him to keep him warm.

"I need to go, but I will be back in the morning. You have to be quiet, though." I told him. Ryze fluffed out his remaining feathers before ducking his head under his good wing. I sighed and rushed out of the cellar and slipped back into my room.

CHAPTER 39

Aleera

I WAS AWOKEN THE FOLLOWING day by the alarm next to my bed. I tossed and turned all night after what Darius had said to me, so my eyes felt like sandpaper. My mind went to the phoenix when I sat up. I needed to steal some breakfast before classes started and quickly check on him. Tossing the blanket off, I heard something slip off the end of the bed with a thump on the floorboards. Walking around to the end of my bed, I found a box. I bent down, picking it off the floor, and turned it over. A sticky note was attached to it, so I peeled it off.

"I already hooked it up to the Wi-Fi. You just need to turn it on. Love, Kalen." Looking at the box, I found it was a tablet. Was Darius aware he had given it to me, and why would he allow it? I pulled it from the box and looked at the shiny device. It was so much better than my old one. Shiny and new. I pressed the power button, and it lit up. No doubt they would track everything I did on it. I knew not even Kalen would be stupid enough to give me a device that could link me to the outside world without parental controls on it.

Despite that, I smiled, wondering if I could speak to my pen pal friend. Would Darius become angry but he was aware, so he couldn't get mad, could he? I dressed quickly and made my way down to the mess hall. The door wasn't open yet, and I had to wait. When they did, the demon that opened them sneered at me, and I gulped, taking a step away from him.

He said nothing but turned on his heel and walked back out to the kitchens. My stomach growled hungrily at the smell of food. He placed the huge trays out, and I quickly grabbed a bowl, filling it with dry cereal. I grabbed another and put some eggs and bacon in before retrieving a water bottle and slipping out before he returned. Although it was necessary to steal food, I felt like a thief. I couldn't live on air alone. After I walked down to the phoenix, he ignored the dry cereal I'd placed in front of him and beckoned at my eggs instead.

"You know that is probably in some small way a relative you're eating, right?" I told him.

He chuffed and pecked at my bowl, and I sighed, placing it on the bed beside him so he could help himself. I chewed on a piece of bacon before eating the dry cereal. When I finished, I opened the water bottle and poured some into a bowl so he could have a drink. He guzzled it thirstily while I pulled the tablet from the back of my pants.

The device was definitely monitored. I couldn't access much on the internet, and half the apps didn't work. Despite it being pointless, I typed in the old chat group name and was surprised it didn't shut me out.

After logging in and trying to remember my password, I discovered my email account was shut down, and I had to create a new one. With a sigh, I typed in the search bar HTIARW. To my surprise, the account still existed. I wondered if the person would still remember me or even want to talk to me. Regardless, I sent a message explaining I had a new account and telling them my old login name. With a sigh, I turned the screen off. "I suppose now we wait," I told Ryze. He nudged me with his beak, eating the rest of my eggs.

When the siren blared, signaling the start of classes, I groaned and got to my feet, saying goodbye to my not-so-feathery friend. Climbing the stairs, I waited for there to be no noise before slipping out and over to my first class, which was with Tobias. As I walked down the hall, I was snatched and instantly thrashed as they dragged me into a nearby classroom.

They let me go, and I turned to find it was Darius. "Where did you sneak off this morning?" he asked.

"To breakfast," I told him.

"I checked, and you weren't in there," he snapped at me. I took a step back before noticing Tobias leaning against the wall.

With a roll of his eyes, he pushed off the wall. "Can we get this over with? I have a class to teach," Tobias said in a bored tone.

I glanced between them, wondering what he meant when Darius grabbed me. The moment he wrapped his arm across my chest and jerked me against him, I shrieked. Darius tucked me against him. He grabbed my wrist, offering it to Tobias, who snatched it in his tight grip while I struggled against Darius's hold.

"We warned you last night this was necessary. Now, remain still," he snarled next to my ear.

I stopped, and Tobias sank his teeth into my wrist. I looked away while he fed off me. Though his grip only tightened, and I started feeling light-headed after a few minutes.

"Enough, Tobias. Let her go," Darius snapped at him, but he didn't. Instead, he sank his teeth in again, making me whimper.

"Tobias, I said enough!"

Tobias growled at him when Darius yanked my arm away, making me cry out as his teeth tore away from the flesh. Tobias went to attack, but Darius flicked his wrist, and Tobias hit a barrier and froze. My eyes widened, and Tobias appeared stunned. Darius then bit his wrist and jammed it against my mouth. I turned my face, not wanting his blood.

"Now! That shield won't hold long," Darius growled, and I opened my mouth, hating the idea of drinking his blood directly from him. I sputtered, and he ripped his wrist away before shoving me away. Only when he did, he yanked me back toward him before reaching down the back of my pants and pulling out the tablet.

"Where did you get this?"

"It was on my bed. Kalen gave it to me," I told him. My body tensed, and I flinched when he examined it. He glared at it before thrusting it back at me.

I hesitantly took it before he looked at Tobias. "Go, before I change my mind," Darius spat at me, and I rushed out.

CHAPTER 40

Darius

I WAS ON A WARPATH as I hunted Kalen down. Lycus jumped as I entered the bedroom, not expecting my burning anger. My eyes went to Kalen, and so did Lycus, as I pinned him with my stare. Kalen rolled his eyes, and I wasn't sure I liked this attitude he was developing with Aleera here.

My steps were purposeful as I stalked toward him. He didn't move, and it was clear he expected my anger at what he had done but also didn't care for it. Lycus moved quickly as I approached Kalen, stepping into my path before reaching him, and my chest smacked against his. Lycus growled at me, and his eyes flickered to his beast.

"Move, Lycus!" I snarled while glaring at him. Lycus, however, only pressed closer. The anger coursing through him matched mine as a growl rumbled from his chest. The threatening noise was a warning not to push him too hard, or he would bite.

"You won't touch him. You can try, but I won't allow it," Lycus sneered as he stood chest to chest with me.

"Have I ever hurt him?" I asked, but his gaze hardened like steel before he spoke.

"No, but when it comes to her, you can be erratic and I don't like what I am feeling from you." His words shocked me. Did he not trust me with our mate? I would never hurt them, at least not purposely.

"Chill, Lycus. He is just upset because I gave Aleera a tablet."

Lycus's brows scrunched together as he glanced over his shoulder at our mate. "You what?"

Well, maybe I was not the only one that could be erratic. Now Kalen was keeping secrets from Lycus. It was apparent Lycus didn't like that either. He turned toward our mate, folded his arms across his chest, and glared at him.

"She won't try to run," Kalen answered confidently, not even bothering to look at Lycus, who frowned. I hated to be the one to tell him, but Aleera would run the first chance she got. I could see it clear as day, and he was a fool for believing otherwise.

"I deleted half the software. The only people she can contact is the old chat group we created, besides the castle portal, not that she has tried to open it yet," Kalen answered.

"And you didn't think to tell us?" Lycus growled at him.

"You would have said no," Kalen answered, looking over at him before leaning forward, reaching into the coffee table drawer and pulling his phone out.

"Yes, because we don't want you talking to her. Remember what happened last time, Kalen? It isn't worth the risk," Lycus said, marching over to him and snatching the phone from his hand.

Kalen sighed before standing up, and Lycus unlocked his phone. Standing behind Lycus, I peered over his shoulder when Kalen snatched the phone from his grip.

"Use your own!" Kalen snapped at us.

"I don't like this, Darius. Tell him!" Lycus said, turning to me. I scoffed and looked at him.

"What, now you are on my side?" I asked him.

"I didn't know he gave her a device." Turning to Kalen, he continued, "I don't want you talking to her without us. You stepped out of line this time, Kalen."

"Lines should be stepped over, Lycus, so stop being a dick. I already uploaded and logged in on all your phones. You can monitor everything if you want," Kalen answered.

Lycus muttered under his breath before pulling his phone out and unlocking it.

"I want nothing to do with this. You monitor their conversations if she tries to talk to him," I told Lycus.

"I still don't like this," Lycus muttered, opening the app when it suddenly dinged.

"Who is that? I swear if you are talking to other people, Kalen, I will put you over my damn knee," I snapped at him, seeing an unusual thread pop up.

Lycus clicked on it. "It's Aleera. She opened up a new account."

Kalen sighed, and I eyed him. I knew he was hoping she would open up her old one and realize it was him she spoke to for all those years.

"So, this over-your-knee thing is still a possibility?" Kalen taunted with a devious smile on his lips.

Lycus raised his eyes to him with a smirk on his face. I clicked my tongue before moving toward Kalen, where he sat on the chair. I leaned over the back of it, and he looked up at me and smiled; his hand reached out for me.

"Maybe later," I told him before pressing my lips to his. He gripped the back of my neck and ran his tongue across my lips. I growled at him, my cock twitching to life, making me want to bend him over and fuck his tight ass. My groan made him smile against my lips, and I kissed him deeper, my tongue invading his mouth. All too quickly, I pulled away before I got carried away and made good on my desire to fuck him senseless. Kalen pouted, and I pecked his lips.

"Behave. I love you," I told him, and he sighed as I stood up. Lycus watched us before adjusting the crotch of his pants, clearly turned on.

"Monitor them," I told him, and he nodded as I approached him.

"I still don't like it," Lycus said, looking over my shoulder at our mate.

"I know, but I have to get to class," I told him, kissing the side of his mouth. "Watch him."

"Always," Lycus mumbled against my lips before I walked out to give hell to my morning class. It would be hell too because I was in a mood, and Aleera would want to behave because I was bound to snap at some point.

CHAPTER 41

Aleera

FOR THE PAST THREE days, I had felt terribly sick. I didn't know if it was because I had only been getting half a breakfast a day since I shared with Ryze or because of the bond. The siren for the next glass blared, and I groaned. I wished I had a theory class all day; I would have even put up with Darius and Tobias's torment. The last thing I felt like doing was that damn obstacle course.

Darius looked over at me and placed my head on the desk, not wanting to go. I felt hot, and my skin was clammy. My stomach was twisting violently, and I was hungry as well as pained.

"Aleera, next class," Darius said, and I looked up at him.

"Can I go back to my room? I don't feel well."

"Class now, or you won't see Kalen after dinner," Darius snapped at me and hauled my ass out of my seat. Seeing Kalen was the only thing I looked forward to besides seeing Ryze. I gripped the desk as a wave of dizziness washed over me, and Darius watched me stagger to the front of the class before turning his gaze away.

"Asshole," I muttered under my breath.

"Want to repeat that?" Darius growled behind me, and I looked back at him.

He glared at me and went to get up. I quickly rushed out the door. Making my way down the corridors, I felt my stomach heave up my throat, and I ran to the closest trash can before throwing up in it. *No, please,* I thought as I lost my breakfast. I wiped my mouth on the back of my hand and staggered to the bathroom. I drank from the tap, knowing that I would stumble across someone if I went to the mess hall.

I wet my face, trying to cool myself down after retching. Looking in the oval-shaped mirror above the sink, my face was pale, and my eyes sunken in. My stomach growled hungrily, and I drank some more water, trying to fill it enough to stop the loud gurgling noises. Wetting the back of my neck, I leaned on the basin, trying to force myself to head to the next class.

My tablet pinged, and I pulled it out. My pen pal remembered me, and we had been talking for the last few days. I excitedly opened up the chat.

"How's your day?" they asked.

I looked in the mirror. *Shit!* I thought, looking at my hollow cheeks. I had lost so much weight with training and not eating I was starting to look gaunt in the face. I shook my head, wondering how it was possible in such a brief period.

"Crap, I feel sick and have to go to class," I replied as I made my way out.

They responded with a sad emoji.

"How's yours?"

"Boring. Locked away as usual," they replied.

My pen pal had told me they too were having mate drama, that he didn't get out much.

"Which class are you in next?" they asked.

"Stupid training one with Tobias."

"You really don't like that guy, huh?"

I chuckled. I had told him all about my asshole mates and the nasty shit they did. Well, except for Kalen.

"You wouldn't either if he used you like his personal juice box daily, and you were starving after only getting one meal or half a meal a day," I replied.

"Your mates starve you?" he replied, and I sighed.

"No, but I'm too scared to go to dinner or lunch in the mess hall because of the other men. Last time one put my hand in a boiling pot," I replied.

They didn't reply straight away, so I continued to the obstacle course and walked over to where they were stretching.

"Who did?" came their reply.

"Some dick called Deacon. They will get bored eventually and leave me alone," I replied when my tablet was plucked from my grip. I looked up to see Tobias glaring at me.

"No distractions. Now, get out there," he snapped at me.

I went to ask if I could sit out, but he growled, so I dropped my head and started running. My stomach was sloshing from all the water I drank, making me regret that stupid idea to curb my hunger. *Lesson learned.*

The demons were shoving and pushing as I tried to remain on the track. Running out of breath because bile rushed up to my throat, I pulled off to the side and threw up again. Zac sniggered as he passed me and nudged me.

"Can't hack it, Aleera?" he taunted before I threw up again.

"Aleera!" Tobias called, and I looked up, hoping he would say I could go inside. He pointed to the track, and my shoulders sagged as I turned around. My surroundings spun, and I found the heat made it increasingly difficult to breathe.

The ground felt like it was moving under my feet, and I felt delirious as I stumbled back onto the track.

My harsh, labored breathing rang in my head along with my heartbeat when I felt my eyes roll into the back of my head. I knew I'd hit the ground, but I felt nothing, no pain, nothing as darkness swallowed me.

Someone was tapping my face, my ears were ringing, and I could hear a faint voice calling my name. The sun shone through the backs of my eyelids, and I blinked, dazed, only to look into the eyes of Tobias.

He turned my face from side to side before prying my eyelids open when I closed them. "Yep, you're done for the day," he said, scooping me up in his arms.

I kept going in and out of consciousness, but I was soon inside, the air-conditioning making me shiver after spending hours in the blistering sun.

"What happened?" I heard Darius ask, and I blinked open my eyes to find I was back in my room. Darius shut the door while Tobias placed me on the bed. I could hear them talking but paid no attention.

"Heatstroke, maybe?" Tobias said.

"She complained about being sick in class. She looked pale then, too."

"So, you forced her to my class?" Tobias snapped when I felt his teeth sink into my wrist. I groaned, hoping he wouldn't take much. I was already light-headed enough.

"Anything?" Darius asked.

"No, not poison, but her iron is a little low. I had noticed that over the last few days."

Darius sighed when the door opened again.

"Lycus said she fainted," I heard Kalen's voice. I couldn't remember seeing Lycus, but then again, I didn't remember the walk to the room either.

"Where is he?"

"Making her something to eat," Kalen answered before the bed dipped beside me. He brushed my hair from my face and leaned over me. "You okay?" he asked, and I shook my head. My stomach was beginning to cramp like I had a stitch.

The door opened again, and I knew it was Lycus this time.

"I need to get to class, but I will see you tonight after dinner," Tobias said, making me wonder where he was going. "Oh, I almost forgot her tablet."

"Why do you have it?"

"Confiscated it. She was using it when she came out," Tobias said, and I heard the door close as he left.

"Fine!" Lycus says, sounding angry.

"What's wrong with you?" Darius asked him.

"Later, not now." I looked at Lycus as he sat beside me before Kalen helped me sit up. I leaned heavily against him, and Lycus placed a plate of tomato and cheese sandwiches on my lap, cut into triangles.

"Eat. It will make you feel better," Lycus said, pressing one to my lips. Kalen looked at him funny before he grabbed my tablet at my feet. I tried to reach for it, not wanting him to read my messages, but he placed it on charge.

"Eat!" Lycus snapped, pressing the sandwich triangle to my lips again. I took a bite, and he seemed to relax but insisted on feeding me like a child. I noticed Kalen watching him, just as confused as I was about his strange behavior. When he pressed a third against my lips, I shook my head, hoping Lycus would leave it so I could sneak down to feed my phoenix tonight. He had started to heal and had some feathers coming back. His wing was still injured, but Ryze was on the mend.

CHAPTER 42

LYCUS AND KALEN STAYED for a while, and whatever Lycus was angry about even bothered Kalen as he repeatedly asked what was wrong. Lycus only growled before eventually storming out, saying he had to take care of something.

It was now dark, and I wondered how long they would let Kalen stay. What I was most surprised about was that Lycus had left me alone with him. That never happened; Kalen was always chaperoned around me, but whatever pissed him off must have made him forget that I was alone with him.

"I wonder how long until he realizes?" Kalen murmured, and I looked at him.

"Realize what?"

"That he left me alone with you. Darius will be furious," Kalen answered, and I nodded, hoping I wouldn't cop the brunt of that fury. With a sigh, I stood up, and Kalen looked at me.

"Where are you going?"

"To shower, and you should go before we both get in trouble," I told him. He nodded and got up.

"It will get easier," Kalen said, and I looked back at him. "It's only because they don't trust you and they're too stubborn to see their own flaws," he added.

"What's done is done. It changes nothing. He still killed my parents. No matter what he believed or his intentions, it would have ended up this way," I told Kalen and instantly regretted it when his face turned somber.

"Would you have run if you knew me before?" he asked, and my brows furrowed at his words as I thought them over.

"No, I would have asked you to run with me," I told him. "But I also know you wouldn't leave Lycus."

He nodded and went to say something before stopping himself. I walked into the bathroom and stripped my clothes off when he said nothing. My shirt smells of sweat, and goosebumps rose on my arms as I waited for the water temperature to go up.

The cramping had gone now that I had eaten, and I was feeling a little better.

Halfway through my shower, when I was washing my hair out, I felt a draft and nearly jumped out of my skin when I felt someone bump into my back. A shriek left my lips as I spun, trying to cover myself. Kalen chuckled while I backed away from him, looking nervously at the door leading into his room. When I saw it was shut, I let out a breath.

"Sorry, I didn't mean to startle you," he said while stepping closer. His eyes dropped to my breasts. I was desperately trying to cover them with my arm.

"Kalen," I squeaked, feeling rather exposed. I liked Kalen, but that didn't mean I wanted him to invade my shower. My face heated, and he smirked before dipping his face under the shower spray, and I moved closer to the wall. He reached for the soap before washing his face, and my eyes trailed down his bronze-colored skin. He was muscular but not as bulky as the others. My face heated when I followed his V-line. I pressed my lips in a line and tried not to giggle, not because he was small, but because I had never seen one up close to compare size.

I knew it was stupid, yet I snorted, and he rubbed a hand down his face before looking at me.

"Something funny?" he asked, cocking an eyebrow at me.

He raised his eyebrows at me, and I giggled like an idiot.

"I don't know if it is a good thing you are laughing or if I should feel insulted," he snickered.

I tried to stop, yet it was so strange-looking and veiny. I wasn't a total idiot. I had seen sex scenes on TV before, but never in person. Now, I was so close I could touch it, not that I would.

"Geez, anyone would think you had never seen one before," he laughed, and my giggling cut off abruptly.

Oh my god, how embarrassing. Here I was giggling like some school girl because I was twenty-four and had never seen a dick before. Kalen stopped laughing and stared at me.

"Wait. Please, tell me you have."

I shook my head, and his eyes widened before he suddenly covered himself with his hand.

"Well, this got awkward fast," he said, looking away. "Have you really never seen a dick before?"

"The girls had separate bathrooms," I told him.

"But you're twenty-four." I shrugged.

"Wait, are you a virgin?" I could feel myself blush from head to toe. I had never felt embarrassed about my virginity, but how he said it made me feel inexperienced and naive. Well, technically, that would make me inexperienced, but it still didn't stop my embarrassment. I awkwardly moved from one foot to the other while he stared at me.

"Can you not stare?" My voice was barely audible.

"Sorry, I am just in shock. The others are convinced you ran off with some man."

"I told you I didn't."

He nodded, and I realized none of them believed me, even after Tobias confirmed I wasn't lying. As if I could somehow get away with it. He went to say something when the door suddenly burst open, and a frantic Lycus and Darius walked in. I shrieked, ripping Kalen toward me, using him as a shield. *Could this get any more embarrassing?* I heard their collective sigh of relief.

"Everything alright?" Kalen asked. Neither of them said anything for a few seconds and I was too embarrassed to peek around to see their faces. One of them cleared their throat, and I heard a growl.

"You weren't in the room," I heard Darius say.

"Yeah, because I was in the shower," Kalen said.

"I can see that," Darius said, and Lycus growled.

"Just showering, nothing else going on, Lycus. No need to be jealous," Kalen snapped at him, which only made him growl louder before he stormed out.

"Come on, out. You know better."

"Fuck, why are you being a dick and acting like I am cheating? She is our mate, too," Kalen snapped, and I looked up at his shoulders as they tensed.

"You know why. Now, out!" Darius snapped.

"Well, at least leave so she can put a towel on."

"I have already seen her naked, and I wasn't impressed," he retorted, and I could hear the anger in his voice. My face heated in embarrassment, and I knew his words shouldn't have hurt, but they still stung. It was one thing hearing the whispers in school about my burns, but another when you repulsed your own mates.

Kalen snarled, and the air chilled significantly, making goose-bumps rise on my arms. The tension in the room rose significantly.

"Either you're blind or jealous because I have seen how every man watches her, including you. Do you think I haven't invaded your dreams, Darius? Because they say a lot about how you feel about her," Kalen snapped at him. Darius growled at him while I chewed my lip.

"Out, now!" Darius snapped at him.

"Should we pretend you don't sneak into her room and watch her while she sleeps?" Kalen said, and I gasped.

"Kalen, one more word, and I will put her in the fucking cells," Darius snarled before punching the tiled wall.

"And I said get out," Kalen snapped, and I touched his side. He looked down at me, and I shook my head. He was playing with fire, and the only one that would get burned was me. I knew better. It was sweet he was defending me or whatever he was doing, but it was only going to worsen things.

"No, I am sick of him being a prick," Kalen said, and he turned back to Darius. The shower screen opened. Tears burned my eyes, and I knew Darius was about to rip him out.

I didn't want them to fight, and I certainly didn't want to get caught up in it. So, I bit down on my shame, pushed past Kalen and Darius, and grabbed my towel. I didn't bother looking at either of them and just walked back to my room so I could die of shame without their prying eyes.

I quickly got dressed and heard them arguing, and for once, I locked my doors, not wanting to be near any of them.

CHAPTER 43

IT WAS A LITTLE after midnight before I finally plucked up the
courage to unlock the door leading into the hall. Surprisingly,
they had once again left it unlocked. The key was still in it, but it
hadn't been turned, trapping me inside. The majority of the night
I spent listening to Kalen argue and fight with them over me.

I tried my best to ignore it and not eavesdrop but hearing
the hatred spewing from their lips and listening to them warn
Kalen away from me bothered me. Though I was a little shocked
overhearing Lycus defend Kalen and me because he was furious
about finding his mate in the shower with me.

Something went down in there, and I hoped Kalen was alright.
If any of them did get hurt, I prayed it was Darius. The asshole
needed to know what pain felt like. I would love to be the one
to deliver every blow he had shown to me. He sure knew how to
ruin someone; there was no doubt about it.

Slipping into the hall, I made my way down to the cells. I
carefully opened the door, so it wouldn't creak before making my
way down the steps. Ryze peeked his little head up excitedly before
tilting it from side to side as he looked at me. I could swear Ryze
looked right into my soul. As soon as I sat down, he bumped his

head against my cheek, making a low cawing sound, and I got the feeling he could sense I was upset.

"I can't stay for long, but I saved you some sandwich," I whispered to him before kissing the top of his beak. I held the sandwich out to him, but he nudged my hand away. I tried again, but he did the same thing.

"You don't want it?" I asked him. *He must be missing eating meat.* I needed to see if I could catch some field mice. I sighed a breath of relief when he plucked the sandwich triangle from my hand, but instead of eating it, he stood pressing the old stale sandwich and his beak to my mouth. I laughed, watching as he tried to stuff the stale sandwich in my mouth and feed me. I shook my head, and he puffed out his feathers before plopping down in his makeshift nest. His snake-like tongue licked the back of my hand, and I picked up the dropped sandwich and placed it beside him.

"I have to get back in case they notice," I told Ryze, patting his back. Feathers were starting to sprout along his back, and his broken wing still looked terrible. I chewed my lip, thinking of the wards on the doors upstairs.

If I could just siphon a little bit of power, I could at least heal his broken wing. Then we could get out of here sooner, or at the very least, he could. That thought saddened me. He was all I had here, but it would be selfish to keep him down here when I was already a prisoner. I wouldn't do that to Ryze.

Reluctantly, I got up and left, sneaking back into the castle foyer. I started climbing the steps when I paused midway, looking back at the door leading to the cells. My eyes moved to the wards, and I quickly glanced up to the other levels to see if anyone was around. When I saw no one, I moved toward the doors. Darius's energy oozed off them, powerful and dangerous. Placing my hand on the doorknob, I didn't get blown backward or incinerated, so

I gripped it. *Just enough to heal Ryze, that was it.* Maybe Darius wouldn't notice if I was careful not to take too much. Who in their right mind would attack a castle belonging to Darius Wraith that contained over six hundred demons? You would have to be suicidal to try that.

My hand heated up as I felt for his energy, and I was about to absorb it when a hand went across my mouth and nose, stifling the scream of fright that tried to leave me.

I was ripped backward and away from the door. I tried to breathe, but the hand prevented it as I struggled. It only took a few seconds to recognize it was Darius.

"When touched, the wards alert me of intruders and those who try to escape, Aleera. You wouldn't be stupid enough to try, would you?"

I swallowed and shook my head.

"But, then again, if you weren't trying to escape, why were you at the door?" he growled, shoving me away.

I staggered and barely corrected my footing before hitting the floor. My heart was racing so fast I could hear it.

"You better have a good reason to be down here. What were you doing? Trying to leave?"

I wanted to tell him I wasn't trying to leave, but he would probably kill me if I said I was siphoning magic and if I told him why he would kill Ryze.

"So, let's hear it," Darius snapped at me. I chewed my lip.

No matter what I said, it would get me or Ryze killed.

"Answer, or am I right? Were you trying to leave?" Darius asked.

I said nothing. Sometimes silence was better than words. I was doomed either way, so I was surprised at what he said next.

"Get back upstairs!" he snarled, motioning with his hand toward the steps. I hesitated before running up them like my ass was on fire to get away from him. With a glance over my shoulder, I noticed Darius walking up behind me, so I moved faster, hoping to get to my room so I could lock him out.

Walking down the dimly lit corridor to my room, I gripped the door handle when Darius's voice stopped me.

"Next door," he said, and my brows furrowed. I stepped back, ensuring it was the right door, and it was definitely my room. Twisting the handle, I pushed the door open only to walk directly into Darius. My heart almost leaped out of my chest as he appeared out of thin air. Darius had portalled into my room. My feet automatically took a step back from him and the glare he gave me.

"I said, the next door!" he snarled, stepping out of my room toward me. I glanced back down the corridor where he was before he materialized in my room. I swallowed, turning around to look at the door beside mine. It was their bedroom door.

CHAPTER 44

"You can lock me in," I blurted, not wanting to be stuck in a room with them. His hand gripped my throat, and he walked me backward until I hit the wall. My hands wrapped around his wrist, yet he didn't put any pressure on my throat. He simply held me, his way of telling me he could break me easily.

Darius pressed his entire body against mine, and his stubble brushed my cheek as he leaned in.

"I am being very lenient right now by not breaking your neck. You will be in our room from now on because you can't be trusted." I shook my head, not wanting to sleep in there with them or be anywhere near Darius, Tobias, or Lycus. I didn't want to be near either of them, but if I had to pick a lesser evil, it was him.

"Maybe Kalen can stay in my room?" I asked, and he growled, pressing so close I could feel the heat of his anger seep into me. His aura was suffocating me.

"And tomorrow, when our mates wake up, you can explain to them why you are in our room and what you attempted to do," Darius murmured. I gasped, thinking of Kalen and how much that would hurt him if I said I was trying to escape.

"But Kalen would hate me," I whispered.

"Exactly," Darius snarled before shoving me off. He took a step back and smiled. So, that was his punishment? Why didn't he just kill me? He wanted Kalen to hate me, and I gritted my teeth before glaring at him. But two could play this game.

"Fine, I will tell them then. I will tell them that you came into my room and tried to hurt me, so I ran. We will see who Kalen believes. Me or his fucking sadistic mate?" I smiled and shrugged.

Darius tilted his head to the side, examining me, and I turned toward his bedroom door. "Tobias would be able to tell you're lying. It wouldn't work."

"But Kalen also knows that Tobias would lie for you," I retorted.

He snarled, and I found myself slammed against the wall, the air expelled from my lungs with one harsh puff.

"Either I sleep in your room with you, or you sleep in ours, Aleera. So, fucking pick. And you pull that shit again, I may just kill you. I will not allow you to get between my mates and me."

"Let me sleep in my room."

"So, you would rather be locked in a room with me than in a room with all of us?"

"I would rather have you six feet down and buried, but I don't seem to get what I want," I snapped at him.

He laughed before pressing closer, so close I could feel his lips move against mine. "The only reason you are alive is because of Kalen. The rest of us wanted to kill you. Just remember that next time. Because if it were up to me, I would have let the wolves rip you apart," Darius sneered.

"And if I could go back to that night, I would have let them. At least I wouldn't have to put up with you daily," I spat back at him.

"So, what is it, Aleera? Am I sleeping in your room, or would you rather be in mine where Kalen is?" Darius asked.

"For someone who finds me repulsive, you are pretty insistent on spending the night with me," I said, glaring at him. He went to say something, but I spoke up, cutting him off.

"Or was Kalen right about you sneaking into my room at night? You claim to hate me so much, and if that were true, why the fuck can't you stay out of my room?"

Darius said nothing; he just glared at me. His burning anger made the temperature rise, and I knew what Kalen had said was true.

"He was telling the truth, wasn't he? You hate me yet can't stay away."

"Don't flatter yourself, Aleera. I do hate you, but you are our rightful keeper. I don't get to control the bond, no matter how stupid it feels about you," Darius sneered.

"No, but you control your actions. So, why come in? Or do you have a thing for unsuspecting sleeping girls, some fucked-up kink?"

Darius pounced on me, and I crashed to the ground with him landing on top of me. I tried to kick him off, but he pressed all of his weight down on me. His hand moved, covering my mouth before he shoved his hand in my pants.

I thrashed and hit him. He uncovered my mouth before pinning my hands above my head, holding them in one of his. I glared at him when his hand slid beneath my panties. I hated him, fucking hated him, yet my body reacted to his touch as he cupped my pussy, which suddenly had its own heartbeat. His touch made me moan despite my hatred as his fingers caressed my slit. His touch was rough and forceful when his fingers moved between my folds, and he shoved one inside me.

A scream bubbled up my throat as I went to call out for Kalen when his lips crashed down on mine, almost hungrily. I pressed my lips together, and Darius bit my lips, making me hiss, only for his tongue to plunge into my mouth.

The bond reacted automatically with no say from me, and I moaned into his mouth as his tongue played with mine. Darius slid his finger out before forcing another inside me. The stretching feeling made me jerk when he curled his fingers inside, and I thrashed as he rubbed his thumb across my clit. Tears of embarrassment brimmed as I felt my body start climbing higher despite my protests of not wanting his touch, yet the bond craved it.

My walls clenched around his fingers as he built up friction, and he groaned into my mouth as his tongue assaulted mine. My body reacted, and I tried to think of anything other than his vile touch. However, the bond had other ideas, wanting and craving him to keep going, though my mind screamed for me not to come.

My stomach clenched, and I struggled harder as heat ran through me, making me gasp when he moved his thumb quicker, his fingers soaked with the arousal the bond had caused, and the friction became too much. My walls clenched and throbbed, and Darius kissed me harder, covering my mouth with his and stifling my moans as my orgasm ripped through me.

My surroundings muted as pleasure rippled through me, and my hips moved involuntarily against his hand. His fingers slipped out of me when the high subsided, and I was left humiliated and breathless.

Darius pulled away from me, and his hand slipped out of my pants. "Now, I am guessing you didn't want to come, but it sucks when you have no control over your bond. Just like I have no control over being in your room when my bond is fucking calling for you," he sneered.

I looked away from him, ashamed, when he shoved between my legs, his erection pressed against me, and I turned back to glare at him.

"As you can feel, I definitely feel the fucking bond. I just choose to deny it control, so don't get it twisted, Aleera. The bond may want you, just like yours wants mine, but I will never be yours, nor will I allow you to be mine," he said before shoving off me.

I scrambled to my feet and away from him when his bedroom door opened. Tobias groggily stepped out, glancing at us in the hall.

"What's going on?" he yawned. My cheeks flushed, and I rubbed my arms, suddenly feeling cold.

"What will it be, Aleera?"

I gritted my teeth, no way did I want to be locked in a room alone with him, so I shoved past Tobias and walked over to the couch.

"What's going on?" Tobias asked as I dropped onto the couch.

"Nothing. She sleeps in here from now on," Darius answered while I said nothing.

CHAPTER 45

TOBIAS GROWLED, AND I turned my head to look over the back of the couch.

"What the fuck did you do to her?" Tobias whispered before marching over to Darius. He sniffed him before grabbing his hand, and my face flamed red when I saw him sniff Darius's fingers. Tobias growled and shoved him away before turning to look at me.

"What the fuck? Did he force you?" Tobias asked me, and I saw Lycus and Kalen stir on the bed as he raised his voice higher.

"Shut up before you wake them. I never hurt her. Quite the opposite, actually," Darius snarled back at him.

"That's not what I asked," Tobias growled at him.

"She is fine. Are you hurt, Aleera, in pain?" Darius asked, and I glared at him before turning away as embarrassment coursed through me.

"That's fucked up even for you. You can't force her to do shit like that."

"Says who?" Darius asked.

"You're unbelievable," Tobias spat, turning to face me. He walked over and reached out to me when Darius spoke.

"Don't feel sorry for her, Tobias. She is the one who tried to break my wards and leave. I was merely demonstrating who had control," Darius said, and Tobias's hand that was reaching toward me to do god knows what stopped.

"You tried to leave?" Tobias asked. I pressed my lips in a line, and tears blurred my vision, so I lay down and rolled on my side. I could tell him the truth, but he or Darius would kill Ryze. That much was certain.

"This will kill Kalen," Tobias hissed angrily.

"He doesn't have to know," Darius said.

"Then how do you plan on explaining her being in our damn room?" Tobias asked, and I sat up to see Darius shrug.

"He asked to sleep in her room. This is giving him what he wants under supervision," Darius said, and I glared at him. I thought the whole point was to make Kalen hate me.

"You keep your hands to yourself. Kalen sees you forcing yourself on her, he will fucking lose it, and I want no part of this," Tobias said.

"Fine, as long as Aleera keeps her mouth shut, everything will be fine. Isn't that right, Aleera?" Darius asked.

"As long as you keep the fuck away from me," I snapped at him.

"See? Everything is fine," Darius said, looking between Tobias and me. I curled back up on the couch while Darius wandered off into the bathroom. Tobias came over, draped a blanket over me, and handed me a pillow. I took it when suddenly he cupped my cheek with his hand.

"Why would you do that? Don't do it again. I am not saying what he did was right. It wasn't. But you running?" He shook his head. I just stared at him.

Was he seriously defending him? I slapped his hand away. "You're just as bad as him. Get away from me," I told him, rolling to face the back of the small two-seater.

"We told you that you could earn more freedom if you behaved, Aleera. We only just stopped locking your damn door, and you ran the first chance you got. How are we supposed to trust you?" he asked.

"I wasn't running," I whispered.

"What?" Tobias asked, and I shook my head when he gripped my chin and turned my face toward him.

"What did you say?"

"I wasn't—"

The bathroom door opened, and Tobias glanced over at Darius. I pulled my face out of his grip.

"Aleera?"

"Doesn't matter," I told him.

"Come to bed, Tobias," Darius said as I snuggled under my blanket, pulling it over my head. Tobias sighed before I heard him walk off and climb into bed with Darius.

℗℗℗

The following day I woke to fangs in my wrist as Tobias fed off me.

"Tobias, she isn't even awake," Lycus growled at him, and I yawned, sitting upright while Tobias was still feeding off me. I rubbed my eyes to see Kalen stretching and waking up. Tobias dropped my wrist, and I rubbed it.

"Aleera?" Kalen asked before rubbing his eyes. He looked around at the others, and I saw Darius walk out of the closet half-undressed. He was only wearing pants.

"Surprise. She is staying here from now on," Darius said, and I glared at him.

"Darius said you can't be alone with her, but if you want her close, she stays with us in here," Lycus said, leaning down and kissing Kalen. I could feel Tobias staring at me, but I didn't bother correcting Darius. I knew it would end badly if I did.

"Hurry up and get dressed, Aleera. You have to be down at the mess hall," Darius said before chucking some clothes at me. It was a new pair of jeans and a black button-up top. I looked at him. What were these hush clothes? I shook my head but got up and headed for the bathroom.

"I will take her to breakfast," Lycus said as I reached the door and stopped. How was I supposed to feed Ryze if he was with me?

"She can go by herself," Darius said, and I let out a breath of relief, about to go get changed.

"No, I have something to do anyway."

"Like what?" Darius demanded.

"None of your business," Lycus snapped at him.

"We always have breakfast together," Tobias said, sounding needy, which surprised me.

"I will grab something down there." Lycus shrugged.

I shoved the door open and went to get changed. When I came back out, Lycus was waiting for me. Tobias and Darius didn't look happy about him coming to breakfast with me. Kalen, on the other hand, was pouting.

"Why can't she eat with us?" Kalen asked. *Probably because they hate me*, I thought but stopped myself from saying it out loud. Not that I wanted to stay in there any longer than needed. I wanted out of this room and as far away as possible from Darius.

Chapter 46

"Ready?" Lycus asked me. I sighed and gave a hesitant nod. "I don't see why you can't wait," Tobias snapped at him. "Chill. You can have your way with me when I return." Lycus laughed, going over and pecking his lips.

His way with him? Is that why Tobias was pouting like a child? "I just need to get my tablet," I told Lycus, wanting to escape their doting affections. It wasn't that it bothered me, but I felt like some strange bystander gawking.

"I already grabbed it for you. Come on," Lycus said before pecking Kalen's lips as he walked to the door. I quickly followed him, and I could feel Darius glaring at us as we left.

"Didn't think Tobias would pout over not getting laid," I admitted as we went down the stairs. Lycus shrugged.

"He can be whinier than Kalen. Darius is the worst. He becomes a real fucking asshole when his power gets low, and he is horny," Lycus said, and I stopped.

"Huh?"

"How do you think we power-share, Aleera? We have to fuck each other. It's easier for Darius. He can siphon easier being demonic fae, but now that we are all bonded, we actually like fucking each other."

"Wait, so you don't just fuck to power-share?"

"Ah, no. We are bonded, Aleera. We do love each other, too. We don't just fuck out of necessity. We used to. Well, except for Kalen and I. But now…" He shrugged. I raced after him, trying to catch up.

"So what, you have an orgy for breakfast?" I chuckled.

"No, but mealtimes get us in one place. Besides at night, of course. And Tobias fed off you, which makes him horny," Lycus said.

"Makes him horny?"

"What? Haven't you noticed he gets a raging hard-on every time he feeds on you?"

"Well, I don't usually look at his dick when he feeds on me," I told him as we lined up in the cafeteria. He filled two trays with food and walked over to a table. I stared at him when he sat down because I expected him to dump it and leave me.

"Sit and eat," Lycus said, pulling out the chair beside him.

"You're going to eat with me?" I asked, glancing around at all the faces watching us.

"I said I was, didn't I?" With another glance around, I sat down. Everyone watched us, and I watched them back, waiting for one of them to do something, but no one approached us.

"Aleera, eat," Lycus said, nudging my plate closer. I looked down at it to find it piled with more than what was on his plate. Grabbing my fork, I started to eat while watching everyone.

It wasn't until I was nearly finished that Zac wandered over to the table, and I tensed, wondering what he would do.

"Eating with the traitor, boss man?"

"And what's it to you, Zac?" Lycus asked. I got the impression Lycus didn't particularly like Zac.

"Just curious as to why you're down here." Zac shrugged, and Lycus leaned back in his chair and looked at him.

"And why is that?"

"Because we rarely see Aleera in here, so it's interesting she came in with you," Zac said, eyeing me.

"I noticed she was losing weight. Wanted to make sure she was eating and not missing any meals. Now that you just confirmed she is, I may just need to eat with her every meal. Darius would be pissed if she starved to death," Lycus snapped. My brows furrowed at this weird topic of conversation, and I wondered why he cared if I ate or not.

"Hmm, suppose you're right. Anyway, have you seen Deacon? He never returned last night after he went into town?"

"Probably at one of his hoes' places." Lycus shrugged.

"Yeah, I will keep trying to call him," Zac said before wandering off.

I looked at Lycus, who was glaring at Zac.

"Can't fucking stand him," Lycus growled before getting up. I quickly started picking up my plate and tray when Lycus stopped and looked at me.

"No, stay. Finish eating," he said, and I shook my head.

"I'm done," I told him even though my belly started rumbling hungrily. He looked around at everyone who was watching us.

"Are they not letting you eat?" Lycus asked, and I looked around at all the men in the room glaring daggers at me.

I shook my head. "No, I am just full," I lied, and my stupid belly growled in protest.

Lycus raised an eyebrow at me before turning to everyone in the room. My stomach sank when he growled. *Was he trying to get me killed?*

"No one messes with her at meals. She needs to fucking eat. I hear one word about you tampering with her food or preventing her from eating, and you will answer to me."

"But she is a traitor," Zac protested.

"I don't give a fuck what Darius told you. Mess with her while she is eating, and you fucking answer to me. Is that clear?" Lycus snarled.

"Yes, sir," a few said while some dropped their heads and others nodded.

Lycus turned to me and pointed at the table. "Sit, and finish eating. They mess with you, fucking tell me," he said, and I shrank back down in my seat. Lycus walked out, and I prepared to run the moment he left. Zac got up, and I tensed, grabbing my fork to use as a weapon if needed.

"Fucking bullshit," Zac sneered before leaving.

"Where are you going?" Satish asked him.

"To look for Deacon," Zac called out over his shoulder.

It took me a good five minutes of glancing around only to realize no one approached me; they stared but didn't come over. I ate cautiously while looking around until the bell rang, too scared to move until they were gone. I was sure no one was coming to hurt me. Carefully wrapping up my leftovers, I stuck my head out the door before rushing into the cells to give Ryze some food.

CHAPTER 47

Tobias

SOMETHING WAS GOING ON with Lycus because he never missed breakfast. Where did he have to go that was more important than our morning ritual? I waited for around five minutes before leaving to look for him.

Yet the bond led me to the mess hall. Walking to the door, I noticed he was eating with Aleera. *Now, that was new.* Lycus hated being around her. Moving away from the entry, I waited for him to come out. *Great, he was eating with Aleera when he should be sucking my dick.*

I growled because this hard-on was becoming annoying, and Darius wanted to check the wards, so he couldn't help me out with it. Not only that, I preferred Lycus's warm mouth. The man was like a vacuum. Kalen was in a damn mood from when Aleera walked out the door, so he was out of the question unless I wanted my dick bitten off. So, I had no choice but to wait for Lycus.

I sat on the stairs waiting, bored out of my fucking mind when I heard him become angry and scold all the men in the mess hall.

Eventually, he stormed out while muttering under his breath, and I stood up.

"Finally," I whined, and he stopped looking over at me.

"What are you doing here?" he asked, turning away from the doors leading outside and facing me.

"More like what were you doing eating with Aleera? I thought you said you were just grabbing something, not actually eating with her," I growled at him.

"She has been starving. They haven't been letting her eat," Lycus growled, and I looked toward the door. My brows furrowed.

"What do you mean?" I asked though I had seen she was dropping weight and her iron was low.

"Do you ever bother to open that damn chat link?" Lycus snapped.

I shook my head, wondering what he was talking about.

"I deleted it before Kalen saw, but they have been forcing her to starve. That is just plain cruel," Lycus snarled.

"Who has?"

Lycus tossed his arms in the air, frustrated, and stormed off.

"Wait, I came looking for you for a reason," I called after him.

"Suck your own dick," Lycus called, and I growled, annoyed. *What is it with everyone today?*

I pulled my phone out with a sigh as the siren blared, signaling the start of classes, but since I was not walking around with this all day, I was canceling mine until I found a hot mouth or an ass to put it in; I wasn't picky. I started walking up the steps when Zac stopped me just as I reached the top.

"Have you seen Deacon?"

"Nah, buddy, I haven't," I told him.

He looked down and smirked. "That explains why you canceled class, I just got the notification," Zac teased, and I shoved him.

"Bugger off unless you're willing to suck it."

"Hard pass." He laughed, moving off with the rest of the men. I shook my head at him. He could be an idiot. Just as I was about to climb the next set of stairs, I stopped because I noticed Aleera come out of the mess hall with a plastic bowl.

She looked around suspiciously, and I watched her move back as she went to look up the stairs. *Now, what was she up to?* The creaking of a door had me glancing back over the railing to where she was, but she was gone, and I just looked over in time to see the door of the cells shut. *Now, why would she be going down there?* Tempted to call Darius, I pulled my phone out when I heard the door before watching her sneak back out, only this time she wasn't holding the bowl. My brows furrowed, and I waited for her to leave.

Glancing in both directions, I raced down the steps before stopping by the cell door. Making sure she was indeed gone, I opened it and slipped inside. Trudging down the steps, I flicked the light on only to hear a screech and hissing. My eyes opened wide when I saw a phoenix get to its feet and fall forward in its makeshift nest. Letting out a breath, I realized it couldn't fly.

I glanced at the steps leading up. How did she get it down here without it ripping her to pieces? The bloody thing couldn't fly but looked like it was tempted to attack me as it continued to hiss. I noticed bloody bandages wrapping its body, and my mind wandered to Aleera's words last night.

"I wasn't running," she said, and I chewed my lip, wondering if she was telling the truth. Darius came out before I could get her to answer again but then why would she be trying to open the door? Darius said he'd caught her tampering with the wards. With one last glance, I rushed back upstairs, wanting away from this creepy-ass bird. I hated phoenixes. *Bloody vicious bastards.*

Pulling my phone back out, I decided to call Darius to let him know when I stopped. He would kill it; I had no doubt that he would. He hated them. His father was a right prick, and when he was a boy, he used to lock him in cages with the damn things and let them attack him.

Though he was a good father, as long as Darius did as he was told, his punishments were cruel and uncalled for. I would never understand how he idolized his father the way he did. Darius always thought he was a great father when I could think of plenty of things his father had done that were either just cruel or outright wrong. I put my phone away and glanced at the door.

I could set it free, but someone else would kill it, and I also had the issue of it trying to attack me if I grabbed it. I pondered what to do when I decided to open up this chat thing Kalen had with Aleera.

CHAPTER 48

Aleera

THE CLASSES DRONED ON, and I wasn't looking forward to being in the sun for the rest of the day. Although, for once, I actually made it around the obstacle course. I was pretty proud of myself, yet the cramping was becoming ridiculous.

Lycus called out to me and waved me over. Moving off the course, I made my way over to him. For some reason, he decided to run the obstacle course.

"Did they give you any shit after I left?" Lycus asked me.

"No," I told him.

He nodded. "Good, go to lunch then. After, you can take the rest of the day off."

"Really?" I asked excitedly, and he nodded.

"Just stay out of trouble and away from Darius and watch Kalen for me," he said, and I nodded before realizing he wanted me to go back to their room.

Sulking, I headed back inside and to the mess hall. I felt queasy lining up for lunch, yet no one said anything to me, and I moved to a table closest to the door up the back so I had a quick escape if needed. One thing became apparent, though. They all feared Lycus because not one of them approached me, and they let me eat. It wasn't until I got up that one of them spoke.

"She is getting up." Satish smiled while also getting up, and I recognized Lycus's error. He said not to mess with me while I was eating. That wasn't going to stop them when I wasn't. Satish's leering smile made me gulp. The man was huge and just as intimidating as Zac and Deacon in his black-ops uniform. How they all wore those uniforms in this heat was beyond me.

Cursing, I sat back down and nibbled the corner of the other half of my sandwich. Satish and Zac growled, sitting back down and glaring at me. Once again, I waited for the siren and the voices to fade before getting up. I was expecting them to be waiting outside to torture me but clearly, being late for Darius's class scared them from wanting to get revenge.

Quickly looking around before I ducked down to the cells, I was excited that I could give Ryze some extra food today. I hoped I could keep this up because he would be fully healed in no time if he was getting the proper amount of food required.

I was scratching his belly as he leaned on his good wing when I heard the door open. Ryze hissed, and I grabbed his beak to quiet him.

Fear wrapped around my throat, and my skin itched as I listened to footsteps coming down. I got to my feet, trying to hide Ryze with my body, when Tobias appeared.

"I thought I would find you here. Interesting pet you keep, Aleera," Tobias said, sauntering closer. I stepped back, and Ryze hissed.

"Darius will kill your pet if he finds it," Tobias said, looking around me. I stepped in front of his gaze, blocking his view of Ryze.

Tobias clicked his tongue. "I saw you come down here this morning."

Tears welled in my eyes because Ryze was all I had, and I knew he would hurt him. Tobias stepped down the last step with his hands behind his back.

"Please, don't hurt him," I whispered.

"Him? How do you know it's a male?" Tobias asked, tilting his head as he watched me.

"It's the beak. Females have red beaks. His beak is black," I answered, which seemed to surprise him.

"You like birds?" he asked, stepping closer, and I turned quickly, plucking Ryze off his nest and tucking him under my arm. Tobias stared at Ryze, and the phoenix hissed at him. I grabbed his beak, trying to quiet him, and moved further back into the cell when I noticed that Tobias still had his hands behind his back.

"I will put him in the forest. You don't have to hurt him," I told Tobias. Ryze hissed, and I glanced down at him. "Shh, Ryze..." I whispered.

"You named him?"

I nodded while watching him warily and a hand he had behind his back.

"What I want to know is how you got close to it and why it's letting you touch it. Those things are vicious and hate dark fae," Tobias said.

"They were torturing him, so I saved him. Once he figured out I wasn't going to hurt him, he got used to me," I told him, which was the truth technically.

He tilted his head to the side, and I could tell he was making sure I wasn't lying. "Very well, but you need to keep him hidden if you want to keep him," Tobias said with a shrug while still eyeing Ryze.

"You will let me keep him?"

Tobias nodded before pulling his arm out from behind his back. I noticed he had a cage full of mice. Ryze hissed and squirmed, wanting the mice now that he had spotted them.

"What's the catch?" I asked him.

"No catch. You answer honestly."

I chewed my lip, debating whether or not to believe him. "What do you want to know?"

"Last night, did you try to escape?"

I looked down at Ryze. "No," I answered.

"You were with your... Ryze," he said while reaching into the cage. He grabbed a mouse out by its tail. It squirmed and squeaked.

"Sit and hold onto that thing. It bites me, I won't be happy," Tobias told me.

I sat down, hugging Ryze to my chest, mindful of his wing. Ryze's eyes followed the mouse hanging by its tail. Tobias stepped closer, and Ryze hissed at him.

"You bite me, fucker, I will scorch your ass," Tobias told him.

"Shh, Ryze... He said he wouldn't hurt you," I whispered to him. His snake-like tongue slivered out of his beak, and he licked my chin. Tobias watched him curiously.

"You know they are bonding birds, right?"

I nodded, patting Ryze's feathers and calming him down. Tobias brought the mouse closer, holding it out to him. Ryze struck like a cobra, and Tobias jumped, nearly losing his fingers when Ryze plucked the mouse from his hands.

CHAPTER 49

I GAGGED AT THE CRUNCHING sounds Ryze made, which suddenly made me feel sick.

"If you want to keep him, you have to feed him properly. They are carnivorous birds, Aleera."

I nodded, but I didn't think I could force a mouse to die after seeing how viciously he'd killed it. Tobias tried to pass me one, and I shook my head, feeling my stomach grow queasy.

"How do you expect to look after him if you won't feed him?"

"You couldn't bring dead ones?" I asked.

Tobias looked down at the cage, not watching his hand, and Ryze struck again, plucking the squeaking mouse.

"Fucker," Tobias hissed, sucking his fingers where Ryze got him.

Tobias sat on the ground next to his mouse cage and pulled another one out.

"So, if you weren't trying to escape, why were you touching the wards?" he said, throwing a mouse to Ryze, who swallowed it whole.

"His wing is broken. I wanted to siphon some of the power from the ward to heal it," I explained.

"So, you weren't going to try to use it against us or use it to escape?"

"No, I wanted to heal him so I could let him go. I didn't want him trapped here."

"You aren't letting the bird go, Aleera," Tobias said, staring at Ryze.

"I have no choice. You said yourself Darius would kill him."

"Good luck because the way he is with you, he has bonded to you. You can try, but he will keep coming back," Tobias said, and I looked down at him.

"And you just saved him, and he got used to you?"

I nodded, and he sighed. "So peculiar," he muttered, shaking his head before tossing him another mouse. Tobias chewed his lip thoughtfully.

"If given a chance, would you escape?" Tobias asked me.

"You know I would, so why ask questions whose answers you already know?"

"Maybe because I hope your answer would change, Aleera," Tobias said. "It's okay, I won't tell them you have him here, but you will have to figure out something. Maybe the attic might be better. There is a hole in the roof, and he can get out and fly around when he wants. You can't keep him locked down here."

"And how would I get him up there?"

"I could portal you up, but tell me something else first."

I nodded, wondering what else he wanted to know.

"Did Darius force himself on you?"

I looked away, and he cursed before shocking me with his next question.

"Are you okay?"

My head whipped toward him, and he seemed genuine. I raised my eyebrows at him.

"I mean with what he did, Aleera. I don't mean in general."

I nodded, my face heating with embarrassment.

"Are you embarrassed because he did it or because he made you cum?"

Why would he ask that?

He put his hand up in mock surrender. "Just a question. I could smell how aroused you were."

"Both," I mumbled.

"I'm sorry for defending him. I thought you tried to run, and I was mad."

"Is that why you are helping me?" I asked him.

"No. I hate phoenixes. When I found him down here, I was going to tell Darius, but I knew he would kill him. Just because I hate something doesn't mean I believe it should be killed."

"But torture is alright and abuse?" I scoffed.

Tobias observed me for a few seconds and hung his head. "I don't hate you. I used to, but I realize we need you after seeing you with Kalen," Tobias said.

"But not enough to stop Darius?" I asked.

He sighed. "He is our mate. It will get better. You just have to earn his trust, Aleera."

Tears welled in my eyes, and I looked down at Ryze.

"If you hold him and don't let him bite me, I will give you some magic to heal him," Tobias said, and I gasped, shocked.

"You will give me magic?"

Tobias nodded, staring at Ryze. "Just enough to heal him, but there is a catch."

"What?"

"Take it. Kiss me."

I shook my head, not falling for this shit again. "Forget it," I told him.

"Wow, rejected pretty fast." Tobias laughed, and I glared at him.

"I have already fucking had Darius tear into my bond by telling me to kiss him and then laughing in my face. I don't need it from you, too."

"He toyed with your bond?" Tobias asked, not seeming to like that.

I nodded, remembering how painful and degrading that was.

"I don't want to toy with your bond, Aleera. I just want a kiss, that is all."

"Why?"

"Because I have been fucking horny from drinking your blood all day, and I need something since none of my mates will touch me. Your blood plays havoc with my bond to you. Just come satisfy it for a second until one of them can help me out."

I chewed my lip, remembering Lycus saying Tobias got horny from drinking my blood. "Just a kiss?"

"Just a kiss," Tobias repeated. "Then you can heal your plucked dodo-looking phoenix."

I glanced down at Ryze, who watched me, like he had been listening to our conversation.

"Just one?" I asked. *If it meant helping Ryze, I would do it.*

"One but I want a proper one." He laughed.

"A proper one?"

"Using tongue," Tobias said, winking at me.

"Wouldn't they be pissed off?" I asked him, and he shrugged.

"Kalen wouldn't care. As for the other two…" He shrugged. "Well, they should have sucked my dick this morning. Neither did, so I will take my vices in any way I can," Tobias said.

"I am not sucking dick," I told him.

"Never said you have to. Just a kiss. So, put your demonic pigeon down and come here," Tobias said, opening his arms.

"I don't trust you and if you were so horny, why not just have a wank?"

"Doesn't work like that. I've drunk your blood, and it makes me crave magic. Since you have none and only they do, I have to take it from them but you can make the ache hurt less since your blood caused it by letting my bond have what it wants."

"Your bond wants me to kiss you?" I asked. It sounded ridiculous.

"My bond wants me to fuck you, but I know you won't give me that. So it will have to settle for a kiss. Now, come here," Tobias said.

"And that is all?" I asked again, not trusting him, and he nodded. I looked at Ryze before placing him in the nest I had made and hesitantly got to my feet. Tobias looked up at me from where he sat, not moving, and I stopped in front of him.

I had a flashback of Darius, and my stomach sank as the bond became excited again. Only this time, Tobias gripped my wrist and yanked me on his lap. Ryze hissed loudly behind me and screeched.

"Quiet, bird. I won't hurt her," Tobias snapped as I straddled his waist.

I swallowed, and Tobias rolled his eyes before gripping the back of my neck and pulling me closer. His lips were warm and soft as he kissed me when I felt his tongue trace across my bottom. Tobias groaned and his other arm wrapped around my waist, tugging me flush against him, which made me gasp.

Tobias took advantage of my parted lips and delved his tongue into my mouth. His groan was lewd as his tongue played with mine, wanting me to kiss him back. The bond answered his kiss longingly, and I kissed him back hungrily. His tongue tasted every inch of my mouth when he pulled me closer, deepening the kiss, which made my stomach tighten as arousal coiled within me when he pulled away.

"Like, I don't mind if you want to keep kissing me, but you are supposed to be taking my magic," Tobias laughed.

My cheeks heated, having completely forgotten as I was too busy enjoying the kiss. Tobias smirked and raised an eyebrow at me when I kissed him again. He groaned, kissing me back, and I moved my hand to his neck, feeling his pulse and energy under my palm before stealing some of it when I kissed him deeper.

Pulling away, I gasped at the feel of his magic writhing within me, cold and sweet. I shivered when I felt his hands slide up my thighs to my hips, and I thought he would demand something more, but instead, he lifted me off him.

"Heal your phoenix. Then I will help you get him to the attic," Tobias said. "And don't let him bite me."

"And you won't tell Darius?"

"It will be our little secret," Tobias said.

I turned back to Ryze, excited that I could heal him.

CHAPTER 50

EVERY NIGHT, I HAD spent the night in their room, unable to return to mine. Darius still believed wholeheartedly that I was trying to escape. I wasn't willing to tell him differently for the sake of Ryze, who now lived in the attic. Tobias was right, however. Even healed, Ryze never left. I noticed, though, with each passing day when Tobias would sneak me up to see him and feed him, that he grew larger, which was concerning because he would soon not fit through the hole in the roof.

I still couldn't bring myself to feed him the mice. I tried to give him frozen ones, even thawed-out ones, but he liked them alive. So I was thankful that Tobias had no issues sacrificing the mice for me. Ryze even let him pat him. He nearly lost a finger, and Ryze only tolerated his touch for a few seconds before snapping at him. Tobias was thrilled that he had touched a live phoenix, like it was some sort of acceptance, and he was suddenly a phoenix whisperer.

Tobias opened a portal back to the room, and the moment I stepped through it, Darius was there, waiting, his arms folded across his chest. His temper had gotten worse over the last few days. The more time Tobias and Kalen spent with me, the more furious he seemed to get.

"Where have you both been?" he demanded, and Tobias quickly closed the portal behind us before he could see into the dark attic.

"The library," I said.

"I checked the library," Darius said, and I knew we would have to come up with a better lie.

"Must have just missed us then." Tobias shrugged before pulling a book from his pocket. He tossed it to Kalen, who caught it and smiled. I had no idea when Tobias got time to grab it unless he got it before he went up, but it seemed to placate Darius for now. He muttered under his breath before storming out.

Kalen looked the cover over before flipping it and reading the back. I realized Kalen spent most of his time reading because Darius had pulled him from the classes he taught so that I wouldn't spend more time than necessary with him. Moving toward the couch, I sat next to him when Lycus came over and rolled his eyes before walking off.

"I'm going for a run," Lycus growled.

Tobias sighed before sitting at my feet on the floor. "They're just jealous," Tobias said, resting his head on my knees.

"Of what?" I asked incredulously. *What could they possibly have to be jealous of? They weren't the ones held prisoner?*

"That Tobias and I don't hate you, and we spend more time with you than them?" Kalen said while opening the book.

I sighed. "And why do they hate me, exactly?"

Neither answered, and I knew it was to do with Darius forbidding them from telling me.

"Okay then, why did you hate me?" I asked Tobias.

He shifted uncomfortably, leaning forward before also getting up and leaving. Was I a repellent? What was up with them all today? Tobias had been fine all week, and I asked one question, and he, too, stormed off and into the bathroom.

"Well, can you tell me?" I asked Kalen, and he sighed.

"Nope, because unless Darius agrees for you to know, we are bound by his stupid bond," Kalen growled.

"Huh?" *First I heard of them being sworn to secrecy.*

"He has been our replacement keeper for years. We are bonded to him most, even Lycus and I."

"I still don't understand," I told him.

"The keeper is the glue. Darius is our glue. We draw off him the most, so our bond to him is stronger. He controls the bonds and, therefore, us, in a sense, like a blood tie or another way to put it is, we can't betray him even if we wanted to."

"So, you have no say at all?" I asked, wondering how that worked.

"We do, but only when powerful emotion is behind it. Like the few times we have gone against him."

"What do you mean?"

"Lycus's guilt, when he healed you. Tobias giving you magic the other day."

I looked at him, wondering how he knew.

"Don't tell me. In case you haven't noticed, I am the weakest link. If Darius asks, I will tell him why. I won't be able to lie to him. Therefore, some things are best for me not knowing," Kalen told me, and I nodded. *I'd have to remember that.*

"Wait, how did you know?" I asked.

"Your aura changed. It glowed for a few hours, like you were recharged."

"And now?"

He glanced at me. "Same as ours, though fainter since you have no magic."

I nodded, relieved. "What can you tell me, then?"

"Ask, and we will find out. See what I can say," Kalen told me.

I thought for a second, choosing my questions. "Why does Lycus hate me?"

"He doesn't. He just hates what you did to me."

"What did I do to you?"

"Can't answer, but you already know," he said, and I nodded, saving that for later to ponder.

"What about Darius?"

He opened his mouth and started humming. "Interesting, that is one I think I can speak about. He killed his father for you, for all of us."

"Can you elaborate?"

"Ah…" He tried to speak when his mouth shut. "I guess that is all I can say on that one."

"Fine, um… Tobias then?" I ask, slightly annoyed.

"His brother, and again all I can say," he said, frustrated.

"Was that the man I saw in the picture on the bedside table?"

"Yes, it was his twin."

"Was?"

"He is dead now."

"Let me guess, because of me?"

Kalen's brows furrowed, but he said nothing else.

"Okay, well, can you tell me why everyone calls me a traitor?"

"Because of conspiracy theories surrounding the plague."

"Conspiracy theories?"

"I can't. That is all you get," Kalen growled, resting his head back on the couch. "This is so stupid. Believe me, if I could, I would tell you everything."

"I know," I told him, gripping his knee.

"Okay, your turn. How about you answer some of my questions?" Kalen asked, and I chewed my lip. "Might help get you some answers," he continued.

"You're going to see if I can answer my own questions?" I asked, and he nodded.

I shrugged. What could it hurt if it meant learning more about them? Why not? The door opened, and I almost sighed when Darius entered the room, knowing how this strange game would be over.

CHAPTER 51

*H*owever, KALEN STILL ASKED, and I noticed Darius fall onto the bed. I could feel his eyes boring into the back of my skull.

"Tell me something. You remember the night of the fire?"

I blinked at Kalen, wondering how that helped anything. Yet the look on his face told me he was trying to prove something to Darius or maybe to me, I wasn't sure.

"I remember coming home sick from school. I think I got food poisoning," I told him, and he nodded.

I thought back to that day, but it was kind of hazy. My brows creased as I tried to think. "My mom was angry; she and my father were arguing, and I threw up on the floor."

Why couldn't I remember after that? I remembered my father cleaning the mess up. I also remembered my mother giving me a drink, but that wasn't it until the actual fire.

"What else do you remember?" Kalen asked, leaning forward, and I noticed Darius hop off the bed and walk over to us. He dropped into the armchair across from us and loaded more wood into the fireplace, though I knew he had only come over to listen.

"I remember the smoke woke me, and I remember calling out to my father. He called back and told me to hold on. That he was trying to get to me," I answered.

"What else?" Kalen nodded.

"Just trying to move, trying to get to the door, but I felt so heavy, and my lungs burned. I think I crawled to the door," I told him.

"Anything else?" Kalen asked when the bathroom door opened. Tobias stepped out, followed by a billow of steam.

"I remember burning, which must have been my side. Then waking up to see Darius standing in front of me, his hands out. My mother's screams when the roof fell in and the forest behind the house caught fire but that is it." I averted my eyes when Tobias dropped his towel, catching a glimpse of his ass as he slid some gray tracksuit pants on.

Kalen chuckled as my face flushed. Darius raised an eyebrow at him but said nothing, nor did he add anything about that night. He simply sat back and watched Kalen and me.

Looking over at Tobias, I stared at the burns on his back and his skin, patchy in places. "Your burns. Why didn't you heal them, and why are they so bad?" I asked.

He looked at me over his shoulder before turning to Darius, who nodded at him.

"Because it took all of our power to heal you," Tobias said simply.

I looked at Darius, who had an indecipherable expression on his face.

"Your back would have looked ten times worse than his and your legs. When we got to the house, the roof over your bedroom was partially collapsed. You were trapped on the floor with a beam on you. We dragged you out just before the entire room caved in after breaking the wards that trapped you in there," Darius finally said.

"Wards?" I asked, a little confused.

"Yes, your room was sealed. You could get in but not back out. Tobias is burned because he used his body as a shield while I broke them," Darius answered.

"So, why didn't you heal him?" I asked.

"As Tobias said, we drained our power to heal you. What we had left, we used to cloak you."

I pulled a face. He made no sense.

"That is also why we couldn't find you after your powers manifested. We cloaked you well, even from ourselves."

"Why cloak me at all?" I asked.

"To hide you from the person or people who tried to kill you. What I want to know, though, is why they tried because the only logical reason is that you are my mate."

"And mine," Tobias added.

"Why does it matter if I am your mate?"

"Exactly, Aleera. So, ask yourself this: Why would your parents try to kill you just to stop me from having you?" Darius asked.

"My parents didn't try to kill me, Darius. I remember them trying to get to me."

"You remember hearing their voices? Tobias and I got to you pretty easily by opening a portal into your room. Getting you out? We couldn't open one. So, again, Aleera, why would they try to kill you?"

"They wouldn't. My parents loved me, Darius. I heard my father trying to smash through the floor to get to me. Then you got there whenever you did and killed them. You probably started it," I snapped at him.

"Why would I try to kill my own keeper? Hurt my mate?" he asked, nodding toward Tobias.

I looked at him, and Tobias was watching me. "Maybe you were only after my parents, then? You said it yourself. Our fathers hated each other."

"For good reason. Your parents aren't who you think they are, Aleera," Darius snarled.

Tears burned my eyes at his words. *How could he say that? My parents loved me; I knew they loved me.* "You're wrong. My life was fine before you came in and turned it upside down. My parents would never hurt me."

"And if you're wrong?" Tobias asked.

"I'm not," I told him, and he shrugged.

"If that is what you want to believe," Darius said.

"And if I was under a cloaking spell, then how did the authorities find me when my grandmother died?" I asked.

"Because you lived on one of my family's properties, that's why. I called the school after she passed," Tobias answered.

"Pardon?" *What was he on about now?*

"The house you were taken to belonged to my family. The private school you went to, we paid for," Tobias answered.

"What are you talking about? The Fae Authorities picked me up?"

"They said they were Fae Authorities but they weren't. They were wardens of the school. That school you went to, Darius and I paid for. Your grandmother was broke. Your parents took everything from her just before the fire, cleaned her out not long after we left. So, we took her in when she agreed to care for you," Tobias said.

"Bullshit," I told them, and Darius growled before walking off into the closet and returning with a box. Darius dumped it at my feet and nodded toward it. I rolled my eyes before removing the lid and finding some papers. I pulled them out.

All of them had my school letterhead. My school photos were even there, and most of them were bills for the school fees, thousands and thousands of dollars they had spent on putting me through school. All addressed to Darius and Tobias Wraith, my next of kin.

"Still think we're lying? We have no reason to lie to you, Aleera. So maybe stop lying to yourself," Darius said before walking off.

I dug through the box, pulling out my school files—everything from when I started, even some of my schoolwork. Rummaging through the bottom, I found my grandmother's locket—the only item I could bring with me when I was taken from her house—next to a photo album I had lost when I called on them. It was in the bag I had dropped. They wouldn't even let me take my clothes; they said everything would be provided. I rubbed my fingers over the locket. It had a picture of her with my grandfather and a lock of his hair she had cut off.

"You got this from my room," I told them.

"Yes, when we came looking for you," Kalen said.

"I never knew," I told Tobias, and he nodded when Darius spoke behind me.

"How could you? When you ran before we got there?"

CHAPTER 52

M Y ENTIRE BODY ACHED when I woke up the following day. Every part of me hurt, and I felt like I'd been run over by a truck. It took all my strength to roll off the couch and onto the floor. It took some serious willpower to get to my feet and stagger into the bathroom. My legs couldn't even hold me upright in the shower; the best I could do was sit on the floor. Though the warmth helped loosen up my aching muscles.

When I was finished, I forced myself up and grabbed a towel, only to groan when I recognized my mistake. I had forgotten to bring clothes in with me. I looked at my now damp walked-on pajamas on the bathroom floor, picked them up, tossed them in the hamper, and headed for the bedroom door.

Poking my head out the door, Tobias was nowhere to be seen and probably setting up for the early morning class he had since today was only a half-day. Lycus was not in the room, and I figured he must have gone for a run. However, Darius was still in bed next to Kalen.

Tiptoeing out, I tried not to wake them as I rummaged through the drawers for some clothes. Usually, my clothes were waiting on the end of the couch, so I had no idea where they kept them.

No such luck this morning. Whoever usually got them out hadn't this morning, but it was pretty early still, looking at the clock. Movement on the bed made me look over my shoulder to find Darius spooning Kalen.

They looked kind of cute snuggled together. My stomach twisted painfully, and I turned my gaze away when Kalen rolled into Darius, both moving and rearranging in the bed. Darius groaned lewdly when Kalen kissed him in his sleep. Moving to the closet, I was about to give up and ask where they kept my clothes since they miraculously disappeared and reappeared when I felt warmth rush across my back.

Without even turning, I knew someone was behind me. I swallowed when Lycus's arm reached past me to the shelf overhead. He pulled some tights and a tank top down before handing them to me.

"You're up early," he whispered.

I nodded, feeling very caged in with him standing so close while also in the confines of the closet. I clutched them before turning around. I took a step back, bumping into the clothes hung up in there, when I noticed he was entirely naked. Stark naked, not a scrap of cloth covered him. Lycus stood there, watching me, and I tried to squeeze past him, but he stepped into my path.

"Excuse me," I whispered, not liking how he was backing me into a corner, a literal corner, and a coat hanger dug into my shoulder. I gasped. *What the heck did he want?* It was too early in the morning for their little games.

"You might want to get changed in here," Lycus smirked, and I raised an eyebrow at him.

Like hell was I getting changed in here with him while he was naked. With a roll of my eyes, I shoved past him, and I heard him chuckle. Walking out, I stopped dead in my tracks. Darius and

Kalen were in bed, and Kalen had his mouth wrapped around Darius. A shriek nearly left my lips out of shock. I had been here for weeks, and I had never witnessed them doing anything. A hand clamped over my lips, and Lycus pulled me back against his naked body.

"Next time, you might listen," Lycus whispered with a soft laugh, and my heartbeat was like a drum when I felt him dip his face into my neck, skimming his nose from the back of my ear and down my neck and shoulder, his erection pressing against my lower back. His grip was tight, yet I couldn't tear my eyes from Darius and Kalen on the bed. Like I was stuck in some trance.

"You feel his power," Lycus murmured against my skin. Goosebumps rose all over my skin. He was right. Darius's power oozed out, and Kalen was taking it. Darius groaned, his hand in Kalen's hair while he took Darius in his mouth.

"Darius may let you join him, but he would need something in return," Lycus purred.

It was like someone chucked ice water over me. I bumped backward into Lycus as I tried to get away, stomping on his foot. Darius's eyes opened and settled on me. He had one arm tucked behind his head, and he quirked an eyebrow at me before smiling. Lycus's hand moved from across my mouth, and I turned in Lycus's hold, wanting to dart back into the closet, only I smacked into his chest instead because the wall of a man refused to move and was blocking the door.

"What's wrong, Aleera?" Lycus chuckled.

I barged past him, and he laughed while I became all hot and flustered. That stupid song, *It's Raining Men*, suddenly came to mind. *Naked men, raining naked men, with penises, everywhere.*

"I take it she doesn't want to join," Lycus chuckled, and I glared at his back as he walked away.

Darius laughed at my embarrassment. I dressed quickly, even managed to put my shirt on inside out, and I was sure Lycus handed it to me in the right way. Flustered and wanting to escape the room, I yanked it off, pulled it back, and then rushed out. My eyes automatically went to the bed. How couldn't they? The bed was in the middle of the room, and I had to rush past it, and there they were in all naked sex-god glory.

I gripped the door handle and twisted. The power in the room was making it harder to breathe, yet the door would not open. I knew who was behind it, who was preventing me from leaving.

"Darius, please open it," I whined, not wanting to turn back to face the bed.

Lycus growled behind me, and I knew he was in bed with them now, too.

CHAPTER 53

THE BOND FLARED, WANTING to go to them. I wouldn't have the slightest idea what my part would be in their orgy or what to do with them. I needed to escape before I embarrassed myself or Darius toyed with my bond and made me do something that would probably destroy any sense of hope I had left.

"Come here," Darius said, and I shook my head.

"Leave her be, Darius," Kalen whispered.

"Just shut up and suck my cock," Darius snapped at him, and Kalen whimpered. Almost agonized, though, the sound was more like a moan.

"Aleera," Darius purred, and I fisted my hands and gritted my teeth. *Why does he have to fuck with my stupid bond?* He would know this causes me pain. With a glare plastered on my face, I turned around, and the noise that left me when I spotted them was embarrassing. Lycus kneeled behind Kalen before gripping his hips and pulling them close to him while Kalen wrapped his lips around Darius's cock. Darius smirked like he knew exactly the effect this was having on the bond. My feet moved, and I only just grabbed the dresser by the door to stop myself from climbing on the bed and begging Darius for his power.

"Everything alright, Aleera?" Darius asked, and my nails ached from clutching the dresser.

"Fuck!" Darius groaned, and my eyes moved to the bed to find Darius's hand fisting Kalen's hair while he bobbed away.

"Darius, please," I begged, my speech more like a damn pant as arousal flooded me. I needed to get out of there. He growled but flicked his hand toward the door, and I heard it unlock. Darius wasn't even looking in my direction, too busy, lost in the euphoria of what Kalen was doing to him.

Turning, I ripped open the door and dashed into the hall, slamming the door shut. The strange fog from his magic lifted, and I clutched my knees to catch my breath.

"Are you okay?" Tobias asked, touching my shoulder.

I hadn't even heard him come into the hall, but he stood in front of me when I looked up. Tobias's eyes flickered, and I knew I was flushed, the stupid bond overriding my brain again. Tobias took a step toward me before shaking himself, and his eyes went to the door I had just come out of.

"I need to go to breakfast," I told him, rushing past him even though the bond was trying to pull me back to the room.

୨୧

My bond played havoc all day. The cramping in my stomach worsened; their energy only made it worse in their presence during class, and I felt sick. Darius was smug in every class I had with him. He knew it was torture for me. I would not give him the satisfaction of me begging him, and I knew that was what Darius wanted. No doubt he would be one of those who enjoyed another's discomfort; hell, he enjoyed mine. Though as the day dragged on, something was amiss. My entire body was yearning, and since seeing them morning, it had only gotten worse.

Going to the bathroom to change into my gym clothes, I rushed into a stall and locked the door. We had the obstacle course again this afternoon. Taking my clothes off, I removed my pants and gasped.

Fuck! The shredding, I had forgotten entirely about the shredding as I looked down at my panties. I was spotting which wasn't a good sign. Being the only girl here, I had completely forgotten about it and the fact I had never actually gone through it in the six years, careful always to make sure I had my herbs that prevented it.

Horror washed over me. Keeper women went through a phase, shredding every six months when we shredded all our power in a day. It was like what humans would call a period, only vastly different, seeing as fae didn't menstruate. Still, we had our own version of shredding, and it only happened to keeper women. We would bleed for a day, and then the next three days, we would power-shred.

There was just one issue. I had no power to shred, and I knew it wasn't obtainable, nor could I afford to go through it. Shredding happened when most bond power was shared. During a shredding, you could power your mates with enough power to last until the next one, making them more powerful, while I would be at my most vulnerable.

Yanking my pants up, I knew I had roughly a week to find some devil's bane. I needed the damn root. It would stop it, yet if I asked for that around here, it would get me some curious questions seeing as it was poisonous to demons, and Darius finding out could be lethal.

I was debating whether to ask Tobias or Kalen for it before shoving that idea away, but I knew they would want to know why

I tried to stop it. There was no way Darius would give me power or allow the others to provide me with energy. While shredding, keepers are at their most potent, our magic at its strongest, though we're also at our weakest because we would literally be throwing off power to our mates. I could not even imagine that horror if I had power.

That explained the agony I had been in this morning, though shredding itself lasted a day. I knew that because I had been holding mine off for six years. I could not afford to lose my power without anything to replenish it. So I knew this would be hell. One, because I had no power to shred; two, because they might find out what I was if I did. I had never gone through it to know if I could even mask my white-fae side.

The sun beat down on my skin as I stepped outside. I looked around the area of this place surrounded by forest, and I knew there would be devil's bane in that forest. It was just a matter of finding it. Chewing my lip, I walked out going to the obstacle course; I internally groaned when I saw Darius was taking over Tobias's class today. He made me run track. As the sun started going down, the whistle blew, and he called everyone inside as a storm was fast approaching. I sighed, excited to rest as I watched everyone head in.

Zac walked over to Darius, talking like good friends as they walked back to the castle, and I glared in their direction. Giving the forest a longing look, I turned to head in when I noticed Darius was gone, along with Zac. *What I would give to be able to move so quickly, mist where I wanted.* But no, I had to walk.

CHAPTER 54

THE NEXT DAY WAS no better. Only now I knew it was approaching. I had to think of a way to sneak into the forest. Darius seemed hellbent on torturing me, which wasn't helping. Once again, I woke up to them fucking. I grabbed a sandwich for lunch today and walked outside needing some air. Lycus's threat seemed to be working. As long as I had food in my hand, no one came near me, and I was free to roam.

Sitting on the bench outside in the warm sun, I stared at the forest before peeking around. Everyone was distracted eating lunch, and no doubt my mates would all be eating together. They always did this in the room while I was stuck in the mess hall. Getting up, I was about to head inside when I realized this was my chance. I had an hour before lunch finished, and I could be in and back before they noticed. Glancing at the roof, I wished I could get Ryze to get it for me, but it was also poisonous to him. Poisonous to everyone. More so, to demons, it was lethal. The root was what I needed, and I hoped I had time to dry it out.

I headed for the forest by giving a quick glance at the castle doors and seeing no one. I carried on until the trees covered me. Catching my breath, I hunted for this damn plant. Searching beneath all the trees and brushing back ferns. Scouring the ground for any sign of this purple and pink budded plant. Climbing the small hill, I moved further through the forest. I had no idea how long I had been out here scouring, becoming obsessed with the damn task. Just on the crest of a slight incline among the trees, I saw it.

Excitement bubbled up in me, and I clambered, slipping as I climbed the steep incline. I went to wrap my hands around the stalk when someone grabbed the back of my shirt, sending me flying.

My back arched as I smashed into the dirt next to the tree I was just tossed against. I groaned, and my back arched as I rubbed the spot. The air knocked from my lungs when I heard a thunderous growl, and my eyes opened. I saw Darius reaching for me in a daze, and I lurched to my feet out of pure adrenaline.

"I fucking warned you about trying to escape," he bellowed as I clambered up the incline, trying to get to the plant. *Fuck it.* He looked livid; I would have to show him. I thought his wrath couldn't be worse than it was now, and I tried to grab the damn plant.

"No, the plant," I blurted when he grabbed my ankles, ripping me back down. My head bounced off the ground, and the rock I smashed it on made me see black for a few seconds. I clawed at the earth, screaming as I tried to get to the devil's bane.

"No, listen. I need the devil's bane, just the root," I screamed as he dragged me back toward him. I only realized how bad that sounded after I said it. Admitting to needing something so poisonous to demons that it could kill them.

"Darius!" I screamed as he flipped me by my hips onto my back. My hand whipped out and slapped him hard across the face. He seemed shocked.

I kicked away from him, scrambling up the incline. I felt his hand in my hair only seconds later. "The shre—"

"Enough! Shut up! I am done with your lies," he snarled, jerking me back by my hair. I clutched his hands and tried to explain, but my lips wouldn't open. Tears trekked down my face as he dragged me kicking and screaming from the forest before I felt his magic erupt as he opened a portal.

I felt the portal's pull before I found myself in my old room. Darius tossed me on the bed by my hair, and I felt the strands rip free painfully from my scalp. My scream was mute, I felt it vibrate out of me, but no sound left my lips. I nearly rolled off the bed, and the door burst open as Tobias and Kalen stepped in.

"Get out! You don't go near her. You don't fucking look at her. You don't speak to her," Darius roared as he turned, glaring at Kalen, who stared in horror at what he was witnessing. Blood trickled down the side of my head, and I touched my fingers to it, wondering what I had hit it on.

"What happened? What did she do?" Tobias asked while Kalen was forced out of the room by Darius's command.

"She tried to escape," Darius sneered, and I shook my head and tried to explain, yet the words never left me. Darius had taken my ability to talk.

"She wouldn't," Tobias defended me.

"She was nearly on the fucking road," Darius snarled. *Road? I was near the road.* I was sure I hadn't wandered that far in, but I wasn't paying much attention.

"Aleera?"

I shook my head and tried to tell Tobias I wasn't, trying to explain, knowing he could tell I was speaking the truth.

"Let her speak," Tobias snapped at him.

"She was by the fucking road, Tobias. What else would she be doing so far out? You can tell if I am lying, and I don't fucking lie," Darius snarled at him.

Tobias watched him before his eyes fell on me. "Why? Everything was going fine, Aleera," Tobias snapped and stormed out, leaving me with Darius.

"You always ruin everything," Darius snarled, walking toward me, and I flinched away from his burning rage. Yet, he grabbed the front of my shirt and jerked me forward before fishing my tablet from the back of my pants held by my belt. I reached for it, but he pulled it away.

Tears trailed down my cheeks as he stripped me of everything, only leaving me with a sheet and my bra and undies. He took my tablet, my freedom, and my voice. He took everything.

CHAPTER 55

Kalen

I WANTED TO GO TO her, but Tobias glared at me from where I sat on the bed. Lycus also stood before me, arms folded over his chest as we waited for Darius to return. When the door opened, my eyes darted over to it, and Darius stepped into the room. His aura was burning hot, threatening to set the room on fire.

My mouth opened, and I wanted to ask if he had hurt her, but I quickly stopped myself with one glare from Lycus. Darius removed his shirt before undoing his pants and chucking them in the laundry basket by the door.

"Kalen, I can feel your burning curiosity. I didn't hurt her," Darius said, not that he sounded happy about it.

I knew he had reason to hate her, but I wanted to understand. She seemed so excited for years when I spoke to her about finding her mates. Then once she manifested, she ran, and I didn't believe it was only because Darius had apparently killed her parents.

If she only knew that the army Darius was building was not to take over the rest of the world but to protect her, maybe she wouldn't have run. I wanted to know why she ran. There had to be another reason. She had to have another reason, but instead of letting her explain, they wanted revenge for things she was unaware she had done.

Darius placed her tablet on the bed, and I glared at him. "What the fuck, Darius?" I snarled at him before snatching it off the bed.

"She can earn it back, along with the rest of her possessions," he said.

"The rest of her stuff?" I asked, but he clucked his tongue at my outrage, and I saw his eyes flicker. He could be such a possessive asshole, and I knew half his issue was that he was jealous. I could fucking feel his and Lycus's jealousy.

However, looking over at Tobias, he was livid. He and Aleera had been getting along well, and with one incident, he was back to being a prick.

"What, that's it? You won't say anything at all?" I asked Tobias, and he sat back in his chair and folded his arms, looking directly at me.

"Darius told the truth. I would know if he lied."

"His version of the truth. Did you ask her?"

Tobias chewed his lip and looked at Darius, who growled, and I felt the pang of hurt flit through the bond that we wouldn't believe him. Tobias, also feeling it, looked at me and said, "I trust our mate." His faith in Darius was beginning to annoy me.

"Aleera is our mate too," I told him, and he glared at the burning fire in the fireplace.

"And she tried to run, Kalen," Lycus said, coming over to me and wrapping his arms around my waist. I shoved him off, and he whimpered.

"No, let go. I am sick of you all using the bond against me. I am not just some fuck toy, and Aleera is also mine," I argued when I was suddenly airborne.

Darius grabbed me, slammed me down on the bed, and I struggled under his grip; I knew he wouldn't hurt me, he never did, but he didn't like being spoken back to either.

"She isn't our mate. We are all mates. We don't need her," Darius snarled.

I glared at him, and he pressed his weight down on me. His erection dug into my stomach. He always liked it when we fought him and always enjoyed forcing us to submit to him but not when it came to Aleera. I would fight for her as much as possible anyway but the stupid bond and Darius having complete control, making us solely dependent on him, made that challenging because none of us were strong enough to fight off his orders.

"You will stay away. You remain with one of us at all times," Darius murmured, nipping at my ear, and I groaned and growled, trying to shove him off.

"Stop, I don't want to fuck," I snapped at him, but he ignored me. Instead, he tugged at my belt before wrapping his hand around my cock and squeezing.

"You don't want me?" Darius questioned as he flooded the bond with arousal, making my dick harden in his hand. His power rushed out addictively, forcing me to submit to get a taste of it.

One thing I hated about the bond was the one who handled the power, had all control, and was half the reason we had issues with Aleera. Darius probably even knew that. Yet, as the fog settled, we all became slaves to the bond, to our keeper, to Darius. Like pigeons flocking, they were drawn to him and the bed, and, despite hating him at this moment, I rolled over at his demand.

"You won't disobey me, will you, Kalen? You will stay away from her until I say otherwise?" Darius purred while stroking my length. I gritted my teeth, trying to fight against his will and his hold on me. Yet I would not win against him, and as the pain of denying the bond grew, I gave in.

"Good boy," Darius purred before sucking on my neck and making me moan and push back against him.

CHAPTER 56

Aleera

THE NEXT MORNING, I awoke cold. Darius walked into the room and tossed some clothes at me.

"Get dressed and get to class," he snapped.

I looked at the clothes on the bed and scrambled for them, snatching and chucking them on. Anything for the extra warmth they would provide. I was just thankful he wouldn't make me go to class in my bra and undies. Darius stood in the doorway, watching as I got changed.

He growled when I took too long, and I looked down at my feet, which were still bare. *Great, back to no shoes again.* At least I had pants and a blouse.

"You try to run, you try to speak to anyone, I will retake your voice," he said before waving his hand and giving me my voice back.

Warmth tickled my throat, and I went to explain I wasn't running. The moment my lips moved, he gripped my throat.

"That means speaking to me, too. I don't want to hear it. Now get to fucking class," Darius sneered before turning on his heel and leaving me.

I swallowed and walked down to breakfast, hoping Tobias would feed Ryze. Worrying about him kept me up most of the night, and I wondered if Ryze had managed to catch his own dinner last night when I didn't come up to see him. I made my way to the mess hall. The moment I stepped in, all eyes were on me. I grabbed a sandwich and moved to an empty table.

Something felt off this morning. I didn't know what, but something felt different as I glanced around the crowded room. Leering eyes watched me from where I sat alone in the mess hall. My usual spot was taken, preferring to be closest to the exit where I mainly remained unnoticed. Closer to the door was safest because it gave me an escape route.

Their sleazy gazes had me on edge as they watched me hungrily. I hated this place. There were no other women here. Most of all, I hated being the subject they loved to torment. All made worse by the fact that I was powerless to stop them.

The surrounding chatter quieted down and made me quickly glance around before I ducked my head when I noticed them. Darius had entered the room with my other three mates. They walked to the back of the room and took seats at the back, which I thought was a little odd; I rarely saw them here. It appeared they had something to talk about with their recruits because Darius spoke about some crap that I showed no interest in knowing. Keeping my head down, I ate quickly, wanting nothing more than to get the hell out of here, and worried that if Kalen tried to speak to me, I would be forced to ignore him or lose my voice.

However, the moment I stood up and went to throw my tras into the bin, my muscles spasmed, and my feet faltered as I tried to take a step away from the table. My entire body froze up with one command.

"Aleera, freeze," came a voice. I recognized the voice instantly and dreaded what he would do this time.

I couldn't move an inch, and everyone erupted with laughter. Oh, how I tried, but I couldn't so much as wiggle a toe. What were these savage men going to subject me to this time? They never usually went this far. Usually, they tormented me, chased me, hurt me. However, this was the first time they used compulsion on me, and it felt wrong as every muscle in my body tensed.

My eyes went to my mates at the back. Darius, Tobias, and Lycus watched from the far table. They were always happy to witness my suffering. Kalen, however, glanced around the room before he looked at me and dropped his head.

My stomach dropped when Zac got up from his seat. My lungs constricted at the cruel smirk plastered on his face. Zac sauntered over and stopped in front of me. His eyes hungrily looked me over from head to toe. Zac was the worst out of all the recruits I had come across here. The vile bastard had no boundaries. He was usually behind my worst degradation. Zac walked around me slowly and plucked the sandwich wrapper from my fingers while I remained unmoving.

"Stand up straight," he ordered, and I gritted my teeth. My forced body did as commanded as Zac's cold magic caressed over me. A violent shudder ran through me in repulsion as I tried to fight against the command, but it was pointless. I was a puppet on strings, and he was the puppet master at this moment.

"Nothing to say, Aleera?" he chuckled, and the entire room erupted with laughter. Except for my mates that watched from the back with expressionless faces.

"Nothing I say will stop you. Did you want me to beg? Beg for you not to do whatever vile thing you intend to do?" I spat at him, knowing I would probably lose my voice for speaking.

Being trapped in this place, I learned quickly not to beg. It just made the torment worse when I did. They didn't care that I was female; they didn't care I was powerless. All they cared about was the control they had over me.

"You're right. It wouldn't stop me. The guys and I want you to put on a show for us," Zac said in an amused tone. I glanced around the room to find the men were all leaning forward eagerly; one even winked at me while another licked his lips.

My eyes darted to the table where my mates sat. Not a scrap of emotion was shown on their faces for what I was about to endure. They would not help me, not that I expected them to. They never did. If they just told them who I was to them, if their soldiers only knew. I wouldn't have to deal with this shit daily. However, I knew they would deny it if I spoke up. Darius had threatened to kill me if I told anyone here who I was to them. So, I had kept my mouth shut. They hated me, and the feeling was mutual. Yet, I couldn't bear to see them hurt, so how could they watch my humiliation with no expression at all?

My eyes went back to Zac, who looked me up and down. Was he going to make me dance? What did he mean by a show? I was already on display. How much worse could it get?

"You could always say no?" Zac teased before he scoffed. "Oh, that's right, you can't. Poor helpless Aleera, always so easily influenced, so easily overpowered. Must truly suck being the weakest form of fae," he mocked.

His demonic eyes ran the length of me in a sleazy, obscene way. His gaze stopped at my breasts, and I felt my stomach drop somewhere deep and cold within me. I knew what he was going to say. I prayed I was mistaken, but his words confirmed my thoughts.

"Strip, Aleera," Zac said, his voice coming out like a purr.

I blinked at him, tried to fight his compulsion with everything in me, even though I knew it was pointless. My eyes burned as tears threatened to spill, and my hands shook as I tried to resist doing what he'd asked.

"All of it. I want to see you completely bare."

My fingers forcibly undid the buttons on my black blouse. My breathing became harsher as I tried to resist his compulsion. A sob tore from my lips that sounded more like a whimper. My vision blurred as my top fell open and revealed my black bra. Zac gripped my shirt and yanked it, my shirt tearing painfully from my body under the force he'd used. My scars were on display for everyone to see. The worst was the burn that went from my shoulder to my hip.

The men watching hollered and whistled, and some even poked fun at my burned, scar-ravaged skin. *Was this high school? Were they truly this immature?* They were fully grown men, all subjecting me to this. Worst of all, my mates just watched. Although, I noticed Kalen looked away when my eyes fell on him. He almost seemed guilty, like he wanted to step in and stop it. My fingers were still working to undo the buttons and zip on my black slacks. My eyes stung from the tears that brimmed and spilled over as I bent over to remove my pants.

"Please, stop," I choked out as I stood upright. *How could they all be so cruel?*

"All of it," Zac commanded again.

My entire body shook at his command. My cheeks burned with the humiliation, tears ran down my cheeks and dripped off my chin, and I could hear them all talking and laughing.

My bottom lip trembled as my hands reached behind my back and fumbled with the clasp of my bra. A hiccupped sob left me as it unclipped. I couldn't handle it, so I clenched my eyes shut, so I didn't see their faces watching me. I hoped it was stuck, but of course, it would come undone easily and expose me more.

Zac's hand ran down my arm from my shoulder to my elbow as he pulled the strap of my bra down. My eyes flew open at his touch. His other hand moved to my hip, and I felt the bile rise in my throat. The feel of his hands on me disgusted me. I wondered how far he would take this. Looking over at my mates, Kalen got up and walked out along with Lycus. Darius and Tobias, however, were enjoying my torment.

"Hurry, Aleera, take it off, take it all off," Zac purred as he tugged my bra strap off my other shoulder.

I stared at Darius. *Was this what he wanted? Was this still not humiliating enough?* His eyes darkened when Zac ran his hand up my side before grabbing my breast roughly. He twisted my nipple painfully, making me cry out, and I felt more tears spill over as my bra fell away. The room erupted with whistles and vulgar taunts.

Darius and Tobias could stop this, and I pleaded with my eyes for them to step in, just this once, and not subject me to this. My hands shook violently as they reached for my panties. It was the last article of clothing I had left, the one place left untouched.

My fingers gripped them, and I closed my eyes and went to tug them down when something wet splattered on my face and skin. The sound was so sickening it made my eyes fly open to see blood drops on the floor before more blood pooled around my feet. Zac's command was suddenly gone, and I felt its weight lift when a pair of arms wrapped around me, crushing me against a warm chest.

My entire body shook, and the place fell silent. Tobias's scent wafted to my nose, and a choked sob left me. I hated them, fucking hated them, but his body was the only thing shielding me from the watchful eyes of everyone else. The thunderous growl that echoed around the room made me whimper.

Suddenly, all the windows exploded with Darius's rage; the blast sent shards of glass everywhere before I heard more sickening tearing sounds. Blood washed over my toes, and I heard popping sounds followed by screams. Blood spatter hit me from everywhere, coating me in blood, and Tobias was murmuring something, but I couldn't understand anything until Darius's voice boomed through the room. His words left no room for debate or argument, and I shook as he publicly claimed me.

"Nobody touches our fucking mate," he snarled.

The collective gasp from those present was audible. My toes squelched in the blood, and I looked down and could see Zac's body by my feet. The room cleared quickly; the screech of chairs was loud as everyone took off and ran out.

"Get her back to her room while I clean this up," Darius snapped at Tobias, who turned to steer me toward the portal Darius had opened.

Bile rose in my throat when I saw blood covering the walls and ceiling. There was blood everywhere, along with limbs. Zac and his entire group of friends were dead; the man who licked his lips at me was also dead. A few I recognized that had catcalled and whistled were also blown to shreds, their limbs lying everywhere like they had suddenly exploded. Zac's hands had been removed from his body, his head was almost severed off completely, hanging beside his body, and a hole lay in the center of his chest. Tobias pushed me through the portal, which led to my room. The moment I was in my room, I smacked him.

"You just let them! You just let them do it!" I screamed, smacking and punching him. Tobias whimpered, and my fist connected with his face. Tobias tried to restrain me, but I wouldn't stop. I hated them, hated them; they all just watched. Tobias became angry and pushed me back before walking through the portal again and disappearing as it closed. My knees gave out as soon as he was gone, and I turned into a sobbing mess.

CHAPTER 57

Aleera

MY STOMACH TWISTED, YET I welcomed the pain—anything to stop the memory of them all laughing, anything to stop the sight of my mates just watching. Darius had brought food in earlier and set it down. I just stared ahead; I had no appetite, no will to do anything. Darius lingered, and I remained where I sat. I hadn't moved from the spot since, even though it was now dark and the entire day had passed by.

"You should shower," Darius said. Silence was all he earned in response; I didn't even acknowledge his existence. I didn't care if Darius killed them. He still watched what they did and only interfered at the end; he still allowed them to get to that point. They still allowed them to humiliate me. I heard the door lock when he left.

If he said anything else, I didn't hear him. Eventually, I got up and showered. The blood coating me made me itchy as it dried. I was numb to everything; I couldn't even feel the water beating down on my skin. It offered no warmth. Getting out, I walked back to my room, only to hear the bathroom door lock a few moments later when one of them showered.

I looked for clothes only to remember Darius had emptied my room, and everything was in their room. The only thing left was a fresh pair of underwear and a sports bra from the clothes he had given me this morning. The punishments never ended. I slipped them on before climbing into bed.

All night I shivered, freezing cold from only having a sheet, my teeth chattering after the fire had gone out earlier during the night. I only woke up when I heard the cawing sound of my phoenix, making me jolt upright. I rushed toward the window, trying to shove it open, but the damn thing was stuck, and I saw him fly to the window next door.

He had done it before, but Tobias luckily shooed him off before Darius spotted him. I wondered if Tobias had fed him for me but since he was at the window, I doubted he had. I tapped on mine to get his attention and divert him away from their window. Panic seized me, and I banged louder. I knew they were all in there fucking, judging by the power that emanated from the room and seeped under the bathroom door. I could also hear the shower running in the bathroom.

It was only moments later that I heard the glass shatter, and my eyes flew wide as Ryze, looking for me, barged through and broke their window. I hit the door so hard that I nearly knocked myself out in my panic.

The shower cut off, and I started pounding on the door, praying they would open it. I could hear Ryze screeching, Darius's angry voice, Lycus yelling, and things being smashed. My heart sank, and tears blurred my vision. I burst through when the bathroom door finally opened, nearly slipping on the wet tiles.

I didn't know whom I barged past because all I cared about at that moment was getting to Ryze, who was squawking loudly. Bursting through into their room, everything was getting knocked over as Ryze flapped around, trying to avoid Darius's magic as he tossed it at him, but he had no escape.

"Shit!" Tobias hissed behind me, barreling into the room as Darius blasted him, and I screamed. The sound was blood-curdling, and Darius scooped him up by his neck, only for him to flap his wings frantically. Ryze turned his head to latch onto his hand. Darius growled and let go.

Ryze was trying to escape when I saw Darius lift his hand, stunning him in the air. My body crashed against Darius as I tackled him, and we both hit the ground. I landed on top of him before turning to look for my phoenix. Lycus grabbed Ryze, who was stunned, holding him by his neck. Tobias rushed over, grabbing Ryze from Lycus, who looked happy to be rid of him.

I let out a breath, got to my feet, and rushed toward Ryze in Tobias's arms as he moved toward the window. I ran over, and Tobias looked at me before his eyes went behind me. Within seconds, I was ripped backward by my hair and dropped on my ass at Darius's feet.

"Fucking kill it and be done with it. Fucking thing broke the window," Darius snarled, and I screamed at the thought, trying to get up only for Darius to growl at me. Tobias looked torn and clenched his jaw.

"What the fuck are you doing in here?" Darius snapped at me before wiping his mouth where my forehead had connected when I tackled him. Blood trickled down his chin, and my eyes went to Lycus and Kalen, who stood around looking stunned by the situation or maybe they feared my phoenix; I wasn't sure.

"No, he's mine! I yelled.

"Kill it," Darius said dismissively, and I wondered if he had heard what I said.

"No, Tobias, don't do it!" I begged.

Darius jerked my head back painfully. My neck craned so far back that I actually fell back against his legs. Darius snarled and let me go. Ryze shrieked again and started flapping, ruffling out his feathers and using his beak to climb up onto Tobias's shoulder. Tobias froze while Lycus gasped as Ryze fluffed out his feathers and puffed before glaring at Darius.

Tobias, too terrified to move, made a strangled noise as Ryze started grooming his beak through his wet hair. I tried to get up to go to him when Darius jerked me down by my shoulders, and Ryze lost it; he flew off Tobias's shoulder and started attacking Darius, clawing at him and snapping his sharp beak at him, tearing him to pieces up with his talons. Tobias, shaking himself out of the stupor, rushed toward Darius as he flung his magic blindly, and Tobias was blasted back.

Sticking my fingers in my mouth, I whistled, and Ryze stopped, flying back to me and settling on my shoulder. His talons dug into my shoulder, piercing my soft skin as I tried to calm him while Darius got up, his chest and shoulders bleeding and torn to shreds. I rushed toward the window to toss Ryze out, only Darius commanded me, and my feet halted. I choked on a sob, and my eyes went to Tobias near the window.

CHAPTER 58

"PLEASE, TOBIAS," I CRIED when I couldn't move my body. He looked torn, and his eyes went to Ryze.

"Please," I begged, tears trekking down my face, and I saw his lip quiver before his eyes went to Darius behind me.

"Turn around, and someone had better fucking explain why that thing just attacked me," Darius snarled behind me.

My feet obeyed his command, and the moment I turned, Darius stalked toward me, reaching for Ryze. Just as he went to snatch him, Tobias grabbed him first, earning a glare from Darius. Ryze screeched as Tobias plucked him off my shoulder, holding him as if he were an oversized chicken, his talons ripping from my skin painfully.

"Kill it," Darius sneered.

"No, please," I sobbed. My knees gave way beneath me, and I fell at his feet. He tilted his head to the side, looking between Ryze and me before his eyes went to Tobias, who turned his head away from Darius's glare. Lycus and Kalen remained still, their eyes not leaving Ryze like they were petrified to move if he attacked. Though he had no magic yet, Ryze was still deadly, especially with how big he had grown in the past few weeks.

"It's a phoenix, Aleera. They are fucking dangerous," Darius spat at me.

"He is hers. She has been looking after him," Tobias blurted, and Darius's eyes flickered toward him. He looked at Tobias, and Darius's eyes turned demonic.

"What! You knew?" Darius asked, looking at Ryze. Tobias sighed and nodded.

"His name is Ryze. Aleera found him injured and nursed him back to health. I knew you would kill him, so I never told you. It's also why she fainted, Darius. She was sharing her food with him," Lycus scoffed, and everyone's eyes went to him while I sat helpless on the floor.

"What?" Darius asked him.

"No wonder she fucking fainted when she was only eating one meal a day," Lycus said from behind Darius.

"Bullshit," Darius snarled, and Lycus shrugged. I had never seen him down there, so how would he know?

"I had to go sit with her the other day. They weren't letting her eat. I also spoke to one cook. He said she only snuck in just as the doors opened to steal food but never went to lunch or dinner, hadn't until I told them to lay off her," Lycus snapped at Darius. I dropped my gaze to the floor. The way he said it, I sounded like I was a thief. Shame washed over me.

"And you didn't think to fucking say anything?" Darius snapped at me, gripping my face and forcing me to look at him. I opened my mouth before closing it. There was no point defending myself, not against him.

I didn't care what he did to me as long as he left Ryze alone. Ryze squawked, and Tobias set him on the floor. The phoenix moved, hopped, and jumped toward me before stopping and hissing at Darius, who stepped back from him as Ryze curled up in my lap.

"You let it bond to her?" Darius snarled, and Ryze hissed at him. Lycus and Kalen moved further away from him in my lap, and I stroked his feathers, calming him.

"How is that even possible?" Lycus gasped, and I went to say because I'd found him hurt, but Tobias stepped in.

"He was nearly dead when she found him. She said he tried to bite her but then got used to her. Somehow he bonded to her," Tobias explained.

"And you didn't think to fucking say anything?" Darius snarled.

"I wasn't going to let you kill it," Tobias snapped back.

"Is this where you two have been sneaking off to every day? To feed that?" Darius growled, pointing to Ryze. Neither of us answered, and Darius snarled.

"Well, she can't keep it. What happens when it awakens?" Darius said, raising his hand, and my eyes widened.

"No!" I yelled, covering Ryze with my body. Darius's feet stopped next to me before my head was jerked back. Ryze hissed and tried to bite him. I held him tighter, knowing Darius would kill him if he did.

"I will do whatever you want. Just don't hurt him," I blurted out unthinkingly.

Darius tilted his head, observing my face. "Anything?" he asked, and I nodded, clutching Ryze, refusing to let him go as he hissed at Darius, who still had a hold of my hair. He shoved me forward, and I let out a breath.

Ryze cawed softly, rubbing his face and beak across my chest, making me remember I wasn't even clothed as I looked down to see I only had my bra and panties on. Goosebumps covered my skin, and I looked at everyone, all of them staring at Darius before my eyes went to him, too.

"If I let you keep it, will you do what I ask?"

I chewed the inside of my lip and saw Tobias shake his head. He scrubbed a hand down his face.

"Darius, no! You have done enough damage today, don't you think?" Tobias snarled like he knew what Darius would ask. I just stared at him, wondering what it was he wanted.

"Yes or no, Aleera? You do as I ask, or I kill your pet," Darius snapped, and I looked at Ryze. His tongue slivered out, and he licked my chin. I looked at Darius, sniffled, but nodded.

"Fuck's sake, Darius!" Tobias snapped.

"Shut up! It's her choice. She could say no, and I kill it, or say yes, and I will let her keep it."

"Until you want something else from her," Tobias snarled.

"He bites me or tries to attack me, I will kill him. Go put him somewhere," Darius snapped at me.

I got up and rushed to my room when he called out again.

"In here, he stays. He moves to hurt me, he dies," Darius said, and I froze, wondering why he kept saying that before looking for a spot to put him.

CHAPTER 59

I LOOKED AT THE OPEN window and swept the glass off before placing him on it. His talons dug into the wood, and the glass crunched under his weight but he didn't fly off. I was hoping he would, but he stayed. Tobias cursed under his breath, and I looked at Lycus and Kalen, but Kalen had a strange look on his face like he was dazed.

"Kalen won't come to your aid, Aleera. He can't. He can speak but he won't help." Tears brimmed in Kalen's eyes, which explained why he moved around wherever Lycus pulled him. It made me wonder what had happened to him after the mess-hall incident.

"Come here," Darius said, and I rubbed my arms against the draft, trying to cover my exposed skin. I hesitantly moved toward Darius, who smirked.

"You said anything." He chuckled darkly, and my stomach dropped, wondering what he wanted me to do. My eyes roamed over his scratched-up torso. He only had shorts on, and I nervously looked at Tobias, who couldn't even meet my gaze.

I gulped, and Ryze shrieked and stared at me.

"You carry on, and that thing attacks," Darius said, and I nodded.

I stopped in front of him, and Lycus looked away. Kalen dropped his head in his hands.

"Shut it, Kalen," Darius snapped at him, which only made me more nervous when I saw Kalen's shoulder shake as if he was crying. *What the fuck have I just agreed to?*

"Wasn't earlier fucking punishment enough, Darius?" Lycus snarled.

"I told you I had nothing to do with that," Darius snapped at him. It became clear why Kalen was silent. They must have argued with Darius over the incident in the mess hall. Darius had warned him away again because the look on his face was defeated.

"On your knees," Darius said, and I looked at him.

"What?" I blurted in shock.

"You want your bird to live, get on your knees," he said slowly and pointed at his feet.

I looked down before noticing his raging hard-on. I gasped and took a step back. Darius raised his hand and pointed at Ryze.

No matter what he forced me to endure, it was never enough. Tears brimmed in my eyes, and I knew what he wanted. It sickened me he would ask for that after earlier. *Wasn't that enough humiliation for one day?*

A sob left my lips as I dropped to my knees in front of him. Ryze shrieked, and I looked over at him, trying to quiet him. He cawed before tucking his head under his wing, and I let out a breath before looking up at Darius.

"Suck it," Darius said, looking down at me. I pressed my lips in a line, and I couldn't help the tears that spilled over, but I remained quiet because I knew if I made a noise, Ryze would attack him. I swallowed and looked at him, horrified, and he raised an eyebrow at me.

"Darius?" Lycus hissed at him, and Darius growled.

"What will it be, Aleera?" Darius asked, and I held back a whimper.

My hands trembled as I reached for his shorts. My cheeks heated, and embarrassment washed over me as I gripped the waistband of his shorts.

"Darius!" Tobias snapped as my tears dripped off my chin and onto my knees.

"No teeth," Darius mocked me.

I tugged his shorts down to his thighs before dropping my gaze, trying to will myself to put his thing in my mouth. I could barely see through my tears as I looked back at him. There was no denying that he was huge.

"Haven't got all day, Aleera," he said, leaning down and grabbing my hand. I whimpered when he forced my hand to grab his cock.

"What's wrong with you? Hurry up. Don't make out you haven't done it before. I know what a fucking whore you are," he snarled, and I shook my head.

"Three seconds or bye-bye, birdie," Darius taunted when I heard a thump, making me jump and look in Tobias's direction to see his fist through the wall. He hissed, yanking it out, and I noticed Ryze watching him before he fluffed out his feather and tucked his head again, only this time peering into the room like an owl watching. Darius thrust into my hand. I nearly let go at the feel, only he grabbed my hand before I could.

"Choose, Aleera," Darius snapped at me. *I'm doing it for Ryze.* I had to do this, I reminded myself, even though I didn't have the slightest clue as to what to do besides putting it in my mouth. My gaze went back to his cock, and I nearly gagged at the size of it. I swallowed before leaning forward on my knees and opening my mouth. Cringing at what I was about to do.

"She's a fucking virgin, you fucking prick," Kalen blurted out, and I froze.

"Yeah, right. She is twenty-four, for fuck's sake." Darius laughed, and I looked up at him.

"Darius, I swear to you she is. She giggled like a fucking school girl when she saw my dick. She wouldn't make that up," Kalen said, and I dropped my eyes to the floor, my cheeks flaming hot.

Darius gripped my chin, forcing me to look up at him. He tilted his head to the side. "Is he lying? Are you a virgin, Aleera?"

My cheeks burned even hotter all down my neck, and my chest became hot as well. I nodded, and he looked at Tobias while keeping his grip on my chin.

"Say it. I swear if you're lying, Aleera…" Darius didn't finish, but the warning was clear.

"Ask her and, remember, I can tell if you are lying, Tobias. You can't lie for shit," Darius told him. He then turned his gaze back to me. "Are you a virgin?"

"Yes," I blurted, closing my eyes, feeling humiliated.

"She is telling the truth, Darius," Tobias said, and Darius jerked away from me, his cock slipping out of my hand. My eyes opened to see Darius had pulled his pants up and was looking at me, horrified.

"But you've done things with guys before?" he asked. I could feel all their eyes on me. Every single one of them had their attention on me.

"No, I never even kissed anyone until I kissed Kalen, if you call that a kiss," I told him, remembering the night I took his darkness.

"Wait. Was I your first kiss? Like an actual kiss?" Darius asked though he sounded appalled.

I looked up at him and nodded.

"And when I—" He gulped and Kalen snarled.

"When you fucking what, Darius?" Kalen snarled, and Lycus growled loudly, glaring at Darius.

"I didn't think she was a fucking virgin, or I wouldn't have," Darius said, and he pinched the bridge of his nose and puffed out his cheeks while shaking his head.

"Please, tell me that wasn't the first time anyone fingered you," Darius mumbled, and Kalen jumped up, furious. I dropped my gaze, mortified that he'd just said that aloud. Lycus grabbed Kalen, pulling him down.

"You fucking jerk," Kalen spat, and his entire body trembled as Lycus wrapped his arms around him tightly.

"I have done nothing with anyone. I was saving myself for my fucking mate until I found it was you lot," I breathed while covering my face.

"You saved yourself?" Tobias and Lycus asked simultaneously, clearly shocked by my words. I nodded.

"I have done nothing besides kissing Kalen, and Darius kissed me and did what he did," I mumbled out that last part. "And I kissed Tobias," I said, hoping they would stop their embarrassing line of questioning.

"Wait, you have all kissed her?" Lycus asked, and I looked at him as he looked between the three of them. "Well, nice for someone to fucking tell me," Lycus snapped before sitting on the edge of the bed and folding his arms across his chest. It almost looked like he was pouting.

"To be fair, I wasn't really with it when she kissed me," Kalen told him, nudging him. Darius ran both hands through his hair and breathed out loudly. "Get up," he said, and I got to my feet, trying to cover myself. I looked at Ryze, and Darius followed my gaze and sighed.

"Just sleep in the bed with us. No one will touch you," Darius said.

"Darius?" Tobias said, shaking his head.

"I said no one will touch her. She wants to keep her bloody… Ryze, she sleeps in the bed," he said before biting his lip. I nodded. As long as I didn't have to suck anyone's cock, I could live with that.

"Can I have a shirt, please?" I asked. Darius's eyes ran the length of me, and he motioned toward their cupboard. I rushed in and grabbed a shirt and an extra one for Ryze. When I turned around, Darius stood in the doorway. I took a step back from him and tugged the shirt on, not liking how his eyes lingered on my breasts. When he didn't move, I went to step past him, but he grabbed my arm.

"I… I wouldn't… if I had known, I wouldn't have done it… I—" He stopped and looked away before nodding and letting me go. I was pretty sure that was his version of an apology. He stared at me, and I could see the guilt on his face. He let out a breath before stepping aside so I could pass him. I rushed past him, going to the couch and making a mini-nest out of Kalen's shirt.

I whistled, and Ryze flew over before burrowing down in it. Darius stared before shaking his head like he couldn't believe I was touching it like it was a puppy and not something that could tear us apart. Turning around, Darius wiped the blood off his chest with a wet cloth Tobias had handed him, and I stared at the bed, wondering where I was supposed to lie.

"Lie where you want," Darius said, climbing into bed.

I looked to Kalen, who patted the spot between him and Lycus. Darius was on his other side, and I figured I was safest with him and Lycus. So, I crawled in between them. Kalen pulled the blanket up, and Lycus lay stiffly beside me like he was afraid of touching me. Only to be squished against me when Tobias climbed in beside him. I sat up, trying to get comfortable, and Kalen wrapped his arm around my waist, tugging me closer while Lycus rolled on his back and placed his arm under the pillow I was using.

"I won't do anything. I can keep my hands to myself," Lycus growled. "And apparently my lips,' he added, earning a growl from Tobias.

I lay down, tucked between Lycus and Kalen. Lycus tossed his arm over me and onto Kalen, and I sank between them, enjoying their warmth and relieved my phoenix was alright.

CHAPTER 60

THE NEXT MORNING, I woke up to somebody nudging me. With a groan, I rolled to find Lycus stiff as a board next to me and looking at the ceiling. Fingers jabbing in my ribs had me turning to look at Kalen, who was also perfectly still. I yawned and rubbed my eyes, only for him to nudge me again.

"What?" I groaned, rolling on my side. Lycus whimpered behind me, and Kalen lifted his hand, jabbing it in Lycus's direction. I peered over my shoulder to see Ryze leaning down off the headboard. Ryze's head turned from side to side as he scrutinized Lycus's face. His long snake-like tongue slivered out of his beak and up the side of Lycus's face, who paled considerably as it ran across the shadow of stubble on his cheek.

I giggled at how terrified he looked. He didn't even blink like he was too scared to. The corner of his lip opened.

"Get it, get it away," he grumbled, and Ryze cawed loudly in his face. Lycus's eyes slammed shut before he peeked one open to Ryze's beak, nearly touching his nose as he leaned down.

"Ryze, leave him be. You are scaring him," I yawned, and Ryze puffed out his feathers and shuddered. I sat up only for him to jump off the headboard onto my shoulder. His talons dug painfully into my shoulder.

"We really need to cut your nails," I hissed at him.

"There is no *we* about it. I ain't holding that thing down while you go at him with scissors," Lycus hissed, now able to move without being stared down by Ryze. I rolled my eyes at their fear while Ryze snapped his beak at him, making him flinch and jump off the bed and away from him.

Kalen rolled away from me, not even willing to sit up with him sitting on my shoulder. A soft thud reached my ears as he hit the carpeted floor.

"And you're supposed to be the big scary Wraiths. Scared of my baby phoenix," I chuckled before blowing kisses at Ryze, who immediately dropped his head, pressing his beak to my lips so I could kiss it.

"I have seen them pluck the eyes out of a demon, and I mean pluck them out! With their tongue! Like a scoop of ice cream. You are bloody nuts even to touch it." Lycus shivered just as the bathroom door opened up, and Tobias stepped out. Ryze flew off my shoulder and over to him, making Kalen duck and drop to the floor, a shriek leaving him as he covered his head with his hands. Tobias grunted as his talons dug into his shoulder, and Ryze banged his beak on top of Tobias's head.

"In a minute, let me get dressed," Tobias groaned, moving around the room and finding his clothes, with Ryze perched on his shoulder. Ryze had gotten so big his tail nearly reached the floor even while perched on Tobias, who was easily six feet tall. Looking around the room, I noticed Darius wasn't there, only for him to step out of the bathroom a few seconds later with a towel wrapped around his waist.

"Good, you're awake," he said, walking out only for Ryze to nip him when he walked past. My heart leaped into my throat, but Darius waved his hand at him, shooing him.

"Control it, Aleera. I don't like them, and that is the second time this morning it has taken a chunk out of me," Darius hissed, wiping his shoulder where Ryze got him.

"He picks up on her. He knows you scare her. What do you expect?" Tobias said before opening the window that I noticed was now fixed.

"You fixed it already?" I asked.

"Magic!" Kalen said, wiggling his fingers, and I frowned before sighing and moving to the end of the bed, only for Ryze to fly over to me. This time, Lycus dropped to the floor as Ryze swooped past. Darius growled, stepping over him.

"Get a grip of yourself. It's a bloody bird," Darius snapped at him.

"Eyeballs, they eat eyeballs," Lycus growled at him.

"Nope, they eat mice mainly," Tobias said, turning around with one in his hands holding the cage. I didn't even notice that he had brought it here. He tossed the mouse, and Ryze struck and chomped it like a cobra.

"I think I am going to be sick," Kalen murmured, turning a little green. Ryze licked his beak clean before flying toward the open window, and I shrieked, knowing there were probably demons downstairs out and about.

Usually, he goes out late in the afternoon. Rushing to the window, I peered out to see a few jogging the perimeter, but he flew up onto the roof. I sighed, a breath of relief leaving me.

"Can we swap classes this morning?" Darius asked Lycus while looking over at him. Lycus's shoulders sagged, but he nodded.

"Why, where are you going?" Tobias asked him.

"In town… Aleera," Darius said, turning his finger in the air, wanting me to turn around. My brows furrowed when I saw him grip his towel, and I turned my back on him.

Lycus smirked at me, folding his arms across his chest. "What class has Aleera got this morning?" he asked.

"Mine," Tobias said.

"Swap?" Lycus asked, and Tobias growled at him.

"Why, what class has Darius got this morning?" I asked while taking some clothes Kalen had managed to retrieve for me. Tugging the shirt off over my head, I tossed it on the bed before pulling the tank top on over my sports bra, only to find them all staring at me. Lycus cleared his throat as I pulled the shorts on.

"Um, what were we talking about?" Lycus asked, and I huffed.

"What class are you taking over from Darius?" I asked, shaking my head.

CHAPTER 61

"A PRACTICE ONE," LYCUS ANSWERED.

"Then definitely not going to leave a theory class, only to have my ass set on fire for a few hours," I told him.

Tobias smiled triumphantly, like he'd just won some prize, and Lycus groaned, stalking off into the closet to get changed. Darius wandered in after him, and I got ready to head down to the mess hall when Darius came out throwing me a shoebox. I caught it, and my eyes lit up. *Finally, shoes again.* I pulled the joggers out, only for him to hand me some socks.

"You go to Lycus's class this morning," Darius said.

"But—" Tobias whined, and I snatched the socks off him.

"Shut it," Darius snapped at Tobias. I slipped the shoes on before standing up and moving toward the door, pissed off I would spend the next two hours getting burned.

"Where are you going?" Darius asked as I moved past him.

"Breakfast, where else?"

"You will eat with us from now on."

"And join your morning fuck-fest? No thanks," I told him.

"No one is fucking. I have to leave for a couple of hours. You eat with us from now on. All meals are with us. I don't want you in the mess hall," Darius said, pulling a jacket on before pecking Lycus's lips as he walked out of the closet dressed in blue faded jeans and a blacktop. Then he left.

After breakfast, I sulked the entire way down to the training fields. Glaring at Lycus's back, everyone murmured and watched me cautiously as I followed him, not willing to leave his side. Tears burned my eyes at the memory of all these men seeing me nearly wholly naked.

Lycus moved to the center and told everyone to partner up. Nobody stepped forward to partner up with me, and I thought for sure I would sit this one out.

"Aleera, you're with…" Lycus's eyes scanned around before he called Gerald over. "Gerald, with Aleera!"

I pressed my lips in a line, and he looked over at me before looking at Lycus. This fucker refused to let me serve myself. He was always on kitchen duty.

"But—" Gerald whined.

"You're with Aleera," Lycus told him, and he dropped his head and stormed over.

Everyone moved into their circles, the ones we weren't supposed to step out of, or it was instant point deduction. Too many point deductions, and it was a fail. I was obviously failing miserably in all practice classes.

"This is bullshit, Lycus. We hurt her, Darius will fucking kill us. I can't spar with her," Gerald said, motioning to me.

"You can, and you will. No repercussions. Fry her," Lycus said, and I took a step back as Gerald's eyes sparkled at me. My back hit a wall of muscle, and I glanced over my shoulder to see Lycus. He ran his hands down my arms, and I felt his magic zapping against my skin.

"You're a pyro," I murmured, feeling my skin warm.

"And electro," he murmured before I felt the urge to pull on it. I had to stamp down the desire to take it. I had tasted his power before but wasn't sure what he could do with it.

"Take it," Lycus whispered below my ear before pressing his face into my neck. His hands moved to my wrist before his fingers locked between mine.

"But Darius?" I worried.

"I wouldn't be able to give it to you without him saying so," Lycus murmured against my shoulder.

I looked at Gerald, and he tilted his head to the side. In fact, I noticed everyone staring in our direction at Lycus's closeness to me and his arms wrapped around me, his hands holding mine.

My only issue was trying not to let my white magic show, which wasn't a major issue. I only used my dark while masking my lighter side throughout school, but it had also been six years of not using magic. Yet, as I felt it caress over my skin, I gasped before squeezing his fingers slightly. His magic bled into my skin, making me gasp and warm all over; my toes curled in my shoes at the sensation as it rushed through me.

My entire body shivered, and Gerald smirked at the challenge; his smirk dropped when I smiled back at him like a Cheshire cat, and I let go of Lycus's hands. Lycus stepped back and out of the circle. He stood on the side between us, and I flexed my fingers when Gerald spoke.

"Ready, Aleera?" He laughed, and I turned my palm up, creating a fireball in my hand, molding it into the shape of an arrow. I giggled as it heated my skin, and I looked over at him to see his eyes grow wide when I felt the jolt of a zap and looked over at Lycus as electricity zapped through the flames in my hand, sizzling around the flame arrow I'd created. He nodded to me before I turned to face Gerald, letting the fire morph back into a ball, tossing my fireball in my hand.

"Oh, scary. Let's see what you got then. Sneaky Lycus," Gerald taunted, yet I couldn't get the smile off my lips, much too excited to play this game now. I laughed at his words and challenge, which he seemed amused about. In school, I had to mask how good with fire I truly was, making sure my grades were mediocre and didn't draw attention to the fact I had more power than most before I manifested. Here I didn't have to mask my strength, just my lighter side. As I turned the fireball into a lava one, my eyes gleamed with that knowledge. Gerald gulped and took a step back.

"What's your highest heat record again?" I asked him, and he folded his arms cockily because he held the highest record in the class at four thousand degrees Fahrenheit.

"Four thousand," he laughed.

"You're so fucked," I giggled, and his laughter stopped.

"What's yours then?"

"You're about to find out." I smiled before setting the ring surrounding us on fire.

CHAPTER 62

ERALD JUMPED AS THE ring around us caught fire, the heat warming us while my eyes glowed with excitement. How I had missed having magic.

"That's the best you got?" Gerald taunted. I smirked before feeling the tether to my power strengthen, morphing it before I lifted my hands out to the sides above my head before tossing them down.

The flames exploded in a cylinder-shaped wall around us. The fire flew toward the sky, higher than the castle's tallest point, and I chuckled while Gerald's mouth fell open. I couldn't see those standing outside our circle, but the murmurs at my reach with the flames had them gasping in shock.

"Pretty sure I just broke the record for highest," I giggled.

"Not the hottest," Gerald said with a cocky grin.

"How hot is cutting fire again?" I asked him.

"Yeah, right, three thousand seven hundred?" he murmured, admiring my towering wall of flames.

"I burn hotter," I whispered, and his smile fell as he looked over at me. Moving my hand, he watched as I turned my palm up before the flames burned brightly, turning purple and blue. I watched as he squinted from the harsh rays of light it emanated. Clenching my fist, the wall of fire plunged toward the earth, burrowing deep into the rock's surface. However, maintaining it on the ring's outer edge took some concentration as I cut the circle out, burning a hole through the ground and turning the rock into molten lava. It bubbled up, spewing out of the gaps as I cut a ring around us, leaving us in the center.

In contrast, lava bubbled and bled from the earth. Everyone jumped back, as did Gerald, before nearly tumbling into the gap behind him before jumping toward me.

It stopped with a twist of my wrist as I felt myself growing weaker from not having used that much power in so long. Gerald noticed my exhaustion as the lava darkened as it cooled, and he smirked.

"What's wrong, Aleera? Can't hold it long?" he chirped before shrieking as I flicked my fingers toward him and engulfed him in flames.

He danced, trying to extinguish the flames covering him as I controlled the fire enough not to touch his skin, only burning his clothes and hair. Still, the shriek of terror from him had every-one laughing as he jumped around like his ass was on fire. As he shrieked, patting himself down before rolling on the ground, my own giggles made the flames cut out, momentarily distracting me.

He stopped thrashing, only to see he wasn't burned, just very naked and looking like a hairless cat. Even his eyebrows were gone. I snickered, and Gerald glared at me.

"Pretty sure I just broke your record. Do you want another demonstration, Gerald? I'm pretty sure I can melt you down. Shall we see what you're really made of?" I challenged him.

Gerald growled and jumped to his feet, rushing toward me like an enraged rhino. Lycus stepped over the gap. I cut into the ground and into his path. He halted instantly, nearly tripping over himself in his effort not to run into Lycus's wall of muscle.

Gerald growled, glaring at me over Lycus's shoulder.

"Issue Gerald?" Lycus asked, and Gerald looked between Lycus and me before sneering and turning on his heel. He stalked off while cursing under his breath.

Lycus then turned to face me, a grin on his face. "So you're a fire element," he said, his eyes sparkling with the knowledge. That made me a little nervous because they might start questioning if I showed any ability in any other element. Lycus held his hand out, and I sighed, knowing he wanted me to give it back, or what was left of it anyway.

"I would let you keep it, but—"

"But Darius," I answered for him, and he nodded. I rolled my eyes before brushing my fingertips over his palm and giving his magic back to him. Turning around to follow him back inside, I stopped when I noticed Darius standing by the edge of the field with Tobias and Kalen. Looking over at Lycus, he shrugged.

"They came to see if you were indeed a fire element like all of us," Lycus shrugged.

"You're all fire?" I asked.

"Yes, we all have a low ability in all elements. Fire is our strongest manifestation, except for Darius. He is a dark elemental. Tobias has a few other gifts, the compulsion and his ability to tell if someone is lying. He can also manipulate a person's emotions," Lycus explained as we walked toward them.

"What about Kalen?" I asked, already knowing he could read auras.

"Fire, but he is a lot weaker, being that he is just a pure dark fae. He can also read auras better than anyone I have ever met. Tobias's twin was almost as good as Kalen at reading auras."

"Tobias's twin? The one who died?" I asked.

"What makes you think he is dead?" Lycus asked, and I shrugged.

"The way Tobias acted when I asked about him but also, I think I have seen him before," I murmured, trying to remember why I felt that way. Lycus said nothing, or maybe he wasn't allowed to answer the underlying question for that one.

"So, Kalen… besides the auras?" I asked, and he shrugged.

"He has a low manifestation in all. He seemed like he had never manifested. Maybe it was his upbringing? Although he's a strong empath which is unusual for dark fae. It makes him a better observer of emotions," Lycus said, and my brows furrowed. We stopped by Darius and the others.

"I looked through all of your records. I didn't find anything that indicated you were strong with this element or any other for that matter," Darius said. I shrugged, and he studied my face intently for a moment.

"Do you have any other gifts besides being able to harness the fire element?" Lycus asked curiously.

I cleared my throat, especially knowing Tobias was right there, and I wouldn't be able to lie without him noticing straight away. I couldn't risk questions that would let them know I was a harmony elemental. That would really grind Darius's gears if he knew I would be as strong as him with magic, possibly stronger, seeing as I still wasn't aware of the limits of my magic if given a chance to use them.

CHAPTER 63

"WHAT'S THE NEXT CLASS?" I asked, changing the subject. Darius eyed me suspiciously, and Kalen stared at me. His eyes were more around my body than on me, so I knew he was assessing my aura, making me nervous about what he was seeing. I was careful not to let it touch my lighter side, but I wasn't sure exactly how auras worked. I could feel them but not see them the way he did.

"You have a theory class with Darius," Lycus said, oblivious to the strange questioning tension surrounding us.

"Come on, we will be late," Darius said, though the look on his face never changed. I reluctantly followed him to the classroom.

When Kalen wandered into the room with me, I stopped and looked at him.

"Darius said I could join you." He smiled, bumping my shoulder and pointing to a desk next to Darius's. With a sigh, I pulled the chair out and sat in it. Kalen sat beside me.

The lecture was boring, and I felt extremely exhausted and heavy. Kalen nudged me halfway through.

"You okay?" he whispered, and I nodded, feeling sluggish.

Only a few minutes after he asked, my stomach cramped and twisted painfully. Forgetting about the shredding with my excitement of being trusted with magic earlier, it wasn't until I felt my underwear dampen that I gasped.

Moving my legs, I hoped I had imagined it. When I did, horror washed over me, and I glanced down at my jeans to find a small red stain on my inner thigh. Glancing around the room, everyone was deep into discussing whatever the heck Darius was talking about. Sweat began to bead on the back of my neck as the cramping got worse, and I felt nauseous. My chair screeched as I slid it back before running from the room.

"Aleera?" Darius snapped, but I didn't stop. Instead, I took off, wanting to get back to my old room. *Please, please, please*, I prayed before I felt my pants become saturated. The sounds of people walking in my direction had me rush into the first bathroom I came across.

I bolted into the cubicle, locked the door, and dread filled me. *How did I forget?* I felt the blood drain from my face when I found my pants completely soaked; I could feel blood trailing down my legs and filling my shoes.

For six years, I had put off the shredding, and now I knew why they said not to. Still, I had no choice. However, I regretted that now, as my feet became slippery on the tiled floor. I looked like I was bleeding to death, my blue jeans now soaked red; frantically, I started ripping toilet paper out of the holder, trying to clean it up. It was no use, and I was mortified. How would I get back to my room, and what would happen tomorrow when it was over and I started shredding my non-existent power?

Struggling to see through my blurred vision from the bloody tears I was shedding, I tried to clean the mess I was making, the tiles beneath me pooling with blood. My tears made the mess worse. It was another side-effect of shredding; our tear ducts changed. Our entire body changed for the shredding. Even my tears had turned to blood.

Giving up, I sat on the toilet. I had no idea how long I was in there, but I couldn't bring myself to open the door and have everyone see me like this. It wasn't bad enough that I was tormented daily and now had to be tortured over something I had no control over. Shame washed through me.

"She hasn't run. She wouldn't, Darius," Kalen told Darius as I heard everyone searching for me in the halls outside the bathroom. My face heated at the idea of them finding me in this state. Yet, I was in too much pain and too embarrassed to ask for their help.

I wiped my bloody tears. I knew I was smearing blood over my face, but what else could I do? The tears wouldn't stop, just like the damn shredding wouldn't. My stomach felt like it was twisting in knots. I would be stuck like this for at least the next twenty-four hours, although I wasn't sure since I had avoided this for six years on the run. If this were anything to go off, maybe, it would last longer.

"Fucking find her!" I heard Darius scream angrily at someone before hearing Tobias's voice, and my stomach dropped.

"Can anyone else smell blood?" he asked.

Darius's yelling was cut off. I listened to the bathroom door jiggle. My heart beat frantically in my ears as the door was pushed open.

I stood up, trying to find an escape, but found none when I heard it creak open all the way. I held my hand on the cubicle door. Tobias growled, and the sound was more like a savage beast.

"Get him out!" Darius snapped at someone.

"Is she hurt?" I heard Kalen ask, and my cheeks flamed when I heard one of them sniff the air.

"Aleera, I know you're in here. Open the fucking door. You don't just run out of my class," Darius growled.

"I said get him out!" Darius roared. I heard a struggle, then the door shut as Lycus was pushing who I assumed was Tobias out of the room.

My lip quivered; my vision blurred worse and tinged red.

"Aleera, open the door," Darius snarled, pulling on the handle. A sob tore out of me as I panicked, looking between the gap that went to the next cubicle over, but I was not going to fit through it.

Darius growled before kicking the door. It flew inward, and I screamed at the bang before dropping down and trying to cover myself. Blood coated the floor and me, my hands covered in it from trying to clean it up, and Darius gasped. Yet I couldn't even look up to meet his gaze. I was far too embarrassed.

"Is she alright? What is it?" Kalen asked.

I looked up to see Darius just staring at me before looking over his shoulder at Kalen, whom I couldn't see.

"She is fine. Just go," Darius told him.

"What?" Kalen asked.

"I said go. Go check on Tobias," Darius told him.

"What? No. Aleera?" Kalen stepped closer, coming into view. He gasped as he peered into the cubicle.

Darius growled at him, but Kalen pushed past him before reaching for me. I pulled my bloody hand away from him when he tried to grab it. Kalen looked over his shoulder at Darius, and I swallowed at the pitiful look they both gave me.

"Find her some fresh clothes," Darius murmured, putting his hand on Kalen's shoulder, who didn't look like he knew what to do. Hell, I didn't even know, and it was my body. Kalen nodded before rushing off.

Darius crouched down, and I looked away from him. "This is why you wanted the devil's bane. You weren't running, were you?" Darius asked. I swallowed and nodded, and he sighed.

"Come on, let's get you cleaned up," he murmured, and I looked at him, horrified at the thought of stepping out of this cubicle.

"I am not going out there. They will see me," I panicked before pressing my face into my knees. However, the tears wouldn't stop making this already gory scene worse.

Darius moved beside me before I felt his hand smooth down the back of my hair. Never in all my life had I been so embarrassed. I was just glad this didn't happen in the mess hall; I thought that was the most embarrassing thing I would face. *Oh, how wrong I was.* Darius sighed when I felt arms go underneath my legs and behind my back, making me jump and try to move away from him.

"Stop, don't. I'm bleeding all over you," I cried, flustered.

Darius ignored me and just scooped me up off the floor. "It's just blood. I'm not squeamish," he murmured, pressing his face into my neck.

I looked at the mess on the floor, knowing someone would see it when I felt his skin heat. He moved his fingers, the tiles catching on fire. The blood staining the floor evaporated and burned off the tiles before I felt the room shudder. He turned, stepping through a portal and into the bathroom attached to our rooms. He sat me on the edge of the bathtub before turning toward the shower, just as Kalen suddenly rushed in with towels and clothes before coming over to me. He cupped my face in his hands.

"It's fine, nothing to be embarrassed about," Kalen whispered before kissing my forehead when I noticed Darius started stripping his clothes off. Kalen glanced out over to him, and he bit his lip.

"Find some feminine products. Surely we have something here she can use until I can take her to town," Darius said.

Though, I doubted that. *What would an army of men do with feminine products?* Kalen rushed out and shut the door while I peered over at Darius, who stood with his briefs drenched in my blood.

Darius tested the water temperature with his hand before walking over to me; he stopped in front of me before gripping my arms and pulling me to my feet. My face heated, my skin was prickling with heat, and my stomach cramped. I hunched forward slightly, the pain unbearable, when Darius started undoing my pants' button and zip. I grabbed his hand.

"Don't. This is embarrassing enough," I muttered, but he shook my hand off, ignoring me, and I was forced to grab his shoulder when he shoved my pants down that were sticking to my skin. I hissed, feeling like I was suddenly waxed.

"Sorry," Darius murmured before gripping my panties and tugging them down. I stepped out of them, looking anywhere but at him, wishing the ground would open up and swallow me whole.

I removed my top coated in blood from crying when I felt Darius undo the zip in the middle of my sports bra, making me quickly clutch the front closed.

"Seriously? I have already seen them, just like the rest of you," he said.

I sighed before turning and tugging my arms out of it. Darius moved toward the shower and motioned for me to get in. I stepped into the shower; the warm water helped, and the floor turned red as my humiliation washed down the drain along with any dignity I had left. Darius stepped in behind me and moved the shower head higher so it sprayed toward the wall near the seating piece before sitting down on the shower recess.

He gripped my wrist, tugging me onto his lap. I tried to get off him, but he wrapped his arm around my waist, holding me in place before reaching for the soap. My stomach cramping made me squirm when I felt his hand heat against my stomach. The extra heat helped, and I leaned against him.

"You should have reminded us of the shredding. Why didn't you say anything? I would have made sure we had feminine products."

"I was going to stop it. That's why I wanted the devil's bane."

"That's how you managed while running?"

I nodded, and my body tensed as pain rippled through me, and he pushed harder on my stomach, his hand heating more.

"I will take you to town once we find something to hold you over," Darius murmured behind me. Blood trailed down his legs from me sitting on his lap, my eyes moving to the steady stream, and I tried to wash it off when he grabbed my hand, tugging it back onto my lap.

"It's fine, Aleera. It's not the first time I have been covered in blood."

I shuddered at the memory of the exploded demons and gory, bloody limbs from the mess hall when he tore apart Zac and his friends for their wandering hands. The door opened, and Lycus and Kalen came in, holding fistfuls full of cotton buds and medical supplies.

"Really, Kalen, a Band-Aid?" Darius asked, and Lycus nudged him.

"I found a wound dressing?" Lycus said, holding it up, and Darius growled at him while shaking his head.

"Find a wash cloth or something. What the heck is she going to do with a Band-Aid?" Darius said while I was too busy staring at the wall. It was sweet that they were trying to help, but they were just making an already awkward situation more embarrassing.

"Out, you are both bloody useless. Where is Tobias?"

"In the room, trying not to come in here and gobble her up," Kalen snickered.

"Out, both of you and get my car ready," Darius told Lycus, who nodded.

"You're driving into town?"

"Yes. Now, go," Darius hissed at them, and they both left.

"Do you want to come with me? I am not really sure about buying tampons. Wait, do you use tampons?" He shook his head, obviously finding this topic of conversation just as awkward.

"No. I have never shredded before," I told him, my face flushing.

"Well, we can both be clueless together then."

CHAPTER 64

EVENTUALLY, THE PAIN RIPPLING through me eased enough that I could stand without wanting to double over. Darius quickly washed while I grabbed my towel. Despite being mortified at the situation I found myself in, Darius didn't seem as horrified as I would have expected.

He wrapped a towel around his waist before removing his briefs and tossing them in the hamper. Kalen had set out some clothes for me on the counter, and I moved toward them while Darius looked below the counter, rummaging around before pulling out a face washer. He tore it in half before folding it.

"Not ideal, but it will do until I can get you to town or maybe rolled-up toilet paper?" he said, holding up the torn face washer. I nodded, my cheeks flaming. Hey, at least he was resourceful.

"Get changed. I will meet you in the room," Darius said before walking out.

It felt like I was wearing a diaper. I was paranoid that I looked like I was walking like a cowboy who'd spent the last week riding bareback across the country. Yet it worked and held in place, but I definitely wouldn't be doing any strenuous exercise with this thing stuck between my legs.

Opening the door, I froze. Tobias was sitting in the armchair by the fireplace. Ryze was lying on his chest while Tobias stroked his tummy feathers. His long tail feathers ran down his legs to the floor.

"I'm fine, Aleera. You just caught me off guard. I won't hurt you," Tobias said. Ryze, hearing him speak, rolled onto his tummy.

"I swear he thinks he is a lap cat," Tobias chuckled, and Ryze puffed out his feathers before flying over to me and perching on my shoulder. He played with my hair using his beak and made a cooing noise. Lycus and Kalen were sitting on the bed just staring at Ryze while I scratched his feathers. Darius walked out of the closet dressed in jeans and a black shirt. Ryze hissed at him as he drew closer, and Tobias tossed Darius a set of car keys.

"I don't get it. For years, you have been our keeper and never went through a shredding," Kalen murmured. Darius stopped in his tracks and blinked before raising an eyebrow at him.

"I am male and technically not your keeper. She is," Darius said, pointing to me. Ryze snapped at his pointed finger and hissed at him while I tried not to giggle at Kalen's question.

"I'm checking," Lycus said, pulling out his phone while Kalen looked over his shoulder.

"You can't be that stupid. How many times in the last six years have you seen me bleeding every six months?" Darius said with a shake of his head.

"Well, it's roughly every six months when you lock us in the room and fuck us every which way from Sunday," Lycus said.

"Ah, yeah, last time, I couldn't sit properly for a week," Kalen mumbled, earning a laugh from me. Tobias snickered before appearing thoughtful.

"Huh, that is true. He does have a point," Tobias laughed. Darius shook his head when Kalen pouted, looking over his shoulder, reading whatever Lycus was looking at.

"So it should only last a day, then you shred power. Did you know that the power shared can last a year and is at its strongest for the mates during the shredding? That it amplifies threefold?" Lycus told us. I chewed the inside of my lip when Kalen spoke.

"Shouldn't you have been keeping track of that sort of stuff?" Kalen asked, and my face flushed.

"She has never gone through it before. I was wrong the other day when I said she ran. Aleera was trying to find some devil's bane," Darius admitted, rubbing his thumb across his lip and looking at me.

Lycus nodded before looking up at him. "Yes, it says here that the root will stop the shredding if brewed and ingested." His brows furrowed before he continued. "Aleera, that stuff is still poisonous. It could have killed you if you drank too much and it has severe side effects, like delirium, vomiting, hallucinations, and a whole list of them."

"Wait, she was looking for the devil's bane? Did we hear that right? Did Darius just admit he was wrong? Shit, get your phones. We need him to repeat that so we have evidence," Lycus taunted. Darius growled before walking over to me and stopping in front of me. Ryze hissed at him.

"Stop it. I am not hurting her. Now off, so I can take her into town," Darius said, holding his arm out for Ryze to climb off. Ryze hissed, his long tongue snaking out and flicking at Darius's face, but I caressed his tummy feathers. He turned his head, pressing his beak to my lips before climbing onto Darius's arm, which surprised me.

Darius gulped and walked very stiffly toward Tobias, where Ryze jumped off him and back onto Tobias's chest. Tobias huffed at his weight landing on him. At the same time, Ryze shook himself before rubbing his feathery head all over Tobias's shirt.

When Tobias didn't scratch his feathers, he bit him, making Tobias hiss.

"Okay, bloody bird, I will scratch your damn tummy. Roll over," Tobias hissed, rubbing the spot Ryze had bitten. Darius shook his head at Ryze before walking toward me.

"Even the bloody bird gets kissed before me," Lycus mumbled, making me look over at him. Darius growled at him before his eyes moved to mine.

"Can you just kiss that idiot so he stops pouting and getting jealous of a damn bird?" Darius growled.

"I don't want no sympathy kiss, Darius. Fuck off," Lycus snarled at him, and Darius shrugged, unperturbed by Lycus's whining.

"Come on," Darius said, coming to take my elbow when Ryze shrieked, flying over to me again.

"Bird, you can't come," Darius snapped at him.

"How come we don't just portal? Wouldn't it be quicker?" I asked him, trying to get Ryze to go back to Tobias.

"Quicker, yes, but we also need to grab a few things, and I am not a pack mule. Besides, we will need to keep our reserves strong for when you shred tomorrow," Darius answered. I gasped and took a step back.

"Pardon?" I asked, and Darius stopped looking over at me.

"You will need our power to shred, Aleera."

"You will give me power?" I asked, and everyone stared at Darius, shocked. Darius said nothing, just looked between us all before raking his hand down his face.

"Can we just go?" Darius said. However, I now had something else to worry about. If Darius allowed me to shred, there was no way I would be able to hide what I was. That scared me the most. My mother always told me to keep what I was hidden, and shredding would be doing the opposite.

"Ryze, you can't come," Darius told him, and Ryze hissed at him, refusing to get off. I tried passing him to the others, but Lycus and Kalen nearly jumped out of their skin when I offered Ryze to them. Darius shook his head, and Tobias got up and walked over to me.

"Come, I will take him downstairs. He probably wants to go fly," Tobias said, following us out. Kalen and Lycus also followed but kept their distance from Ryze, who was quite antsy inside the castle. He flew off my shoulder and out of a window, and I sighed.

We made our way downstairs when I heard screeching, and my eyes widened. I took off running for the doors, missing a few steps in my haste.

CHAPTER 65

RUSHING THROUGH THE DOORS, I could see Ryze perched in a tree, and two men stood below it, trying to hit him with a fireball. I gasped in horror and ran over to stop them when Tobias came up behind me.

"You touch that fucking bird, and it will be the last thing you ever do," Tobias yelled to them, and they both stopped and looked over their shoulders at him. Tobias looked furious, and Darius wandered out.

"But it's a phoenix," one said.

"That bird is off-limits. Now, go!" Darius snapped, coming up behind me while I raced over to the tree and looked up to see not only one but another higher up. It looked older, and I was surprised they didn't notice it among the orange-red leaves of the tree as it tried to blend in. Darius talked to the men, and Ryze flew down before Darius yelled out to me.

"Aleera, no!" he said, making me look over at him. Ryze dropped onto my shoulder, his weight knocking me forward onto my knees. My eyes went to my mates, who were all frozen. Ryze rubbed his head and beak onto the back of my head, checking to see if I was alright, when suddenly the tree came to life.

What I thought were leaves were actually feathers, and about ten huge phoenixes suddenly dropped on the ground around me. They were towering over me, and these weren't juvenile ones; they had the power to rip me to shreds and tear me apart if they chose to. Everyone froze as the birds surrounded me, and even I shook, terrified, when I saw all four of my mates' hands begin to glow. My eyes widened when I saw they were about to attack the birds. Horror washed over me at the danger I was in but also fear for these beautiful creatures.

Ryze, playing with my hair, squawked, and the birds backed up a little. I threw my hand up. "Stop!" I screamed to Darius as he went to blast them with magic. My heart beat like a drum in my ears, pounding loudly as I moved slowly.

"They won't hurt me," I called to them before slowly standing up so I didn't spook the birds and make them attack me. I hoped what I said was true because I could see their curious gazes watching me. Phoenixes were lethal birds. Standing, they were nearly taller than me. The recruits that watched approached us, and I could see the hunger on their faces, eager to rip the birds apart and absorb their power.

"Don't let them hurt them," I murmured, watching the recruits grow nearer, and Darius glanced around, also noticing we had drawn a crowd. One of the phoenixes turned its head, observing Ryze perched on my shoulder, his feathery tail wrapping around my body like a snake. Ryze hissed at them.

I scratched his tummy feathers, and my breathing became ragged when one hopped closer. Lycus moved, and Kalen's head tilted to the side, observing me. His hand smacked into Lycus's chest. My hand shook as I held it out to the phoenix, and the other ones drew nearer.

The phoenix's tongue flicked out. I felt a jolt sliver up my arm, making me jerk my hand back to realize it was giving me power, a small jolt of its energy. My eyes widened. I had never seen so many phoenixes in one place before when Kalen gasped. I could feel the bird's magic writhe through me and mingle with my white magic.

"They won't hurt her," Kalen murmured, his head tilting from one side to the other. Darius, Tobias, and Lycus looked at him as if he was insane. My heart pounded, wondering what he saw when the phoenix exchanged power with me. I swallowed, hoping he wouldn't out me to the rest of our mates who didn't notice the small exchange, but Kalen, I knew, would have seen it in my aura.

"Call them off, Darius," Kalen said, looking over at him.

"They will rip her to shreds," Darius hissed at them.

"I said call them off. I don't ask for much, Darius, but you will do this for me, for her. Call them off, and tell them to leave her birds alone," Kalen growled, glaring at him.

"She can't keep them all," Darius hissed. Lycus paled as he, too, looked questionably at Kalen, who wasn't giving anything away.

"That isn't up to you. It's up to them. Now, call your recruits off," Kalen repeated, and I had never seen him look so determined.

"Take them to the roof," I whispered to Ryze, who screeched at the other phoenixes. The other birds all watched him, and some drew nearer trying to touch me, their feathers bumping against my legs when Ryze flew off my shoulder, and they took flight after him.

The demons went crazy, and power was suddenly hurled their way as they took to the air. I screamed when suddenly Tobias and Darius moved as if in sync and raised their hands. The fireballs smashed into a shield beneath the birds.

"No one touches them," roared Darius furiously at them. "Anyone who does will suffer the same fate you bestow on those phoenixes, are we clear?"

I swallowed and looked toward the roof where the phoenixes were perched, watching us. Kalen rushed toward me, wrapping his arms around me and tugging me closer. He let out a breath, and I watched the demons scatter away from Darius's furious anger.

"Thank you," I murmured to Kalen. Lycus turned to make his way over to us when Kalen looked at me.

"I know what you are," he said, barely audible. I gasped, looking at him over my shoulder. Kalen pressed his head against mine and kissed my cheek.

CHAPTER 66

KALEN SIGHED. "I KNEW there was another reason you ran, but you don't need to hide from us. We would have kept you safe," he whispered.

I glanced at my other three mates, who were making sure the demons left the phoenixes alone. "You can't say anything," I whispered, my heart jolting erratically.

"I won't right now, but you have to tell Darius. He will—" Kalen's words were cut off when Lycus approached.

"That was some of the scariest shit I have ever seen. I thought for sure your eyes were gonna go," Lycus said, then shivered. "I can't believe they didn't attack you."

"Probably because Ryze took a liking to her. They are smart birds," Kalen told him, giving me a knowing look.

"Well, I am not catching mice for all of them. They catch their own damn food," Tobias hissed while Darius stood between us and the castle. He looked between the birds and me, his face taking on a strange expression.

"Come on, we should go. I want to get back before dark," Darius said when I noticed the sleek black sports car parked ou

"You will make sure they don't hurt them?" I asked Tobias when he stopped in front of me. He gripped my chin, pecking my lips.

"Your devil birds will be fine, promise," he chuckled, and I nodded. He let my chin go, and I felt Kalen bury his face in my neck. He pulled my tablet from his pocket, and I looked at Darius, who said nothing but nodded, so I took it from him.

"Please, don't try to run," Kalen whispered into the crook of my neck. I never had a chance to answer him when Darius called out, having unlocked his car.

"Aleera, come on," he said, waving me toward him. Kalen unwrapped his arms from around my waist and gave me a push toward the car. Yet I got that same sweeping feeling from Kalen when I first met him. That fragile state, warning bells saying he wasn't okay. Even Lycus looked at Kalen worriedly, picking up the strange sensation. We all could feel the darkness enveloping him, and I paused midway.

He thought I would run now that he knew, yet he wouldn't say anything to them. Moving toward him, I grabbed his face and pulled it down toward mine while I stood on my toes. I pressed my lips to his and kissed him. His lips were warm and soft, and Kalen clutched me to him. His strong arms squeezed me tight, and he let out a shaky breath. When I pulled away, Lycus stepped closer to him with a worried look and gripped his shoulder.

"I'll be right back," I told Kalen. He looked down at me and searched my face for a few moments. Then he let out a breath, pressing his forehead to mine and nodding before letting go.

"Promise?" he whispered.

"I promise. I won't leave you again," I told him, and he smiled sadly.

"What's gotten into you? You were fine a few seconds ago?" I heard Lycus ask him as I stepped away. Lycus wrapped his arms around Kalen's waist and rested his chin on Kalen's shoulder.

When I reached the car, Darius was watching Kalen worriedly. "He's worried I will run," I told Darius, and his jaw clenched as he turned his head to look at me. He glanced down at the tablet in my hands but didn't say anything or try to take it from me.

"I wouldn't allow that," Darius said, looking like he wanted to go to Kalen. I looked over at Kalen, and Tobias was also walking toward him.

"I know, but I don't think I could leave him again," I whispered, and Darius looked at me.

"You wouldn't try again?"

"No, not without a good reason, Darius and if I did, I'm sorry, but I'd be taking Kalen with me," I answered honestly. He watched me curiously.

"You can't hurt him, can you? Or you wouldn't anyway," Darius said while watching me closely.

"It took you all this time to realize that?" I asked before opening up the passenger door and climbing in.

I slid into my seat and buckled up, and the door opened a few minutes later as Darius climbed in. He looked over at me like he wanted to say something before shaking his head and starting the engine. I watched when suddenly a driveway appeared in front of us. The grass covering it dissolved, revealing the road that led toward the treeline. I closed my eyes when Darius floored it. Peeking my eyes open, I tensed, thinking we were about to smash into the trees. Darius chuckled, and I gasped when the glamor lifted, revealing a long road that weaved through the forest. We drove along it for a while before pulling up at the gates. Darius hit a button on the visor and waited for the huge gates to open.

"Mirage ward," Darius laughed and shook his head. Looking down, I stared at the blackened screen of my tablet and tried to turn it on, but it was dead. Darius leaned across, opening the glove compartment before pulling out some cords.

"One of them should fit," he said before pointing to the USB socket in the dash.

"Thanks," I said while finding the right one so I could plug it in and turn it on. Darius nodded, turning his eyes back to the road, and we continued to drive in a strange silence. After a few minutes, my tablet turned on, and Darius peeked over at me.

"You messaging your friend?" Darius asked, and I chewed my lip, wondering if he was mad.

"That bothers you," I stated.

He sighed and looked over at me. "When we get into town, just stay close. Don't wander off."

"Okay," I said, glancing down at the screen, wondering why he was being weird.

"No, I mean it, Aleera. Stick close to me. There is a reason I don't allow my mates to leave the castle. It's not safe. So, stay close to me," Darius said.

My brows furrowed, and I looked over at him. "Why are you letting me come with you then?"

"Because I don't know the first thing about lady products, and secondly..." He paused and sighed. "I wanted to apologize. Figured you would want to get out of the castle for a little bit. Kalen said it would be good for you to get out of that place for a while."

I chuckled and shook my head. "You can't hurt Kalen either," I laughed.

"None of us can. Kalen is... He is—"

"Special," I offered, and he bit his lip and nodded.

"He is our glue. Kalen is the reason we all held together the way we have," Darius answered, and I nodded.

CHAPTER 67

HE TOWN WASN'T THAT far from the castle. It only took roughly twenty minutes to drive there. The time seemed to fly by as I was busy talking to my internet friend. When Darius pulled into a parking spot out the front of a grocery store that was part of a small shopping complex, he got out and walked to my side. The place was bustling with shoppers as I glanced around.

The moment I stepped out of the car myself, Darius was already at my side before I had even shut the door. He grabbed my hand, and I glanced down at my hand when he laced his fingers through mine before raising an eyebrow at him.

"Don't argue. I want you close," he said, glancing around almost anxiously, which I thought odd. He led me to a small post office first before pulling a key from his pocket and unlocking a mailbox.

"You don't get your mail at the castle?" I asked him.

"Nobody can find it. It's hidden," he said, placing the mail in his back pocket. He dragged me to a few different places, including a pharmacy where he picked up prescriptions for Kalen, and I was surprised to see how many different pills Kalen took. When we were done there, Darius pulled me to the grocery store.

I did, however, notice that anyone who stepped near or in our path quickly scattered. The pharmacy completely emptied of people when Darius entered, leaving only the pharmacist who was familiar with Darius. The grocery store was the same, except even a few of the workers scurried off.

"Do you always get such a warm welcome?" I whispered.

"It has its benefits. Never have to wait in line," Darius chuckled while stepping closer to me and placing his hand on my hip so I was pretty much tucked under his arm. He led me to an aisle that contained feminine products, and both of us stood there like idiots.

"Please, tell me you know which ones to buy," Darius murmured. I picked up one of the colored boxes to read it, and so did Darius.

"What, they couldn't make it one size fits all?" he said, picking up a couple of boxes of pads while I picked up some tampons.

"One size fits all?" I asked him, shaking my head.

"Yeah, why are they different sizes, and how do you know what size to buy?" he asked, holding up two different ones. This was the most bizarre experience of my life and not one I ever pictured doing with Darius.

"Just go with the regular?" I told him, and he looked at the box in my hand.

"You are not using those. You can die if you forget it is in there," Darius said, placing it back on the shelf.

"Huh?"

"Lycus said something about some syndrome."

"Toxic shock syndrome?" I offered.

"That's the one. Stick with the less-lethal kind," Darius said.

I shook my head at his words. Darius grabbed a few different boxes, putting them in his basket. "You know it only lasts twenty-four hours, right? I don't need all those," I told him.

"What if they are uncomfortable?" he said, and I just let him go, letting him steer me toward the next aisle. His basket was full by the time we were done, and he escorted me to the register. The entire time, Darius kept glancing around nervously when his phone pinged, and he got a text message. He pulled his phone from his pocket. Looking at it, he sighed. He looked around for a second before looking behind him.

"I will be right there. Put the rest of the stuff up. If anyone speaks to you, scream," Darius said, wondering off about three meters away to some confectionery stand. I placed the contents out with a sigh before putting the basket back beside the register when the man behind the register spoke.

"Never seen you in here before with Darius Wraith. Family member?" he asked while scanning another item and placing it in the bag before looking at me. *Surely Darius didn't mean to scream if the teller spoke to me.*

Before I could answer, though, Darius put some chocolate bars on the register. "Her mate, so eyes down." Darius sneered at him. My face flushed; the poor guy only asked an innocent question. The man dropped his gaze and quickly started scanning.

"Why are you so nervous?" I asked Darius when I noticed him looking around again.

"Because you're with me," he said before stopping as he stared out the window at something, cutting off what he was about to say.

"So?" I asked, and he looked down at me.

"Usually, I don't bring Kalen or Lycus in here without Tobias. I should have brought someone else with me. You're too exposed," he said, and my brows furrowed.

"Exposed to what?" I asked, looking around at the empty store before turning my gaze to the man serving us. He smiled at me before dropping his head when Darius's hand fell on my shoulder as he tugged me back against him, wrapping his arm around my waist.

"You won't like it if I have to warn you again about looking at her. Fucking do your job," Darius growled. He scanned faster while my face flushed at how rude Darius was to him.

Getting to the car, Darius placed everything in the trunk before walking me to my side of the door and waiting for me to get in before walking to the driver's side.

When he got in, he put a chocolate bar on my lap, and I stared at him.

"Lycus said you would crave sweet stuff?"

I shrugged before opening it. *What girl turns down chocolate? Not this one, that's for sure.* "Exactly why is Lycus googling about keepers' shredding?" I asked him.

"Because I asked him to," Darius said, starting the car.

"And did you have to be so mean to that poor guy? He looked like he was about to wet his pants the second time you snapped at him," I told him, biting into the chocolate bar.

"He is a vampiric fae, Aleera."

"So?"

Darius tilted his head to look at me before looking at my lap. "Remember Tobias when I found you?" Darius asked, and my smile fell. My face heated, remembering how crazed he became.

"Exactly, I don't want him taking a bite out of what is mine," Darius said, pulling onto the road before slamming on the brakes. I lurched forward in my seat and nearly smashed into the dash when Darius's hand flung out, shoving me back before I head-butted it. My breathing ragged when a dark-haired middle-aged man walked out in front of the car.

Chapter 68

*D*ARIUS GROWLED, AND THE man just stared through the windshield at us for a second before walking off and watching us leave. I shook my head and turned to Darius, who was watching the man in the rear vision mirror.

"I need to get you home," he muttered.

"Gosh, he came out of nowhere."

"They always do," Darius muttered, and I peered over at him, wondering what he meant. He never elaborated on his words but kept glancing in all the mirrors as he drove. Finishing my chocolate bar, I pouted, and Darius laughed.

"I got you more in the bag in the trunk," Darius chuckled. We were about ten minutes from home and had been driving on a backroad for about five minutes already.

"Maybe Lycus was right about that one," I said before suddenly everything exploded, and I was tossed forward in my seat. One minute we were driving; the next, we crashed into a wall.

The front of the car smashed into a shield. The windows exploded on impact, and I remembered the sound of groaning metal and felt the glass rain shards on my face before everything went black.

Dazedly I blinked to find the car upside down on the roof. I groaned, my head throbbing, and I stupidly unclipped my belt, falling headfirst onto the roof lining. Blood trickled down my face as I tried to see what had happened when I noticed Darius hanging limply from his seat. Blood gushed from a massive gaping wound across his forehead.

"Darius?" I called, shaking his arm, but he was unconscious. Crawling out of the wreck, glass stabbed into my hands. I stumbled over to his side and opened the door. I kept trying to wake him, but he was knocked out and bleeding profusely. I unclipped his seat belt, worried about a car slamming into us, and he fell from his seat with a groan. The smell of gas filled the air, and I shook him, trying to rouse him awake.

"Darius!" I hissed nervously, looking around for what we had run into, but I found nothing besides the clearing, the forest, and a clear road ahead.

Grabbing his arms, I pulled him out, dragging him to the side of the road to a small clearing among the trees before fumbling in his pockets for his phone. Then a thought came to me. *I could run!* Yet as I looked at Darius unconscious and thought of the others back home, I dismissed the idea before clutching my head that throbbed as if someone had smashed it with a sledgehammer.

My vision blurred as I tried to unlock his phone to call one of the others when I heard a series of whooshing noises. Blinking, I tried to clear my vision. The shimmer of portals glistened in the distance, blobs of black spilling out. A gasp escaped my lips when I heard the snarls, and my head twisted around to see twenty different portals suddenly open up in the clearing and on the road.

"Darius!" I screamed, shaking him when I recognized what they were. *Hellhounds.* They charged at us. I screamed, shaking Darius as they drew closer, trying to wake him. Darius groaned, and they got about twenty feet away. I panicked, crawling on top of him. My lips smashed against his.

Their feral snarls sent shivers up my spine, their black furless huge bodies bounding toward us, all sharp teeth and massive claws leaping our way. Darius's magic slammed into me like a tidal wave, stealing the air from my lungs. It was so cold, like ice, as I consumed it, taking it from him.

It writhed in my veins, and I choked, ripping myself away, unable to consume anymore. A scream tore out of me as four hellhounds pounced on us, about to rip us to pieces. My ears rang from the commotion as I tossed my hands out, slamming them on the ground on either side of us and shut my eyes, waiting for my death when I jolted. The movement rattled my pounding head as the hellhounds collided with the force field I'd created.

The huge beasts growled, trying to find a way past it, when I pushed the walls higher, creating a crystal-clear dome around us. Their massive bodies collided with it, trying to break through. Each hit weakened me as I tried to hold the barrier in place.

Sweat beaded on my neck and dripped off my face; everything ached and cramped at the exertion it took. Digging my hands into the earth, vines started wrapping around the dome as it splintered from the repeated blows.

The vines grew with thorny branches encasing the dome, and the hellhounds snarled louder. The trickling sensation running down my face told me I wouldn't hold it much longer when my nose started bleeding, my blood dripping onto Darius's chest, where I hovered above him while praying for him to wake.

If he didn't soon, I would pass out from using so much magic at once, yet they kept tearing into the vines, ripping them down as quickly as I replaced them. The magic it took to hold them back started running low and faltering when I felt warm hands grip my waist and move under my shirt to my ribs. My eyes flew open to see Darius staring wide-eyed at me, his obsidian eyes watching my face.

"You're a harmony," he whispered before looking at the crystal and vine dome surrounding us. "And an elemental."

At that moment, I felt his hands heat as he gave his magic to me, replenishing it more and trying to keep me strong.

"I can't hold it!" I said through gritted teeth. My vision turned red as I blinked through bloody tears. I could taste my blood running into my mouth from my nose.

"Hold it a second longer," Darius said before moving one hand off my waist and placing it over his mark. I felt a shudder run through me, and the infinity mark on my wrist burned as he used his to call the others.

"Darius!" I cried, digging my fingers into the earth further as black dots danced before my vision, and I felt the dome start crumbling around us. Darius growled when I crashed against his chest. His arms wrapped around me, and he rolled, flipping me onto my back as the walls keeping us safe started to crumble.

"Good girl, but now I need you to remain still," Darius murmured, and I blinked up at him dizzily when he growled. His eyes glowed so brightly, they almost turned silver. His hands hit the ground next to my head, and the noise was horrendous.

The ground was lifting in a wave all around us, and his car alarm started blaring. My head fell limply to the side, and I saw the hellhounds suddenly become air-born and blast backward. The ground split around us as Darius's wave of power made the ground shake and move, sending them flying back. I blinked, trying to remain conscious as my vision blurred.

"Stay with me, Aleera," I heard Darius call out as the sound of portals opening up reached my ears. Heat engulfed me as firewalls suddenly encased us. The sound of pained whimpers pierced through the air and the dots taking over my vision grew larger before taking my sight completely and leaving me blind to my surroundings.

"Darius?"

"Right here with you, you're safe with me," he said above me though his voice sounded muffled, and I tried to nod but couldn't fight the exhaustion as it sucked me under. "I got you."

Those were the last words I heard before plunging into nothingness.

CHAPTER 69

Darius

MY MIND WAS SPINNING as I held the hellhounds off. One stupid mistake nearly cost her life; I should never have taken her out of the castle grounds without the others. I was most shocked that she could have drained me of my power and portalled out and run, leaving me, but she stayed to protect me. I knew something was off about her, but never in my wildest dreams did I think she was harmony fae and elemental on top of that. Not for one second did I ever entertain that idea; she shouldn't exist. Aleera would be a lethal weapon if appropriately trained.

Why would she keep it from us? We would have protected her. However, it made so much sense now why her parents tried to kill her.

"Aleera, stay with me, love," I called to her as my magic faltered after getting hit with a blast of air. I scanned my surroundings as my flame wall suddenly encased us, and I barely covered her body with mine in time to stop the flames from burning her before reinforcing them again.

Come on, Tobias, where are you? I thought just before I felt his presence getting close. Lycus's presence also felt near as my mark stopped burning. Kalen was not here, and I wondered what they did to subdue him to force him to remain home. I knew that man would walk through fire for her. We all would. Whimpers and shouting could be heard all around, yet the shudder against my shield as they bounced off it told me they would get to her if I dropped it.

"Tobias, behind you!" Lycus called out before I heard him grunt. Panic made me drop the shield to find him fighting with the man from town, the same man that walked out in front of my car. There was a vicious snarl as the hellhounds lunged at us, ripping me back to my surroundings and forcing me to drop the shield. My body covered Aleera's head to shield her, expecting the hellhounds to sink their teeth into her any second, yet my thoughts were interrupted by the fierce sounds of flesh being ripped from bone and a mighty furious roar.

Lycus's giant wolf gripped its neck in his powerful jaws, ripping the hellhound back at the last second and slamming it on the ground before he shook his head, ripping out the beast's throat and spraying himself and me in blood. Looking around, I noticed he and Tobias had taken out the others, and the only person left was the man Tobias was fighting. *Fool. Sneaking up on him would have been smarter in case he ran.* Tobias plunged his hand through the man's chest, and his entire body became engulfed in flames. His screams drilled into my ears.

"Idiot," I muttered, thinking his puny air magic was no match for a fire user. Tobias ripped his hand out, leaving the man's burning corpse to fall at his feet. The hellhounds put up more of a fight.

Tobias ran over to us. Lycus's big black wolf also came over, sniffing and licking my face. I pushed his head away, lifting my body from Aleera's unconscious one. He sniffed her, licked her cheek, and nudged her before whimpering when she didn't wake. Tobias came over and ran his hand down Lycus's back.

"She will be okay. Let us get her home," Tobias told him, and Lycus whined while I bundled her up in my arms. Blood trickled from her nose, ears, and eyes from using my magic. The amount she used told me she had never harnessed that much at once. Being an elemental, magic should come easy to her unless she hadn't used it. Tobias walked over to the car, and Lycus shifted back to give him a hand as they pushed it back on its wheels. The car banged and bounced as it was turned back upright.

"She has seen better days," Tobias muttered at my ruined car before he pushed it off to the side of the road. Lycus retrieved the stuff from the trunk and our belongings from the vehicle.

"Yep, need another one now," Lycus hummed.

"The car is replaceable. Lives aren't," I told them, and they nodded before Lycus flicked his fingers at it, setting it on fire. Tobias opened a portal, and I groaned as I staggered toward it with Aleera in my arms. Tobias came to take her from me, but I pulled away, unwilling to let her go, and he looked at me questionably.

"She saved my life. She could have run, but she didn't."

"Goes to show how wrong you were about our girl," Tobias chuckled.

"We were all wrong. She is an elemental harmony fae," I told him, and the shock on his face was apparent.

Lycus chuckled. "Yeah, right, there is no harmony left, and what would be the chances of finding a harmony that was also an elemental? Impossible?"

I stared at him, and he looked at Tobias, who nodded to him that I was telling the truth.

"What?" Lycus stuttered.

"Aleera is an elemental harmony fae. She took my magic and protected me while I was out. I woke up to her above me holding them off," I told him.

"Fuck!" Lycus cursed, and so did Tobias. This meant the war we were fighting to protect her had more meaning; now, the stakes were higher. If anyone found out about her, she would have an entire world of fae after her. It was bad enough that I was stuck for years, going through tests to recreate the elemental status until I said no more. Not like they could force me when I could melt their insides with a click of my fingers. However, with Aleera, no amount of fear for what she could do would stop the council from coming for her.

Stepping through the portal, I found Kalen shackled by Lycus magic. If looks could kill, we would all be dead for forcing him to remain behind. Tobias flicked his fingers in his direction as we stepped into our room, releasing him from the hold of Lycus's magic. The moment he was released, he stood up and punched Tobias.

"How fucking dare you!" Kalen snarled at him while Tobias rubbed his jaw before grabbing his throat. Lycus flopped on the bed, and I turned my attention back to Tobias, who pressed his lips against Kalen's.

"I will let that slide, but don't push me, Kalen. It's unsafe for you," Tobias growled before tugging him closer and embracing him. Kalen's eyes went to Aleera in my arms as he tried to escape Tobias, who sighed, releasing him so he could rush over to take her from me.

He hugged her close, burying his face in her neck and laying her beside Lycus. "You gave her magic?" he asked, and I knew he was assessing her aura when a thought occurred to me.

"You knew she was a harmony fae, didn't you?"

Kalen growled but nodded. "I noticed earlier when one of the phoenixes power-shared to her." He said it so matter-of-factly, like he hadn't kept it from us.

"You didn't think to say something?"

"Not my place to say. I figured she would tell you when she trusted you," Kalen said, leaning down and kissing her before adjusting her on the bed so her head was resting on Lycus's shoulder.

"She needs magic, Darius. She won't run," Kalen said, looking over at me.

"I know. She could have, but she didn't," I told him, lifting my shirt to find a piece of the door trim stabbed into my side. Tobias hissed as I groaned, ripping the piece of metal out before his hand covered the wound as he tried to heal me.

"Save it. I will heal on my own. Save it for Aleera," I groaned, sitting down and holding my hand to the side to stem the bleeding as I waited for it to heal. We all kind of sat around in silence, everyone shocked at what we learned when Ryze flew in the window and shrieked as he landed on the windowsill.

Chapter 70

$\mathcal{B}$LOODY BIRD, SHE IS fine," I told him, and he flew over to perch on the headboard. He leaned down, looking at her and licking her cheek, caressing it with his beak while Lycus remained frozen, only for Ryze to lick his temple. I snickered when he paled.

"Having a taste test for when he plucks those eyes of yours out?" Tobias chuckled before whistling to Ryze, who flew over but instead of going to Tobias, he perched on the arm of my chair, looking down at my bleeding wound before looking at Aleera and back at me.

"She is fine. You bite me, I will smack your damn ass," I told him while he eyed me with his creepy beady eyes. He then took off out the window, and we all relaxed; that was only momentarily because he came back but with the big fucker that we thought would kill Aleera. My fingertips fizzled as it squeezed through the window and everyone froze to see what it would do.

It hopped down on the ledge, walking across the carpet like an oversized fucking chicken, its long tail still outside the window when it stopped beside me. Its eyes roamed over me, and Ryze cawed at it, nudging the other phoenix, who tilted its head to the side. They were such intelligent birds, but they scared the crap out of me.

Its beak opened, and its long tongue slivered out split at the end. Going in two different directions, I leaned back, wondering what it wanted, and my eyes darted to Tobias. When its tongue suddenly zapped my hand, the buzz of its magic shot up my arm, making me jump. Then it spoke.

"Welcome," it said, and I gasped before my side heated.

The phoenix then turned and jumped back out the window, and Ryze jumped up to perch on the armchair, nudging my side with his beak. Looking down, I found my wound closed, and my mouth fell open.

"Lira..." Ryze tried to speak before sneezing. He was still too immature to pronounce words. I knew they could talk but had never actually witnessed one speak. Then again, I tried to avoid the bloody things, too.

"That big bastard spoke, right?" Lycus pointed to Ryze, and I nodded.

"Now we know why we suddenly have an infestation of phoenixes. They sense the white fae. They sense their own magic," I told him, looking at Aleera, who was passed out still.

Ryze flew over to her, sitting beside her and resting his head and neck on her hip like he was some kind of lap cat wanting cuddles from its mother.

"I need to shower," I groaned, getting up and walking to the bathroom. I showered quickly when the sounds of arguing reached my ears.

"Of all the days they want to argue, it has to be now," I muttered, wrapping a towel around my waist and shoving the door open.

"No, you're doing it wrong. It has to go the other way," Lycus says, and I noticed Ryze was gone, and they were huddled together arguing over something.

"How does it stick, though? It says it will stick. And where are these wing things?" Tobias said, showing Lycus something on his phone while Kalen held a pair of Aleera's panties, and Lycus was holding up some of the pads.

"What the fuck are you doing?" I asked, walking over to them.

"She was bleeding through her pants. We tried to wake her," Kalen said, and I glanced at her. *Fuck. Probably from using so much of my magic before she shredd*ed. I peered at what they were watching on the phone—some YouTube tutorials.

"Ah, we have to peel the back thing off," Lycus said, turning the pad between his fingers.

"Now what?" he said, and Kalen leaned over to peer at the screen. I shook my head, snatching her panties and the pad from Lycus's hand.

"Bloody morons," I growled before placing it in the underwear and folding the wings over the sides.

"Have you used them before?" Kalen asked, and I raised an eyebrow at him.

"Common sense, fool," I growled at him.

"Now, how do we put it on her while she is passed out?"

"We could always lay a tarp under her," Lycus said, and Tobias snickered.

"What? We could. Then we won't have to worry about her freaking out if she wakes up while we're undressing her." I shook my head before walking over to her to remove her jeans. "Get me a cloth," I told them, quickly cleaning her and placing the panties on her. I tucked the blanket around her, and Tobias climbed under the blanket, tucking her close. Standing up, Kalen and Lycus were staring at me.

"What?" Tobias rolled his eyes.

"Darius cared for his mother for years. Stop staring at him like that," Tobias snapped at them.

"Granted, my mother wasn't a keeper, so I never had to deal with her shredding. But it was pretty much the same thing, so stop staring at me," I growled. Kalen shook his head before climbing in bed beside Tobias.

"We know that. It's just odd seeing you caring for her. Almost feels like you had a brain transplant," Lycus snickered.

"Shut up," I told him, going to get changed.

"You think it was the council that time," Tobias called out.

"Who else would it be?" I told him.

"Her parents," he said.

"We masked her."

"Yes, until she used Lycus's magic earlier, it would have been like a beacon for some with those particular gifts."

I mulled over his words. We had been hunting her parents since they tried to kill her; now we knew why they did it. Walking out, I stopped at the end of the bed.

"We have an entire army. I won't let them touch her," I told him.

"But if she knows they're alive, what if she goes looking for them?" Tobias said, brushing his hand down her cheek.

"She won't. We are her mates," Kalen whispered.

"But after everything?" Lycus murmured worriedly. I bit the inside of my lip.

"She wasn't the only one who lost everything, Lycus," I told him. Although, I now felt even worse after she saved me. She saved me despite everything I had forced her to endure.

CHAPTER 71

Aleera

PAIN RADIATED THROUGH MY stomach, so I rolled over, only to be invaded by Lycus's scent. A hand moved across my stomach, heat radiating out of it, and I sighed as the pain eased. I glanced over my shoulder to see Darius pressed against me. Darius kissed my shoulder while his thumb brushed my stomach gently. He tugged me closer, so I was flush against him, his entire body heating like my very own personal hot water bottle.

"It's late. You should try to go back to sleep," Darius murmured. However, I wasn't sure I could sleep knowing he was lying beside me. It kind of put me on edge, yet I was reluctant to move away.

"What happened to the hellhounds?" I asked, confused. I had no memory of returning here or anything since I passed out.

"Nothing. Tobias and Lycus got to us in time," Darius said. The memory of teeth and claws trying to get to us made me cringe. Shivering, I jammed my feet between Lycus's legs in an attempt to warm them. Lycus hissed at how cold they were when I realized I had no pants on. I lifted the blanket and peered under it. To find I only had underwear and one of their shirts on.

"I changed you. You bled through your pants," Darius whispered behind me. My face heated at that thought before shaking it off. I had literally bled on his lap in the shower, and he didn't seem fazed.

"Geez, your feet are freezing, " Lycus hissed before wiggling a little closer and rubbing my thighs and the back of my legs with his hands, trying to warm them. My heart raced with their closeness, yet the bond soared, enjoying their skin against mine. It took everything in me not to reach out and bury my face in Lycus's neck or climb on him. Yet I didn't want to move away from my demon hot water bottle either, especially not now that he was being nice.

"Move closer, Lycus. She wants your scent," Darius said, and I peered at him over my shoulder.

"Demonic fae, love. I'm part incubus. So, I can sense your desire and what you're craving."

I thought over his words and turned back to see Lycus smile slyly.

"I have no issues being all nice and close," Lycus said, his eyes flickering under the dim light from the open fireplace.

Lycus pressed his chest against mine, his entire body touching, and I slid my leg between his, melting against him, suddenly not caring if I looked needy. I just wanted his skin and Darius's heat.

"Go to sleep, Aleera. You're safe with us," Darius whispered.

"You're not mad?" I asked him.

"Mad that our keeper is one of the most powerful faes in the world? Never but now we know we need to take extra precautions," Darius whispered behind me.

His sudden change since the other day was giving me whiplash, and some part of me wondered if he was only being nice because he wanted my non-existent power or because he now knew he owned the ultimate weapon, one he could use to his benefit.

"What's wrong?" Lycus asked, and I opened my eyes to see him staring at me.

"Nothing," I whispered, and I saw his eyes dart to Darius before I pushed my face into Lycus's neck, only to hear him start purring.

The sound soothed my soul as I melted against them while Darius's heat bled through me like my own personal heat pack. I sighed, closing my eyes and snuggling between them, enjoying it for now because no doubt they would probably go back to hating me when I was no longer shredding and of no use to them. So, for now, I would enjoy the bond and worry about its withdrawal when it happened. I knew I would pay dearly for letting them get this close. The withdrawal from the bond would be pure agony, yet I ignored common sense, instead giving into it for once.

I let my eyes close. A few hours later, I was awoken by Ryze, his beak playing with my hair, his tongue flicking over my cheek. I blinked up at him perched on the headboard.

Lycus was still asleep, and I could hear Darius snoring behind me, feel his breath on me, tickling the back of my neck. Rubbing my eyes, I lifted Darius's arm off me, wiggled out from between them, and scooted to the end of the bed. Seeing that I was getting up, Ryze flew over to me and perched himself on my shoulder, rubbing his beak across my cheek and cooing softly.

His weight was becoming heavy, and his talons dug into my flesh, making me hiss. Still, I scratched his tummy feathers as I peered back at the bed.

Kalen was beside Lycus, snuggled against him, also asleep. However, Tobias wasn't in bed, and I couldn't see him in the room. I walked toward the bathroom and turned the handle, only for it to open before I could. Tobias stepped out, having just hopped out of the shower. A towel hung dangerously low on his hips, his hair was wet, and droplets cascaded down his chest from the shower. Some foreign urge to trace the hard lines of his abs rushed over me. My breathing hitched as my eyes traveled lower to his V-line that disappeared beneath his towel.

Ryze shifted his weight on my shoulder, his talons digging into my skin and collarbone, piercing through my delicate skin.

"Ryze, careful," Tobias said, holding his hand out for him to climb on. I was relieved when Ryze climbed up his arm and off mine, only to perch on Tobias's shoulder for a moment before flying out the window.

"We need to cut his claws," I told Tobias while looking down at my bleeding shoulder. I wiped the blood off only to look up at Tobias, whose eyes were glazed over, staring at my neck. Tobias licked his lips.

CHAPTER 72

"T OBIAS?" I ASKED. HE shook his head, snapping himself out of whatever frenzied daze he was in.

"Yeah?" he said. I looked at the bed to see Lycus just climbing out of it. Kalen and Darius lay still, sound asleep. I held up my wrist with a sigh, and Tobias shook his head when I felt heat press against my back before feeling fingers swipe my hair to my other shoulder. Lycus kissed my cheek as I looked over my shoulder at him.

"He wants to feed on you," Lycus growled before his lips trailed up my shoulder and neck.

My breath hitched as sparks zapped and moved over my skin. I tilted my head, giving him better access, loving the feel of his lips on my body. The bond urged me to give myself to him and let him do what he wanted with me, and I wanted to do precisely that. Desire coursed through me so viciously that it made my legs tremble as Lycus pulled me against him. One hand squeezed my breast while the other sat flat against my abdomen.

"You're overwhelming her, Lycus," Darius said, and I blinked out of my lust-filled daze to look over at him as he sat up in bed. Darius rubbed his eyes while Kalen wiggled closer, placing his head in Darius's lap and wrapping his arms around Darius's waist. I watched as Darius ran his fingers through Kalen's hair, and I suddenly wanted to crawl back into bed to be with them.

"Someone wants to shred," Lycus whispered, and I looked up at him behind me. Lycus smiled seductively, and his eyes turned obsidian as his big hand cupped my cheek, tilting my face toward his. I swallowed when his eyes darted to my lips. He smiled mischievously, leaning his face closer; his breath fanned over my lips teasingly, nearly touching, but waiting to see if I would pull away.

When I closed the distance, his rich cinnamon and smokey scent enticed me, my lips brushing his plump ones, wanting access. The noise that left me when his tongue brushed mine sounded needy as I turned in his arms, kissing him hungrily.

He smiled amusedly against my lips as I mauled him. My tongue tangled with his, and I kissed him deeper. Lycus's huge hands gripped my thighs, hoisting me up. I wrapped my legs around his waist, and my arms went around his neck.

One of his hands slid up my back to my neck as Lycus kissed me harder, dominating my mouth as he tasted every inch, devouring my lips in a soul-destroying kiss. Heat rushed through me, and I gasped, pulling away from him breathlessly. Lycus smiled smugly, and his eyes flickered. He gave me some of his magic, just a taste, and I wanted more. His magic writhed through me, tickling my insides.

A moan escaped me, my eyes falling shut when warmth seeped into my back, stopping me from falling backward at the sensation rolling through me. It slivered in my veins; it felt empowering though it flickered and tried to mingle with my white magic, making me bite my lips as I fought the urge to let it meld together. *Oh, how I wanted it to.*

as I pulled back away from him.

His power was like ice in my veins, so cold and intense that it made my heart stutter, and I gasped for air as I swallowed down the power bleeding into me and mingling with ours; mine was fighting to change his, while his powerful magic was fighting to change mine. His power danced with mine, playing with it, teasing mine, and making goosebumps rise all over my body.

"You little minx, you stole it," Darius chuckled, and I giggled, worried he would be mad, but he just seemed amused.

Kalen roared with laughter behind me. "Not such a big wicked demon after all," he said behind him, making Darius smirk before glancing back at Kalen. His laughing cut off when Darius growled. My heart lurched in my chest when Darius pounced on him, causing him to shriek, and I flinched, about to help Kalen when Lycus's lips nipped at my chin.

"Darius is playing with him. He won't hurt him," Lycus purred, and he was right as I watched Darius pin him to the bed before his lips crashed against Kalen's.

Kalen writhed beneath him while also trying to escape him. Darius chuckled, pinning his wrists above his head. Darius's hand was moving between their bodies, and arousal smashed into me when I saw him squeeze Kalen's cock through his boxer shorts. Kalen groaned and rocked his hips up against him. I couldn't tear my eyes away from them, loving seeing this playful side to them. Darius's tongue slipped into his mouth briefly before he pulled up, a teasing smile on his lips, and Kalen pouted.

"If you want it back, take it," Darius teased, making me realize Darius had just stolen his magic.

"What do you want to do, love? I take you over there to them. You won't be leaving the bed, or do you still want to shower?" Tobias purred behind me.

That was suddenly a tough question to answer because I wanted both things.

"Or one of us could join you?" Lycus purred. Darius and Kalen glanced over to see what I would choose.

"In that case, I choose Kalen," I giggled, and Tobias huffed behind me while Lycus growled, scrunching his face up before smiling. Darius looked down at Kalen beneath him.

"Maybe you can steal mine back from her," Darius purred, leaning down and nipping at Kalen's lips before kissing him. I could see the exchange this time, paying attention as Darius gave him back his magic, Kalen's aura growing stronger before Darius let him up. Lycus placed me on my feet and stepped back. The bond urged me to chase him, bring him back to me; it craved his touch.

"He's all yours," Lycus chuckled as Kalen came over to me. His eyes roamed over my face and down to my bare chest, his breathing becoming heavier, and I watched his eyes darken. I reached for him. Despite craving his touch, I was gentler with Kalen, unable to be rough with him, yet I felt he craved roughness, like some part of him got sick of everyone treating him as if he was made of glass.

Kalen grabbed my throat before I could touch him, ripping me toward him before his lips crashed against mine. That was when I realized that Kalen didn't crave roughness; he desired control, something the others rarely gave him, and I had no issues letting him have it as his mouth dominated mine, devouring my lips while his grip on my neck grew tighter.

"Kalen, gentle," Tobias whispered, but I shook my head, knowing Kalen wanted this, knowing he needed it.

His mouth went to my jaw and neck. The heat of Tobias pressing against my back seeped into me and his concern for me.

"He's fine. Leave him be," I moaned when his grip became rougher, his fingers digging into my breast as he squeezed it with his other hand before pressing himself against me.

My breathing became labored when I felt his teeth sink into me over their marks; I hissed at the pain because his teeth were blunt compared to Tobias and Lycus's. I clutched him closer, feeling the bond wash over me, Kalen's emotions bleeding into me along with his magic when he pulled his face from my neck.

His eyes were closed, and my blood ran from the corner of his mouth. He sighed, and I gripped his chin, tilting his face down toward mine before licking the trail of my blood back to his lips before kissing him. Kalen smiled against my lips as my tongue delved between his. All too soon, he pulled away.

"Three down, one to go?" he breathed, brushing his nose against mine.

CHAPTER 74

TOBIAS MOVED BEHIND ME. His lips pressed softly to my jaw, and I tilted my head, giving him better access. My eyes fluttered closed at the sparks rushing over my skin, making goosebumps rise over my body as he left open-mouth kisses on my skin, sucking and nipping at my soft flesh. His teeth grazed and teased as his arms wrapped around my waist, firmly holding me against him.

Kalen's lips crashed against my own, his tongue demanding as it moved between my parted lips, tasting every inch of my mouth. Their touch was invigorating and empowering as their magic passed between us with each touch and gentle caress. I ran my hands across Kalen's warm chest, loving the tingling sensation beneath my palms and the feeling of his arousal from the bond.

Tobias growled, the sound sending a cold chill up my spine as his teeth pierced my flesh and nearly caused my knees to buckle. My eyes rolled into the back of my head as his tongue lapped at my neck, his grip becoming stronger. His bite was no longer painful but pleasurable, and I pushed back against him, my lips pulling away from Kalen's as I moaned at the euphoria coursing

Darius's scent reached my nose. His masculine smokey scent wrapping around me made my eyes open to see him watching me. Kalen stepped out of his way and moved toward the bathroom door. He opened it, and I heard the shower turn on a few seconds later. Tobias pulled his fangs from my neck, and I felt a little light-headed as the ecstasy of his bite faded and forced me back to reality.

"Go shower before they get carried away," Darius whispered. His eyes flickered, like he was fighting his own urges to mark me. His hands fell on my hips, and he turned me toward the bathroom, where I could see Kalen already in the shower.

I gulped when he turned and wet his face. His body looked like it was hand sculpted. Kalen was by far the smallest, with his height and muscle, more athletically built, and leaner. Yet his softness was what made him so appealing. That and the calmness I found when with Kalen. Whereas Lycus looked like he lived in a gym despite never seeing him use one; his werewolf DNA was strong, and he was all muscle on muscle. Darius's body, you could tell, was lethal, bulky, and hard-pressed behind me. He and Tobias were built similarly, both towering over the rest of us.

"Are you just going to stand there?" Kalen asked, raising an eyebrow while I gawked at how perfect he was. He smirked, his hair falling in his eyes now that it was wet. He ran his fingers through his hair, flicking it out of his face as he turned back to wash himself.

Darius pushed me through the door, making me stumble. His hand on my stomach caught me before I face-planted onto the tiles because I stared off in a daze, too busy perving on my mate. Darius laughed softly behind me.

"Kalen is delicious to look at," Darius told me, and I nodded stupidly. I was pretty sure he could have said anything, and I would have nodded, still focused on Kalen, my mind refusing to comprehend anything or anyone else.

"Kalen, stop. She can barely function," Darius told him, and I felt the trance that gripped me lessen, making me blink rapidly.

"He was fiddling with your aura, pulling on it," Darius murmured when I felt his fingers trail along the waistband of my pants. I gripped his hands.

"You're not bleeding. I checked you early this morning while you were asleep," Darius told me, and I sighed. I knew I should probably be embarrassed, yet I found I was anything but. Darius slid them down, and I quickly stepped out of them.

"I will get some towels for you both," Darius murmured, and I gripped his wrist as he turned to walk out. He stopped looking at me as I turned, pulling him toward the shower. His eyes moved behind me to Kalen.

Kalen's wet hand gripped my hip as he tugged me to him. His skin was hard and warm against my back as he pulled me under the shower spray. He detached the showerhead, and I shivered when the spray blasted through my hair as Kalen wet it.

Yet I stood waiting to see what Darius would do when I let his hand go.

"Would you like a written invitation, Darius? I don't think she could be clearer unless she said it," Kalen asked him as he hooked the showerhead back onto the wall.

Kalen grabbed the soap, his arm wrapping around my waist as he lathered my skin with his hand holding the soap. Citrus and vanilla flooded the room as the steam heated the place, making the mirror fog.

Darius turned and walked out, and I sighed. *Invariably, one step forward and ten back with him.* Turning in Kalen's arms, he smiled down at me before dipping his face lower, his lips brushing mine softly when heat moved across my back, seeping into me. I pulled away from Kalen to see Darius step in behind me when I glanced over my shoulder.

His hot skin brushed mine as he closed the shower screen behind him. His hands moved to my hips, and Kalen's hands trailed up to my ribs, softly caressing my sides when he turned me to face Darius. Kalen's hand moved to my breast, fondling it, and I leaned back against him, only for Darius to take a step closer. His face was barely inches from mine as he watched Kalen's hands exploring my body, touching and caressing.

I placed my palm on Darius's chest, the heat radiating from him hotter than the water I stood under. Darius looked down at my hand and stepped closer, his lips smashing against mine. His hand moved from my hip and went to my hair as he pulled me closer, deepening the kiss. His lips devoured mine, and I had to pull away for air.

CHAPTER 75

$\mathcal{A}$S HE STEPPED CLOSER, Darius's lips moved to my neck, so his entire body was flush against mine. Kalen's erection dug into my lower back, and Darius grabbed my hair in his hand, tugging at it and forcing my head back. His tongue flicked my earlobe. He nibbled on it, teasing it with his teeth, making me moan when Kalen's hand pressed between Darius and me on my stomach.

Kalen's fingers trailed down between my legs when he cupped my pussy with his hand, squeezing it, making me shiver as sparks rushed straight to my clit. Lust coursed violently through me when his fingers parted my lower lips before shoving his finger inside me. My legs shook with the sudden intrusion as he slid his finger in as deep as possible, making Darius groan and pull away to look down at Kalen's hand, teasing and playing with me.

"Gently, Kalen," Darius said before his hand covered Kalen's, slowing his movements. Darius pulled Kalen's hand gently, guiding his finger inside me. Both of them were playing with me, and my arousal spilled out of me, coating Kalen's finger and hand as I writhed between them. I gripped Darius's arm, my legs trembling as he moved Kalen's hand faster.

"Curl your finger upward," Darius growled, watching Kalen's hand, and he did, making me cry out as his finger brushed some part I did not know existed, causing a breathy moan to leave my lips, and my eyes fluttered closed.

"That's it," Darius murmured, making my eyes open to find his eyes watching my face when I felt his finger slip inside me alongside Kalen's. His finger was warmer and longer as he slid in, matching Kalen's rhythm and guiding Kalen to the same spot that made the warmth pool in my lower stomach and my body tingle.

My walls clamped down on their fingers, and Kalen's arm tightened around my ribs, keeping me upright. My nails dug into Darius's arm, earning me a growl when Darius's lips swallowed my moans as his and Kalen's fingers moved quicker. The feeling they were stirring up within me built quickly, and Darius kissed the side of my mouth.

His tongue teased the seam of my lips. "Can I mark you?" he murmured against my lips, making my eyes snap open when he asked for permission.

"You're asking?" I said, a little shocked.

"Maybe I should have all along," he whispered before his finger curled inside me, making me shake and cry out. He smirked. My face heated, and my head rolled back against Kalen's shoulder behind me.

"Is that a yes?" Darius growled, his teeth grazing my jaw and down my neck where all their marks lay.

"Yes," I answered breathlessly.

His teeth sank into my neck over their marks, sending me over the edge. My moans resounded loudly off the tiled walls. My inner walls clenched around their fingers as my pussy pulsated, my orgasm rippling over me, making my knees go out from under me.

Darius stepped closer. Kalen bore all my weight on his arm that was securely wrapped around me, trapping me between them. Their fingers slowed as I rode out the orgasm that washed over me in waves when I felt Darius's teeth smash through the barrier and merge with all their bonds.

His magic smashed into mine, wanting to return to its owner. His cold power bled into my veins quickly, tangling and dominating mine, only for mine to fight back and morph and change his, turning his magic from ice cold to warm as it slivered through me strongly. Darius's emotions bled into me like a tidal wave.

Shock and awe were the strongest, followed by his longing. Only he now genuinely realized what it meant that I was a harmony fae. Both light and dark coexisted as one, mingling and blurring the lines between what should be impossible but yet somehow fit like pieces of a puzzle, and Darius just gave me the last piece.

Darius pulled his teeth from my neck, and his eyes flickered oddly, the color changing from black to gold then flashing before turning black again. He cupped my face with his hand, and their fingers slipped out of me. Darius kissed me softly, sucking my bottom lip into his mouth, making me gasp at how gentle he could be. "Four down, four to go," he whispered against my lips, and my brows furrowed at his words.

"We all belong to you now, so now you get to choose if you belong to us," Darius murmured, pressing his forehead against mine. I wrapped my arms around his neck, tugging him down to kiss him. He answered instantly, and I heard the shower screen open up.

Kalen shuffled around behind me, and Darius pulled me closer, allowing Lycus and Tobias to step into the shower with us. Lycus turned one of the other shower heads on, adjusting it as it wasn't

as the need for Kalen's power overwhelmed me. It was like the bond craved him, yet subconsciously, it went with whom I would have chosen first. It was an odd feeling.

Darius let me go, and the moment he did, I attacked Kalen, the bond overwhelming me. Kalen's nervousness hit me like a slap in the face when Darius grabbed me, pulling me back down, his magic moving through me again and sedating me. Yet still, my hips rocked against Kalen, my legs locked around his waist.

"Her bond wants you, Kalen," Tobias told him, but the fire coursing through me became painful the more he denied me, and I groaned as my arousal spilled out, coating my thighs.

But Kalen just stared down at me, and I whimpered. Kalen bit his lip, looking down at me. I wondered why he was denying me, the bond screaming out painfully for him, but he just stared down at me. The feeling through the bond was almost fear.

"Maybe Tobias should," Kalen murmured. Tears pricked my eyes at Kalen's words. The bond recoiled in my chest, making me cry out. My back arched at his rejection as pain rippled through me when Lycus moved onto the bed beside me, his magic flooding into me as his hand moved across my stomach, the bond relaxing under his touch. I fell back against the bed, humiliated at the way my bond was reacting. Tears stung my eyes.

I couldn't even speak. Everything became based on instinct and the feeling of my bond tugging on theirs. It became clear why everyone always said you needed your mates when shredding. It was agony and uncontrollable; I was at the mercy of my bond, overcome by instincts I was not used to.

"Calm, he is scared, Aleera. He isn't rejecting you," Lycus murmured before leaning over and kissing me softly and sucking on my bottom lip.

He nibbled on it before pulling away and smiling back at me.

Darius's hands still cupping my face warmed me up more, his magic bleeding through me, trying to calm my frantic bond. I saw Tobias kiss Kalen's shoulder. Kalen turned his head to face him, to look at him, and Tobias kissed him. The sight made my bond flare stronger, saddened Kalen would give in to Tobias, but not me.

"I know you want him. He will give your bond what it wants. Kalen has never been with a woman. Just give him a second," Darius purred, leaning down and kissing me softly. His words startled me for a second, and when he pulled away, Kalen was staring down at me with a worried look on his face, and his cheeks flushed.

His embarrassment hit me, and my bond calmed, reacting to him. I wanted to comfort him and tell him it was okay; I was a virgin, for god's sake, and not many were at the age of twenty-four, especially not a damn keeper.

A purr escaped me, a noise I wasn't aware I could make, my bond rushing out like an aura and reassuring him. Kalen sighed, closing his eyes and tipping his head back. My body felt foreign doing things I had no control over. The urge to comfort my mate became overwhelming, and I felt the tension start to leave him.

"What are you worried about? Hurting her? I can assure you right now you won't, not while she is like this," Tobias chuckled, nodding toward me writhing on the bed.

Kalen looked down at me, and his face took on a darkened expression, his eyes flickering, and the room chilled slightly, reacting to his mood.

And for the first time, I got glimmers of his aura. I had never seen one, and I knew it was because I was filled with his magic. However, Kalen's was black as coal, and fractures like shattered glass crackled within it. Darkness, his aura, was tainted by the darkness that sometimes took over him, showing how close he lived to the edge of this world and death, a limbo between the light and darkness that swirled within him.

"Yes, but mostly about what she will see," Kalen said, and Lycus cupped Kalen's cheek with his hand. His thumb smoothed under his eye.

CHAPTER 77

"*I*T WON'T MAKE HER love you any less," Lycus told him. Their words confused me, and I tried to process what he meant. I wanted desperately to ask, yet my tongue felt thick in my mouth. I glanced at Darius, who had an indecipherable expression. Worry etched on his handsome face, a crease forming between his eyes as I stared up at him questionably.

Darius licked his lip, and his eyes went to mine and softened slightly. "There is a reason they are called keepers. They are keepers of more than magic, Aleera. You get their magic, but you also get all their secrets, even the ones we haven't told each other." Darius murmured the last part as if he had just remembered that. *Was that what Kalen was worried about?* I knew that already, so why was he so scared of me learning about his past? The atmosphere in the room changed now that Darius spoke up. A nervous ripple coursed through all of them as they watched me.

"Kalen doesn't have a good one, Aleera. I know you are probably having trouble keeping a singular thought, but you should know not one of us has a stellar past," Lycus whispered while leaning over me. He brushed his nose against mine and pecked my lips. My hands gripped his arms, tugging him closer and deepening the kiss. Lycus palmed my breast before rolling my nipple between his fingers as I kissed him.

Hands smoothed over my thighs, and Lycus pulled away from me just as Kalen gripped my hips, yanking me closer to him.

His eyes flickered at me, and he purred, a cocky grin splitting onto his face. Kalen pushed my legs further apart before grabbing his cock in his hand. He ran the tip between my glistening wet folds, making me arch my hips, wanting him to sink himself inside my tight confines.

Lycus growled, and my eyes darted to him to find him watching Kalen tease me by running his cock between my lips, parting them. Lycus leaned down, and Kalen moved slightly as Lycus's mouth covered my throbbing pussy, his hot tongue brushing my clit, making me cry out and buck against his lips. Lycus growled, sucking on my clit, and I watched Kalen run his fingers through Lycus's hair.

My hips rolled against his fiery tongue. Arousal made my muscles tense, and heat pooled in my belly, desire coursing through me. My thighs became slick as my juices spilled from me, coating his lips. Lycus pulled away, and Kalen gripped the back of his neck, bringing Lycus's lips to his and kissing him. Tasting me on Lycus's lips, Kalen let him go, and my breathing became harsh as the bond grew impatient.

Kalen looked down at me and smirked before running the tip of his cock between my pussy lips again teasingly, stopping at my entrance. Tobias moved onto the bed on my other side, his lips latching onto my nipple, making me moan, and his hand fell on my knee, pulling my leg further open.

Kalen's hand fell on my thigh, spreading my legs wide apart as he moved closer and pushed the tip in. I gasped at the feeling. Tobias pulled away, and I saw Kalen watching me as he slowly pushed inside me, stretching me around his thick shaft. His cock grazed my inner walls, gliding smoothly, coated in my juices. My pussy gripped him, and he groaned. His eyes flickered before shoving inside me, his hips flush against me.

Kalen stilled before watching himself slide out of me, and his eyes flicked to mine when I moved my hips, forcing him back inside. Darius growled, his hands moving to my shoulders before letting me go. His magic let me go, and the bond was flooded with primal desire. Kalen smiled darkly, gripping my hips and slamming into me.

I reached for him, my hands wanting to touch him. I felt the bed dip as Tobias and Lycus moved when Kalen gripped my hands, lacing his fingers through mine and shoving them into the mattress above my head. His lips crashed against mine hungrily. My tongue fought him for dominance as the bond flared. I rolled my hips in sync with his thrusts, and I moaned as bliss rolled over me when he flooded me with his magic, giving me all of it, bathing me in it. My bond tangled with his, and my chest warmed at the feeling coursing through me.

Kalen's lips moved to my mark, and he sucked on it, earning a moan from me when sparks made my entire body buzz. His hard length slid in and out of me, slick with my arousal from the building friction. Kalen groaned when my walls clamped down around him. His lips returned to mine, and my fingers squeezed his as he drove me closer to the precipice.

As he tasted every inch of my mouth, Kalen's tongue became demanding, and I was overwhelmed with the friction and his magic slivering through me. My entire body heated, and my breathing turned to a pant as I rolled my hips against him when my bond took over completely, hungry to mark him and claim him.

Kalen growled when my magic shoved out, and I overpowered him, flipping him on his back. Kalen barely sat up in time before I climbed on top of him. My legs straddled his waist, and Kalen's arms wrapped around my waist, slowing me as I sank down on him.

A sigh left my lips at the feel of his cock filling me, and my head rolled back at the pleasurable feeling, only for a set of lips to swallow my moans as Tobias's lips covered mine. Kalen rolled my hips against him, his lips going to my breast, his teeth tugging at my nipple as his tongue swirled around it.

My stomach coiled with tension, and heat washed over me. My inner walls quivered as the first ripple effect of my orgasm washed over me. Kalen groaned, and Tobias's lips left mine, only for Kalen to grip the back of my neck, bringing my lips back to his. His kiss was hungry, and I shattered.

My pussy was pulsating and gripping his cock when Kalen's lips pulled away from mine, and he groaned as warm jets of semen coated my insides, and his movements slowed just as I sank my teeth into his neck.

Fireworks exploded behind my eyelids as his soul bled into mine, giving me every piece of him. His magic was no longer his or mine but ours. My bond calmed, and I moaned as his blood flooded my mouth and coated my tongue. Kalen's cock twitched inside me as he clutched me closer. My orgasm was prolonged by the feeling of his magic flowing through both of us, and my cries seemed endless as I rode out its effects.

I gasped, pulling my teeth from his neck. Kalen cupped my face in his hands, and the room spun, warping the colors around us. I felt like I was falling when Kalen kissed me gently. "I love you, and I never stopped," Kalen whispered, pulling away, and he sighed, pressing his forehead against mine.

"So, please forgive me," he whispered. His words made no sense to me until I was plunged into the darkness of his memories. I was aware I was being moved and could feel their hands touching me until I was no longer feeling anything but experiencing something else entirely. I was being thrown into new surroundings, ones that I wasn't familiar with. It was at that moment that I realized I had traveled back in time to Kalen's memories.

CHAPTER 78

IT WAS LIKE WATCHING A timeline of the most significant
memories he had, those that shaped him into who he was
today. A glimpse into the depths of who Kalen truly was and the
things that haunted him, made him happy, everything that made
Kalen, Kalen.

His earliest memory was horrible. At first, I was an outsider
watching until the vision warped, and I was suddenly Kalen,
seeing the world through his eyes. Feeling what he felt, enduring
what he endured. I found myself running into some room with
gray walls with peeling wallpaper, exposing the mold-covered
walls beneath. Beds lined the room in rows, large bay windows
overlooked the city, and the room was ice cold.

He crawled underneath his bed by the window only to be
ripped out by his ankles, his nails clawing at the wooden floorboards, making his fingertips bloody as they tore away his finger-
nails. His screams were horrendous and hurt my soul. The fear he
felt made my heart race, and at first, I had no idea what he was
running from until he was rolled over.

It was other children. Kalen was crawling on his hands and
knees, blocked by legs and backed into a corner. The kids huddled

around him in the corner of the room. He tried to cover his ears with his hands over his head as they screamed and taunted. Throwing things and kicking and hurting him. Most of his childhood was spent being bullied relentlessly for being the weakest among the fae. But Kalen wasn't just the weakest; he was also the smallest among his peers.

The bullying was horrendous, the things they did to him. Setting him on fire, urinating on him, beating him bloody, and the teachers or those responsible for looking after him turned a blind eye to it or outright condemned him by telling him he deserved it. Kalen's childhood was tragic until one day that changed everything for him. Kalen looked worried as he sat in the playground by himself, and a new kid walked out the doors.

He thought it was another person to add to the list of bullies he already had. The boy reminded me of someone, and it didn't take long before I recognized who he was. It was Lycus. He was younger in this memory. Lycus was just a boy, like Kalen. Only he was frighteningly bigger, and Kalen watched, horrified as he argued with one of the teachers before stomping off to sit on one of the bench seats. Lycus watched the other children play, his eyes falling on Kalen, and Kalen dropped his gaze, cursing himself for making eye contact with the scary-looking boy.

When the bell rang to signal class, and he had to return to the orphanage, he ran for the doors, hoping to go unnoticed. However, Kalen knew his bullies wouldn't give him a day off when the one he hated most stepped into his path. The boy was a teenager and almost looked too old to be still in the orphanage Kalen called home. Kalen had to have been at least half the other boy's age.

As the bully stepped out the door into the concrete playground, he took a step back. Kalen's eyes scanned his surroundings, looking for an escape. He noticed Lycus watching curiously from where he still sat, ignoring the sound of the school bell. Kalen ran for the door across the quadrangle, only for the teenage boy to tackle him.

Kids rushed out the doors, circling and taunting him while the other kid gripped the front of his shirt and repeatedly punched him, making his nose bleed, and his eyes blur as they swelled. Pain rippled through me as I experienced what he did, the helplessness and the acceptance. Kalen didn't fight back. He knew it was useless and only brought on more pain.

So instead, he just took it. He thought the boy would surely kill him that day. He promised Kalen he would before he aged out of the system. Kalen accepted it. In some ways, he hoped this was it, the day his torment ended. Just as his bully gripped his head in both hands, Kalen closed his eyes, knowing his head was about to be slammed into the pavement. Yet the deadly blow never came.

Instead, the weight holding him down was gone, and a collective gasp was heard from the surrounding crowd of children. Kalen's eyes flew open to find his tormentor beside him on the ground, and the new kid that had arrived was punching into him, the bully's head bouncing off the ground as Lycus pounded his face with his fists. Blood spurted out of the bully's nose and mouth, covering the new kid.

Kalen was shocked but also petrified that Lycus would turn his attention to him when he was done. Lycus's eyes were a demonic black, and he foamed at the mouth in rage. Kalen just lay there and stared, too scared to move. Lycus growled loudly when Kalen's bully fell unconscious.

The other kids scattered and ran away in fear as Lycus stood upright, breathing heavily before his gaze turned to Kalen, who cowered away from him as Lycus stepped over the kid. Yet instead of offering Kalen a fist, he offered him his hand and pulled him to his feet.

"Are you okay?" Lycus asked him and Kalen just stared at him. No one ever asked if he was okay, and he suddenly found himself mute for another reason.

"You got a name?" Lycus asked him. Kalen nodded, and Lycus raised an eyebrow at him.

"Well, are you going to tell me or can't you speak?" Lycus asked him.

"Kalen," he stuttered out.

"I'm Lycus," Lycus told him, and Kalen looked down at his bloody bully lying unconscious on the ground.

"Come on, let's find a first-aid kit," Lycus told him, grabbing Kalen's arm, but Kalen shook his head, pulling away. Lycus stopped and stared at him.

"I will get in trouble. The teachers don't help," he whispered to Lycus. That seemed to anger Lycus, who chucked his arm over Kalen's shoulder.

"They'll help, or I'll make them."

"They won't listen. They don't care," Kalen murmured nervously.

"I'll make them listen," Lycus told him.

Kalen looked at Lycus, and he smiled, flashing his canines. "Because if they don't, I'll bite," he said, and Kalen laughed, letting Lycus lead him back inside.

After the day he met Lycus, they were joined at the hip, drawn to each other. Lycus always defended Kalen and taught him how to protect himself as best he could. However, when they were both fourteen, Kalen's mental health declined, and his depression worsened until Lycus got sick of watching him hate himself.

His teacher had hit Kalen across the knuckles with a cane when he was trying to explain the work to Lycus beside him. Kalen's knuckles split open, and Lycus lost it, standing up and ripping the cane from his teacher's fingers. The man was cruel, hated Lycus and Kalen, and used any excuse to punish them. Lycus pulled the cane from his hand before wailing on him with it. Lycus was then shot with a dart gun after one of the students raced into the halls to alert security. Kalen watched on helplessly as Lycus was then hauled away to the infirmary, and Kalen wasn't allowed in with him, so he waited by the door for him to wake up.

"Kalen! Now!" his teacher called to him. Kalen was waiting in a corridor for Lycus when he heard his name called. Kalen pushed off the wall he was leaning on as the burly vampiric fae stalked toward him. Kalen glanced at the door where Lycus was before turning his attention to the headteacher.

"Follow me," the man said.

"But, Lycus—"

"I am not here for the were-fae. Now, hurry up," the man said, turning on his heel and walking into the gymnasium. Kalen followed. He had never had issues with the headteacher; he was only new to the orphanage, so he didn't suspect anything wrong. When he entered the gymnasium, his math teacher sat on a chair. Lash marks covered him where Lycus had beaten him.

A few other teachers stood off to the sides as they entered, and Kalen followed behind, thinking he would probably be issued the cane. He got the cane. Not a piece of his skin was left untainted when they finished beating him. This was their punishment for Lycus. They knew Kalen was Lycus's weak spot and the only person he cared for, so they hurt Kalen to teach Lycus a lesson. Then they fed on him, nearly killing him before dumping him outside the infirmary door for Lycus to find. A few days later, Lycus had enough.

CHAPTER 79

"*P*SST, WAKE UP. WE are leaving," Lycus said, shaking Kalen's shoulder and waking him. Kalen groaned and rolled over to see Lycus hovering above him.

"What's wrong?" Kalen whispered, sitting up and rubbing his eyes while yawning.

Lycus grabbed Kalen's face, which was still covered in lash marks. "We are leaving. We are better off on our own," he told him, pulling Kalen's pajama shirt off and dressing him. Kalen's sleeping medication made him extra groggy and almost nonfunctioning.

"Where will we go?" Kalen mumbled, trying to lie back down when Lycus grabbed him under the arms forcing him to his feet.

"Anywhere they can't touch you," Lycus growled before chucking a bag over his shoulder.

Kalen, doped off his face from the medication, woke up later at the bus stop, having no memory of the walk there. It was freezing cold, snow covered the ground, and Lycus was rubbing his arms, trying to warm him up. The motion having woken Kalen, he peered around, confused.

"Shh, go to sleep," Lycus murmured. Kalen trusted Lycus to keep him safe, so he did just that.

They lived like that for years, living day to day. Taking any odd jobs they could find. Lycus, at one stage, even became a male stripper to get them by. His werewolf genes made him appear older than he was, and as much as Lycus hated it, he did more than just strip for the filthy old pub tarts as he called them to get them by until he realized he was hurting Kalen. I was then shoved into one of Kalen's happiest memories.

Lycus had just come out to the kitchen at the back of the strip club where Kalen was washing dishes, covered in sweat with money stuffed in his briefs. Kalen hung up his apron as his shift ended before stalking off out the back.

"Kalen?" Lycus asked, chasing after him and pulling clothes on as he chased after him, but Kalen hated seeing Lycus with women and found it made him jealous. He didn't know what to think of the strange feelings he had for him. He thought it wrong to feel that way.

Trudging home in the snow, they were currently sleeping in a tent at a nearby park, both still too young to rent a place, and neither had ID.

"Kalen, did something happen?" Lycus asked him, catching up to him, but Kalen ignored him and kept walking home. When they got to the small park at the back of the pub, Kalen unzipped the tent and climbed in, sitting on his makeshift bed.

"What's gotten into you?"

"Nothing."

"Well, something is wrong," Lycus said, sniffing himself. He shuddered; he hated how they pawed at him, hated the things he had to do, but he did them so they could survive. When Kalen didn't answer, Lycus growled before stomping out of the tent and toward the toilets. There was a shower in there, but it only had cold water. Still, it was better than nothing. When he returned, Kalen continued to ignore him.

"Kalen," Lycus said, and he looked up at Lycus. He passed Kalen a burger he must have gotten on his way home. Kalen sighed but took it. Lycus sat across from him, eating his own food.

"You were in the red room," Kalen muttered, taking a bite of his sandwich. Lycus shrugged like it was no big deal.

"Filthy whore, she was married, too," Lycus said, his eyes flicking to Kalen's.

"What?" Lycus asked, but Kalen shook his head, going back to eating his food.

"You have been really strange lately. What's gotten into you? Have you run out of medication? I can pull a double tomorrow," Lycus told him.

Kalen muttered under his breath, and Lycus growled at him. Kalen knew he was annoyed. They told each other everything. Well, except for one thing; he never told Lycus how he felt about him. When they finished eating, Lycus rummaged through their bags, looking for Kalen's sleeping pills, and sighed.

"You are out. Why didn't you say anything?" Lycus asked.

"I don't want you selling yourself. I hate their smell on you."

"It's just sex. It's no big deal," Lycus said before he sighed.

"To me, it's not! They are using you!" Kalen screamed, and Lycus seemed startled by his outburst. Kalen hardly raised his voice, and he was quick to apologize.

"I'm sorry. Forget I said anything," Kalen muttered, rubbing his temples. He could feel a headache coming on.

"I don't mind. It is fine," Lycus told him. "I will speak to Bill about doing more shifts."

Kalen cursed, getting to his feet to storm out of the tent.

Only Lycus gripped his arm, tugging him back. "What did I

say this time? What is wrong?" This time he was becoming angry with Kalen's lack of answers.

Kalen's face heated with embarrassment. "I'm being stupid. It must be my meds," Kalen told him with a shake of his head, turning to leave the tent so he could shower. Kalen froze in the shower, and by the time he got out and returned to the tent, he was shivering and regretting showering in the first place. His teeth chattered as he rubbed his arms, and tonight it was snowing, making it just a little chillier. Kalen hated the cold.

Lycus was reading with a flashlight between his teeth when he entered. Kalen fell onto the sleeping bag beside him, and Lycus looked over at him before lifting his blanket and throwing it over Kalen. Lycus would sometimes shift, knowing his fur would keep him warm and help warm Kalen.

"I'm fine," Kalen growled.

"You're freezing," Lycus told him as Kalen wriggled beneath his blanket. Lycus placed his flashlight down before sighing and moving closer to Kalen.

"I can shift?" Lycus offered, but Kalen felt guilty about their argument and believed he didn't deserve a friend like him.

"Man, this tent is fucking boring when you are so quiet," Lycus said, lying down.

"Why don't you go sleep with one of your whores? I am sure they will keep you entertained," Kalen spat bitterly, not meaning for the words to spill from his lips.

"What the fuck is your problem?" Lycus snapped at him before gripping his shoulder and flinging Kalen on his back. He glared down at him.

"Fucking answer. I am sick of your snide comments. Do you think I want to fuck them? It's a job. It keeps us fed," Lycus snapped at him.

"Well, you seem to enjoy it, or you wouldn't keep doing it," Kalen growled.

"Ah, for fuck's sake. If you have something to say, Kalen, fucking say it. I am sick of guessing where your head is at," Lycus said.

"I don't want you fucking them. You earn enough without fucking them," Kalen told him.

"Your medication is expensive. It's the only way to cover it."

Guilt smashes into Kalen. "I don't need them," Kalen said, but Lycus growled.

"Yes, you do. We tried that, and you went into withdrawal and had a fucking seizure."

"Not if that is what you have to do for them. I hate that you fuck them!"

"It's just sex, Kalen. It means nothing to them or me."

Kalen shoved him back and sat up. "You keep saying that, but I can't stand knowing the person I love is fucking some bitch just to keep us alive. I fucking hate that they use you. I hate living like this. I hate seeing you with them!" Kalen yelled, blurting everything out, only realizing what he had said when it was too late to take it back.

Lycus tilted his head to the side curiously. "You love me?" he asked.

Kalen's face heated, and his eyes widened in fear. "No, you know, like a bro—"

His words were cut off when Lycus pounced on him, a scream bubbling up his throat. He had pushed Lycus too far. Lycus would abandon him, too, he thought, then Lycus kissed him.

"You love me?" Lycus mumbled against his lips.

Kalen said nothing, in shock that Lycus's lips were pressed to his. He had always secretly wondered if they were as soft as they looked but his kiss was rough as he forced his tongue into Kalen's mouth when he didn't answer.

"Is this what you want, Kalen? You want me?" Lycus asked, pulling back to look at him. Lycus was rocking his hips against Kalen, who realized Lycus had an erection. Kalen gasped, and Lycus watched him breathe heavily, an unsure look on his face. For once, Lycus looked scared.

"Please, say something," Lycus said to him.

Kalen looked away from him. "What I want is wrong," Kalen murmured.

"Then I guess it is wrong for me too to want the same thing," Lycus said.

Kalen looked at him, thinking Lycus was playing with him. "You're not grossed out?" Kalen asked.

"For wanting you, too? No! I always have. I just didn't want to act on it. Didn't want to lose you, in case you didn't feel the same way."

"You want to be with me?" Kalen asked, confused by his own words.

"I wouldn't be here if I didn't," Lycus told him before smiling and dipping his face closer to Kalen's.

He pressed his lips against Kalen's, his tongue moving across the seam of his lips. Kalen's lips parted before Lycus deepened the kiss.

"Just so you know, I love you, too," Lycus whispered. That was one of the first times Kalen felt truly happy. He got a glimpse of happiness. It was also the same night Lycus marked him.

Now that Lycus was aware sleeping with women hurt Kalen, he stopped, which sent them back to having nothing. Lycus was okay with that as long as he had Kalen. Kalen, however, felt he was ruining Lycus's life. Stopped him from becoming who he could become, and when their magic manifested, fear rushed through

Kalen when he saw Darius and Tobias's names appear on their wrists. The marking was made more shocking when they realized they were mates all along.

I watched the memories play out before stopping again. One of them slowed down, and I was sucked into it. It was a week after their eighteenth birthday. Both of them were sitting at the park under a tree in the sweltering summer heat. Kalen had felt faint all day from having not eaten. Neither of them had found anything much to eat, and the days were so hot now. Lycus was too weak and dehydrated to try to get to the forest outside the city so he could hunt for them, and Kalen was withdrawing from having no medication that day.

"Maybe they will help?" Lycus murmured.

"Are you insane? That is Darius Wraith. He will kill us," Kalen murmured. Everyone knew the Wraiths, and even they feared the Demonic Fae King.

"We don't know that. We are technically his mates," Lycus said.

"Yes, if he wanted us near, he would have called on us by now."

"Well, we haven't exactly called on him. Besides, I don't see much bad stuff about Tobias in the news. He might come?" Lycus told him.

"No, it isn't worth the risk and what about that reporter? Tobias killed him in front of the cameras. I thought fate couldn't fuck us over more, so to prove me wrong, they had to fate us to the two most influential families, a fucking Demonic Fae King and a vampiric prince? Seriously, Lycus, they find us, either would kill us or me, anyway; I am the weakest link."

"We don't know that," Lycus said, sending a flare of magic into his infinity mark before Kalen could stop him.

"What have you done?" Kalen gasped, horrified, as his mark tingled. He looked at it. My name was faint on his wrist, unlike the rest.

"Anything has to be better than living like this," Lycus said, only the tingling stopped, and Lycus huffed.

"See? Told you," Kalen muttered when they felt the mark stop. "I wonder who rejected it," Kalen said, a little sad. He rubbed his wrist before lying back down and resting his head on Lycus's shoulder.

"We'll figure it out. Maybe once she comes of age, they will accept us," Lycus murmured to him. They both fell asleep, and Kalen was later woken up when someone kicked his foot. He yawned, shaking his head and sitting up. He peered down at Lycus when someone cleared their throat.

Turning his head, he came face to face with Darius crouching next to him in a suit. He eyed Kalen's mark on his neck before looking at Lycus. Darius's brows furrowed while Kalen tried to shake Lycus awake, petrified. His heart was pounding in his chest when he noticed Tobias standing behind him, also staring at them.

Lycus groaned and sat up before noticing them and ripping Kalen behind him with strength that clearly indicated what Lycus was. Darius tilted his head at Lycus, looking him over.

"Are you the one who called on us?" Darius asked.

"Yes," Lycus said while Kalen was worried Darius would kill him for it.

"Why are you at the park? Do you live nearby?" Tobias asked, and Lycus looked up at him. Tobias tried to look around Lycus at Kalen, who was peering over Lycus's shoulder.

"We live here, but you can go. He didn't mean to call on you," Kalen blurted.

Darius looked up at Tobias, who nodded to him before Darius stood.

"Come on then. I can't leave you here knowing that," Darius told them.

Lycus looked at Kalen over his shoulder.

"Where would you take us?" Kalen asked, wondering if they were being led to their deaths.

"Home. Now, come on. I wanted to come earlier, but I was in a meeting. Now, hurry up. I have another in an hour and need to get you set up back home before I go," Darius told him.

"You will let us stay with you?" Lycus asked, a little shocked.

"Well, I won't have my mates living in a park. Now, hurry up," Darius said, checking his watch.

"Don't leave him waiting he is insufferable when he is pissed off. He can hold a grudge like he bloody invented the word," Tobias said, clicking his fingers.

Darius took them in, provided them with everything they ever needed or wanted, and looked after them despite his father clashing with Lycus constantly. Yet, Darius was always quick to get on Lycus's side, which often turned into a power battle. Darius barely won against his father, no matter how much he copped a beating in the arena that I now recognized as the outdoor obstacle course, though it was a simple training arena back then.

Darius's father saw Kalen as a weakness, proven when Kalen nearly got them all killed in an ambush. He ran after Lycus thinking he was hurt, but he was being the bait. It almost cost them all their lives when Kalen alerted everyone to their location. It was declared after that night that Kalen wouldn't go on the scout teams. He would remain home in the castle, which just added to his depression until Darius handed him a tablet one day.

"What's this?" Kalen asked, looking up at him.

"The school opened up a buddy system. Lycus said you were bored."

"You're lying," Kalen accused, observing Darius's aura. Darius laughed and nodded.

"Yes, I am. Tobias opened up a buddy system at the school, made it mandatory, and you have been assigned a friend to talk to, give you someone outside this room to speak with when we aren't here," Darius said, kneeling between Kalen's legs. He handed the tablet to Kalen, and Kalen took it from him curiously.

"Lycus won't like me talking to random people," Kalen told him.

"This one he approves of," Darius told him.

"What would I say, though? I don't do anything. I am useless," Kalen said, and Darius growled at his words.

"Don't speak like that. Don't listen to the shit my father spouts about, but talk to her. She is waiting for a response. The school logged her in this morning. She will be waiting to speak with you."

"It's a girl? I can't speak to a girl," Kalen said, handing back the tablet.

"You can because she is our keeper, our mate. You can't hide from her now, can you?" Darius laughed, and Kalen bit his lips nervously.

"You think she will want to speak with me?"

"She has no choice but, yes, Kalen. You are worthy of your mates, of her, or the fates wouldn't have given her to us," Darius told him. Kalen sighed when Darius spoke again.

"No names. You must not tell her who you are. That is the rule of the school, not ours, by the way." Darius nodded, and Kalen unlocked the tablet.

"I thought you said no names," Kalen asked, staring at the pen name. "You told her yours." Kalen laughed.

Darius smiled slyly. "No, I didn't."

"HTIARW is Wraith spelled backward, definitely your name." Kalen laughed.

"Our name. You are a Wraith now, too," Darius told him.

"What?"

"We all have to take a name, so what better name than to take the name of the Demonic King? No one will dare touch you when you share my name," Darius told him. Kalen sniffled and nodded, his thumb brushing over the tablet. Darius turned to leave his room when Kalen spoke.

"Darius?" he called out. Darius stopped and turned to look at him.

"Thanks," he said, holding up the tablet.

"No thanks. We are mates. What's mine is also yours," Darius told him.

Kalen nodded and watched as Darius left. Even with Darius's words, he still felt unworthy.

Kalen messaged me, and I replied. At first, I felt obligated to until I was just as obsessed with him as he was with me. He was the highlight of my day, and I was his. Until I stopped replying.

◈◈◈

Kalen was excited because he would meet me today, and he waited patiently, but today he couldn't contain his excitement as the memories moved along. That excitement died along with him. Five years, and he was able to tell me who he was, only I never replied, and he spiraled.

I was the last rejection he could take, so he hung himself. He believed he ruined everyone's chance to have their keeper. He convinced himself he was the reason I ran. Then he convinced himself they would be better off without him. So, he repeatedly killed himself, becoming more unstable each time he came back to find I never came back for him.

My heart broke, knowing I was his last straw, a life of rejection, and the one person who should love him most. His keeper never came for him. No. Instead, I ran from him, and in turn, I killed him. That knowledge burned my soul, marred my heart, and broke the spell I was under as I lurched forward, ripping myself out of his memories and into the present world. Kalen sat next to me, staring at me.

"It was you all along," I whispered. Tears glistened in my eyes before spilling over. "I never ran from you, Kalen. I was trying to find you, find my internet friend," I told him, and he sucked in an unsteady breath.

Kalen dropped his head. "You're not mad I didn't tell you?"

I shook my head. "No, I am mad I ran," I told him before throwing myself in his arms.

CHAPTER 80

Kalen

She was out cold for hours, her shredding had died off, but we all knew it was only a matter of time before it returned. There were four of us after all, and until she completed it entirely, it would only keep returning, though the first part seemed to have worn off.

"Try to get some sleep," Lycus murmurs behind me, yet all I could do was stare and watch her eyelids move as she watched the disaster of my entire life unfold.

I hated myself, hated that being our keeper, she would have to endure all my misdoings, all my failures, and most of all, I hated that she would know. She would see how truly pathetic I am. Aleera would know that I am weak. I had nothing to offer her, and I worried she would be upset that she was cursed with a mate like me.

Lycus growls, gripping my face and tilting my head to look up at him. "Get some sleep!" he growls, but I shake my head, gnawing on my fingernail while staring back at her sleeping body.

"Leave him be, Lycus," Tobias says as he gets ready for bed. He climbed in beside Aleera, tucking her tiny body against him. She reacted instantly to him, rolling into him and clutching his arm as she whimpered at whatever she was living through in my memories. Lycus squeezes my shoulders, kneeling behind me as he watches her.

"She will be fine,"

"I know that. It isn't what I am worried about," I whisper, and he leans down, resting his chin on my shoulder and wrapping his huge tree-trunk arms around my waist.

"Then what is it?" he asks, nipping at my mark.

"You're not weak!" Darius snarls, and I glance at him over my shoulder. He was sitting by the fire, glaring at it while Ryze perched on the back of the armchair, watching him.

"Is that what you think?" Lycus growls at me. His anger erupted through the bond, and I hung my head. Darius always read me too well. They all did. Darius, however, was usually the most observant.

"What if she thinks I am?" I murmur.

"You are not weak. Never say that again. You know I hate when you talk like that." Lycus snapped.

"Lycus, calm down," Tobias scolded as Lycus trembled behind me, fighting the urge to shift at my words. Yet I couldn't help but believe she would hate me for being weak, hate me for not telling her it was me all along that was talking to her, hate me for them hating her for what I did.

"Lycus, go for a run," Darius snarled, making me jump when he ripped Lycus off the bed just as Lycus shifted into his gigantic black wolf. His claws ripped apart the rug as he skidded along it.

Tobias clucked his tongue while Darius glared at him and pointed at the door. Ryze hissed and squawked at at the huge werewolf. Lycus's anger grew, and his werewolf instincts took over, making him savage. No longer in control, he lunged at Ryze, but Darius snatched him off the back of the armchair before his powerful jaws wrapped around the bird.

Tobias pointed to the door, and Lycus growled, his claws scratching the floor up. Lycus pivots and runs out the door when Tobias moves with inhuman speed and opens it.

"What's wrong with him?" I asked. He didn't usually lose control like that.

"He is picking up on her anger as well," Darius says and I look at Aleera and put my head in my hands. She thought I was weak; I knew she would. I wasn't like them. I wasn't powerful. I wasn't strong.

Darius steps closer, holding Ryze in his hands like he is holding an oversized chicken. Instinctively, I cringe away, and Ryze flaps his wings. Darius lets him go, and Ryze flies over to perch on the headboard. His tail flicked over her arm as he petted her like she was his pet, not the other way around. "Crazy bird," Darius mutters, climbing on the bed beside her. Ryze hisses at him, but he waves his hand at him.

"Hate me all you want. Just do it quietly," Darius snaps at him. I shake my head, but Ryze seems to listen, huddling in his feathers like an owl watching with wide eyes, but he remains quiet.

Darius leans his face closer, sniffing her neck before sighing and laying back. He pats his chest with his hand while looking at me expectantly, but I don't move.

"One!" Darius says, and I ignore him, not in the mood to cuddle. I was antsy and irritable.

"Two!" I pick at the blanket, watching her squirm as fear floods me through the bond from her.

"Don't make him get to three, Kalen," Tobias hisses behind me and nudges me toward him.

I roll my eyes and look at Darius, who raises an eyebrow like he was daring me to disobey him before pursing his lips. He lifts a finger, motioning for me to come to him, and I growl before crawling closer. Obviously, I didn't move fast enough when Darius ripped me on top of him.

"Stop your pouting and sleep," Darius growled before pressing his lips to my forehead. His hand was warm as it trailed up my arm gently.

"You're not weak," he whispers, while I trace the scars on his chest with my fingertips.

I looked up at him, observing his aura, but I could see he was worried about something. His aura was black but flickering red oddly.

Everyone had color in their aura, depending on the emotion. Mostly everyone was a shade of black or grey, sometimes blue. Looking at Aleera's was like looking at a bubble when the sun hits it, a mirage of every color you could think of. Observing Darius again, he was nervous about something.

"What are you worried about?" I asked him.

"Nothing that concerns you, now sleep,"

"Only if you tell me," I tell him, and he growls, squeezing my arm before he sighs.

"She will know all my secrets, just like she knows yours,"

"You worried she will find out about your father?"

"No, something else," I could tell he wouldn't answer any more than that and sighed before looking at Tobias, who curiously watched Darius.

Darius grabs my hand, placing it over his heart and holding it there. "Try to sleep. I will wake you when she is up," he says before I feel his magic wash over me. I melt against him, letting his scent soothe my anxiety.

A few hours later, I am woken by screams; I lurch upright, and so do Darius and Tobias. Lycus, having returned, growls, stepping over me, his eyes on the door. Blinking, I see it is still dark, but definitely early morning. The light outside was lightening, and I could just make out the trees in the distance.

"For crying out loud. What now?" Tobias groans, tossing the blanket back and climbing out of bed. Something was going on downstairs. Darius tapped my arm, and I rolled off him. He leaned down, kissing my lips softly, his tongue forcing its way into my mouth as he kissed me. All too soon, he pulls away before ruffling Lycus' fur as he climbs off the bed.

"Stay here," he says, grabbing a shirt and tugging it on as he follows Tobias to the door. They leave, and I look at Lycus, who starts to shift back before moving off the bed toward the closet. Sitting up, I see Aleera was still asleep, but her eyelids moving rapidly when she shot upright, scaring the crap out of me. She blinks, her eyes trying to adjust to the light.

"It was you all along," I whispered. Tears glistened in her eyes before spilling over. "I never ran from you, Kalen. I was trying to find you, find my internet friend," she tells me, and I suck in a breath.

"You're not mad. I didn't tell you?" I ask her.

"No, I am mad I ran," she says, tears roll down her cheeks before she threw herself in my arms.

I wrap my arms around her, squeezing her tight. She didn't hate me, and I had never felt more relieved. Feeling the bed, I watch Lycus climb on the bed. He kisses my cheek before running his fingers through her hair, and Aleera turns her head on my shoulder to look at him.

I kiss her nose, hugging her tighter when Lycus runs a hand down her sides before pinching her chin and pulling her head off my shoulder. Her lips part, and he kisses her gently at first before his tongue invades her mouth, making my cock twitch beneath her.

"Thank you," Lycus whispers, pulling his lips from hers and she looks at him oddly, clearly confused by his words.

"For what?" she asks, confused. Lycus pecks her lips before laying down, pulling us with him.

CHAPTER 81

Darius

ALL NIGHT I WAS awake. I couldn't sleep. I had completely forgotten about the true meaning of keeper. She would know our darkest secrets, even the ones not even my mates knew, and some I kept were unforgivable. I was too ashamed to tell them, too afraid they would run from me if they knew the sort of monster I truly was. I could feel her so easily through the bond, feel her fear as she lived through what Kalen endured.

Feel her burning anger at what they did to him. I wondered what she would think of my past, how much she would turn against me once the truth was out. We all had secrets, but none of them kept the secrets I did. None of them had done what I did.

They all thought they were monsters. I was the biggest monster of all. Hearing the door push open, I see Lycus walk in. His wolf sniffed the air before coming over to the bed. He climbed up, laying across Kalen and me. I stroke his fur, and he purrs, resting his head on Kalen's lower back, his tail swishing back and forth in the air happily. Tobias flicked his wrist toward the door closing

Tobias watched me. I could feel his eyes on me, feel his burning curiosity. I knew he was also worried about Aleera knowing his past, knowing about his brother. At the same time, he wanted answers too. Some part of him wanted her to know what she took from him. He may act like he has forgiven her, but I know he hasn't. I could feel it festering inside him, yet the bond was irresistible, and he was done fighting it.

We all had lost something because of her, maybe not directly because of her, but what would happen when they learned everything started with what I did. All of it was my fault. Everything that happened was my fault. I never should have gone looking for her. If I had known whose daughter she was, I would have waited until she came of age before seeking her out.

I was not expecting her father to answer that door. What were the chances that I would be bonded to my father's greatest enemy's daughter? Aleera was his best-kept secret, but knowing what I know now. I was certain he was the one that unleashed the plague. Hearing a commotion downstairs, Kalen jumped, sitting upright.

I grip Lycus's fur as he growls and stands glaring at the door. Tobias gets up. "For crying out loud. What now?" Tobias growls, stalking toward the closet. Shaking my head, I push Lycus back so I can get up before kissing Kalen when he rolls off me. Getting up, I walk to the dresser.

"Wait here," I tell Lycus and Kalen. I grab a tank top, pulling it on before walking out of the room and down the corridor. Tobias cursing as the racket grew louder as the recruits freaked out about something downstairs.

"What time is it?" I asked Tobias. He pulls his phone out of his pocket. "5 am," he growls, shaking his head. We walked down the stairs to the next level. The recruits were freaking out about something, and I could see them all looking out the windows. Some even rushed back up the stairs to their rooms.

"What the fuck is going on?" I boomed, leaning over the banister and looking at the ground floor. They all froze, looking up at us, and Tobias cursed while a few pointed out the windows. All of them are too stunned to speak, and Tobias growls.

"Back to your rooms!" Tobias snapped, his voice echoing like a thunderclap, and they took off.

Waiting for the stampede of men to scatter, we descended down to the next level. Grabbing one of the stragglers, I yanked him toward me.

"What is going on?" I snarled at him, and his mouth opened and closed like a fish as he shook. I shoved him away, looking up to see haunted peering faces staring back at us.

"You call yourselves an army?" I bellowed angrily.

Tobias turned toward the double doors. Some ran. Others shrieked when someone on the top level spoke up. "I wouldn't go out," he said, and Tobias froze, looking at me and I, him. He looked out the windows, and I moved to the wide double doors and glanced out but saw nothing.

"Fucking bunch of pussy's," Tobias snapped. He shoves the doors open and stalks outside, and so do I.

"I swear if this is a fucking prank, I am opening veins," Tobias snapped as we stepped outside.

Looking around, we saw nothing. Shaking my head, we started walking toward the huge obstacle course to find what they were scared of.

"You have been quiet tonight," Tobias states, nudging me.

"Just thinking,"

"You're worried about her finding out her parents are alive," Tobias says, and I sigh. That wasn't what I was worried about.

"You might as well tell me. We will find out anyway," Tobias says as we stop at the edge of the obstacle course. "What the fuck is that?" Tobias says, looking at the climbing wall. He points, and I follow his finger to notice something torn apart and bloody perched on top of the wall.

Sniffing the air, it was definitely blood. I growl, stalking toward it to see better, yet the closer we got, the more unidentifiable it became.

"You going to answer?" Tobias asked as we climbed the hill toward the center of the obstacle course.

"What if I did kill someone?" I ask, and Tobias stops. He looks at me, and I look toward the forest, unable to meet his gaze.

"I think she would understand you killing your father, Darius,"

"Not him," I admit. Tobias seems taken aback, and his shock hits me through the bond. I swallow, and he steps closer before grabbing my arm and shaking me.

"What did you do?" he snarls.

"I killed him," I tell Tobias. Though I had a reason, it was also a reason for her to hate me when she found out.

"Who?"

"Her father," I tell him. Tobias lets me go and tilts his head to the side.

"No, I was there. I would have seen you do it?" but he also knew I wasn't lying was just hoping I was.

"It was when I went back in," I tell him.

"Darius!"

"So you fucking killed them?" Tobias snapped.

"No, her mother got away, and she is lucky she did because I would have killed her too, but," I tried to explain.

"You killed her father?" he asks again and I nod.

"Fuck Darius! How could you keep this from me?"

"She already assumed I killed them, and I didn't think. He was a fucking elder," I let out a breath.

"He is also guilty for unleashing the fucking plague. You could have told me!" Tobias forever, my defender. I swallowed guiltily, I never killed him for what he did to Aleera but what he said to me.

"Fuck! Darius, she would be pissed knowing they were alive, but to find out you actually did kill them,"

"Her father, her mother is still alive," I tell him, and he clutches his hair and curses.

"Anything else I need to fucking know?" he asks and I press my lips in a line.

"There is more, isn't there?"

"You're unbelievable," he says, storming off toward the obstacle course. Tobias climbs the climbing wall, grabbing whatever it is and ripping it off, letting it fall to the ground in a heap.

"We agreed on no secrets, Darius! What else?" He snaps before jumping from the top and landing beside me.

"Darius!"

"Shut up," I snap, squatting next to the torn apart creature or what was left of it. Tobias growls and walks off, and I see him pick up something on the other side of the wall before tossing it at my feet. It was a cow head. I take a step back.

"It's a cow," Tobias says, and I look at the climbing wall.

"Now, how did a cow get up there?" I ask, and Tobias growls.

"How else? It is a fucking prank. I am going to kill them," Tobias says, storming off back toward the castle in a burning rage. I didn't know who he was madder at, me or the recruits. Climbing the hill again, I get to the peak, and Tobias was further ahead when color caught my eye, making me peer up at the roof. My feet stop in horror as I gasped. I look at Tobias, unaware of what is right above him. Opening a portal, I appear beside him and grab his arm.

"What?" he snaps, and I point to the roof. Tobias looks up and takes a step back.

"Fuck me!" he gasps, and I look around at the trees and tap his shoulder. Tobias turns, his eyes also going to the trees. How we missed it, I did not know.

"That's impossible. They are almost extinct," he whispers.

"Apparently not. They were just waiting for their master," I tell him, turning back to peer up at the roof.

"There are hundreds of them!" Tobias shrieks.

"Explains the dead cow," I tell him, nearly choking on my spit.

"What do you think they want?" Tobias asked.

"Geez, I don't know, Tobias, go ask one? What do you think they want?" I snap at him.

"Aleera!" We both say simultaneously.

"She has a fucking army of them," Tobias murmurs. "Well, you better hope you don't have too many secrets because she unleashes those things, you're fucked," Tobias says, storming off toward the castle doors.

"And I ain't feeding them," he calls over his shoulder. I looked up at the roof, and I could not see a single tile. Hundreds of phoenix's all perched like a sea of flaming color, every inch of the roof was obscured by them.

But if this was after obtaining her power and marking one of us, what would she bring when she owned all of us? More importantly, if they could sense her, who else could?

Author Note

For those who made it to the end and wish to continue, Book 2 Tasting Darkness will be available on Kindle in November. If you can't wait, you could always jump onto the ireader app where I post chapters as I write them. The link is below.

https://abs.ireaderm.net/zyhw/u/p/api. php?Act=facebook&bid=52003007&p2=120161&locale=en-us

Also, don't forget to follow me on Facebook and insta.

Insta @jessica.hall.author

FB https://www.facebook.com/jessicahall91